10/16

# MORE

# MORE

## A NOVEL

## HAKAN GÜNDAY

### Translated by Zeynep Beler

Arcade Publishing • New York

Library of Congress Cataloging-in-Publication Data

Names: Günday, Hakan, 1976- author. | Beler, Zeynep, translator.
Title: More : a novel / Hakan Gunday ; translated by Zeynep Beler.
Other titles: Daha. English
Description: First English-Language Edition. | New York : Arcade Publishing, 2016.
Identifiers: LCCN 2016025295 (print) | LCCN 2016033224 (ebook) | ISBN 9781628727074 (hardback) | ISBN 9781628727081 (ebook)
Subjects: LCSH: Refugees--Fiction. | Human trafficking--Fiction. | BISAC: FICTION / Literary. | FICTION / Coming of Age. | FICTION / Thrillers. | GSAFD: Bildungsromans.
Classification: LCC PL248.G766 D3413 2016 (print) | LCC PL248.G766 (ebook) | DDC 894/.3534--dc23
LC record available at https://lccn.loc.gov/2016025295

Jacket design by Laura Klynstra
Front cover photograph © AP Images

Printed in the United States of America

# MORE

If my father weren't a killer, I wouldn't have been born . . .

"Two years before you were born . . . there was this boat named *Swing Köpo*, I've never forgotten . . . Belonged to a son of a bitch by the name of Rahim . . . Anyhow, we load the goods, there's forty heads at least. And one of them is sick. You ought to have seen the way he was coughing! He's done for! It's anybody's guess how old he is, could be seventy, could be eighty . . ."

If my father weren't a killer, I wouldn't have been one either . . .

"I even told him, what use are you anyway? Running, migrating somewhere? What would it matter if you got where you're going? You want to go through this torture so you can die? Anyway . . . Then Rahim said to me, come along, we can shoot the breeze on the way back. Back then I had nothing to do, I hadn't bought the truck yet . . ."

If my father weren't a killer, my mother wouldn't have died giving birth to me . . .

"Every once in a while I'd lend a hand smuggling migrants. I'd get to know the business and also make a bit of cash . . . I said all right, fine. So we board, we're out in the open sea . . . short while before we make it to Khios, a storm breaks out! The *Swing Köpo*'s already a lost cause as it is! We went under before we even knew it . . ."

If my father hadn't been a killer, I would never have turned nine and sat down at that table with him . . .

"I look around, everyone's scattered everywhere, screaming and yelling . . . These guys are from the desert, what do they know of swimming! You see them once, and then they're gone. Sinking like stones, all of them. Just drowning . . . at some point I saw Rahim, his forehead's covered in blood . . . he's knocked up his head somewhere on the boat . . . You should have seen those waves, like walls! Rolling up like they would swallow you! Then I saw that Rahim was gone as well . . ."

If my father hadn't been a killer, he wouldn't have told me this story, same as I wouldn't have been listening . . .

"I would have started swimming except I'm thinking, which way? It's the dead of night. I struggled quite a bit . . . But no, even keeping my head above the water is an issue. I keep bobbing up and down . . . I said, Ahad, my man, this is the end! You're done, you're a goner . . . then all of a sudden, between two waves, I saw this white thing . . . There's this dark shadow on top of it . . ."

If my father hadn't been a killer, I never would have had to learn that he was a killer . . .

"Turns out it was that sick guy . . . You know, the geezer I was telling you about . . . He's got a buoy that he's clinging to . . . I don't even know how I swam, but I made it over to the guy . . . I grabbed the buoy and yanked it out of his hand . . . He just looked at me . . . reached over like so . . . so I shoved him . . . Grabbed him by the throat . . . Then a wave came and carried him off . . ."

But my father was a killer and all of it did happen . . .

That night, my father told his story so slowly his words dissolved into the air between us like those intermittent silences that slipped from his lips. In fact, it was for that reason they were not nailed, but as good as screwed into my memory. Round and around they spun as they lodged into my mind. Or into whatever was left of my mind . . . Now I wonder if my father hadn't been a killer, whether I would have had no father at all. For only a killer could have been a father to me. The passage of time made this clear . . .

He never talked about his murder again. He didn't need to. How many times do you confess the same sin to the same person? Hearing it once is enough. Enough to cause you to slowly rise from the table and lie down in your bed although your eyes remain open . . .

Why now, I remember thinking that night. Why tell it now? Was he telling it to me or to himself? Maybe that was the only life lesson he was able to pass on to his nine-year-old son. The only vital information he had. The only true lesson of life: survive! I remember, too, the moral I found in that story: Don't tell anyone how you survived . . . No one should talk about where they're from. I remember weeping. No one should talk about the breaths they've stolen from others. I was nine. I couldn't have known . . . that you survived so that you could tell people about how you survived . . . Then at some point, I remember picturing the moment my father grabbed that old man by the throat and pushed him. Thinking, that old man must have had an Adam's apple just like my father's . . . asking myself, had my father felt that lump in his hand? Had that old man's Adam's apple left a mark in my father's palm? When he stroked my cheek, would I catch it too? Next I remember sleeping. And then waking . . . then, the breakfast he had prepared me, and the slap, and the command.

A slice of bread . . .

"What did you make out of what I told you yesterday?"

"It was either you who would die, or that man . . ."

Two slices of cheese . . .

"Good . . . so tell me . . . what would you have done?"

"Maybe that buoy could've helped us both . . ."

A slap . . .

"Eat, don't stare at me like that! Wipe those eyes!"

"OK, Dad."

An egg . . .

"If I wasn't around, you wouldn't be either, do you understand?"

"Yes, Dad."

Three olives . . .

"Good . . . don't ever forget this! Now tell me, what would you have done?"

"I would've done the same as you, Dad."

A sliver of butter . . .

"Everything I do in this life, I do for you."

"Thanks, Dad."

A command . . .

"Now you know that this business is about survival of the fittest, you're coming with me today!"

"OK, Dad."

It turns out Father had been looking for a novice. One who would belong to him to the flesh, bones, and marrow. It seems he would rather become accomplices with his own son than split his profit with a stranger.

"You're coming!" he said, so I went. That summer, as soon as I got my report card, I became a people smuggler. At the age of nine . . . it wasn't really that much different than being the son of a people smuggler . . .

Now I wonder if maybe he was drunk when he told that story. Recounted his way to lucidity, then realized it was too late . . . Maybe my father simply had a crippled sense of remorse and a mean streak, that was all. Maybe he was that way because of his own father. And *he* was that way because of *his* father . . . and *he* was that way because of *his* . . . and *he* was that way because of *his* . . . Weren't we all children of survivors after all? Children of the survivors of war, earthquake, famine, massacre, epidemic, invasion, conflict, and disaster . . . Children of swindlers, thieves, murderers, liars, informers, traitors, of those first to leave a sinking ship, who yank buoys out of the hands of others . . . those who knew well enough to stay alive . . . those who would do anything, anything at all, to stay alive . . . If we were alive today, did we not owe it to that someone in our family tree who'd declared, "It's either me or him!" Maybe this wasn't even the reign of wickedness. It was only natural . . . It only seemed unwholesome to us. But there was no concept of ugliness in nature, or of beauty. Rainbows were rainbows and no science textbook had ever disclosed any information about how to get to the end of one.

Ultimately, it was two corpses that carried me into this life: the wish to live and the wish to let live . . . The former was my father's wish, the latter my mother's . . . And so I did live . . . Did I have any other choice? Surely . . . but who knows, maybe this is just how the physics of living goes, and somewhere it's written:

*The Physics of Living 101*
*Every birth equals at least two deaths. One to do with the wish to live, one to do with the wish to let live; two deaths.*

*For the newly born, however, those deaths must ensure that he lives his life unaware that he is even breathing.*

*Otherwise, said person will be made up of war and ends every day as a corpse.*

Yes, maybe my name is Gaza . . .
And I never thought about committing suicide.
Except, at one point . . . I felt it.

Now I'm going to tell myself a story and believe only that. For every time I turn and look to the past, I see it's changed again. Either the terrain is diminished, or its history compounded. In this life nothing stays in its place. Nothing is content with where it is. Maybe nothing has a place really. That's the reason they won't fit into the holes you leave them in. All the while you're measuring away and digging holes in just the right size, but it doesn't work a damn bit. They all wait for you to blink. So they can run off. Or switch places and drive you insane. Especially your past . . .

And now it's time . . . time to tell every single recollection once and for all, seal it off. Because this is the end! I'm never going to turn and look back again. Not even in the mirror, I'll look it in the eyes. With every word I'll nibble at it until I've eaten it up. Then I'm going to scrape it off my teeth with a toothpick and grind it under my soles. That's the only way to comprise only the present . . . otherwise the body I live inside will do anything to stop time! Because it knows everything: that it will die, that it will decay. . . who was the piece of shit that told it this? The body knows it'll croak and disappear! In fact, that's why . . . clamping its jaws on to life like a rabid dog, it makes me repeat the same mistakes time and time again. Time and time again! To buy some time through those déjà vus that take me back to the past, even if for an instant . . . but it's over.

When I finish my story and am silent, I'll only make new mistakes from then on! Mistakes so foreign they'll kick time into full gallop! Mistakes so unknowable, they'll turn wall clocks into magnetized compasses! Mistakes no one's heard of, let alone made before! Mistakes as great and recondite as the discovery of a lost continent or extraterrestrial life! Mistakes as extraordinary as men who make machines that make men who make machines that make machines! Mistakes as tremendous as the invention of God! Mistakes as unanticipated as the second-biggest invention following God, that of *character*! As magical as the first mistake of a newborn! A mistake as deadly as being born! That's all I want . . . and maybe some morphine sulfate.

Turkey is only the difference between the East and the West. I don't know which one you'd have to subtract from the other to leave Turkey, but I do know for sure that the distance between them is equal to Turkey. And that was where we lived.

A country whose geopolitical significance was discussed daily by politicians on TV. Before, I couldn't figure out what that meant. Turns out geopolitical meant a decrepit building, pitch dark on the inside, that buses with glaring headlights used as a rest stop in the middle of the night just because it was on the way. It meant the huge Bosphorus Bridge, 1,565 km long. An enormous bridge passing through the lives of the country's inhabitants. An old bridge, one bare foot on the Eastern end, the other shoe-wearing foot on the Western; all kinds of law-lessness passing over it. It all went straight through our bellies. Especially those referred to as *the immigrants* . . . We did what we could . . . to make sure they wouldn't get stuck in our throats. We swallowed and sent them on their way. Wherever it was they were going . . . commerce from border to border . . . from wall to wall . . .

Needless to say, the rest of the world also did its part and provided them with the desperation necessary to start running from the place they were born to the place they were to die. Every variety of desperation. Desperation of every length, width and age . . . As for us, we simply carried out the demands of our country's latitudes and longitudes. We carried to paradise those who'd escaped from hell. I believed in neither. But those people believed in everything. From birth, practically! After all, they assumed: if there is famine-afflicted, war-wracked hell on earth, there must surely be a heaven as well. But they were wrong. They'd all been played for fools. The existence of hell wasn't necessarily proof of heaven. Yet I could sympathize with them. This was what they'd been taught. And not just them, everybody . . . a dazzling tinsel-framed painting was being sold to the entire world population. And in that painting, good sparred with evil; heaven with hell. Yet there was no such war and never had been. The vitally crucial war between good and evil, expected to endure until the apocalypse, was the biggest ruse known to mankind. A ruse necessary to ensure the absolute effectiveness of authority and social order by the shortest route possible. For if the simultaneous existence of good and evil within every person were not generally accepted, the identities of everyone in whose name people had died, meaning every leader who ever lived, would start showing stains. There would be confusion, clashing thoughts, and no one would ever give their life for anyone else again. But that's not how it worked out and so it became that the simplest way to get people to fight one another to the death was the war between absolute good and absolute evil.

Those who said, "You're the good ones!" actually meant to say, "Go and die in my name!" while those who said, "You're the ones who'll go to heaven!" meant, "Those that you do in are going to hell!"

Hence heaven and hell, good and evil, split the creature called man down the middle and created a vendetta between the two halves, turning him into a total dolt. So it was that the formidable salesmen of the past were able to wrap lifetime-guaranteed servility in the sacred theory of conflict and sell it to free people. Getting submissive dogs to fight and kill other submissive dogs was the whole point! It wasn't that darkness was against light, nor was it vice versa. There was one true conflict, relevant only to biology: death or life . . .

In the illegal transportation of people, that was really the only thing to be mindful of: that the number of living persons delivered be the same as the number picked up. Other than that, it didn't matter how many of them had run from hell expecting to get to heaven. We were carrying meat. Just meat. Dreams, thoughts, or feelings, these weren't included in the pay we were receiving. Perhaps if they'd paid enough, we would have carried those with caution too. I, in fact, could have willingly adopted this mission and made sure the dreams they'd dreamed up back in their homes—or in whatever hole they were born—didn't break during the ride. A few Hollywood movies would have done the trick. It would have secured their faith in heaven. Or, to implement the classic, time-honored method, handing them a holy book. To only one of them, though, as it goes in history. So he could tell the others. He could tell it any way he liked . . . In fact, I would have done it all for free, but I wasn't old enough and didn't have the time. Because there was always work to be done.

"Gaza!"

"Yes, Dad?"

"Go, get the chains from the storage."

"OK, Dad."

"Get the locks too."

"I will, Dad."

"Don't forget the keys!"

"They're in my pocket, Dad."

I was lying. I'd lost them all. But I hadn't imagined that I'd get caught. I got two slaps and a kick for it, as a matter of fact. How was I to know that father sometimes had to chain them up?

"Gaza!"

"Yes, Dad?"

"Go get the water, pass it out!"

"OK, Dad."

"Not one per head like you did last time! You give two people one bottle, got it?"

"But, Dad, they always say . . ."

"What?"

"More!"

I was lying. Yes, they always said, "More!" because that was the only Turkish word they knew, but the issue at stake here wasn't the water being in demand, but my diminished profit. I'd begun selling the water we normally gave out for free. Without my father knowing, of course . . . I was ten now, after all.

"Gaza."

"Yes, Dad?"

"Did you hear that? Did somebody just yell?"

"No, Dad."

"Guess I must've imagined it . . ."

"Guess so . . ."

I was lying again. Of course I'd heard that scream. But it was barely two days since my discovery that a certain appendage I possessed wasn't only for pissing. Therefore my only wish was that we'd get the job done as soon as possible so I could go back behind the locked door of my room. There were twenty-two adults and a baby in the back of our moving truck. How could I have known that that cut-off scream belonged to a mother when she realized the baby in her arms was dead, before the others clapped panicked hands over her mouth? Would it have mattered if I did? I seriously doubt it because I was now eleven.

There's no absolute way of knowing how people smuggling began. But if you take into account that it's possible to undertake such a task with just three people, it's possible to go way back in human history. The only rewarding line in an otherwise useless book I read years ago was: *The first tool man used was another man.* So I don't suppose it was a very long time before somebody put a price on that earliest tool and sold it to others. Accordingly, the beginning of people smuggling on earth can be dated as: first possible chance! After all, since it also encompasses pimping, it's the second oldest profession in the world. Of course I was unaware that we were upholding the traditions of such an ancient line of work. All I did was sweat all the time and do the best I could to follow my father's orders. Yet transportation was really the backbone of human smuggling. Without transportation there was nothing. It was the riskiest and most exhausting step of the process. The later part where the immigrants were stuck in a den, worked eighteen hours a day making fake purses, were made to sleep on the ground, and even got fucked if they struck someone's fancy, was child's play compared to what we did. We were the true laborers of the people-smuggling industry, working under the heaviest conditions! First of all, we were under constant pressure. The ones making the delivery, the ones picking it up, the middlemen, they were all after us. Everyone held us accountable for the smallest setback. Time was never in our favor, and everything that could possibly go wrong at first always pretended not to and then went wrong sevenfold. It wasn't that the operation was so complicated, but as it goes with illegal work, no one trusted anyone else and every step had to be taken as painstakingly as if we were in a field of glass.

The goods came from the Iran border three times a month, were joined up with the ones from Iraq or Syria if there were any, and sent out to us. They usually came in an eighteen-wheeler. A different one every time, of course. Occasionally the goods were divided up and parceled out to vehicles such as trucks, pickup trucks, or minibuses. A man named Aruz organized the entry across the Iran border and the departure of the goods. He was probably *President of the Administration Committee of the Executive Counsel of Coordination for Aiding Persons in Unrestricted International Roaming in Return for a Determined Fee in Compliance with the Tariff of the People's Revolutionary Movement as Part of Covering the Free Living Expenses and Democratic War Expenditures of the Board of Directors' Command Dedicated to the Perpetuity of Leadership and the Indivisible Totality of Kurdistan* of the PKK, or something. The *determined fee* required for *unrestricted roaming* was whatever came from the heart. It included the heart. Or the kidneys, plus expenses, or whatever . . . all in all, if you were to ask Aruz, he would have said that he was one of the PKK's ministers in charge of smuggling. But he was responsible only for people smuggling. Drugs, petrol, cigarettes, and guns were handled by other ministries. Which was the way it should be: duties that were different in objective should also be set apart managerially. Otherwise everything would get tangled up and poisoned. After Turkey's exemplary Ministry of Culture and Tourism—which was as bizarre a title as Ministry of War and Peace—no one wanted to repeat the same mistake. When two opposite concerns, one completely occupied with money-making and the other with unconditional support and conservation, were brought together under the same ministry, culture was reduced to nothing more than a dried-up giveaway pen, and tourism the halfway erased logo of a five-star hotel on that same pen. But who cared? Not Aruz, that was for sure! Every bit as much an expert of commerce as of violence, Aruz's approach to tourism was totally different. First of all, he ran his illegal travel agency empire by telephone only. By eating phones, I mean.

That was the presumption, because I could never make out what he was saying with his drowned hippo's voice, and would repeatedly say, "I kiss your hands, Uncle Aruz!" or sometimes, if I was in a bad mood and felt like pissing him off as well, ask, "How's Felat?"

When the name of his child, who was nothing like his dream son, came up, he might start grumbling like a beached whale, but would generally just make a sound that might have been laughter, and ask for my father. That, I'd deduce from his having stopped talking. Really, there was a love-hate relationship between my father and him. They could talk on the phone for hours. I think it was also out of obligation. After all, it was impossible for them to backstab each other over the phone.

The backstabbing in question meant of course a part of the goods being missing or being shown as missing. I knew that my father didn't smuggle out some of the immigrants he received and sent them instead to Istanbul. These were sold as slaves to some form of textile production or other, or some form of consumption like prostitution. Then my father would revert his tone from almighty judge to almighty accused and moan to Aruz about the fake disasters that had befallen us and resulted in the loss of the goods. And since every single calculation was made per head, Aruz would bellow like a rhino at least half an hour, then mumble a threat and hang up on my father because he knew he'd never find a more reliable trucker.

In fact, at some point, as a precaution against all this, he'd begun having numbers tattooed on the right heel of each immigrant and keeping a photo archive of these. When one vanished, he'd ask, "Tell me the number, which one was it?" He liked this photo business so much, one day he called my father to say, "Find number twelve!" and when rolling up number twelve's pant leg, revealed the words "Up yours," Aruz laughed like a baby elephant.

What was up my father's was, of course, the recent victory of the football team Aruz supported over his. The papyrus scroll used to deliver the message was an Uzbek in his twenties. I don't know why, but he also laughed. Maybe he was a lunatic. Actually, I think they were all lunatics. All those Uzbeks, Afghanis, Turkmenians, Malians, Kyrgyzes, Indonesians, Burmans, Pakistanis, Iranians, Malaysians, Syrians, Armenians, Azerbaijanis, Kurds, Kazakhs, Turks, all of them . . . because only a lunatic would put up with all this. All this meaning, in a sense, us: Aruz, my father, the brothers Harmin and Dordor, who were captains of the ship that took the immigrants to Greece, the men with guns that increased or decreased in number depending on the tide of crime rates, and all the other basket cases I didn't yet know by name, lined up on a road tens of thousands of kilometers long to carry tons of people hand over hand into the world . . .

Especially the brothers Harmin and Dordor. They were the strangest people I could ever hope to meet in this life, and I really loved them. Because with them, it was like life didn't exist. When it had no rules, life slowly dissolved into the air. Time, morals, my father, fear: it was all gone. They were barbaric enough to turn any modicum of civilization they encountered into a desert, make a gigantic mirror out of its sand, and write farewell messages onto it with lipstick-colored blood. They both took me by the hand and brought me many times to the end of humanity and back, but regrettably, on our last trip, forgot about me and left me there . . .

Yes, my father was a merciless man and of course Aruz, being an orangutan, had an inner world as big as a plastic model of the earth. But the brothers Harmin and Dordor were something else. A pair of Arthur Cravans! Their grand total was four meters and two hundred fifty kilos. Yet despite all that meat, their voices were tiny. They always whispered so I had to rise up on my toes to hear what they were saying. They were constantly tattooing each other, and I'd strain to see what they were drawing. After a while I realized that, naturally, it was the same sentences every time:

*Born to be wild*
*Raised to be civilized*
*Dead to be free*

It was written all over them. On their legs, arms, the backs of their necks, their feet, hands . . .

"What does it mean?" I'd ask.

"It's all names of broads!" Harmin would say.

Dordor, who could tell I didn't buy it, would say, "It's in old Turkish, pal, Ottoman!" and laugh.

Three years would have to pass for me to learn what those words meant. Harmin told me the morning after the night Dordor was killed, stabbed sixty-six times by four of Aruz's men. In his usual whisper:

"We must have been around your age . . . We went and stowed away on a ship. Wanted to travel the world. Anyway . . . One day we dropped anchor, we're in Australia! Let's go ashore, we said. But no! We just couldn't. Man, we said, what the hell is this? We don't feel well, we're dizzy, feeling sick to our stomachs . . . The mere mention, going ashore, and we go white as a sheet . . . You know how people have fear of the sea? You get seasick . . . turns out we'd begun to get landsick. We asked if there was such a sickness. No, they said. They didn't have it but we fucking well did! After that we always stayed at sea. Years passed this way. So you see, we never did travel the world! We traveled the sea. . . Remember how you used to ask? 'What do these tattoos mean?' That's what they mean . . . This entire story . . . This is the Turkish version. One day you can go and learn the English one too . . ."

"Where'd you learn English, then?" I asked.

"At the Belconnen Remand!" he said. Seeing I didn't understand, he added, "Prison . . . in Australia."

"But you said you never made it on land!" I began to say, and he snapped, "We didn't! We went under it."

I hadn't understood a word of that. I thought he was messing with me as usual. I couldn't comprehend. Turns out whatever sickness it was that he had, he was contaminating me too. On the front steps of the morgue where Dordor lay, no less . . . Then he went off to shoot Aruz, of course. But he couldn't kill him and died . . . As for myself, I learned English. So . . . now I know that they're both free. Not on, perhaps, but beneath the land they'd been trapped under . . .

I was twelve, and the regular presence of Near-Middle-Far Asians in my life meant I now had the ample geographic knowledge of a Gypsy. The teacher pointed me out in class and said, "That's it! Look, your friend Gaza examines the world map in his free time. It wouldn't hurt if you did the same as well. There's more to the world than just where you live, kids!"

Then all the kids, with the exception of Ender, with whom I shared my seat, gave me predatory looks and emitted a smell furious enough to necessitate opening a window. They really hated me. That I was sure of. They wanted to beat me up. They weren't quite sure if they could, though. For they'd heard some small, nauseating tidbits. About me and my life and my close and far circles. In any case, the fluctuating bouts of violence, during which I, as the target, would just sit there cross-legged, didn't take long to abate. For one day Harmin and Dordor came to pick me up from school and showed off their four-meter height, and the juvenile hate I was besieged by folded in on itself and sank into definite silence.

The only one talking now was Ender. Only he told me things and asked questions he wouldn't be able to get replies to, and kept chortling to himself. His father was a gendarme. A sergeant. I knew him. Uncle Yadigar. Every time he showed up when school let out, he'd take a chocolate bar out of his pocket and give it to Ender, saying, "Break it in half, son, give some to Gaza." Then as I munched away, he would bide me, "Why don't you come to our place, look, your aunt Salime made meatballs," to which I'd shake my head and walk away.

He knew I was Ahad's son, obviously, but I was sure he couldn't figure out what the hell Ahad was. Maybe that's why he kept inviting me to his home. To get words out of me in exchange for meatballs. But I had no mother and I could make meatballs on my own. For the past two years, no less . . .

Uncle Yadigar the Heroic Sergeant! He really was. He'd grabbed up and saved two children from the midst of a forest fire two years earlier, and his right cheek had been completely burned; he'd been awarded a medal. Ender had even worn that medal to school one day, and all the kids whose fathers were olive growers, grocers, tailors, picklers, stationery sellers, butchers, patrol policemen, guardians, restaurateurs, furnishers, or dead gnawed off the jealousy coating their lips, collected it at the edge of their tongues, and spat it onto the ground. Ender, who was already an outcast because he talked to me, was ostracized even more—and this meant out as out could be—leaving the son of the smuggler and the son of the gendarme to their own in a class of forty-seven. But Ender was so stunted he failed to register all this and continued to chortle to himself. As for me, I was sure it was my insides, rather than my face, that were breaking out in spots. For slowly but surely the immigrants were beginning to make me nauseated.

Whenever I saw those people; who clung to one another and made microscopic squeals at the smallest noise, or whose pupils quivered as if they had some mysterious strain of Parkinson's, or who kept trying to smell the forthcoming moment with their broken, sunken-pen noses, who emitted nothing other than the word "More!" even though they never stopped talking, who were buried in seventeen layers of sweat- and then soot-stained fabric and stuck their heads out of their textile tombs only to ask for something; I would say: "Fuck off already!" To their faces, in fact. It wasn't like they understood. Even if they did, they'd just sit and thrust their chins into their chests.

When Ender asked me, "What are you doing this weekend?" I couldn't very well say, "I'm going to smuggle people, is what I'm going to fucking do!"

And when I said, "I'm helping my dad," he'd rattle off all the places I always wanted to visit, saying, "I wish you could come too": the movie theater in the city, the amusement park in the neighboring town, the game hall in the shopping mall of the city, one of the two Internet cafés in our own town . . .

Ender had nothing he had to do! All he had to do was home-work, and eat his mother's meatballs, and maybe go to Koran class! I worked like a dog! I collected the plastic bags immigrants shit into and buried the shit behind the warehouse, bought bot-tles of water in twos and loaves of bread in threes from all the stores in town so that our shopping wouldn't attract attention, emptied bins of immigrant piss, ran from pharmacy to phar-macy since they kept getting sick, never even stopped for a min-ute. I was worked into the ground just because someone felt like going to another country! I even had to give back the copy of *Robinson Crusoe* I'd borrowed from Ender because I hadn't had time to read it.

As a matter of fact, I'd only been curious about the book because he'd summed it up as, "There's this slave merchant, he gets washed up on a deserted island . . ." The second I heard that, I'd wished I could get washed up on a deserted island too. After all, I could be considered a slave merchant, and I was sick of both: of slaves and of mercantile! All I wanted was for my father to scold me over my report card like a normal kid, and not because I forgot to activate the air conditioner we'd just had installed in the back of the truck!

This wasn't like forgetting to turn off the lights when you left the house. I'd caused the death of an Afghani by not turning on the conditioner. He was twenty-six, and he'd made me a paper frog. A frog that leaped when I pressed down on it with my finger. His name was Cuma, which meant "Friday." The Afghani's, not the frog's. I found out years later that Robinson had a Cuma of his own. But since Friday was a book protagonist, how could he possibly be anything like Cuma! For he would never be found asphyxiated in the back of a truck nor give a paper frog as a gift to the child who'd turn on him like a snake. Of course, had Robinson and Friday existed, our lives would have seemed like a novel to *them*. That was the problem. Everyone's life seemed like a novel to someone else. But they were all just lives. They didn't turn into novels through mere divulgence. An autopsy report perhaps, at most . . . a feature one. Libraries were full of them: feature autopsy reports. Bound or unbound, they all told the story of paling skins. A man was made of skin and bones, after all. He would either eventually wrinkle or break on the way. Or be an Afghani named Cuma to die like that pondering rock of Rodin's. Cuma who died on a Sunday . . .

And I felt so bad I finally caved and went to Ender's for meatballs. But it didn't help shit. In fact, sitting at that table and watching that family made me feel even worse. The meatballs were delicious, though. If I had had a mother, I'm sure she would have made them that way too. "Would you like more?" she too would have asked. "Some more?" Maybe then I wouldn't have hated the word "more" as much. When I got up to turn the meatballs in the pans, due to habit I suppose, my mother would say, "That's not for kids, leave it," just like Salime. Like a kid I would sit and the sizzling oil wouldn't burn my hands and blister the spaces between my fingers. The way it did every time . . .

They said there was ice cream, but I didn't stay. I got out of there. Yadigar didn't ask me anything. Not my father's health or how his business was holding up. All he said was, "Eat. You need it," like he knew everything. Really he was right. We were all growing. No matter what their age, everybody. The entire world. We were spinning our way into growth. Our heads spinning . . . That was why we ate and should eat. Each other and everything. We needed it. So we could grow as quickly as possible. Grow as quickly as possible and croak and leave space for others. So a new epoch could begin. One that was preferably not like this one . . . because we could tell we wouldn't amount to shit. We weren't that dumb . . . not *all* that dumb . . .

I was home. Father had gone to the industrial area in the city to get the brake linings of the truck replaced and wouldn't be home till the evening. Just as I was contemplating how terrific it was to be alone and that I should definitely be alone when I grew up, the phone rang. I could tell it was Aruz by the digits on the small blue screen. I'd memorized his number. I didn't want to take it. He would ring three times at most, then get bored and hang up anyway. But the ringing didn't stop. Four, five, six . . . We weren't home, damn it! Why didn't he just give up and call father's cell? Was it that he'd already called father, wasn't able to reach him, and was now trying the house? But father would always have his phone at hand. Had something happened to him? Had the police caught my father? The gendarmerie?

I'd gone deaf with anxiety.

"Hello, uncle Aruz?"
"It's me, Felat!"

Aruz's son, Felat. He was my age but for some reason older than me.

"What?"
"Gaza, it's Felat!"

"Felat? Are you all right?"
"Fine, fine. What are you up to?"
"Never mind that, talk to me! Where've you been. What's happened?"
"What can I say, father beat me up and all that, and then sent me to my uncle's. They stuck me in a room. I just sat there . . ."

Upon finding out that the village they had vacated years ago on the state's orders was now, again by instruction of the state, habitable again, Aruz and the elders of his 260-person following had gotten together for a family meeting, during which Felat, who wanted nothing to do with this reverse migration and didn't want to leave the city, and a few nutjobs in his leadership, had gone out to the fields and torched the houses of their great-grandfathers. Since these fanciful arsonists whose ages ranged from nine to fourteen hadn't been as *meticulous* as those who, in their time, had burned similar villages with so much precision they could have been following a "Village Burning Directive," the fire grew and they were collared before nightfall. The gendarmerie even prepared a report stating that the incident was in no way connected to any state institution, official or unofficial, and had Aruz sign it, and the fire took its exceptional place in the smoky history of the region. I hadn't heard Felat's voice in four months. Now he was talking about running away.

I remembered so clearly. It was the holy night of Berat. Father was at me again, nagging, "Get up and call your uncle Aruz, wish him a blessed night!" So I had been forced to call him. When the phone rang a few times and I was about to say, "No luck, Dad, he's not picking up," a child's voice came from the other end:

"I'm running away, man! I'm going to get the fuck out of here!"
"Hey, you ran away just last year! Where're you going now?"

"Brother?" he was saying. "Is that you?"

"I'm Gaza," I said. "Who're you?" I asked, and he hung up on me.

"That should be Felat . . . Aruz's little boy," said my father. "Whatever then, you can call him tomorrow," he said and left. For the mosque.

Half an hour later in the same evening, Felat had called us back and his first question had been: "Is my brother there?"

"No," I had said. "Who's your brother anyway?"

"Ahlat . . ."

"There's no such person here . . ." Then we were silent . . .

"You're Felat, right? Uncle Aruz's son."

"Yeah . . . who're *you*?"

"I told you, I'm Gaza . . . My dad works with your dad. That's why I called him, for the holy night . . ."

"How should I know, man, should I maybe come over to yours?"

"What're you going to do over here, kid?"

"Or should I go to Istanbul? The nephews live there. But they're even bigger dopes!"

"Is your dad there?"

"No, he's out."

He had begun to cry. Abruptly. As if he'd collapsed to the ground . . .

"Felat? What's wrong?"

"I've run away from home . . ."

I didn't catch this because the words were tangling up in his sobs.

"What?"

"I've run away from home!"

If I'd been an adult, I'd have asked him where he was right then, but I wasn't.

"Why?"

"I don't know, I just did . . ."

"So what're you going to do?"

"I'm going to sell the phone . . . then I'm going to go someplace . . ."

That's how I knew how Felat happened to have his father's phone. It was looking for its new owner so it could sponsor a voyage to God knows where.

These were the words of a thirteen-year-old . . .

"Your dad'll kill you for sure this time, kid!"

"I'm already fucking dead!"

After that phone conversation a year ago, in full knowledge that he wouldn't make it far in the darkness of night, Felat had dried his wet face on walls on his way back home, called me again two days later using their house phone this time, and we had resumed talking.

"Don't be stupid, man, you're not dead!"

"Let's run away, Gaza! Come on, let's go together!"
"Go where?"
"How should I know, man, let's just go someplace . . ."
"Forget it, kid . . . Maybe later . . . Like, in a few years . . . Let's finish school first, at least . . ."

Even though we didn't really take in what the other was saying, being two kids who'd never kept diaries; we'd begun to tell. Things we couldn't tell others . . . It was in our second conversation I found out that Aruz had saved my father in his phonebook as Ahlat. A brief inquest by Felat revealed that Aruz's unlawful business associates were saved in his phonebook under the names of dead relatives. It was his security precaution. But the situation was different with

Ahlat, his eldest son. There'd neither been funeral prayers for him, nor a grave. In these times and regions where people you saw in the morning disappeared by noon, he'd vanished as if he'd never been. So he'd turned into statistical data and taken his place in the missing persons quota of the nation's history of counterterrorism. Clearly Ahlat was dead, but Felat had never been able to accept that. That was why, on that night he ran away, seeing his long-lost brother's name on the screen of the ringing phone had made him freeze. In those few seconds, the only person who'd never stopped believing Ahlat was alive even had a dream: to protect the older brother who'd been taken into custody and tortured time and time again, Aruz sends him away and tells the family, "He's dead!" But of course father and son maintain contact, even if only over the phone. Here's proof: he calls . . . That was why Felat had answered that phone almost expecting to hear a sacred voice. When he hadn't, he hadn't given up that poisonous hope and tried again half an hour later. Unfortunately, he had only been able to talk to me . . . I hate that natural disaster called hope, that makes the world's most desperate children dream the biggest dreams!

There was nothing I could say. Nothing at all!

"You know what, Gaza?"

"What?"

"My dad is sending me to the mountains."

"To the mountains, what?"

"You know what I'm talking about! To join the guerillas! He said they'd man me up over there."

"No kidding!"

"I really don't want to go, man . . . What the hell am I going to do there, man!"

"Gaza?"

"What?"

"Look, kid, if I become a guerilla . . . what if I run into you?"

"What d'you mean?"

"Look, don't go to the army, man!"

"The army, what're you talking about? That's years away . . ."

"Don't go anyway . . ."

"Are you crazy, kid, what are the odds of us both ending up in the same place in this country?"

"Don't be so sure . . . at least send me a photo."

"I don't have a photo of myself, kid."

In those years cell phones were only good for talking and maybe texting. It wasn't yet clear why anyone would pay hourly rates for the Internet, and cameras were still too large to be affixed to computers. Felat and I had never seen each other's faces.

I really didn't. The only photograph at home was of my mother.

"You don't say? I have a whole bunch but they're all at the gas station . . ."

Aruz's only legitimate business: selling gas . . .

"Felat, calm the hell down! Maybe your dad's only saying it to scare you. Maybe he won't send you away . . ."

Even I didn't believe what I was saying. Felat also ignored it and kept trying to come up with a solution to the problem.

"Damn, how am I supposed to recognize you up there then? How can I tell. . . I've

He'd really got it! He was always good at finding things. He was an inventor. Even at the most desperate of times, even if really stupid like that village-burning plan, he always managed to find an escape hole and float through it. Or at least tried to . . . I had no choice but to accept . . . I actually felt pretty good for having a friend who was this frightened of the possibility that in the future he might kill me without realizing it.

He'd never talked about this girl. I'd never heard of her. But this wasn't the time to call him out on it.

To this day I don't know why I said it:

got it! A password! Let's find a password!"

"All right. What'll it be?"
"How should I know. You tell me."
"Remember how I told you about this girl? The one who liked me . . . her name was Çiçek . . ."

"And?"
"I'll call you Çiçek. And you . . ."

I really don't.

Could this be the reason?

I don't think so!

"I can call you Cuma."

"Cuma? What d'you mean, Cuma?"

"It's Friday today!"

"That's good, but don't you forget . . . I'll call you Çiçek, you'll call me Cuma. We'll know right away who it is, and we won't shoot each other . . . all right?"
"All right!"
"It's Father. I'm hanging up!"

He said and vanished from my world. When that phone call was over, the rotting teeth of life completely severed the delicate thread holding us together. I neither talked to Felat again, nor joined the military . . . I did, on a few occasions, call "Cuma!" into a crowd. In hopes someone would call, "Çiçek!" in return . . . but no one ever did. No one replied to my password. Except, one day I did come across an article in the paper:

*A young Kurdish man of Swedish citizenship murdered by relatives in Stockholm, on grounds that he was gay . . .*

Although a rarity, some parts of the world still treasured persons more than the events surrounding them; so the details of the victim's love life or even his identity weren't disclosed. Plus up until this part, the news was pretty commonplace. The killing of homosexual relatives was basically an ancestral sport to some families. What was not commonplace, though, was this:

The victim's will included, right under his wish to be cremated, a request to be wedded with his lover, identified by name, in the likelihood that he was killed by his relatives or parties solicited by his relatives.

In Sweden it was legal for gay people to marry, but in no country of the world was marriage a right available to the dead. The lover who was named in the will took the matter to court immediately to make this marriage happen. With its main themes of death, humanity, romance, and the meaning and tragedy of life, so began one of the most Shakespearean lawsuits in history.

The cowards who squirmed to make sure that the rest of the world could also be crushed under the reign of the moral code they themselves couldn't stop hauling around were quick to build their opposition. Their mouths and tongues became loudspeakers blaring that *living* homosexuals shouldn't be allowed to marry, let alone dead ones. Especially the nameless relatives of the deceased, scattered over three continents . . . They who had assumed that murder could put an end to any love affair were so infuriated by their victim's parting gesture that Swedish flags were already catching on fire on various sidewalks of the world. During this time of foaming saliva and soaring affronts, the expected decision was announced on an unexpected morning:

No case had been made against the marriage of the gay lovers, one of whom was dead and the other alive . . . At least half a kilo in ethical weight and wrapped in a very long rationale, the decision could be summed up as:

As long as it wasn't with a legally impermissible entity—an animal, a child, etc.—as long as no third party was hurt—in cases where there was an ongoing marriage prior to death, for instance—and with the certified consent of both parties, everyone could marry whom they wanted. Dead or alive . . .

The unprecedented decision of the Stockholm District Court was an inspiration to all homosexuals, mostly immigrants, who were being threatened by families or acquaintances, leading them to write single-clause wills immediately. The practice surged out of the borders of Sweden with the velocity of a vaccination against a lethal disease. Future prospects arose in Sweden for homosexuals who'd tried to bury themselves in every desert charted on the map, as deep down as possible, so they wouldn't be seen. For the event that someone anywhere in the world was killed due to their homosexuality, volunteer lists were made in Sweden of people who were ready to marry them. Homosexual people from all over the world who felt themselves under threat picked the name of a Swede from the list, wrote it in the form titled *Posthumous Marriage Request,* and sent it to the foundation in Sweden. This newly established foundation was named *One More!* That by itself summed it all up. In capital letters, too:

"You killed your relative because he was gay, but see, now you have one more gay relative! Will you kill him, too? Then you'll suddenly have one more gay relative. Then more and more and more . . ."

It was a symbolic reaction, of course. Yet weren't all hate crimes of the world grounded in symbolism? Weren't the victims attacked because of whatever it was they symbolized for their murderers? A hate crime wasn't a *personal matter*. It was an objective kind of violence. Hating the victims didn't necessitate taking the time to know them in person. Taking a few hits of the pandemic hate floating in the air would suffice. In this way it wasn't so different from the past, current, and future wars that would be waged over symbols. Yet if those symbols were to be swept out of the picture, all that would be left would be a territorial dispute concerning the distribution of resources. All the wars of the world were basically civil wars. But democracy and liberty and religion and sect and the flag and every symbolic ideal imaginable rippled so alluringly in the wind that it was almost impossible not to be swayed by them. On the streets, in the trenches, anywhere the darkness of the night and systemic violence could reach, all was symbolic. Except the blood that was spilled. Although even that might have been symbolic . . . It did inspire the color of many flags . . . the whole symbol-laden world was a shitty alliance dipped in gold paint. When all those symbols fell off, it would reveal the conspiracy underneath. Because there always was one. Just like the one in Sweden . . .

A few months later, all of this international movement was abruptly cut off by a piece of razor-edged news. A rusty razor at that . . . The *Velvet Mafia*, an invisible organization composed of homosexuals with political and economic power of the caliber of mythical gods, were exposed as having blackmailed and bribed the board of the Stockholm District Court into running the famed decision through. That power-hungry arrogance, fearful of deadly consumption unless it reigned over every single thing, had shown up once again and in trying to save the applecart, shit on it instead. Soon after that day, all dead-living marriages were annulled. Only one of them remained still valid: *symbolically*, that is . . .

In the end, the one who had made it all possible, the owner of that initial will, inside his urn of Roosendaal china, was wedded to his lover in a magnificent ceremony for all the cameras to see, and had his revenge on the murderer who was now in prison and all those who had hated him in life. It was only then that his name was made public. Or rather, his moniker: *Blomma* . . . it meant flower in Swedish. Çiçek . . . was Felat?

Or was he just one of the bodies unearthed every spring by wild animals from the bottoms of hills following one of the PKK's interorganizational execution festivals? If so, had he mentioned me in the *self-criticism* he'd given in a last hope of survival, which would now be filed away in the organization's archive of *Pre-State Bureaucracy* persuasion? Perhaps he'd made it to counselor status in the expertise of confession and was busy chasing debentures in Istanbul . . . Or had he committed suicide? Or had he already run off to a quaint corner of the earth and sat gazing at sky-tinged seas . . . I doubt it . . . If I've learned anything from this disease called life, then he was sitting in Daddy's chair, holding Aruz's phone in his hand. It's that simple . . . The new Aruz wouldn't remember Felat any more than he remembered me or our password . . . I was the only one living in the past, no one else. I was alone in that mausoleum of horrors that no other living thing would set foot in. Horrified . . . because I'd turned into my father, too! I was Ahad! I was worse than Ahad, in fact . . .

Yet on the other hand, *blomma* . . . did that not mean *çiçek*? Çiçek . . . Cuma, then! Felat! Cuma! Against chance, Cuma! Against the predictable flow of time! Against all odds, Cuma! It's Gaza, Felat! Cuma! Don't kill me! Cuma!

Sawdust makes me nauseated. Whenever I see sawdust on the ground, I know a life of filth has been lived there. The shed where cock fights were held three days and two nights a week, the broken-down tavern one slipped into by ducking under the shutters during Ramadan, and where I learned to knock back a couple shots and screw up my face, the police station that was open 24–7 and where I stayed for two nights, though I didn't sleep: they all had sawdust.

Kandalı was the town we fought one another to live in. I'd come too late to see the days it had been called Kandağlı. The letter Ğ didn't wait for me and had long taken its leave. Seated in the middle of Kandağ, which resembled a couch more than it did a mountain, and thus not a recipient of much wind unless it one day chanced to get lost, Kandalı was a small town that everyone insisted on calling a county. Perhaps calling it a county brought them close, if only phonetically, to the possibility of living in a city. In reality Kandalı was a town-sized pit where the humidity was practically a glass curtain, so you had to part it with your hands to move forward, measure it with scales instead of a barometer. A flowerpot that couldn't pull any more than its weight in population, where anything that overgrew would dry up and croak before long. It was a place of olive consumption, of olive tree harvesting, of downing a spoonful of olive oil to fortify oneself for rakı drinking. And sawdust was all over the place.

Wherever I looked I saw sawdust scattered everywhere, so that whatever was about to be spilled would be easier to sweep up later. There was sawdust in all of its five town buses, four coffee houses, its one main street, and numerous small streets no one cared to count. Sawdust in the houses, sawdust in the shops, on the soles of shoes and the knees of children, everywhere. All of Kandalı was covered in sawdust like it'd rained from the heavens. So that nothing would be left of Kandalı and of us . . .

It was in the back of our truck as well, of course. I scattered it on and swept it off. I did it so often it felt like it would stay in my life no matter where I went in the world. Maybe that was as it should be: the whole world should be covered in sawdust! That would make it easier to sweep up entrails spilled by knife, sword, or lead, or the blood from the rape of girls by baton, prick, or fist, everywhere in the world. Because sawdust was magic! It absorbed everything and was cleared away with the sweep of a mop. That was what sawdust did: it sucked up the shitty past and cleared the ground for an even shittier future.

Our own sweet home was at the end of a two-hundred-meter-long dirt road just past the sign at the town exit, one side of which read "Welcome to Kandalı!" and the other "Good-bye!" As for some reason my father refused to have the road paved, we'd emerge at the main road covered in dust. So I'd made a sign reading DUST STREET and tacked it up at the entrance of the road. The sign had been so well received even the postman had written it in his address book. Henceforth our address was Dust Street, Kandalı. No number, since ours was the only house there.

I even hated our address. If it were a living thing, I'd kill it! Anyhow . . .

Our plot of land was one and a half acres. Left to my mother by her father who'd died when she was just a girl. It was basically as if the plot were the only relative I had besides father. We had no one else. I had absolutely no knowledge of the whereabouts or activities of my father's family. Father didn't tell me anyhow. All I knew was that he'd come from far, far away. He had up and come to Kandalı from Bosnia or Bulgaria or South Africa or some other place I couldn't care less about, maybe lost his family on the way.

He must have seemed interesting to my mother because his looks differed from that of the town average. He was pale, with eyes of even paler blue, and he was handsome as a cat. Genetically speaking he was a dickhead. So it hadn't taken him long to catch my mother in his web, and then I was born. And when mother died, it was my turn to fall into the web. I don't know if at any point in his life he had a legitimate job. Perhaps he had gotten into this line of work at nine, like me! Ultimately, all I knew was that the house, shed, and the reservoir underneath the shed were his places of business and that he occasionally transported vegetables and fruits. For the sake of giving the impression he was working, I suppose . . .

Aruz's eighteen-wheelers took off from Kandalı into the depths of Asia Minor, arrived at the entrance of the village of Derç that was three hundred kilometers away, and drove along the Derçisu Creek, in the winter a thousand times its summer width, before entering the forest. The road ended a few hundred meters in, but the huge eighteen-wheeler would already have been swallowed up by the surrounding red, black, and stone pines, becoming invisible. That was the exact point at which the fifteen-minute run of transporting the goods would take place and, having nothing to do except open and close the vault doors,

I'd breathe in the fragrances of thyme, sage, and lavender and imagine burning down the whole forest so it would smell even more strongly. That was the precise spot my father had buried Cuma. Among the lavender . . .

That morning, I'd neglected to turn on the conditioner when I was supposed to, and then forgotten about it completely. According to father's plan, we were to put Cuma on the boat toward nightfall and then return to Derçisu to pick up new goods. Father must have counted on me, since he didn't check the back when we were setting out. But when we made it to the cove where the boat was waiting and opened the back, we'd encountered not Cuma, but his corpse. This had forced my father to make a decision. He would have to either bury Cuma somewhere in the cove and be late for the delivery, or take him to Derçisu and figure it out there. He chose not to be late. And to give me a lesson . . . thus I'd had to ride to Derçisu not on the passenger seat next to my father, watching the road, but in terror in the back, trying not to look at Cuma's corpse. For hours on the road—trying to stay as far away as possible from Cuma's constantly shifting corpse . . .

When we got to Derçisu, my father dug away like a beaver and quickly buried Cuma. That was why the forest was as cursed to me as it was sacred to the immigrants. Because there they were one step closer to their goal. When their transition to the truck was complete, there was a brief transaction, then the same three hundred kilometers back until we entered Dust Street. We'd park the truck in the shed and open the doors of the vault. As we opened the lid in the corner of the shed, we'd say, "Come on!" and even if they didn't know the words, our gestures would immediately tell the immigrants what to do and they'd disappear through the hole just wide enough for a human to fit through.

Father had had the reservoir installed two years ago. Due to the security necessities of the chaining method—that was dependent on the steps prior and subsequent to the delivery, which could end up being delayed—he'd decided the shed was no longer suitable. So he'd called in constructors from Barnak, a village two hundred kilometers away, and told them, "I want a water reservoir." He'd even drawn a water pipe from the main grid to the reservoir so they wouldn't get suspicious. Although the men had pointed out that the reservoir should be nearer the house for the stability of the water pipes, they hadn't been too insistent since my father was paying their wages. When he said he wanted a cast iron door, they hadn't made a peep, since it was much more costly than a simple iron door. It wasn't their problem if some nut wanted to seal off his water reservoir like it was a manhole!

When the lid was installed, further confirming my status as a sewage worker, we had at our disposal a hell pit large enough for two hundred people to fit in, provided they sucked in their bellies and stayed close to one another. A perpetually warm tomb where the tropical maps on the damp concrete walls and the ponds accumulating on the floor constantly shifted places and shapes. A cell lit by the diffused shadows of spiderwebs rather than by the bulb I had to replace two or three times a week. A cellar we used to age people in . . .

Yet the immigrants, who'd traveled who knows how many thousands of kilometers to get here, never paid attention to the décor and immediately lined up to sit on the wet floor like they came here every day, resting their heads between their palms and taking up their pose of the waiting. The perfect waiters! They could wait days, weeks, months without tiring. Once they rested their heads on their palms, they disengaged like space shuttles and sank into a strange sleep until they were woken up again. A kind of standby mode that wasn't quite like sleep . . . auto-anesthesia!

Since experience had taught me that sitting on that wet floor eventually gave them diarrhea and left me with longer sawdust-sweeping duty, I handed out pieces of newspaper and

Styrofoam. Then, for obvious reasons, I'd put buckets in front of them. One per family. One per set of friends. I'd ask the lone ones, "Who would you like to shit with?" They wouldn't understand, of course. I couldn't be bothered to explain.

Just as I was headed to the six wooden steps leading up from the reservoir to the shed, one of them would step forward and ask. They usually had a spokesman. Someone who could string together about four words in English or who'd had the right mind to learn useful words in the languages of the countries he'd be traversing. Someone clever . . . I'd know what he was asking, of course. But I'd pretend I didn't. "When?" he'd say. In all the languages he knew. He'd ask when they'd be setting out again. I'd tell him to forget about it and concentrate instead on the more pressing issue of what the hell they were going to do when they had to use the buckets in a few hours. He'd make nothing of this long reply and repeat his question. I'd ignore this again, of course, and walk out. I'd return with a clothesline for them to stretch from the hooks on the walls and an old sheet to hang over it, and hand these to the spokesman who'd be in my face again. As he stared dumbly at me, unaware that he'd just been given the materials to partition their home measuring twelve by six meters in perimeter and twelve meters in height, and fashion a toilet for themselves, however primitive, I'd already be up in the shed, pulling the lid down. They'd very well figure out the curtain thing by themselves. I'd never encountered anyone who hadn't. Leave people with no resources and they'll make a rocket out of innards!

Depending on the situation, they'd stay in the reservoir half a day or two weeks, and then be on their way. Dordor and Harmin were the ones who determined this. With respect to the course of the pattycake they played with the coast guard, they'd decide on a date for the departure of the boat and call to give my father the code for the place and time of their meeting. And one night the lid would open, a route ranging from fifty to two hundred kilometers would be traveled, and they'd jump on a boat on one of those coasts of the Aegean that looked like it had been gnawed on by wolves and vanish into the darkness . . .

That was the whole job. It wasn't much . . . But on that morning . . . There was more. That morning, there was more than more! My awakening was more. The way I got out of bed, the way I walked, it was more. The way I washed my face and walked some more, again; more. I was immersed in something similar to happiness. My hands, my eyes, and what I saw were more. There was something about me that made me forget about my life . . . something more . . . It was love.

There was a party of twenty-four in the reservoir. As Dordor would say, a parade! They'd been there for two days. Among them the one who'd dipped me into that something more, the world's most beautiful girl . . . She must have been around my age. Or maybe a year older. Maybe two. She had black hair. Black eyes . . . I didn't know where she was from, but I wanted to ask. Her name, age, what she liked, what she wanted to be when she grew up . . . I couldn't get her out of my mind ever since I'd seen her passing from the eighteen-wheeler into our truck. I couldn't sleep. I held my breath without realizing it, leaving myself breathless, then chortled to myself like Ender used to do. I didn't know how to fall in love but felt it must be something like this: planning like I was preparing for a robbery . . . chasing the right moves, the right places, the right moments . . . It wasn't that much different from hunting. In fact, the man who'd made the first leopard print must have thought the same thing. Love had to do with hunting. What woman would want to look like an animal otherwise?

Time was running out. Dordor and Harmin might send word any minute, and the most beautiful girl in the world would disappear in a matter of hours. I was waiting for father to leave the house, but he just wouldn't. It was like he was

nailed down! So I decided to ignore him. This was a big decision. Very big! I'd take my only chance that day and place a bet
to the possibility of my father not going down to the reservoir.
I was a born gambler. A million to one odds was enough for
me. That, and I was counting on the fact that Father woke
around noon, came around in the afternoon, started drinking
before nightfall, and made me do everything shed- or
reservoir-related. So I might not have been that big a gambler.
I've always felt more like a gambling ticket anyway. I was even
willing to put in my will that my bones be made into gambling
tickets. That wouldn't be halfway bad. At least, it wouldn't be
against my nature!

All I'd thought about the last two days was how to make the
world's most beautiful girl happy. Obviously I didn't have much
to offer her. I had a necklace of my mother's. A gold chain with
an angel on the end. I could give her that. But what use would
it be to her, given the situation she was in? I needed something
more real. That's when it occurred to me that all they'd been eating was the sandwiches I gave out. I made them. Tomato-and-
cheese sandwiches. That and I gave them water. For free, even! So
that the world's most beautiful girl would see what a thoughtful
person I was. I couldn't tell if she noticed, though. It didn't seem
that way. She didn't even look at me, even though I did everything I could to prolong my time in the reservoir. Still, she was
having the worst days of her life. For now . . .

Anyway . . . I'd made up my mind. My present to her would
be a nice meal, one that left its taste in her mouth for the rest
of her journey and reminded her of me. But what was a good
meal? For me, it was meat . . . would she like that too? Also, was
it romantic to give food to someone? Maybe that, and to let her
out of the reservoir so she could breathe for a while . . . without
Father knowing. That was the most knightly I could be in my
current circumstances. I didn't know how much more dangerous

you could get with the one you love. Because it couldn't get more dangerous than that for me.

I was up early that morning. I'd dressed quietly and left the house because I was sure my father was still sleeping. Yet when I shut the door and looked out at Dust Street, I saw something that upset all my plans. On a chair at the beginning of the dirt road was Father, just sitting there. There were about forty meters between us and his back was to me. He seemed to be waiting for someone to come from the direction of the main road. Yet he was so still I thought for a second he might be dead. Maybe that was a wish, I can't say for sure. With every step I took in his direction, I tried to think up a lie so I could go into town. I'd just come up to him silently when I saw that his chin was practically on his chest. He was sleeping! He'd fallen asleep on that chair. He'd probably drunk till morning and passed out. I had no idea why he was seated to face Dust Street. Why ever he had been drinking *there* when he had the whole yard to get drunk in? I didn't care a bit. All I cared about was that he was passed out . . . I passed him discreetly and took off running when I was a good distance away. Sadly, I arrived in town to realize it was still too early. Upon which I paced the pavement in front of the three restaurants on Kandalı's main street until they opened up shop.

One was a kebab joint, the other fish. The last one made casseroles. When noon came I started going back and forth between them. A waiter, thinking I had no money and was too embarrassed to say so, said, "Come, let me give you some soup."

"No," I replied, "thanks."

I had other things on my mind and no one could possibly understand. I was looking for something that wouldn't lose its taste when it got cold on the walk home. In the end I wasn't able to decide. So I went into all the restaurants and ordered food. While I waited for them to prepare it, I watched the girls on the street. Their hair, clothes, shoes . . . so I'd get an idea . . . The world's most beautiful girl sat in that hell of a reservoir in just a sweater. I should get her a T-shirt, I thought. I went into a shop and examined at least thirty T-shirts like I'd never seen one in my life. I'd never bought a girl a T-shirt before, after all. When they asked, "What size?" I was struck dumb, and bought two T-shirts emblazoned with an angel like the one on my mother's necklace. In two different sizes. I was so flustered doing all this that my hands shook and I kept scattering change whenever I took money out of my pocket. I think I was also grinning like an idiot . . .

When I went back to the three restaurants and collected the bags, I realized just how over the top I'd gone. I'd bought food enough for five people. I didn't get hung up on it. My only goal now was to make it to the reservoir before any of it got cold. I began running. I stopped twice on the way to put the bags down because I burned my hands. I thought at some point that my father might still be sitting in the same place. But then I thought that the sun was now so high up that it must even have woken up a drunk like Ahad, and I kept on running. When I got to Dust Street, neither the chair nor my father were there. They were gone . . .

So I was able to get into the reservoir without Ahad catching me. It occurred to me then that I hadn't gotten anything to drink. There should at least be Coke to wash it down. There was a bottle of it in the house. On my way out of the reservoir, my father busted me. A gun in the hand of that other guy I didn't know. I was accustomed to both. To strangers and to the guns in their belts. I didn't get hung up on it. I only started praying internally, "Not now! Don't let them leave now, please! Let them stay one more day!" because such strangers usually materialized before departure. Since I doubt the existence of a godly power in favor of illegal immigrants and those who transport them, I don't know who I was praying to. As they walked to the arbor behind the house, Father turned and yelled:

"Where the hell have you been! Go, clean the trailer and throw down some sawdust!"

He referred to the enormous box behind the truck as the trailer. I preferred to call it a vault. It felt more logical. It was a vault! A vault we put humans into, saved humans in, always locked the doors of, and constantly emptied and filled up . . . Didn't we do everything in our power to make sure it didn't appear to be a vault? The huge AHAD LOGISTICS—FRESH FRUIT AND VEGETABLE TRANSPORTATION inscription on the outside, wasn't that for this very reason? It was like a crap painting hung up on the wall to disguise the vault underneath . . .

"All right, Dad! I'm going!"

What or whoever it was I had prayed to must have heard me, because my father's command was ordinary and quotidian. Not a command pertaining to departure. A command given for the sake of commanding. One of the commands that came to his mind when he saw me. A way of communicating with me because he had no way of saying, "Hi, son, how's it going?"

As soon as my father and the stranger were out of sight behind the house, I doggedly dashed inside. I grabbed the bottle of Coke, a glass, a fork, and a knife within seconds. I left quickly and just as doggedly ran to the shed.

It was now time for the second phase of the plan: setting a table. The truck was parked in the middle of the shed and didn't leave me much of a choice where to place the metal table that my father used for his carpentry. It was right next to the entrance of the reservoir. I collected the hammer, screwdriver, screws, and nails that were on it and put them on the floor. I wiped clean the tabletop with a dirt-blackened cloth. I knew there was a stool somewhere in the shed that took me at least ten minutes to locate. Just when I'd dragged it up to the table, I realized that it was wobbly. I considered finding a piece of cardboard to steady it, but abandoned the idea for the sake of time. I wouldn't have minded sticking my foot under it so the world's most beautiful girl wouldn't wobble on it and be uncomfortable. Then I'd get to stand behind her as she ate and even put my hand on her shoulder. I took the food out of the bags and set it out on the table. I set out refreshment towels, packets of salt and pepper, napkins, fork, knife, glass, and Coke and took two steps back . . . Yes, it seems I had set a table. Or it seemed that way to me. All the stuff and I—we were ready. The T-shirts hidden under the truck I'd give her after the meal, in place of dessert.

I opened the lock on the lid with the key in my pocket and went down into the reservoir. I was so excited I could feel my heart pulsing in my forehead. As soon as they saw me, the ones who still had the energy to stand got up and surrounded me. As always, they thought it was time to take off.

Waving both my hands, I said, "No! No!" in English.

They sat down as if an avalanche had come down on their shoulders. Then I saw her. The world's most beautiful girl. She'd pulled her knees to her chest to prop up her head, and her arms were wrapped around them. She didn't look at me until I'd gone up to her. She lifted her head only when my shadow eclipsed her. I took a breath as large as my courage and held out my hand. She didn't understand. I bent down slightly and took her right hand. She began to shake her head, left to right.

"Don't be afraid," I said.

With my free hand, my face, my gaze, and everything I had . . . But she didn't understand. None of them did. The woman sitting next to her, whom I took to be her mother, began shouting. Shouting something at me . . . then a man joined her. Then another woman. Then all of the rest of them. But I didn't listen. I thought that they would understand. I even smiled. Smiling, I looked them in the face and held on to her hand. Then suddenly the world's most beautiful girl began to cry and pull herself back. Right then I felt hands on my shoulders. Hands trying to pull us apart. They were all over me. They wanted to wrench me away from her. And I was forced to let go of her hand. In turn the others let go of my shoulders.

"Fine!" I said. "Okay . . . *no problem!*"

I spun around and took a step. But I didn't get far. For the woman I'd thought to be her mother was standing in my way. She uttered two syllables and spat in my face. Then she got out of my way, and I just walked. I passed twenty-four pairs of murderous eyes, went up the stairs into the shed, and locked the door. I wiped the spit off my face with the back of my hand and stood still for a few seconds. I looked at the table. At the food . . . It was still steaming, albeit slightly. Or I was imagining it? I sank down on the stool and almost fell off because it wobbled. I got my balance back and put my elbows on the table. I rested my head between my hands, closed my eyes, and understood who I was . . .

Of course I knew before that day what kind of business I was mixed up in. I knew in the eyes of those people I was a freak they needed to stay away from. A freak they depended on in their desperation but would never dare to be alone with . . . Yes, it was true, I didn't like them, either. Sometimes I could barely stand their presence. Because it wasn't just them in that reservoir. They might not have been aware of it, but I was stuck in that reservoir with them. Plus my loathing was on the inside only. It was right behind my closed lips. I still did what I could. So they wouldn't get sick, wouldn't be hungry, wouldn't have to live in filth . . . I did everything I was supposed to. Besides, I was just a kid. But it turned out that I wasn't. What had just happened was blaring into both my ears: you aren't a kid! You aren't a kid. . . I couldn't have known . . . I hadn't known . . . I hadn't known I was this loathsome in their eyes . . . I had had no idea I was so similar to the leading men in the rape stories they'd no doubt heard many times from others who had gone, or attempted to go, on the road. I hadn't known they feared me so much. I hadn't known I was so fearsome . . . It would never end, too . . . and now I was left with only two choices: Either I would run from this house, this life, and these people who thought I was a monster and go somewhere far away, or . . .

I stood. I took seven steps to the wall on my right. I knelt down. I opened the lid of a black knee-high box. With some difficulty, I turned the red valve inside all the way to the right. It was the first time that valve had been turned since its installation. The water from the main grid headed through the previously unused pipe toward the reservoir, its boisterous procession gurgling like a deep river. Then it was joined by a banging sound just as deep. The sound of flesh on iron. I looked at the padlock on the lid that was being beaten on. It hardly moved. Only the lid shook faintly with each slam. Or it was just my imagination. The screams rising behind the lid must have been who knows how loud, but I only heard a murmur as if from another planet. As if the reservoir had a gurgling stomach. Maybe that gurgling was coming from me. I went back to the table, sat on the stool, and began slowly to eat. I paid no attention to what I was eating because I didn't taste any of it. I just chewed. And watched the reservoir lid and listened to the sound of the water filling it . . . I didn't think of anything.

When I felt I was full, I opened the packet of one of the refreshment towels. I wiped my fingers and lips until I believed them to be completely clean. I folded up the greasy towel, stuck it back inside its small packet and put it in the bag at my feet. It was a perfectly right time to start smoking. I got up and went to the truck and opened the door on the driver's side. The door had a large cubby full of stuff. I rooted around a bit and found what I was looking for. Father's pack of cigarettes, with his lighter inside it at all times. I drew one out and lit up. Coughed and took another drag. I put the pack back and closed the door. I walked toward the lid of the reservoir lid and took another step. Standing on the lid, I smoked the cigarette until it was finished. Underneath my feet, I thought I felt the vibration from the increased hammering. I took a few steps to the wall and knelt down to open the lid of the black box. I thought of mother. Then of father. And I shut off the red valve. Neither the river nor the noise was left. They both dried up.

I went to the reservoir lid, opened the padlock, and removed it. The hammering stopped that second. Or that's what I imagined. I took the lid by its handles and lifted it as I stood. A couple of screams leaked out and then it was silent. I took two steps back and slowly set the lid down. A meter away, the door to the shed was completely opened. I turned around, walked to the stool, and sat down. But I didn't wobble this time. Because I was aware of all irregularities.

There was a monster in the imagination of the people down there. And I waited for that monster to fuck away with all the humanity that was in the reservoir. I heard a voice, then three, then ten separate ones. Talking. Voices that rode over one another and merged together and rose out of the entrance to the reservoir and rose to the ceiling of the shed like smoke. Then I heard the sound of weeping. Actually two . . . a cry. Then it was silent . . .

I saw a head of hair. Jet black. Then a face. Then shoulders. I saw slender fingers in the sawdust. Then a knee. Then another and there, the world's most beautiful girl was standing. In front of me . . . weeping. But there were no tears in sight. More than that, it appeared to be flowing inside her. Deep. Like the river a minute ago. Perhaps if I laid my head on her chest, I could hear her tears.

But I didn't. I gestured to the table. "Eat!" I said. "It's for you."

She took one step, then six more. She hesitated, then hastily collected the food and began dole it into the entrance of the reservoir. Within a minute, every single thing on the table had disappeared into the entrance. Then she stopped and looked at me. Her eyes met mine. She was trembling.

She took two steps toward me and began to unbutton her dress. This time I could see her tears. They had overflowed at last and were pouring down her cheeks. I looked at the entrance of the reservoir. At its wide-open entrance . . . the bulb must have blown out again. There was no light, nor a sound, nor anyone in sight . . . only, at one point, something that sounded like a sob. From underground . . . a monosyllabic sound reminiscent of the scream of that woman long ago whose baby had died, before it was blocked by the hands of the others.

That day, on top of twenty-three people, a few pieces of Styrofoam, and a few pages of newspaper, I touched a woman for the first time in my life. As I was about to come like my jugular had been cut, staring over her shoulders at the mouth of the reservoir, she shoved me back. She knew better than me what men were. I poured everything that had been pooling up in me on the floor of the shed . . .

She dressed, I dressed. She went into the reservoir, I locked the door. Then I began to sweep the sawdust and its contents off the floor . . . not a trace was left . . . The day after, as they got on the boat, I looked them in the eye. Every one of them. One after the other. No trace there, either. So we were in agreement. They thought I was a monster, and I was turning into one. To top it off, it took them no longer than ten minutes to sacrifice one of their own in my name . . .

On the way back, Father said, "The reservoir was flooded!"

"The men told you," I said. "It should have been nearer the house."

I wasn't in love anymore. I just followed the path. The path those people had shown me. One way. No return . . . I saved the red T-shirts with the angels to buy the most beautiful girls of other worlds. Then I figured out that I didn't need those, either. I realized that the index finger of my left hand was the barrel of a gun. It was enough to point it at someone. If she was someone's wife, they'd find someone else to send me. That was how my knighthood was taken from me at fourteen, piece by piece. But this was never made known, since no one knew in the first place that I'd lived as a knight among dragons and dungeons up until that age. Perhaps only Cuma, but he didn't count. Because he, architect of paper frogs, wouldn't have known even if he had lived: why I hadn't run that day from that house, that life, and those people who thought I was a monster . . . Perhaps because I wasn't named Felat. Because I was a coward . . . So, could a coward be a monster? Of course! In fact, I think only cowards could be monsters. I was the living proof. That was why sawdust made me nauseated. For I was sawdust. Sawdust and splinters. If I'd been spread over the earth, there wouldn't be a single trace left behind . . . I tried. Many times I scattered myself over those women and eradicated them all.

My transformation into a dreadful monster took only five years. I was the sum of my father, Aruz, Dordor, and Harmin. In fact I was more than their sum. I was still a kid, after all. I was fourteen. So the pain of others was just a game to me, and none of the things I experienced seemed real. This made me even more dreadful. I wouldn't have been as affected if I'd been a child worker in another sector, of course. In my line of work, there were no strange chemicals to riddle my lungs or vaporous materials such as thinner that I'd become addicted to. I was in the service industry. The manhole industry! Down in the sewers of the service industry. I was responsible for the facilitation and sanitation of a sewer that transported people. That might be why the capacity for empathy, which I was born with like everyone else, wasn't worth a damn under the circumstances. I couldn't possibly put myself in the shoes of those human-shits. Anyway, I'd already wasted all of that innate capacity to fathom the motives of my father, Aruz, Dordor, and Harmin. There was nothing left behind except my eyes that apprehended their surroundings like a pair of bullets. It was absolutely of no concern to me that the immigrants had names, lives, or blood and nervous systems inside them. I just got angry. Their most minute reaction or smile tore at my eyeballs like poisonous claws. Especially those surreptitious dreams of theirs! Because I could hear them! I could hear those edifices of dream perfectly well! Dreams of happiness in faraway places! Disgusting dreams I inadvertently had a role in realizing!

I'd asked father once. "Can we go as well?" I'd begged him actually. "Dad, let them take us along!" We could have gotten on one of Dordor and Harmin's boats and set foot on distant shores to be born again. "Please, Dad, let's go with them!"

He'd stared. "Our job," he'd said, "is to send the passengers on their way—not go with them!" As if to say that our job was to kill, not die . . .

Upon this, encumbered with the pain of having to stay in Kandalı, I dreamed my own dreams. Sometimes they even became reality. As a matter of fact, they did so many times and it was always exactly as I'd dreamed: I watched them being busted by the coast guard just as they believed their months-long torture of a journey to be over, a step or two short of whatever land they'd been promised. Or on TV or the photos in newspapers.

Many late nights I was so uplifted by the sight of their faces riddled with coast guards' searchlights, I broke out laughing! As I watched them huddle together and freeze like a rabbit with a thousand eyes captured by a thousand hunters, I said, "See?" It was all for nothing! Now off to where you came from, on the first flight! The first time in your lives you'll fly, and to be deported at that! Why don't you fuck off and start all over again! But then my mouth would abruptly shut. Because it would occur to me that they'd just go by us again. Fuck this shit, I'd say! No getting rid of them for good! Why wouldn't these people just stay at their homes? Why wouldn't they stay in their cities? Why . . .Then I'd randomly plant myself in front of one and start hollering.

"Is there a war on your street, huh? Are people killing each other on your front stoop? Go, get outside then, and fight! Get killed or mauled, become a cripple! Is there hunger back where you live? Why don't you have a kid and eat it! Eat yourself! Don't presume to fuck up my life just because you want to up and go to the other side of the world! What do you think will happen when you get there anyhow? They'll fuck the very marrow in your bones! What else do you expect? Because people are waiting for you with open arms, right? Idiot! You aren't worth a damn where you're going, don't you get it? Of course you don't! You'll see! No one will want to sit next to you on the bus! No one will want to be left alone with you on an elevator! No one will return the greetings in that stupid accent of yours you'll never get rid of! No one will want to be your neighbor! No one will let their child associate with your child! No one will want the slightest thing to do with your religion! No one will want to have to smell the reek of your cooking! No one will want you to earn money! No one will wish you more happiness or a longer life than themselves! No one will want to be behind you in a queue! No one will want you to be voting where you're going! No one will want to sleep with you! No one will look you in the eye! No one will treat you like a human being! No one will want to know your name! If they do, believe me, they're just insane or pretending! They're going to hate you so much estate prices will go down wherever you move! Wake up already! Yet you're still giving up your life to get there! You're still working like a dog for years to save up money so you can hand it over to our kind! That goes to show . . . that goes to show that you deserve all your suffering. And that's where I come in! I'm going to show you such a good time that you're going to go and tell it to your piece of shit friends! That illegal immigration realm of yours! That realm with all your whispering among yourselves, 'Who, where, for how much?' That realm you cheer each other on with constant bullshit! And they'll all be talking about *you*! They'll hear about what's happened to *you*! Because you'll go tell them! You'll be crying when you tell them! Maybe you won't even be able to tell some parts of it! You'll be too ashamed! They'll gnaw on your wits! When we're through our time together, anyone else that's considering immigrating won't even dare set foot outside their house! Or else, wherever they want to go, they'll have to travel to do it over the North Pole . . . and I . . ."

And I what? My speech would end somewhere around here. I didn't really have an idea what would become of me in the event that my crazy plan to put a stop to all this somehow happened. All I knew was that my situation couldn't get much worse. To be fair, all these lines were part of a text I was working on. It was just a while ago, for instance, that I'd added the part about religion and the reeking food. In order to obtain knowledge about those countries they'd give up anything to get inside the borders of, I was reading anything I could get my hands on. I needed to know what those fucking countries were like, that they were willing to die to get to or slave away ten years when they did! And everything I learned I put into my speech.

I would usually be standing when I started. It was important to be standing. For they would tend to be on the floor and early on this discrepancy in our heights would let them know who was boss. Another crucial detail was the instantaneous start. It had to be sudden! Bursting out in out-of-the-blue hollering, when they least expected it! Even better, looking at them with a childlike smile right before hollering, which petrified them even more.

Then I'd kneel and bring my face close to theirs. I loved doing that. Peering very closely at someone when only I knew the next move. Violating personal space, that minimum expanse based on interpersonal respect, was a terrific feeling! At first they would avoid looking at me and turn their gaze away but, having to eventually wipe the spittle that was spewing out of my mouth onto their forehead or cheek, would be forced to make eye contact with me through their fingers, even if for a moment. And in that moment, I never saw them. I'd be aware that right in front of me were a pair of eyes, a nose, a mouth, and a person at least twenty years my senior, but I wouldn't comprehend.

That's what I mean when I say that none of it felt real. Only I was real. Just me. This was clearly proof that I wasn't quite sound in those years. But mental health wasn't a prerequisite for my line of work. It was enough that my five senses and muscles functioned adequately. I cleaned the sewer! And if this was my job, I had to become god of the sewers! And that's what I did . . . I did so many things I'd rather never have to remember, when the only chance I have of forgetting is to tell . . . What's more, I did those things so I'd *never have to remember other things* . . . But trying to live today as a way of forgetting yesterday proved to be useless. Quite the contrary . . . the unforgettables that I yearned to forget quadrupled in number. Turns out that one needed to forget about tomorrow in the first place . . . forget so completely that one could believe that every dawn meant a new sun . . . forget so utterly that every sighting of the sun was surely the first and the last. Forget well enough to say, "I believe today's is a bit wider!" or "Yesterday's sun was more oval shaped, wasn't it?" Forget enough to live every day as if it were one's first . . . And to holler: "Which religion doesn't have déjà vu? I'll take that one!" And to be silent: Where there's no resurrection, that's where I'm going to be . . .

When I first laid eyes on Dordor and Harmin, who'd ended up doing one of the world's most detestable jobs when they ought to have been explorers like Juan Ponce de Léon or James Cook, I knew right away that they were nothing like my father or any of the other people in the fabric of crime in which I was only a stitch. Even though I was only nine years old. But their way of conversing and their manners, along with the stories they told, made me associate them with the adventurers in the children's books I'd just begun to read at that time. A pair of adventurers from an era when piracy didn't yet entail gnawing hungrily on a freight ship off the shore of Nigeria . . .

Although they'd sampled the salt of at least four oceans, besieged by nothing but the horizon, they had somehow gotten stuck in the handful of water that was the Aegean. Perhaps they'd dropped by in passing and, having come by the opportunity for easy money, wasted years of their lives between Greece and Turkey, all the while saying, "One last time, then we're done!" I had the best times of my life on the *Dordor* and *Harmin* when their day off coincided with one on which my father wanted to get rid of me. Yes, the boats had been named after their captains. Obviously these were monikers. They'd each picked a noise made by their boats and put them into words. Dordor was named Dordor because his boat made a "dordor-ing" noise! Maybe it was because I never learned their real names that they reminded me so much of the seamen in the books.

Especially during the months of spring, they'd come in the mornings and whisk me away, take me on either the *Dordor* or the *Harmin,* and bring me back to my father only after dark. Both liked to read. They always kept books on their boats. Both smoked constantly. Not that I had any inkling at that age that what they were smoking wasn't tobacco. From morning till night they inhaled a mix of ashen marijuana smoke and cloudy sea air and were either completely quiet or talked as much as if they'd lived a thousand lives. They were the ones who taught me to swim. They taught me to dive, to use the spear gun, everything about the sea's underside and surface. They were a year apart. Dordor was older. Their families were in Istanbul. In Heybeliada. But they never saw them. Perhaps because they'd run away from home years ago. Over some hard feelings or other . . . if Dordor brought it up, Harmin would wave it off. If one asked, "I wonder how Mother's doing?" the other would snap, "Like Father, I bet!" and that would be that.

They read Jack London. But not the Jack Londons I used to read. Theirs were different. They preferred the novels of Jack London that I was to discover years later, in which every *White Fang* rotted and fell out one by one . . . I wished night would never fall. That it would never get dark and they'd never have to take me back. That we could stay at sea forever! Drop anchor anywhere we liked, fall into the water wherever we pleased! Neither had ever gotten married. No woman could have shared that watery life. They were no older than thirty. Two overgrown juvenile delinquents. Two overgrown water plants . . . flowers, after Felat's fashion.

They were the only ones I could ever tell . . . the only ones . . . what one of the immigrants did to me back when there was no reservoir and the immigrants were being held in the shed . . . or, to be more accurate, what he did while the others watched and did nothing . . .

It wasn't just the innocents that left the countries of their birth. It wasn't just those fleeing from *bad men* . . . The *bad men* themselves also fled! Our shed also accommodated criminals who were wanted in their own countries and set to serve sentences of who knows how many years. Thieves, murderers, rapists, and child molesters . . . and I had to be alone with them . . .

I was ten. The age when I'd had the idea of selling the water. I held out my hand for the money. He held my hand and pulled me toward him. The other laughed. They all got lumps in one cheek. As if they were holding eggs inside their mouths. I thought they must be ill. Turns out it was *khat. Khat*, that Yemeni shit. Shit that also had a Latin name: *catha edulis*. A type of amphetamine. The kind that one can't stop chewing on all day . . . I tried to run. I tried to get away, to shout, to bite, to hurt him. I couldn't. I tried to disappear. Like a magical kid. I tried to be blind and deaf. I tried not to understand what was happening to me. I couldn't. There were red rivers in his eyes. He pulled up my pants and zipped them. He buttoned the button and put the money in my pocket. I tried to think of other things. I couldn't. I tried to cry, to run off crying, to find my father, tell my father everything. I couldn't. It might have been because I was selling the water. Because Father might be mad if he found out . . . He pushed a wad of grass into my mouth. It wasn't an egg in his mouth, I saw then. He chewed and his eyes got even redder. I chewed and nothing happened.

The prints stayed on my forehead half the day. His finger-prints. I waited for them to disappear. They didn't. They sank into my skin and bled into my forehead. I tried to sit down for two days and couldn't. Then in secret I bled . . .

How ever did I tell Dordor and Harmin, how was I even able? Maybe I didn't know what I was saying. Perhaps I was simply raving . . . They both listened. They exchanged glances and said nothing. The only thing they did was to not take me back that night, telling Father I was to stay on the boat. I stayed there three days, in fact.

When it was time to leave, the men in the shed came out of the back of truck and, walking right past me and staring at me the whole time, got on Dordor's boat. Then Dordor and Harmin returned the following morning with an empty boat, just like always. Aruz called my father the same day and told him that the goods hadn't been delivered to Greece. Not knowing how to reply, my father asked Dordor, who in turn said:

"We killed them all. Whatever we owe you, we'll pay."

My father was once again at a loss for words because neither Dordor nor Harmin told him why they did it. They were both seaman enough to be able to keep a secret. I wonder to this day why they didn't tell my father the truth. Probably because they knew it wouldn't make any difference. Maybe it was because they didn't even trust their *own* father!

When Aruz received the news, he said, "This is the last time! The first and the last! I won't excuse this kind of thing ever again! Tell them to send the money!"

Dordor paid Aruz for the six heads lost during delivery, and Aruz then returned it to their relatives. One of them, however, the oldest one who watched, was from a clan in Libya. A clan that was a regular in other trafficking services of the PKK as well. Since Aruz was under the impression he could talk his way around any-one at any time, he didn't take the situation seriously at first and said the ship had sunk. On Aruz's orders, Dordor even sunk the *Dordor* a week later. But the Greeks, hoping to blackball the PKK on a drug deal they had going with the Libyans, downright poured salt into the wound by claiming the boat was in great shape and couldn't possibly have sunk. This created a complication that was beyond Aruz's control and in the realm of other trafficking deals. Aruz tried to withstand the pressure for as long as he could, but that turned out to be only four years. When he saw that diplomacy was no longer enough and that the issue was getting too dangerous, Aruz called Dordor one night to say:

"I like you both . . . We've done business for years now . . . but I'm at my last straw here. Now . . . decide. You or him? One of you is enough."

He was asking them which one of them to kill. He was a businessman after all. He had in mind to keep doing business with the one who survived. I don't know how they made the choice. Actually, I have an idea . . . One night four days before Aruz's men showed up with their knives, as we sat on the boat, Dordor had taken a drag off his joint and looked up at the stars, and then spoken:

"You know what we used to do? When a tour boat or something went by, we'd wave at it. Then we'd check out who was waving back . . . how many of them were chicks and all that. Sometimes it was only dudes waved back. And we'd say, man, even from this far away, the broads can tell we're not much to look at . . . We'd do odds and evens over the ones who waved . . ."

Maybe that was how they decided who would die. Or perhaps Dordor never told Harmin about his conversation with Aruz and kept all the short straws to himself . . . He had continued:

"You know that inn with the two doors, the one the minstrel Aşık Veysel speaks of? That's the reason for the constant draught in this life! That's the reason I'm always cold. Guess I might as well go and shut a door."

He went and shut the door behind him. He was stabbed sixty-six times and photographs of his corpse taken to be sent to Libya. The photographs were taken from angles that clearly showed the stab wounds. That was the order. Because the bastard had been sixty-six years old at the time he watched me get fucked, and at the time he died.

Some of it father told me. Some Harmin related to me. I started to say, "Why didn't you run!" but Harmin laughed. I couldn't think of a thing to say. It was all because of me . . . I would have apologized, but I said nothing. Harmin himself left soon after anyway. To shut his own door. Only his books were left behind. He left them all to me. Then there was only me. And all those corpses . . .

**Were you in any way affected by being molested at the age of ten, Gaza?**
Who're *you*? Just kidding! Of course not.
**Are you sure?**
It's not like this kind of thing only happened to me!
**Yeah, but still . . .**
Let me tell you a secret! No one knows . . . but all ten-year-olds get molested.
**Are you serious?**
Yes!
**Then what happens?**
They turn eleven.
**Well, how come no one else remembers but you?**
Because it's healthy!
**What's healthy?**
Rape is. You know the stages kids have to pass through? For a healthy development? Rape is one of them. That's why no one remembers. If there's something you can't remember, you can bet it's something healthy!

**But you remember.**

Because you keep reminding me, fucker!

**You're just fooling yourself, Gaza.**

You don't say. Of course I'm fooling myself. Have got any other choice?

**Obviously you've been affected by that molester. You've been affected plenty. Please admit it.**

Fine, I admit it. But only because you said please.

**Thank you . . . how do you feel now, then?**

Same as always.

**Which is?**

Like *khat*!

**I beg your pardon?**

Like I've been chewed up! Like I'm being chewed on. Like I might be chewed on any minute now, that's how I feel.

**Then there's only one thing you have to do . . .**

What's that?

**Have yourself spat out.**

How?

**Cause pain.**

To who?

**Whoever's mouth you're in, that's who.**

But he's dead. Dordor and Harmin killed him.

**The dead can't chew, Gaza.**

They damn well can.

**Believe me, they can't. Some other mouth is chewing you.**

There is no other mouth.

**There is . . . the shed.**

The shed! Don't be ridiculous! Whose mouth is that then?

**You father's . . . Ahad's mouth.**

Never thought of it that way.

**It's my job to think, Gaza. Not yours.**

What's my job, then?

**To kill me.**

That's what you always say. Please, stop saying that.

**Fine . . . but only because you said please.**

Thank you. How do you feel now, then?

**Same as always.**

Which is?

**Like a paper frog.**

There were two alternatives to transporting illegal immigrants: in the first, the goods, that is, the person, would be delivered to the recipient and do forced labor in that country in order to pay off their transportation fees. In the other, the recipient *was* the goods and would, in return for a one-time-only payment, be taken where he was going and left to his own devices! Since the world was changing, however, the first model was becoming more commonplace. The equilibrium of income between regions of the globe was fast approaching the ratio of *life: no life* between the earth and the moon, so compared to one side of the illegal immigrant transportation business, the other became fleshier and fleshier with each passing day. Another reason for this was its potential for even more profitable side-trades. The utilization of illegal immigrants as illegal laborers in the manufacture of illegal goods meant an extraordinary advantage in sustainable economy and sustainable *evil*. For even evil required a certain amount of effort to sustain it. You couldn't expect human nature to do everything! Anyway . . .

The costs of illegal manufacture were lower even than exportation costs out of China. Because of this, in fact, so much profit was expected of the exchanges to be made in the target country that transportation, and in some cases even accommodation, were basically free, and illegal transportation services, also symbolically priced, were in the ascent. From Kabul to Marseille or Islamabad to Napoli, the free worker shuttles took off, shuttling back and forth between continents. This meant even more broken-nosed profiles passing through our shed. Those harboring dreams of freedom in the country they were headed to were replaced by those who had acquiesced to being put to work for years so they could save just enough for a cow per year and send it to their families. Of these half were aware of all this as they embarked on the journey, while the other half, oblivious to what was to come, imagined themselves to be on their way to get a piece of the pie. Illegal immigrant transportation had become indistinguishable from slave trade. When one examined the eminent techniques of the industry, violence came forward like the sun. Still, as it was too difficult to uphold the old, exhausting, and time-consuming traditions of receiving slaves in return for won battles or setting up markets for human auctions, the contemporary world had channeled its energies into that miraculous device, willpower. Though establishments that used traditional methods of violence and provided capital for the sex industry did still endure, the most powerful means of human trafficking was persuasion. This was of course also a type of violence, but at least when all was said and done, it didn't leave as much of a mess.

Ultimately, the general behavior of those who came in and out of the shed suggested, besides the fear brought on by ambiguity and illegality, a docility loaded with dreams of cows—the average weight of which, by the way, is five hundred kilos. This entailed the emergence of a new breed of immigrants with even more of a slump to their shoulders, heads even more bowed in compliance, and in a positive correlation of poverty/compressibility, took up even less space in the shed, who carried their own rations for fear of having to pay for food, no longer talked to one another as much, and lastly, constantly made sly little plans. As a result, they weren't much distinguishable from the slaves in ancient Egypt. We'd collectively gone back in time! After seeing that new breed, in fact, I never once again believed that the pyramids had been built by extraterrestrials. It didn't take me long to realize that the pyramids had been built not *by* humans, but *from* humans. Long story short, and thanks to the support of the macroeconomy policies of G-8 and G-20 member nations, I was now G-1 and pharaoh of that seventy-two-square-meter shed. The only difference between me and the child pharaoh Tutankhamen was that I didn't wear stupid makeup. Or a skirt . . . As a pharaoh, all I needed was money. Enough money to help build my pyramid! I was at the age, no, *past* the age to be stealing from my father! But there was no possible way I could make alterations to the shed without his knowledge. Therefore, first of all, I needed to persuade Ahad. He was on the phone in the arbor. With Aruz, of course. I waited patiently for them to shut up. Two months had passed since I'd gotten the news of Harmin's demise at the hand of the parasites on the back of the hippopotamus he'd gone out to hunt. June, which I'd hated, since much like insects, the immigrants increased in number in the summer, had come around again, but this time I wasn't so upset that school was out. I had my heart set on supremacy after all.

Finally father hung up and, fixing his customary unseeing gaze on my face, asked: "What is it?"

"The shed," I said.

"What about the shed?"

"I made a list. Take a look . . ."

He picked up the paper I placed in front of him and read only the first item before he asked:

"What is this?"

I had to stay calm. If he saw my eagerness, he would figure it all out. He always did. He figured out even the nonexistent. He was like a primitive animal with the ability to sense an impending earthquake. Right behind those dead blue eyes was a radar tuned to my inner world. My father was a weapon created for the sole purpose of ruining me. A technological wonder! An unmanned aircraft of sorts! Or whatever, just anything without a person inside. Yet still I was prepared! I myself had a few tricks up my sleeve . . .

"You know how you mentioned that there'll be more people coming in this year and we should enlarge the reservoir? I think that instead we might install all this. Now, the real issue isn't the numbers. Because some way or another, they can squeeze in. That's not the problem. Plus until now the most we got was, what, a hundred people at the same time. And the reservoir handles that, easy. The actual problem is: when the numbers go up, it's out of the question to do daily errands. Especially when there's a baby or an old person or whatever, I can't get anything else done. And you know how they sometimes get into fights with one another . . ."

I was doing perfectly well up until this point. In fact, just a few months ago, I had been two strides away when a Lebanese man attempted to suffocate another Lebanese man with a plastic bag over his head. It was later revealed that they had both come from Beirut. One was a Shiite and the other Sunni. Sunnis had blown up the marketplace in the neighborhood of the Shiite, while Shiites had blown up the mosque on the Sunni's street. Two madmen at least as unfit to be near each other as an Ulster Volunteer Force militant and an IRA militant, and somehow they'd escaped notice and were put in the same group. Of course we'd only been able to find all this out through Aruz's transla-tion over the phone. It was decided after impromptu tele-trial that both were to have their hands tied until they reached their final destination. They were more than welcome to strangle each other once they got to wherever it was they were going. Besides, even if they didn't, their children would keep on strangling one another. Sectarian wars were like fashion trends. They repeated themselves every twenty years. In the Middle East, at least.

Since people in the West had long known to dress for their shape, they only spilled blood for the sake of the acidic colors of things like fossil fuels. But since it was especially difficult to get bloodstains out of the carpets of the European Parliament and the White House, they didn't let the fighting inside their homes. Still, they were also only human, and like all humans were itch-ing to war with their peers. And so they whispered to each other, "Meet me outside after class!" and as soon as they set foot outside the Western civilization, saw no harm in grappling inside other people's houses.

Though of course it was different with Israel who, believing itself to be the Greenwich of politics, wanted not only clocks but even the seasons to be tuned to its liking and expected everyone to wear the clothes suited to the ensuing climates. For Israel was a neurotic, black-robed desert ninja that emerged from its own mist and flung Stars of David this way and that.

And finally there was Turkey, a bulimic, depressed girl that saw herself as fat in her mirror to the East and emaciated in her mirror to the West. For two decades she ate without pausing for breath, got fat, and, stricken with guilt, made herself vomit for another two decades until her throat bled so she could start eat-ing again.

I was aware that generalizations were a pathological incli-nation, but then a people generalized itself the day it founded its state. We were living in too organized a world to avoid generalizations. It was too late! We preferred to be bought and sold in bulk. If you liked a handful of the fabric, you had to buy the whole thing. Just like in the textile industry. Or, to be more accurate, the spiderweb industry . . . As it came to show, everything had to do with fabrics. From the blindfold of Justitia, goddess of justice, to the flag, everything was a matter of fabrics. The few native Amazonians who had managed to stay naked owed the tranquility in their expressions to their lack of fabrics. The lack of tranquility in mine as I spoke to my father, on the other hand, I owed to being cut from the same fabric as him . . .

"But if we had a camera . . . I could just put the monitor in the shed and keep track of things there. If something were to come up, I could go take care of it or, I don't know, come tell you. Of course when you have the camera, you'd also need a light. Three fluorescent lights would be enough. See, I wrote down all the prices. Also I was thinking we can maybe put in a little partition. You know, instead of that curtain we make them put up. Plaster would do the trick. They get into a lot of fights over the toilet too. Some guy was staring at this one, staring at that one, that sort of stuff . . . I took the measurements and looked into the costs of that as well. Matter of fact I say we make a partition for the toilet, then this other partition. Say we put a ring on the wall of that one. You know how sometimes one of them freaks out, we stick him in there and chain him to the wall . . . We don't need to hire anyone, either. I can take care of it all. And a fan. Because it stinks to high heaven in there. Which wouldn't be a problem, but then someone passes out and you have to deal with that, it's a waste of time! I think the less we have to do with the drugstore, the better. Look, here's the cost for the fan. You can get floor fans. Three is enough. The trick is to avoid getting them sick . . . If I could just figure out a solution to the toilet issue too! I mean some sort of sewage link . . . but that's too much work. No matter, we can keep doing that the old way . . . Now look, we'd need just about this much money to enlarge the reservoir. But see, all this adds up to just this. I say we don't need to stick out our necks that much at all. It'd be enough to get these . . . What do you say?"

He wasn't saying anything. Yes, I had prepared well for my presentation, but there was never any knowing what Ahad would do. He was even apt to say, "Is this what you've been wasting time on when you could've been studying!" and land one right in my face, even though he didn't care a bit about my school situation. But for the moment, he was content to just stare at me. It was as if he were seeing my face for the first time in his life. Maybe he was. He was seeing me for the first time. He stared . . . stared . . . and spoke:

"Well done, kid!"

I expelled my breath in part from each nostril so he couldn't tell how much I'd been holding in. And of course, my heart started beating again. And it was then that a miracle happened and he placed his hand on my shoulder.

"Are you sure you'll be able to handle it all?"

"I will! Don't you worry. When's the next shipment coming in?"

"In two weeks."

I was reduced to a gibbering fool by his easy assent to my proposal. And this was proof:

"In two weeks I'll turn that reservoir into a paradise, I will!"

He laughed. I laughed too. That his fourteen-year-old son was so enthusiastic, or even passionate it could be said, about the family business, must have moved some cells somewhere inside him. Perhaps for the first time since I was born, he was proud of me. He didn't say that, naturally, but it was exactly that kind of moment. I would be happy to be proud of myself even if he wasn't. After all, Ahad had already begun peeling bills from the sheaf he'd brought out of his pocket. Then all of a sudden he stopped and asked:

"How's school?"

I was so taken aback that I babbled.

"It's holidays, Dad."

"I know that, kid! I want to know how it's going—did you pass?"

"I got the letter of commendation, Dad."

A few more bills were peeled away from the sheaf. It appeared that I was about to get an award. The world had really turned upside down! In my elation I'd forgotten to mention that I was top of the class. I'd forgotten to mention that, as a matter of fact, I'd even been handed a stupid book called *Robinson Crusoe* as a prize for having the highest average in the entire eighth grade. On a very insidious whim, I'd even considered mentioning that Ender, son of the Heroic Sergeant Yadigar, had gotten such bad grades that he was nearly expelled, but been unable to do even that and was left only thinking it.

"Well done!" said Ahad. For the second time! As though he was sparing my life. "What grade are you in now?"

How was it possible to hate someone this much but still want his approval just as much? How was it possible to house these two urges inside the same body? Who could know the suffering that was taking place inside me just then? The fight that was being fought? How violently they were laying into each other? What kind of a war was it? It was gruesome, surely. That must be why I was feeling nauseated. Yet the moment I opened my mouth, it was clear who the winner was:

"Ninth . . . first year of high school."

Unable to gain dominion over the tongue, vanquished in a blind battle of denial, the hatred of the losing side withdrew into the barricades to multiply even more. I could hear its footsteps. It was going to search for a way out. And out it would go, at first chance. It would either become an act unleashed in a weak moment or a thousand curses to spew from my mouth. It would either land on Ahad or whomever else it would be that I happened upon . . . all hatred ended up at the same place in the end: tomorrow. It could wait. It would wait. I would wait with it. I was a true coward after all. And hatred was the coward's vengeance. I was an expert! One blacked out, sank into his chair, and hated himself to death. But he would be the first to die. From a brain tumor! A vengeful tumor! A tumor the size of a marble! From too many fantasies of vengeance. Unfulfilled vengeances. Unfulfilled, vaporized vengeances. We breathed it all in! We'd absorb it through our pores if we could! The air of vengeances comprised of curses hurled behind backs . . . and a bit of oxygen. Not enough to kill. Enough that you'd still be good for something . . . Of course human life was sacred but only as long as it was good for something. Consequently life was only as valuable as the value of the thing it was good for. So if someone were to up and cover that cost, the life in question would thereby become redundant and expendable. It was all mathematics. Only subtraction, actually. If I could subtract my hate from this life and behold what was left, the whole story would be over. Because the only thing from then on would be daily life . . . and maybe some morphine sulfate.

"You're old enough to be going to high school, already?"

"I dunno . . ."

"You're old enough to hoist yourself on that girl, aren't you, though!"

What had he just said? I hadn't heard that!

"Come now, come now, don't blush! I don't mean anything by it, but you should be careful. You could catch a disease or something . . ."

I still couldn't hear!

"Take it easy, kid! I said I don't mean anything by it! But if you have to do shit like that, at least lock the door of the shed!"

That I'd heard. And only because there was a command in his words. It was habitual.

"I will . . ."

He laughed . . . How much had he seen? Had he watched until the end? I couldn't think about this now. Later! I should be laughing. I should be doing whatever he was doing. I laughed. Or something close to it . . .

"You're not mad at me that I didn't let you take that exam?"

Presumably he was talking about the exam that would have won me a bursary to study at one of the finest high schools in the country. I had taken it without his knowledge. I myself didn't know what I would do when the results were disclosed. Was it possible to leave Ahad? Was he leavable?

"No, Dad, how could I be?"

"What'd that son of Yadigar's do, did he pass? Ender, was it?"

And then, this question. This question that made me forget it all. It was that easy, then! That he'd seen me have sex with the world's beautiful girl, nor anything else, was exempt. It was all gone. I couldn't believe it. It was as if he'd asked because he'd heard me. I recounted Ender's ineptitude with such ardor that my drool wilted the piece of paper I'd written my list on. Truly, I was no different from Ahad. I was just as indifferent to everything as he was. It was just taking a while for me to face the facts, that was all. One needed time not only to adapt to the world he was born into, but to himself as well.

Then I took the money and left . . . It was enough to flee anywhere on the first bus. But I returned with the equipment. My hands were full, my mind empty. Then it was the opposite, and I got to work in the reservoir like a veteran electrician. I did my best and still didn't receive an electric shock. I knew then that I was electric. If I had a dog, I would have named it Tesla. Or vice versa . . .

I was in the reservoir day and night for two weeks, and finally the gates opened on hunting season with all their glory. My ant farm was ready. And it was erected on just the place, the ants' route: the Silk Road . . . a matter of fabrics!

Right on the morning of the day I was planning to promote myself to deity of a reservoir full of people, Yadigar crossed my path. I'd been shopping in town and was on my way home with bags of groceries. He didn't cross my path, exactly. He pulled up next to me his blue car with GENDARMERIE inscribed on the side and rolled down his window. Looking perfectly healthy from where I stood, since his burned cheek was facing the other way, Yadigar glanced at the bags I was carrying as he spoke.

"What's all this? Got visitors?"

Among the many things I was able to do effortlessly and while standing on one foot was, of course, lying.

"There's this family in need, in one of the villages. It's for them. My father said go buy some things . . . so I got this. We'll be taking it over now."

"Good of you to think," said Yadigar.

Then he was silent. But Yadigar had a peculiar habit. He'd say something, then stop and stare you in the face. As a man of few words and much staring, he was like some kind of champion unnerver. Or it seemed that way to me. I was the one with the kind of life to hide, after all. What did he mean to say? It was good of us to lie? What was good of us to think? Would that be all? Were we done talking? Could I resume walking? In truth the only thing that gave me hope at that moment was that his engine was still running. It's possible no engine sound since has given me such strength.

I was just about to say, "Give Ender my regards," and take the first step when he asked, "What village?"

"I don't know, Uncle Yadigar," I said. "My father said, but I forget now."

My only hope dried up the instant I had thought my reply would suffice. Yadigar turned off the ignition and killed the engine. It appeared that we would keep talking.

"We should let the prefecture know. Maybe they'll put you on an allowance or something."

"Sure," I said. "I'll get the details and let you know."

After all, poverty was within an arm's reach for us all. An elbow's reach, in fact. As soon as we began groping for a family in need, we'd bump into one before we even finished reaching out our hand. If there was the need, we could easily find one and stick it under Yadigar's nose. But right now the only thing bumping was my heart. It was like a wild animal trapped inside my rib cage. The bags were heavy, but I didn't want to put them down. After being abandoned by the sound of the engine, it was the only move I had left, however puny. Putting down the bags would be a sign that I was willing to continue chatting. At least that's what I thought. This juvenile, private precaution prevented me from wiping the sweat off my brow, as both my hands were full. And now Yadigar was staring at the sweat. He was watching a particular drop of sweat. The one trickling between my eyebrows and heading for my nose. It had reached the tip of my nose and begun quivering there when Yadigar finally spoke.

"It's hot!"

"I should go, Uncle Yadigar, my father's waiting."

"Come, let me drop you off."

"Thanks, I'm already almost there."

He opened the door and got out. I had nowhere to run.

"Give it here," he said, taking the bags off my hands and opening the door to put them in the backseat. I was frozen, at a loss for what to do. It was my turn to talk little and stare much. Yadigar took his seat, shut the door, and turned to me. "Come on."

There was to be no zeppelin to swing down a ladder and lift me into the sky, nor a horse that would materialize out of nowhere and come running the second I whistled. All those adventure novels I had read were a bunch of crap! I was the only thing that was real! Even an earthquake would have been enough! An earthquake just strong enough to flatten a few villages, kill a bunch of people! But that didn't happen either, and I was the only one who shook. And that only because I slammed the door a bit too hard when I crossed in front of the car and got in next to Yadigar . . .

This time the only thing I could see was his nonexistent cheek. How fast can a person think? What's the speed of thought? I had no idea, but I was trying to calculate everything at once. We'd make a little way, turn into Dust Street, and arrive at the house. Perhaps I should jump out of the car as it slowed to a stop and yell, "Dad! Dad! We're home!" Perhaps I should pretend to faint. Perhaps I should rat out Ender for having started smoking! All this was racing through my head when I saw Yadigar give the steering wheel a full turn. We spun in our spot until the nose of the car was pointing at the town. The opposite direction of my house. I turned to him, but he was no longer interested in me.

"Uncle Yadigar, my house . . ." I began, and he said, "There's something I have to do. Let's take care of that first."

I was relieved. The animal in my rib cage was somewhat tamed. Whatever it was he had to do, I could maybe find a way to call my father while he did it. I could go into some store or another to call him. We went into town and cruised through the shopping street. I was expecting him to slow down. But he didn't. His only possible destination from here on was the Gendarmerie's station at the other exit of the town. That was where he went and stopped in front of. He turned off the ignition, stared at my face for a half minute before saying, "Come," and got out of the car. Since I couldn't lock myself inside the car and stay there until I died, I had no choice but to get out as well.

For a split second, I glimpsed the guard on duty stand fast and salute Yadigar as he walked past. He must be so scared of Yadigar he couldn't even take his eyes off him. When I climbed the five steps to the entrance of the building and turned back to look, he was still watching us. I wish I hadn't looked! For the fear in that private's eyes reinforced mine to start punching the walls of my rib cage all over again. All I could do was follow Yadigar. He was two steps ahead. I felt as if everyone was looking at me. The handcuffed man that we walked past and the soldiers on either side of him and everyone.

We passed through a hall and approached a set of stairs. We went down the steps and entered yet another hall. A short one. There was a pair of iron doors at the end. Stopping in front of the one on the left, Yadigar took out a set of keys from his pocket and opened it. As he was in the way, I couldn't see what was inside.

Yadigar turned and looked at me. "Go in," he said. He took me by the shoulder and pushed me in, and only then I could see what was inside. There was nothing. It was a cell. I took two steps and stopped. Yadigar's hand was still on my shoulder. I turned my head to look at his face over that shoulder. "You just wait here a bit now," he said.

So at a loss for words I was that I could only ask the most stupid question in the world: "Here?"

"I'll come pick you up once I get this thing done. Then I'll drop you off, all right?"

Would it have helped then if I cried "help"? Or would that just get me murdered by a lunatic named Imdat?[1] I'd found myself in such unreasonable circumstances that anything was possible. Yadigar made two moves. In one he stepped out of the cell, and in the second he locked closed the door. Next I heard the sound of a key. A key that spun inside a lock and was briskly withdrawn . . .

I don't know why, but the first thing I did was hang my head. That was when I saw the sawdust. Around my feet . . . another sawdust swamp . . . I felt like I would sink into it and suffocate. Perhaps that would have been for the better. Yet unlike Dordor and Harmin, I was capable of staying aboveground, always. I could never sink. At least, that was what I thought then . . . but none of that mattered now. I was really inside a cell. What's more, I certainly didn't know what I was in there for. I thought that we'd been caught, of course. Of course I was certain that our whole web of crime had been uncovered and that I'd rot in jail for years! But all I wanted was to rot outside! There was only a steel bench in the cell. And some writing on the walls, and some jumbled drawings. It didn't even have a window. That was when I noticed the lightbulb over my head. It was similar to the one we had in the reservoir. I hadn't been paying attention when Yadigar presumably turned it on when he opened the door. Perhaps it had been on the whole time. Our lives were ruined, and I was standing there, staring at the lightbulb.

"All right!" I said. "All right, calm down!" And I tried to calm myself. This I tried to do by walking. As I paced the cell, tracing the walls, I continuously reminded myself of my age. "Who's going to do anything to you?" I reasoned. "Let's say you went on

---

1  Turkish for "help," also a boy's name.

trial, how many years would you get anyway? You're not even eighteen!"

Then I began pacing faster and was completely convinced I'd be in jail till I croaked. As a bonus I'd get convicted of rape! Nothing would be left unseen, and that, too, would be exposed! And it wasn't even rape! It was just a person's self-sacrifice unto me in keeping with the circumstances. Or others' sacrifice, whatever. But who'd listen to me? And the worst came last: attempted mass slaughter! Because I'd turned on the valve!

"Yes," I said. "You were going to drown them, they'll say! You were going to kill them all!"

I imagined I'd be imprisoned just for having been born! And since I couldn't possibly have been more terrified, my pulse inadvertently began to slow. So had my pacing. In fact, since I wouldn't be able to leave the cell no matter how fast I paced, it was most reasonable to just sit on the bench. I went over and sat. But then I began jogging my knees on tiptoe. Both knees jogged as if they were trying to drill into the ground. Eventually they too slowed and stopped. All that was left were me and my pulse.

That was the moment I said, "Fuck it! Fuck it! It's for the best! You couldn't get away, but look, you're free now!" Yes, the wind inside my skull was starting to change direction. Different thoughts were filling its sails. It was really a miracle! All this! What I'd always wished for was happening. I'd be free of my father and those sickening immigrants forever. I'd never have to see any of their faces again. It was incredible! It was the rope ladder swinging down from a zeppelin to carry me into the sky! It wasn't exactly the way I'd imagined it, but if I were to get away, it would be thanks to this cell. Then at some point, it occurred to me that I might be a sleepwalker. Had I in all probability gotten up one night and gone over to Ender's to tell Yadigar everything because I'd desperately wanted us to be caught?

No, no, I was reading too many novels! It was what it was! I didn't care the least how we'd been caught. What mattered was that being caught would absolve me of the horrible things I was to do! It really was divine intervention! If Yadigar had never shown up and I'd made it home . . . all the things I'd thought up! The things I'd planned! All that preparation! Those fantasies of ant farms! The things I was going to do to those people! How could I have been so mad! How? I really was saved! The Heroic Sergeant Uncle Yadigar, he really was a hero! He'd protected me from myself and prevented me from living the rest of my life in a pit of self-loathing! I'd stay in this cell as long as he liked! As long as he liked, no buts about it.

Then I'd go on trial and tell them everything. How Ahad forced me, and everything! I'd even say he'd threatened me. They'd believe me for sure. I'd say he beat me. Yes, it made a whole lot of sense. And it wasn't lying. Fine, so he didn't hit me as much as he used to, but he looked at me like he might at any moment. How I wished he'd given me a sound beating recently! It would really work in my favor to have a few bruises here and there! Or, say, a cigarette burn! He'd never done that, but in the paper I'd seen news of people doing that to their children, God knows how many times.

And in that enchanted moment, I remembered the pack of cigarettes and the lighter I had in my pocket. In my excitement I'd totally forgotten about them. Not being a full addict yet I hadn't acquired the habit of lighting one every half hour, so it hadn't occurred to me. How about some burns! On my arms, my legs . . . it would be awesome! The more Ahad denied it, the more the judge would be convinced!

"He puts out his cigarettes on me, uncle judge," I'd say. Or should I say your honor? No, uncle was better. Definitely! "I don't know why he does it, uncle judge. And with all the ashtrays we have!"

I was laughing now. It was all resolved. All had come to light and the subject was closed. I was every bit an inventor as Felat was! I wished there was a way I could reach him and tell him about my invention! I think Dordor and Harmin would have been proud! They'd run away from their father, and I was going to make sure mine would be in prison longer. Wasn't that just another way of running away from one's father?

"He made me do it all, uncle judge! I love my father really. But he always ordered me that I should treat people badly. In fact, once, there was this girl and he . . . I'm so ashamed . . . and he watched! He made me open the valve, on top of it! He would have made me drown them all. I stopped it. Don't do it, Dad, I said, have pity. Just look at my arms! He smoked a pack a day, put out half of it on me. With all the ashtrays we had!"

Perfect! In a word, perfect!

"Ask my school, every year I get a letter of commendation. I get a commendation every semester! I'm expecting a really high score on the high school entrance exam as well. I just might make the top hundred! You never know. If you'd let me, I'll enroll in the school I'm about to get into. I can board there! There's burns on my legs as well. Can I show you?"

"No, son, that's all right. It's all clear," the judge would say. "Your father is inhuman, it's clear. Of course, son, wherever you want to go, please, go! But first we need to get those burns treated!"

"Thank you, uncle judge," I'd say. "The burns are of no importance, I'm used to it!" And right then everyone in the courtroom would start crying, and maybe even applaud me for my courage. In their eyes I'd be an angel who'd made it in one piece from the devil's house . . . and who was to say I wasn't?

The cell no longer seemed as terrifying to me. I was grinning to myself. I even felt good enough to get up and examine the writing on the walls. The cigarette burns could wait. I could take care of it in a little while. I got up from the bench and began pensively strolling with my hands in my pockets, as if I were on a beach. Contemplating the walls. The first wall I got in close to had intermingling forms. I couldn't quite make out what they were. But when I looked harder and traced the lines, I realized I was face-to-face with a prick. It was then that the cell's magic reasserted itself, and the words that would elevate me to the highest step of my angelhood began to spill like confetti over my head.

"Lastly, uncle judge . . . I don't quite know how to say this, but . . . I was ten . . . One day my father . . ."

"Don't cry, child . . . calm down . . . Now tell me. Yes, your father?"

"My father did terrible things to me . . ."

"What terrible things?"

"First he began to touch me. Then he took off my pants and undressed me . . . then he held my . . . thing. He began to stroke it. He rubbed it on his face. He kissed it . . ."

At that point I wouldn't merely walk, I'd absolutely fly out of that courtroom on a pair of wings! I wouldn't even have to say the rest. But what if they wanted proof? How could I prove all this? It was four years ago. True, the fingerprints of that Lebanese guy were right behind my brow . . . but no one else could possibly see them but me. And there were no other marks on me. Of course, if I could shove something up myself and make it bleed a little . . . then . . . I could even say, "He did it yesterday!"

**Gaza, what are you doing?**

I'm trying to save my life, fucker!

**Is that how you're going to save your life?**

It's none of your business!

**Use your head, is this how you're going to save yourself?**

Why don't you come and save me then!

**I'd come if you hadn't killed me.**

They're sure to ask about you too! What am I going to say?

**How'd they know about me?**

What if they find you?

**My corpse? Don't be silly. Don't you remember how your father buried me? Who'd ever find me in that forest?**

That lavender sure smells good, doesn't it?

**Sorry, since I don't have a nose . . .**

So what am I supposed to do? How do I get out of this shit?

**You curse too much . . . I think right now there's not much you can do. So just stay calm and wait it out. Maybe Yadigar really has something to do and he'll come pick you up once he takes care of it.**

Cuma . . .

**Yes?**

I'm sorry.

**Don't be sorry. I'm fine. The lavender does smell nice, by the way.**

Ever see my mother?

**No.**

Neither have I . . . You know what?

**What?**

She ran away from home the night she was going to give birth to me. She went to the graveyard in our town.

**Why?**

To get away from Ahad.

**What's that got to do with anything?**

She was going to give birth to me, and then bury me . . . in the graveyard . . . and then run away.

**Who told you this?**

My father . . . he found my mother in her last moments. Before she buried me . . . she had lost a lot of blood . . . and then she died.

**Your father was lying to you, Gaza. I don't believe for a second that this could be true. It's a story he made up so you'd feel indebted to him your entire life.**

I think so too.

**Don't you ever believe it.**

I already don't . . .

**And don't try to put out cigarettes on yourself. Don't you even think of it. It wouldn't help anything.**

But I've already done it, Cuma . . . look.

**Throw away that cigarette! Throw it away at once!**

I think all children should be born in graveyards and buried right away. It'd save them the trouble.

**Gaza, you've destroyed your arm! Quit it, stop!**

Then they'd all go to heaven. Just like you. They told Ender at Koran class you have the chance to repent until the last second. No matter what you did! Allah might always accept.

**Gaza, listen to me! Throw away the cigarette!**

But like, say, if you kill someone, he can't repent. He wouldn't have the time! He didn't know he was going to die. Or I don't know, it happens real fast. Say he was going to repent, right? Maybe Allah would accept him? I wish someone would kill me too . . . but real fast! Strike me in the back! So I wouldn't have the chance to repent . . . and I could go to heaven . . . because if I were to repent now, it wouldn't work, I know it . . . so I could only go to heaven if someone took away my chance to repent. Do you understand? I'm not that dumb. Not *that* dumb! I've got my own ways . . . Also you said yourself, you don't have a nose, so how could you smell the lavender! Besides, I don't really think you could ever go to heaven! Remember what you said to me? You said to go hurt those people! You said, that reservoir is your father's mouth!

**Gaza!**

What!

**I didn't say those things.**

Then who did?

**What do you think?**

Did I say them? Is that it?

**You're talking to yourself, Gaza.**

So, I guess I'm talking to myself . . . Look at the state of my arms! Why don't they hurt! Why don't I feel anything? Why does it feel like they aren't mine? Tell me! I guess these arms belong to someone else, don't they?

**Fine, Gaza, okay . . . those arms belong to someone else. Who?**

**Your mother . . . they're your mother's arms. She dug the hole she was going to bury you in with those arms . . . all right? Are you happy? You got what you wanted. You've learned the truth. How do you feel now?**

Same as always.

**Which is?**

Like my mother's necklace with the angel.

**I beg your pardon?**

Like I'm around my mother's neck, strangling her.

**Are you serious?**

I'm telling you I'm an angel made of gold. Of course I'm serious!

**So why do you feel like that?**

Because I didn't kill my mother for vengeance. I killed her so I could survive. She wanted to bury me as soon as I was born. But I was born with such a vengeance I spilled all her blood! Isn't that strange? That she died giving birth to the baby she was planning to kill . . . Of course, I'd have to be out of her belly in some way or other for her to be able to kill me. So I'd have to be alive, even if for a moment. Maybe she only wanted me to be alive in that moment. In wanting me to be born as soon as possible, she really wanted me to live. Maybe she didn't even know it. But she wanted so badly to expel me from herself! To expel me and deliver me to life! And she got what she wanted. She got at least half of her wish to give life to her baby so she could kill him. I lived . . . If in being born, I hadn't spilled so much of her blood and taken her life, she'd still have found a way to kill me for sure. Maybe she'd have strangled me with a plastic bag before I was even a month old, just like that Lebanese man. "It's either me or him!" I said. Do you understand, Cuma? Either me or him! Like my father! Like all those who survived! Surely you have someone in your family who was like that. I bet it was thanks to him that you were born. Whoever it was that said, "It's either me or him!" Don't be upset . . . I know you're in heaven . . . and I could have been there too, but it was not to be! I wish my mother could have buried me when I was a baby! When I was free of sin! It would have been as if she'd buried me right into heaven, wouldn't it? But what can you do . . . if I can't go to heaven when I'm dead, then I'll go to heaven and die there! Come and let's put some burns on my mother's legs!

Two nights. I spent two nights in that cell. Without sleeping a wink. Its door opened four times. Four times I thought I'd leave. Each time I sprang to my feet and bolted to the door. Like the immigrants in the reservoir . . . four times I was wrong, because all they did was put a plate of food in front of me. A different soldier every time . . . I tried to ask questions. I tried to talk, to shout, to cry. But none of them listened. Like me in the reservoir . . . then the iron door opened a fifth time and this time I didn't move an inch. I just raised my head. Yadigar stood in front of me. And so did my father . . .

"Come on," said Yadigar. "Time to go home . . ."

I got up and walked past them. I climbed the stairs. I passed through the hall. I left the building and without waiting for my father to catch up, started running. I was crying and didn't intend to stop. I was going to run for as long as could.

As I ran through the shopping street, Ahad pulled up next to me with his truck and said, "Get in."

I stopped. First I looked at my father's arm hanging out the open window of the truck and his face, then the pavement I stood frozen on. Trying to catch my breath . . . when I saw the sawdust on the ground, I knew there was nowhere to run so I got in the truck.

We didn't speak at all on the way back . . . Only I glanced at my father at some point. Since I didn't know what else to think, all I thought was how much our faces looked alike. Maybe we didn't look that alike, I'm not sure. But he looked as sleepless as I was. He'd been sweating too. Who knows what had happened while I was in that cell? How had he felt? Maybe they'd put him in another cell . . . Whatever trouble we had gotten into, it must have been too disastrous to talk about before we got home, I thought, and kept silent. Together we kept silent. Then once we were inside the house, I asked:

"Dad . . . have we been caught?"

He laughed. He was opening the fridge to get himself a beer.

"What're you talking about, 'caught' . . ."

But I wasn't laughing. For the first time in my life, I yelled at my father. Even then all I could manage was: "Dad!"

He turned around like he'd been struck, and his smile slowly sank into his lips. He unscrewed the cap off the beer and tossed it onto the kitchen table. Then he poured the beer down his throat. He wiped his mouth with the back of his hand and spoke.

"There's nothing to worry about . . . It's just that that son of a bitch Yadigar wants more money . . . understand?"

I didn't.

"He wants money for what?"

He turned his head to gaze into the distance, but since the walls prevented that, his gaze ended up on me, and he took a breath. He expelled the same breath with the words, "Have a seat then." There was a chair on either side of the table. They sufficed for us since we didn't have anyone else. I pulled out the one near me and sat. He sat across from me . . . He took another swig from his beer and stared at the bottle in his hand as he spoke.

"So you've been to have meatballs at theirs."

"When? Where?"

"To Yadigar's . . ."

"To Yadigar's? I dunno . . . I might have . . . I guess it was like two years ago."

"Were they good?"

"The meatballs? I wouldn't remember . . ."

"Salime's a good-looking woman, she is . . . though it wouldn't hurt if she were a bit thinner . . . What was their house like?"

His eyes were still fixed on the bottle that he held with both hands. And it was obvious he wasn't seeing the bottle. He was seeing something else. Something I couldn't see. Like those lines Rimbaud wrote hundreds of years ago, that I was to read years later: *And I've seen, sometimes, what men only dreamed they saw.*

"It was a house . . . just a regular house . . ."

"Say . . . what was their furniture like? Their television . . . their sofas . . ."

What was my father seeing in that bottle?

"Nice, I guess . . . I remember the television . . . You know those large screen ones? We even hooked up Ender's PlayStation to it . . ."

"How did they seem? Were they happy?"

Why did he want to know all this? Who cared?

"I think so . . . yes."

"You see, I'm the one who pays for that happiness. Every last scrap of shit you see in that house comes out of my pocket!"

Since my mind was still in the cell where I'd left it, I wasn't comprehending. I was just a scared child and nothing more.

"Why?"

"Because we've already been caught long ago, Gaza . . . years ago. How do you think we stay out of trouble so easily? Ever wondered?"

The door of the custodial cell in the lower floor of the gendarmerie station opened. My mind shot out of the cell and into my skull, and I understood both the mathematical reciprocity of the speed of thought and what my father had just said.

"You bribe them?"

"How the hell did you ever get that commendation?"

Okay, fine . . . so Yadigar had taken me hostage so his inducement would get a raise. I could understand. On top of it, he'd done it in front of all those soldiers, using the custodial cell of the municipality's command headquarters as his private dungeon. I could understand. So Uncle Yadigar, the heroic sergeant, was not only the station's commanding officer but the warranty certificate for the crime machine built in cooperation in our quaint little town, and run by us. I could understand. Anyway, there were no heroes. I could understand. I just couldn't understand why I had to stay in that cell for two nights.

"Okay, so why didn't you give him the money right away and get me out?"

He raised his head and took his eyes off the bottle for the first time since we had sat down and looked at me.

"The first rule of business . . ."

"And that is?"

"Negotiations . . . we were negotiating."

Obviously I hadn't been expecting this! So I yelled at my father for the second time in my life:

"I've been there for the past two days, in that place that's like our reservoir, just sitting there without sleeping! And you're telling me you were negotiating?"

Frightened of the volume of my own voice and the possibility of what could happen, my tongue instantly swerved in the direction of a lie:

"And all that time I was worrying about you! Wondered where you were! Thinking, what if they took my father too!"

He laughed as if he were sighing. He took a swig of his beer and put the bottle on the table before he replied. "Why, Gaza? Why worry about me? You worry about yourself, son. Fuck me!"

He must've been seeing that thing that I couldn't see, again. But I was starting to get sick of this. Of all those things I couldn't see and of constantly being left in the dark. I made one last effort. One last time.

"How could I do that? How can you tell me not to worry! You're my father!"

He stared into my eyes, as still as a bust, which then cracked, and a smiling Ahad emerged from within. An Ahad that just kept on smiling without saying anything, and shaking his head as if he didn't believe me . . . I hated my father. He'd let me stay in that cell for two days just so he could pay less to that jerk Yadigar. Two days of sheer hell! He didn't care about me at all!

"Dad, I took the exam. And I'll probably get into a school in Istanbul. I'll be leaving at the end of this summer . . ."

My voice had shaken so much the last syllables hadn't quite made it out of my mouth, but fallen onto the table and shattered. In truth I was counting on that table as well. I could pull back and run if he as much as made a move. But he didn't do anything. He just continued to look at me and smile.

"I know. Your school's principal called the other day. He's the one who told me. Your boy is very smart, he said. Very intelligent. As the school administration, we'll do the best we can, he said. If I'd only pay attention to his education . . . a bright future is ahead of Gaza, he said. He'll grow up to be a great man!"

I must have blinked twice at the most as I listened to this. It had taken that long for all I knew to be replaced by the unknown. I was in a new world now. A new planet. And this one also had gravity. That much I knew, because I wasn't rising from my chair. But did it have oxygen as well? Could I breathe? I tried.

"So you knew?"

"Yes."

I tried again.

"May I go then? Are you letting me?"

"Sure, you may go . . . Help me just till the end of the summer, and then you can go off to your school, get a proper education."

I could definitely breathe. In fact, there was so much oxygen it was making me lightheaded. What was more, on this new planet, I think I loved my father.

"So why didn't you want me to take the exam?"

"To see."

"See what?"

"If you're anything like me . . . Because if it was me, I'd never have listened to my father. He could say whatever he liked, I couldn't have cared less . . . and neither could you. Isn't that right?"

Maybe it had all happened during my stay in the cell. As I burned myself with a quarter pack of cigarettes the earth I had been living on had been pulled out from under me and replaced with a new one. Maybe they'd affixed a new tablecloth to the end of the enormous tablecloth that was the earth and yanked it away. Or the earth, for an instant, had spun too fast. That was how it had been possible to replace the tablecloth with a new one without breaking anything. Perhaps we were all standing on the new tablecloth of the earth and vowing that we wouldn't stain it this time around . . .

I could have searched for ten years right then and still wouldn't have known what to think. I just looked at my father. His hair, brow, eyebrows, and eyes . . . but we couldn't look each other in the eye. For he was looking at my wrist. My right wrist that was resting on the tabletop. He was looking at one of my blisters, one that was left uncovered by the long sleeve of my shirt. An engorged blister. It didn't look good. I knew. For the past day and half, I'd been watching every moment of my skin's struggle for regeneration after I'd turned it into a battlefield . . .

I had to think of something to say in case he asked. For that I needed to push aside what he had just said and clear some space in my head. Then of course there was an arm that must be removed from the tabletop. A right arm. I had just started to withdraw it when my father placed his hand on mine. Now we met each other's eyes. He was smiling. I smiled back . . . I couldn't remember the last time he had held my hand. Maybe when crossing the town's only main street. Years ago . . . that he was holding my hand again after so long might well be for the same purpose. To take me across. Into another life . . .

Just as I was looking into his eyes and smiling, picturing the life across that road we would cross together, a volcano erupted in my wrist. Its lava seared everywhere it spilled and an armor of pain encased my body in seconds. I could neither draw a breath nor part my lips to scream. My father was pressing his left thumb down on the blister so hard that it was my eyes' turn to be engorged. Two blisters with blurred vision. They burst immediately, and tears made way down my cheeks. I tried the only thing I could and grabbed my father's wrist with my left hand to pull it off. But I couldn't budge it. I sprang backward out of the chair but that was also no good, as Ahad ended the discussion by placing his other hand on my left one. And so we presented a new picture to observing eyes. A father-son tableau built of senses. A father and son in the kitchen of a house, facing each other, looking at each other, their hands joined on a tabletop. A father and son holding on to the love between them with all four hands so it wouldn't escape . . . and I'd seen the earth from afar many times. In documentaries. A bright blue, bright green, bright white sphere suspended in the pitch-black void of space! There was absolutely no way of telling that on it, children were getting fucked! From that distance you could see neither the wars where heels were blown off, nor the peaces where tongues were ripped out. You could hear neither the screams nor the lies. A slowly revolving sphere, silent, peaceful. They say that what really matters is your perspective. Bullshit! I, for one, was looking at life and all else under a microscope and it all looked terrifying. A swarm of viruses! Microscopic serpents and dragons! An army of bacteria that writhed and twisted as it searched for flesh to latch on to! If I'd been able to open my mouth, I might have let out a burly scream. I might have opened a scream-sized hole in the pain coating my pores and mouth in order to draw in somewhat of a breath. But I was more like a child whose jaws were locked on the brink of freezing to death. All I could do was let out a snarl as thin as a single hair. It was all that could squeeze out between my teeth. Right then there was thunder:

"I'll kill you! Who the hell are you to think you're going! Who the hell do you think I am that I'll let you leave so easily! Do you have any idea what I went through for your sake? To raise you! The things I've done to look after you! Do you know why there's no woman in this house? Why I never married? Your mother was about to bury your ass! She would have buried you alive! I never allowed a woman into this house so no one would ever hurt you again, or touch you! Now you up and tell me, I'm leaving! I'll break your jaw! As long as you have your father, who loves you to death, you're not going anywhere!"

I really did make the top hundred. I came in forty-third place in all of Turkey, in fact. While they knew very well that my success was no thanks to them, all my teachers smugly congratulated me. All the notable people of our town, so far behind the times that they were unaware the race of humanity was long finished, raised money among themselves so I'd be able to uphold my academic life in the best way possible and made promises they'd each give the most they could. And the governor gave me a wristwatch with four dials, two of which were broken. That moment took place in the main room of the Government Office, was photographed and published on the first page of *From Kandalı to the World,* the local biweekly, inside a red-and-white border. The space it took up was only slightly smaller than the space where they published Atatürk's only photograph, taken at Kandalı at every anniversary of Kandalı's emancipation from enemy invasion. I knew where the photograph, in which Atatürk was captured in conversation with Kandalı locals, was taken. It was the entrance of the village of Nazkur, thirty km away from the center. The very site of the news that, due to the news about me—*Kandalı on a Blessed Crusade*[2]—was allocated a matchbox-size space on the page. On that village road where Atatürk had once stood, a trailer carrying the season's laborers had tipped over, leaving five dead and six injured. And certainly the same season every year in Kandalı saw workers blooming in every color. Therefore the discrepancy in value between these two pieces of news was due to no one knowing the people who had died. These workers with a life expectancy of three months, whose seeds had been planted very far away although they bloomed in Kandalı and dried up in a trailer, had lived elsewhere and never read the paper called *From Kandalı to the World.* In that sense it was perfectly natural that these casualties, who piqued the interest of no Kandalı resident save for the few farmers whose fields they had worked on, be left outside the red-and-white border. Only the doctors, nurses, and assistants at the public hospital of Kandalı were, naturally, rather distressed by the matter. After all it was highly tiresome to have to stare blankly at people who tried to tell them things in a language called Kurdish that they didn't understand. To make it worse, unlike the flowers that bloomed in the same season as them, the workers stank. As if they'd begun decaying as soon as they were born. In reality we were also the same, but

---

2  A play on Gaza's name, which in Turkish means "crusader."

since they only lived three months, their decay was visible, and it reeked.

Ultimately the focal point of the paper and Kandalı was the photograph that also featured me. Standing behind the governor and smiling was Yadigar. You couldn't really tell from the photograph, but I was actually looking at him. He in turn was looking at the district police chief. The district police chief was looking at the district gendarmerie commander. The district gendarmerie commander was looking at the mayor to his right. He in turn was looking at my father, who definitely didn't want to be there. And my father was looking at the governor as if he would have slit his throat, because in his eyes the governor was a child thief. No one in that photo was looking at me. For the governor in his turn was looking at the watch he was handing to me. The face of the watch showed quarter past three and both the hour and minute hands were pointing and looking at the elderly janitor standing in the corner. The man, whom my father had informed me was the janitor, had been caught with his eyes closed. And so the entire chain of gazes ended at his wrinkled eyelids. It was an unbelievable photograph! An unbelievable scene! Of course I was unaware at that time of its likeness to the scene in that fresco of Da Vinci's that I was to see in a book years later . . .

*The Last Supper* . . . the last! Not because Christ had the last meal of his life at that table. The last because Christ was the main dish at that table. The first and last really! Because Christ's first and last bite was consumed that evening. So with no Christ left, God, in his desperation, would reveal himself . . . but throughout the meal God was neither seen nor heard. The twelve apostles, their bellies full but their souls empty, placed the bones in front of them into grails to leave them at the mercy of dogs but still God would not appear. Just when they thought they'd killed the goose that laid golden eggs, they heard a voice. God spoke:

"Is there man?"

The apostles were so excited they first exchanged glances and then cried in unison, "Yes!"

"Are there then any believers of man?"

They were at a loss for words, and their gazes slid to the animals that were crunching the bones of Christ.

"Dogs!" they hollered.

Upon this there was a pause and God spoke again:

"If the only believers left of man are dogs . . . then there are bound to be ones among them who catch rabies and become enlightened."

And as soon as He was finished, the dogs ran off, foaming at the mouth, and all that was left inside a small grail were Christ's skull and three bones . . . Those who had dined at that table and watched it all to death said, so that no one would know the truth, "We'll tell another truth!"

Judas was the only one who said, "No, I can have no part in such a lie."

And he took the grail, with the last remainders of Christ, and left the table. As Judas sank into the quicksand of regret with each step, the remaining eleven apostles instantly thought up a story. This story would contain neither the contents of Christ's meal nor what they had heard God tell them. On the contrary, this story would have Christ make the highly inviting suggestion to "eat my flesh, drink my blood," but no one would eat or drink of him. Most importantly, Judas would be the traitor of the story. A traitor who'd left the table and gone to turn in Christ to the Sanhedrin Council.

So Christ would be crucified and no one would know that he'd been chewed up and consumed by his apostles that night. Essential details would further be added to the story for plausibility. Such as the number of the pieces of silver Judas received in return for his betrayal: thirty! Fearful that Judas might tell the truth, the apostles came to agreement on the story they had built and told the lie, which they referred to among themselves as *another truth*, to everyone who crossed their path.

But Judas was in no state to utter a thing. Whenever he opened his mouth, he was overcome by guilt. Even if he were to tell, who would believe him? Eleven against one! He didn't stand a chance. He could endure neither the lies that were starting to be spread about him nor the truth he had witnessed. He stopped in front of the first wishing tree he came upon and buried the grail he was carrying underneath it. Then he hanged himself from the thickest branch of the tree . . . and a dog came upon the tree. It began digging and became rabid as soon as it reached the bones. Then another dog and yet another became rabid. Upon seeing this, the peasants dug a deeper hole, tossed the grail into it, and covered it with rocks.

But since they were unable to keep their mouths shut, they told of the cursed grail that turned rabid anyone who came near and brought about the crucifixion of Christ, even if only in whispers. The story was shaved into shape like a sculpture as it moved through the ages and from ear to ear. Who would want their village to be remembered by a cursed grail? Thus the first thing to be forgotten was the spot where the grail was buried. Then Judas was eradicated from the story. After all, it was a sin to even mention his name. All that remained was a grail that had belonged to Christ. And it came time for the bones and skull in the grail to evaporate. Due to technicality, it was easier to start the tale, "There was once a grail." instead of, "There was once a skull and three bones inside a grail." The story's reach depended on it being easy to remember.

Lastly, the word "curse" from the story became *sacred* because it scared children. In fact, with time that grail took on the form of bowl, or chalice. After all, those that had buried it were long gone and there was no one around to belie what was told. And so in order to recover what one generation had thrown into a hole and covered with rocks to get rid of, other generations started wars and called them the Crusades. Everyone's after it still. Even if they don't know it, they're all after gnawing on whatever is left of Christ and hearing the voice of God . . . but what could He say even if He did speak again? Would the answers to the questions be any different after all this time? Weren't dogs the only believers in man? Was there any point in chasing after the Holy Grail just to hear the tone of God's voice? After a skull and three bones!

As I left the Government Office, that was about as much as was left of me, you see! A skull, three bones, and empty space, that was all. A Gaza filled with nothingness or nothingness encased in Gaza . . .

Certainly with such doors open in front of me and the population of an entire town behind me ready to push me forward, it would have been only right for me to cross that threshold and receive the education I deserved. But I didn't and so remained rooted in Kandalı, that wormhole, like a thousand-year-old tree. Even despite the fact that my situation had been taken over by the town the minute the school principal disclosed my score and things had immediately progressed outside Ahad's control.

So I could have escaped . . . but I couldn't. Simply because my father had said he loved me . . . pressing down on the blister on my wrist all the while! If Ahad loved me, it didn't matter that I didn't love myself. I couldn't leave Ahad . . . perhaps I hadn't wanted to leave in the first place. To leave and get away from that reservoir . . . I had merely distracted myself with the possibility of leaving. For actually my father, me, and the reservoir, we were the Trinity itself! We were the *real* Trinity! My father and I were an eight-legged insect. We scrambled over the wet walls of the reservoir. We had been speaking the same tongue from birth. No one could understand this tongue, that served only to speak of the reservoir, except for us. Other people may have been created or spewed into the sky out of some white hole in the solar system but we were different. We were the only living things on Earth that had come to life through evolution. Whereas other people were different probabilities of one soul, we were the beginning, middle, and end of one probability! We lived in a place only accessible by holding your breath. Outside the universe. In the reservoir . . . our mothers had shot us at the world. We had been born as bullets and whizzed around in the reservoir to pierce the stomach of whoever happened to cross our path. Our range was our lives. Our name was the Story. We were about two men and a reservoir.

But the paper *From Kandalı to the World* didn't care enough to cover the *renunciation* chapter of the story. More accurately, it specifically didn't care. Because at the head of those who had promised to aid my education came the owner of the paper. Therefore some foray into the matter might have cost him! Also, the memory of Kandalı was known not for its capacity for forgetting but for misremembering! Before long they started believing that I'd gone to Istanbul and always remembered it that way. And when they saw me on the street, they remarked that I looked like that boy who had gone to Istanbul . . . and I went back to my reservoir and hung on one wall a large clock with a white face, of which the second hand ticked every 150 milliseconds because I'd messed with the mechanism. A clock that slowed down time by one and a half.

The immigrants didn't have blisters on their wrists that you could press. Their wrists had watches. And I collected those watches the moment they got off the truck. They never had phones. For fear of getting robbed, they swathed themselves in fabrics with a thousand secret pockets and carried only meager amounts of money on them. I wasn't interested in money. My preoccupation was with time. I was interested in the immigrants' gradual decline into head-bashing as they looked at that clock and the minutes that just wouldn't pass. Only then would they know the pain Ahad inflicted on me with one finger. If I couldn't put myself in their place . . . we would just have to try the opposite. Not just the opposite, we would try everything . . . They would teach me about humanity. I in turn would share my pain with them. If my father had said he loved me . . . then this was our only salvation. Then of course we could all commit suicide and end the matter. All those immigrants and myself. But out of all the religions, they had to believe in the ones that forbid suicide! I was aware of all their minute calculations. I wasn't that dumb. Not all that dumb! Perhaps because I didn't put on the watch that the governor gave me and jump on the first bus to Istanbul . . . I was that dumb, dumber, and dumbest! Because what I always kept on my person, rather than the watch, was Cuma's paper frog. It didn't even leap anymore when I pressed onto its back. The only thing it did was talk to me in an imitation of Cuma's voice. Or I was simply hallucinating and what was talking was the picture on the paper Cuma had folded over and over into a frog. A picture he'd drawn himself. The picture of a mountain. Or a hill. Or a reef. Two cavities in its slope that was like a straight wall. And a statue inside each cavity. Around them, other reefs and other dark cavities. Black dots resembling cave entrances. In his Turkish comprised of three words he had said, "Me, home!" It didn't make a bit of sense to me. I'd thought he was crazy. Huge statues carved into a reef and a Cuma that lived in one of the tens of holes in yet another reef!

Seeing that I didn't believe a single word, he had laughed and begun folding the paper . . . how could I have known? That there was a valley called Bamiyan in an area called Hazarajat in a country called Afghanistan and that people there lived in caves carved into the reefs by Buddhist monks 1500 years ago? How could I have known that every morning, since the sixth century, they woke up to two statues of Buddha, one fifty-three and the other thirty-five meters tall, also carved into the reefs? How could I have known that the larger one, Buddha, was the *Vairocana* that represented the embodiment of the void, and that this could be derived from looking at the posture, or the *mudra*, of the statue? How could I also have known that Buddha came from the Shakya Dynasty, and that was why the smaller statue was named *Shakyamuni*? And who could know who it was that spoke to me? The frog, or one of the two Buddhas? Who knew? That every time I looked at the two giants in that picture, Dordor and Harmin came to mind . . . in truth even I didn't know. I didn't know why I thought of them when I looked at that picture. Maybe it was because they had been two colons that rose up on either side of me and held up my childhood. Because once upon a time they had stood on either side of me and prevented life from crashing down on me . . . maybe there was yet another reason that I thought of them . . .

"You know what?" Harmin had said. We were sitting on deck. The sun seemed about to come up, and the sky changed colors as it rose and fell.

"A vicious cycle never disappears. It just expands and makes itself forgotten. Why? Because what you call a cycle is just your basic circle. It takes so long to make a full tour that you don't even notice you passed the same spot twice. Sometimes the vicious cycle grows so much you don't live long enough to get back to where you started. One keeps galloping on it like a blind horse. Thinks he's going in a straight line. That he's making progress. Even thinks he died while making progress and breathes his last in peace! Blindness is imperative, of course! Otherwise you'd know you're running around in circles. That's why old people lose their eyesight, you see? So they won't know they're passing over the same spot twice. Blindness is a natural defense against the vicious cycle. A mechanical response! Like life itself . . . In fact, that's why life is so boring! Because life is also just a response. Now, take a look around you! Everything antagonizes life! What you eat, drink, say, the breaths you take, everything! So that's life, only a response against that! Against death first and foremost, of course! They must have taught you at school. What's the basis of science? Cause and effect, right? You know what that means? It means nature's tenacity! Everything's a matter of tenacity. Especially life. And that's the very reason life is as boring as watching a team of tenacious parasites that think just getting to be in a game is as good as a consolation goal. So you don't need hope or a purpose to survive. It's enough to know you're going to die. You're alive because you're in danger. You're alive because you're dying by every second. That's all. That's the meaning of life: fear of death! Are you following me?"

I didn't. How could I have understood what Harmin was trying to say? I was thirteen. Maybe twelve.

"So, if you really want to live, you really want to have a purpose, you first have to shake off that fear of death! Fear of death, you know, the meaning that comes for free when you receive life, that they push into your hand the minute you're born, you've got to toss it away! Only then can you be free! Only then can you go and find the true meaning of your life! Now make me a promise."

"Okay," I'd said.

"You're not to ever fear death. Because that fear, that's the one thing in this world that can blind you!"

"Promise," I'd said. "I won't."

He had laughed. Then he'd rolled himself another cigarette.

"Well, do you know how not to fear?"

"No," I'd said.

He'd shown me the tattoo on his wrist: *Dead to be free*. But I didn't know English. Yet.

"Death includes life, Gaza. You know what they say, starting something is half of finishing it. So is being born. Half of dying. It's enough that you accept that. I'm not asking you to believe.

Because there's nothing about that to believe. That's nature for you. It's enough that you see . . . see that you're dead already and accept it. The rest will come."

"What about you?" I'd asked. "Aren't you afraid of dying?"

"Me? I'm a fool that's afraid of even treading on the ground. All I do is sit around like this, on this boat! You know the lotus flower? It looks like the lily. I'm sitting on the water just like one of those. So is Dordor . . . he's also sitting . . . other than that we don't do a damn thing."

That I thought of Dordor and Harmin every time I looked at the statues in that picture of Cuma's didn't merely have to do with their being two giants. There were also the lotus flowers . . . I learned about it years later. Why lotus flowers rested on the water and Buddha's palm . . . I found out that their implications, as various as their colors, started out in wisdom, passed through enlightenment and rested in mental clarity before ascending to peace. I learned how they held their breath to dive into life's depths and that, naturally, frogs lived among them. Frogs that looked as if they'd been folded out of wet paper . . . it took a while for me to find all this out. After all, I was finding out as I went along. Finding out as you went along made the journey longer, of course. But I wasn't in any hurry. No one was running late to where I was going. They couldn't have if they tried. There was no running late for those that knew where they were headed. If the destination at hand was somewhere you could be late or early to, it wasn't even worth setting out. If Harmin had been with me now, he would have said, "Those that fear death are the only ones that make appointments. They're the only ones with purposes that require making appointments. They're bound to graduate in four years, go insane if they don't have a job in six years, buy a house some way or another in ten years, and walk out of life in fifty years via one of at most ten varieties of death!" And since

Harmin being on one side of me meant that Dordor was on the other, he would then noisily add:

"You'd think they made a fucking appointment to be born! What's all this about appointments and being late and being early! If you can find a way, walk! Or sit down and stay sat! You know the lotus flower?"

If I were to say, "Harmin already told me, Dordor," he would first give me a look and then take a drag from his joint before he spoke:

"Just wait till you hear it from me! Say, now I'm curious! How am I going to tell it, I wonder?"

I watched the group of thirty-three scatter to different points of the reservoir where they let themselves sink to the ground. Dragging their backs down over the wall, they squatted and sat. Only one remained standing. A young man, the frame of his glasses broken passing through God knows which hole and taped in the middle. He caught my eye. He raised his index finger the way I once had in school to ask permission to speak and said:

"I knows Turkish."

"So do I," I said.

He laughed.

I didn't. I asked: "What?"

"When are we go?"

At least he could put together something resembling a sentence.

"What's your name?"

"Rastin."

"Are you all from Afghanistan?"

"Yes. But different different. There is Tajik, there is Pashtun . . ."

"You can understand them all, right?"

"Yes."

"Then you're going to be my translator."

"Okay . . . tell."

"Not now. That's all for now. I'll come back later."

"When go?"

"I don't know, Rastin."

"Your name?"

"Gaza."

He laughed and spoke. "Gaza? You are mujahideen?"

He extended his hand. I assume we were supposed to shake hands. Below ground! I could try. I extended my hand as well, and we shook, as though we'd been introduced on an ordinary day for an ordinary reason. I even said, most likely out of habit, "Pleased to meet you."

He laughed again. "No death, no pleased."

"What?"

"When mujahideen die, then pleased."

I would have left, but he wouldn't let go of my hand. I didn't get people who shook hands for so long. They'd cling on to the accosted hand as if they'd waited to hold it their whole lives. Also, instead of practically dying of exhaustion like he should have been, he was still peering into my eyes and laughing as if to convince me that what he'd said was amusing. Just as I was about to withdraw my hand and leave he asked:

"You, student?"

"Yes."

I was lying.

"Me also student. Kabul University. Law."

I pulled my hand away as soon as he loosened his scrawny fingers, every bone of which I could feel. I pulled back a little too fast. His hand was left hanging in the air. But I didn't care. After all, we weren't about to be friends.

"I'm going to give you some buckets now. You can hand them out."

"Bucket?"

"No toilet, only buckets, you understand?"

The smile covering his entire face vanished in an instant. That the topic had suddenly come to his bowels, and the shittiness of the situation he was in, right when he had believed himself to be in an everyday social interaction, had punched a bucket-sized hole in his pride. I was able to tell things like that now. I could feel how stung those still capable of shame were. I hadn't been able to set foot outside Kandalı in fifteen years, but people from at least three continents had come to my doorstep. Some had not only come to my doorstep but walked all over my feet too, but by now I knew them all. There wasn't a variety of immigrant I was unaffiliated with. This Rastin, most probably, was one of those that left his country on political grounds. Because they were the most likely to wear broken glasses. Since every policeman that crossed their path would find a way to break them! To make sure they wouldn't read any more books. But Rastin got himself back together.

"I see, bucket! You collect sample, for test!" he said, and laughed again.

I didn't reply. I just shook my head and left . . . I locked the door to the reservoir and went to sit at my desk. The metal table in the shed was my office now. My father's carpentry was in the past. There was a monitor on it where I watched the reservoir and took notes on the groups. I even had a computer next to it along with a printer. In its memory were hundreds of files. In those files, information about the hundreds of people that had passed through the reservoir . . . First of all, I'd divided up the groups by the duration they stayed in the reservoir: there were four main sections, *2, 7, 14,* and *Over 14 Days.* Because the greatest variable of their behavior was the duration of their stay in the reservoir.

So, their reservoir lifespan . . . They displayed a distinct change between day two and five. But when they finished out seven days and started to think they might have to stay another seven, their reactions quickly changed too.

Aside from that, the number of men and women was also important. I had three subsections called *Male Majority*, *Female Majority,* and *Equal*. The groups where women were predominant in numbers were more patient and extraordinarily resilient in the face of ever more difficult circumstances. In groups where men were predominant, the rate of me being presented with the woman I wanted to fuck, surprisingly, was higher.

Also, the numbers of the people in the group was also a key element. For that I had four files named *5*, *15*, *30*, and *Over 30*. It was extremely difficult to undermine a group of five or play them off against one another. But it was possible to make a lynch mob out of thirty people within three hours of arriving at the reservoir. Or, whereas crowds of more than thirty people unhesitatingly sent me the women I wanted, groups of five were willing to put their lives on the line to prevent that from happening.

And besides all of this, I had files opened under the names of *Nationality, Ethnic Origin, Average Age, Level of Education, Profession, Amount of Food Consumed, Endurance to Thirst*, and any other measurable attribute pertaining and imaginable to man. For I had something very important now: time. I had left school. With my father's arms, and my own hands, I'd strangled my educational life. It was all for the best, really. Because I'd started at another school. A school that had humanity for all the subjects. What was more, I could read all I wanted. Though I wasn't interested in adventure novels any longer. When I went to the bookstores in the city, I beelined to the shelves no one went near and flipped through books no one cracked open. On the trail of every author whose name appeared in Dordor and Harmin's shady books, I spent the money that my father gave me, now upgraded from allowance to salary, and sank my teeth into my finds like a vampire to suck on to the very last word. Of course other people also read the human-related theory hidden inside those books. But no one else had a full laboratory of humans right underneath their feet, as I did. There was a huge difference between listing on fine-quality printing paper the probable reactions of an adult against the rising temperature of a crowd, and experimenting with and observing it. A difference the size of reality!

I was fifteen and had neither a conscience nor any friends. On his first week at the private school he was enrolled in with his share from the bribes taken by his father, Ender had been subjected to disciplinary punishment for extorting money from his classmates. A month later, he had gratuitously lit up a cigarette in class and started a fire, though small, and was expelled three months later for punching a teacher. Now and then I glimpsed him pacing up and down the only main street of Kandalı with the other cactus-kids that were rooted here. Ender also no longer cackled to himself. He never laughed at all, actually. His brow, crushing down his eyes, gave the impression of having either just left a fight or being about to enter one, while the cigarette sticking out of the corner of his mouth made it seem as if he were looking to star in an animated film called *The Kandalı Mafia* or something. And even more strange was that I'd heard Yadigar tell my father in conversation:

"Everything I do, I do for my son!"

Where had I heard that one before . . . ? But Yadigar was serious. Yes, he himself might be sunk into everything illegal up to the badges on his shoulder, but all he wished for really was for Ender to grow up to have a life in which he answered to no one. For that he wanted to make sure his son receive the antibiotic that was *a good education*, which had been forsaken from him in his time. No matter that the mere mental image of said reception made Ender sick to his stomach!

Yadigar was also a dreamer. For the status of junior officer that he would never deem worthy of Ender didn't exist in the army only. Even heads of state were sometimes junior officers. In fact they took their orders not from above but from other heads of state, who in theory were of the same rank as themselves. In the end, despite all the conscientious tear-soaked wet dreams Yadigar had about his son, Ender's sole career plan appeared to be becoming part of the Kandalı Mafia. But what Ender didn't know was this: the Kandalı Mafia was his own father. Along with Ahad and myself . . . Perhaps there were others, but for now I had no interest in them.

When we ran into each other on the town's only main street, I only nodded to him imperceptibly and wondered at how it was that he had transformed from the clueless little boy who had been my desk mate into a black shirt. His transformation had even given me inspiration for a new research topic. The only explanation for Ender unexpectedly donning all black and starting to wave around a string of prayer beads as if he would have poked out someone's eye with the marker was a quest for power. To be the only holder of power in any territory he entered. Spreading fear through the evocation of violence and becoming powerful through spreading fear. In this way, once he gained the power he was looking for, the flaws that he loathed in himself and held responsible for making him an outcast in school, would disappear forever. This would be made possible by the other boys that now accepted Ender as their leader. Ender as leader could claim that the sun rotated around the earth, and no one would contradict him. Because the first condition of accepting someone else's monopoly on power was denial. Denial of oneself and of facts. And especially denial of the shortcomings of one's leader. Therefore the only way of Ender, as a fool, to be respected and to live his life without anyone telling him to his face that he was a fool, depended on him being the only authority in his colony of vermin. Yes, the issue was that simple.

But it didn't end there. Because all of this was connected with another issue: one's internal wish to rule. It was about the wish to have power over others or to become an authority of any scale . . . Why was it that in some this wish was lighter than their shadows, when in others it was dense enough to hemorrhage a thousand veins? How did it come about that some people felt like sorry sons of bitches unless they reigned over everyone else? Was authoritarianism a virus? Did the immune system of society have to collapse for it to arise? Was leadership addicting? If so, who was the dealer of this drug, how much for a dime, and did achieving the same effect every time require increasing the dose? Lastly, why did man, that toy, take himself so seriously and thrash like a beached fish for the sake of being taken seriously? In all probability the answers to these questions were based in the fear of death, as Harmin had explained. For the individual who found the meaning of life in a fear of death, this was a way to feel invincible: to become an authority. It was a subject much deserving of contemplating and experimenting on. After all, Enders were all around. From one-on-one dealings to political relations involving millions, all around. Every single one was after the tiniest opportunity they could come across. Every day we walked past secret tyrants who had been lying in wait all their lives to seize and overtake power at its weak moment and might die waiting. They might even be those closest to us. In our families, among our friends, everywhere. Who would dare call out another for a dictator? It didn't exactly show when they were walking down the street by themselves! Or sitting in a reservoir with their heads between their hands . . .

The thirty-three-person group that included Rastin had come into my life at the exact time I had been having these thoughts. It had actually done so as a bit of an exception. It was the month of February. Judging by the fact that they hadn't waited for the summer to flee their country, they must have been in quite a hurry. They could at least have waited for spring when the prices would have decreased somewhat. Contrary to the legal tourism industry, high season for illegal excursions was the months of fall and winter. After all, mountains waiting to be scaled would be made taller by the snow, and all the roads leading to death made shorter by the ice. It couldn't be accidental that they disregarded all this and set off anyway. In fact, it must have been something so certain it had made them forget everything else they knew.

My father had gone to the city for four days. To meet with Aruz's men. They were going to discuss the captains that had taken Dordor's and Harmin's places. The blokes were useless. They cooked up trouble constantly. It wasn't that surprising. There wasn't much of a chance that the fishbowl called the Aegean would carry on its back two water lilies of the likes of Dordor and Harmin ever again. Anyway . . .

So I was left alone with the reservoir dwellers for four days. They would also not be boarding the boats for at least two more weeks. I'd heard my father say it. That meant I had at least fifteen days' worth of material to work with. I could start the world's most scientific study right away! It needed a title. I opened up a file on the computer and named it *The Power of Power*.

My project was really quite simple. I would imagine the reservoir as a country. The group would be its people. I'd play on the living conditions, maybe grant some stipulations to a few among them, and measure the general reaction. There were hundreds of computer games along these lines, I knew. But the reason other kids continued to play those games was because none of them had a reservoir full of people at hand. That was what those kids didn't know . . .

Firstly, they had to have a leader. In the life above the reservoir, the real one that is, there were various ways to determine this. For instance, the most physically strong person could be leader. And for that they'd need to spill one another's blood, maybe even kill—which method my father would never condone, as it meant losing goods. I could forget about that . . .

Or whichever was richest could be the proprietor. Yet I also couldn't take that road, since after all these years, I knew that the amount they carried on themselves was very little or more or less equal . . .

That left the method that was perhaps the most interesting: determining the leader by vote. Democracy! That was the most logical. In the end, the society-leader relationship wasn't much different from the situation of a human and an animal trapped in the same cage. In dictatorship the door of the cage would abruptly open and a hungry lion would be shoved inside. But democracy entailed freedom for a person to choose what kind of animal they would rather be trapped with. A carnivore? An herbivore? An omnivore? One that roams by itself? One that hunts in packs? A endangered species? Can it be domesticated? Such were the questions that arose. The fact of the cage, the animal, and the locked door remained, but there was nothing to be done about that. The facts of life existed at this level for now. Also, while in a dictatorship the animal must remain in the cage until it died; in a democracy it would only remain so until the next election. One could count the fang marks on one's body, consider how much flesh or how many digits one had lost, and thus decide whether or not cage life with the same animal could be continued . . .

Yes, the reservoir dwellers would have the right to choose their leader. In fact, maybe the people of the reservoir deserved democracy much more than the ones in real life. The reservoir was a real cage, after all, and those people were aware of the walls surrounding them as surely as they were able to lean their backs against them.

But the ones in real life had no idea. Especially not of the fact that they were living in a cage! When they looked at a map, they only saw lines. Red borderlines. As a matter of fact, they were so used to the borders of the cage they failed to recognize as a cage that they would die and be resurrected over and over in order to protect them. Preserving that cage was a matter of honor, and they used the ties of citizenship to lash themselves to its bars by the neck.

Perhaps they were right. After all, there wasn't much left in the name of humankind worth making into a matter of honor. It was too late to make honesty into a matter of honor, for instance. If the facts of biology were to change overnight and lying were to kill one immediately by brain hemorrhaging, the world would empty so rapidly there'd be room anew for dinosaurs!

Or, for example, it also couldn't make a concept such as fair allocation of resources into a matter of honor. It couldn't presume to up and exclaim, "Either you see to it that there isn't a single hungry person left on the planet or I'll kill myself! I can't stand to live such a wretched life!"

Children especially couldn't be made into a matter of honor. Was there anyone on this Earth who had ever said, or could presume to say, "I saw him putting children to work so I shot him down, Your Honor! It's a matter of integrity where I come from!" Or, any law that counted facilitating child labor as extreme provocation and would thus see a reduction in the murderer's sentencing?

So, even matters of honor had to be somewhat grounded in reality. It made much more sense for them to concern women and their virtue, so to speak! That was a much more realistic matter of honor! Or a blood feud! Or the disputing of one's religion of choice! Or the criticizing of one's ethics! Or the tampering of the borders of one's cage of residence! These were much more logical issues and wouldn't pose an inkling of a threat to sustainable economy. So it seemed that the trash bin called human history, filled with methane gas ready to go up in the first explosion of the third world war, was now brimming with issues that couldn't be made into matters of honor. No matter that the borderlines of the world map would appear extremely claustrophobic to any sane extraterrestrial, there was nothing to be done. Yes, those borders were as claustrophobic as a three-person elevator, but there were ways to forget one was in an elevator in the first place. Like endlessly taking it up and down. That was how the people trapped inside those borders passed the time. Going up and down and up in that elevator called *homeland*. And by peering into other elevators through the doors that opened at every floor . . . the reservoir dwellers had it worse, obviously. They were stuck at −1 and going nowhere.

I was watching through the screen. They just sat there without talking. Only Rastin remained standing, still as a statue. I was just trying to figure out what he was looking at when he raised his head and met my eyes. Out of the six cameras in the reservoir, he looked at the one closest to him and waved. Then he went to find an empty spot and sat down. He took a pen and paper out of pocket. He began to write.

**He's like me, isn't he?**
I don't know.
**I think he is . . . Look, he's constantly scribbling something down like I used to do. So I guess a Cuma passes through this reservoir every five years.**
Could be . . . Cuma?
**Yes?**
Why were you running?
**Never mind.**
They were going to kill you, weren't they?
**I said, never mind.**

120

Was the government going to kill you?

**The government is a word, Gaza. People kill.**

But you would've been killed, wouldn't you?

**You'd like to think that I died on the very road I took to evade death. So you can make yourself feel even worse. So you can feel even guiltier. You were ten, Gaza! You were just a small child. Stop thinking about it.**

I'm not thinking, I'm feeling . . .

**I don't like the games you play with these people.**

I know.

**Then don't do it. Look how tired they are. God knows how scared they are . . .**

No one is more tired and scared than me, Cuma! No one!

**Really? You should think about your mother! Have you ever been scared enough to kill your own child?**

Remind me of that one more time and I go open that valve and dispatch those people by drowning!

**I remember the days when you used to tie pieces of *simit* to the tail of your kites to try and feed the birds in the sky . . . You've come a long way, haven't you?**

You can't remember that, Cuma. That was before I killed you. Now shut up and watch! Watch and maybe you'll learn how the government you said was just a word can be used in a sentence!

"Gaza! We are go?"

"No, Rastin, we're still waiting to get word. But there's another issue at hand. You need to choose a spokesman."

"Spokesman?"

"Yes, you need to have a leader."

"Why?"

"Because you're going to have to make some decisions for the road that's ahead. You're a crowded group. No one will ask you individually what you want. So, among yourselves, you need to choose someone you trust so he can speak for you. So he can do the negotiating, you see?"

"But we came Turkey. No problem."

"I know, it's what's from here on that's the problem! The real journey starts once you get on those boats. Whatever, it's up to you . . . I'm just saying. The people you'll come across on the way to where you're going won't be like us, Rastin. Do you know what danger means?"

"Yes."

"Then let me put it this way: a lot of danger!"

With that I left Rastin, whose eyes had become the points of two questions marks, and exited the reservoir. He'd begun talking with the others by the time I took my place at my desk. Using the word danger had been a good choice. The best way to stir people into action with the minimum of information was to convince them that an obscure threat lay ahead for them. Rastin most probably hadn't made anything of what I'd said but thought it was serious business anyway.

There was an old man in the group. He appeared to be the eldest of the thirty-three. Most of the faces were turned in his direction. After all, they came from a territory of earth turbid with clans and believed that the best way to measure a man's wisdom was by the lines on his face. Yet I knew kids younger than me, the napes of their necks were like alligator hide from working in the fields all day. Having a lot of wrinkles meant nothing. Getting old was more like the last phase of the living disease. A phase where mental health was lost and replaced with the disagreeable certainty that one would never find what one had been searching for in life. Elderly people were those who had become fully aware that they'd been duped and it was too late for everything. A society run by one of them could only be one that died with them, complaining and in agony.

The old Afghani spoke laboriously from where he sat and everyone listened to him. Then suddenly Rastin looked at one of the cameras and began waving his hands to call me. I would have heard him if he had spoken. Of course, he couldn't have known that the cameras also transmitted sound. Likewise he couldn't have known that when I turned on and spoke into the microphone in front of me, my voice would come out of the speaker in the reservoir. That was why Rastin and the others were so startled that they jumped. Because I might have been a bit loud asking, "What is it?"

Rastin immediately figured out the contraption and gave it a try. "Gaza? You are hear me?"

"Yes, Rastin . . . have you picked someone?"

"Group not understand. Why is danger?"

"I can only say that to whomever it is you pick. You'll also know, of course. Because you'll be translating. We shouldn't scare the others unnecessarily, right?"

As soon as Rastin related this to those around him, there was a rippling in the reservoir. Everyone started to talk at once. They could neither hear nor understand one another. I could see it. I didn't have to know Pashto to recognize desperation and fear. Especially with a dark secret in question that concerned all their futures, it had taken panic only a few seconds to fill up the reservoir like poisonous gas. This was because of the circumstances they were in, of course. They were in such an illegal and illogical situation that they reacted much more rashly than a people passing their lives between home, work, and school. They were after all on a journey that trapped them between the place they came from and the place they were heading to. They'd left everything behind that they could afford to lose and the only thing they had left was their bodies. Their only valuable was themselves. And in that situation neither conventional ethical norms nor logical decision-making devices were valid. When a person's only wish was to make it from one point to another, no matter what, every psychological and social theory caved.

For example, their fears were thousands of times that of the apprehensions of the regular people of a regular country. That enabled me to reap the reaction of every one of my moves instantly. Last year, when I was yet a student, I'd been sent to the fast chess tournament in the city because I was school champion. We had only three seconds for every move. I'd made it to the finals. A private schooler had sat across from me and kept turning around to look at his father throughout the whole game.

The man was at least as excited as his son. I don't know why, but I let the kid win. Then the man came up and embraced his son. Maybe it was only for the sake of seeing that . . . whatever. So due to the fast reactions of the reservoir dwellers, I was once again chasing three-second moves.

And a woman in her forties with a child of seven or eight in her lap, that I hadn't noticed up till then, shouted at the top of her lungs and shut everybody up. Then she pointed to Rastin and said something. Most probably she wanted him to speak. That was what Rastin did and he did so for about five minutes. Then he stopped and gestured at the old man. At this, from different spots in the reservoir, ten hands that I could count went up. The election had begun!

The middle-aged man sitting next to the elderly man, whom I took to be his son due to the fact that they had agreed to shit in the same bucket, counted the hands. Then he said something to Rastin. Rastin pointed at himself and expelled a long sentence before he was silent. At that twenty-one hands were raised in the reservoir. Since the only child in the reservoir wasn't yet of voting age, his hand had gone up to be grabbed by his mother and pulled down. The elderly man had motionlessly stared ahead of him in both votes, but Rastin had had no qualms about raising his hand for himself. I've always found it unbecoming for a person to vote for himself. It's one of the two most repulsive things in the world. The other is a Hindu playing cricket.

"Gaza! Are you hear?"

Rastin was calling to the camera. I had started to say, "Yes, Rastin," when the Afghani sitting next to the elderly man suddenly stood and started to yell. Now I was certain he was his son! It wasn't hard to guess who he was yelling at. He was clearly yelling at the owners of the twenty-one hands that had gone up a minute ago. He was even unable to control himself at one point and tried to attack Rastin, but the others intervened. But other champions of the old man had come to life. Of course, the ones who had been regular people up until the point they morphed into Rastin's crowd a minute ago had also straightened up. In a matter of seconds, a weird fight had erupted in the reservoir where you couldn't tell who was laying into whom. It was weird because the election didn't even have an actual topic. They didn't even know what purpose the chosen one would serve. That left someone they had chosen for reasons they didn't know. But there were others who were enraged out of nowhere at that *someone* because the candidate they had supported hadn't been chosen. They were going through the first phases of democracy. They believed in the vote, but didn't trust the result unless their candidate came on top. Then that woman in her forties, once again, shoved the child off her lap and unleashed a keening scream that ruptured every eardrum in the reservoir, and all was calm even if only for a short while.

The woman had this specialty. First she let out a shock-factor scream, and then she would start to cry. Her voice fell to pieces as she cried, and she would dissolve into sobs by the time she sat down. It was a sufficiently functional technique. For she had a sacred accessory: the child. The child that she shoved away when she got up to stand, that she grabbed by the arm and pulled in as she sat down, and then tipped over to press into her chest. But as all this was going down, the child never took his hand out of his mouth and merely watched his mother. He was like some kind of taxidermy. Maybe he was a midget pretending to be a child. Maybe he was her husband and not a midget pretending to be a child, I don't even know. You couldn't really tell from where I was sitting . . . I wasn't interested in the details.

The only thing that concerned me about the images I was seeing on the six cameras, on my screen divided into six, was that the peace they'd had up until a half hour ago had been fucked over by politics. Politics was like a foreign substance in one's body, after all. It was as synthetic as a platinum rod. It was the biggest obstacle in the way of the natural progress of society's division of labor. It was against human nature. But then humanity itself was against nature. So there wasn't much to do about that.

Rastin, upon seeing that the objections against the election results had dissolved into silence, looked up at the camera across from him. What had happened had no importance for the old man, but judging from the looks in the eyes of the ones around him, it was evident they would never forgive Rastin. Rastin couldn't even look at the camera for more than the three seconds it would take to speak, kept casting nervous glances at the spot the opposing side was congregating in for fear of an ambush. When he saw that opposition was limited to hasty mumbles and the shaking of heads, he finally relaxed and spoke.

"OK, Gaza. I, leader . . . tell . . . what is danger?"

"Now, Rastin, the ones with you can't hear what I'm about to tell you. I'll explain first, we'll come up with a solution, then we'll see. All right?"

"All right."

"It seems the ones taking you into Greece want more money. Apparently there's more policing on the sea, you understand? More risk, and because of that, more money!"

"But we, we give money, in Kabul. They say, okay."

"I know. But it looks like you have to pay more."

"No, Gaza. No money."

His constant use of my name was starting to get on my nerves. Why, I don't know.

"You're sure no one has any money?"

"Sure! They tell us, do not take money to road. It is better."

"All right then, here's what you can do. You're thirty-three people now. You paid $8,000 per person, right? Now they want $2,000 more from you. So in total you have to pay $10,000 for each. That leaves a shortage of $66,000. Say you negotiate out of the sixty-six thousand but the rest is still fare for six people. So what you paid at this point is only enough for twenty-seven people. So only twenty-seven people get to continue on the way. So above everything else you'd have to pick the six who stay behind. *You* have to, really. Because if you tell them all this, there's sure to be a scene. But if you tell me who stays behind, we'll tell them that they'll take the next boat after you people leave, and then send them back to Afghanistan. Do you understand what I'm saying?"

I was sure Rastin understood me very well. I knew from the many Afghani students that had passed through the reservoir that Kabul University had a department of Turkish Language and Literature. No matter what department they had studied in, in general they would have dabbled in Turkish classes. At the very least they'd know a few words. But Rastin's Turkish surpassed them all. It was possible he had come to Turkey before, maybe even lived here. But that wasn't in my area of interest. I wasn't interested in anyone's background aside from myself. I was fifteen and clearly the world revolved around me. Like a housefly! And if it continued to revolve that was only because I didn't crush it in my fist!

"I not understand! Gaza?"

Rastin was trying to appear to have forgotten Turkish in four seconds, but the sweat on his brow, glistening under the strong light of the reservoir, told me he wasn't doing a very good job.

"You're to choose six people. They're to stay here and then go back to Afghanistan. Or you'll pay $66,000. Do you get it now?"

"Yes," said Rastin. But he was about to cry.

"Can't you pay two thousand per person?"

"No, no, too much money. No one have money. Not other way?"

"Actually maybe . . . you can also do this. I don't know how these guys do business. They'll take a kidney too. One of those cost around twenty thousand. So if you choose three people, you can take care of this thing with three kidneys."

Rastin's eyes, growing wider with every word, had almost come to overflowing the broken frame of his glasses.

"A minute! A minute! What is kidney?"

"You don't know what it means? Should I check a dictionary and tell you the English or something?"

"I knows, I knows, kidney! But, Gaza! No!"

"Fine, then the last solution I can find is this: give the guys two women, you carry on. But you have to give them those younger ones. Not the one with the kid."

It wouldn't have surprised me if Rastin passed out then.

"Is not possible! Is not possible! No!"

"Then I'll go tell my father. You're all going back. Okay?"

"Gaza! Gaza!"

"Yes, Rastin?"

"I give. One kidney enough?"

Had he really said this? Would he be that selfless? For a group of people, one-third of which would have torn him to pieces, no less! I had to make a move in three seconds. With those words the chessboard had suddenly taken flight, grown to the size of the shed's ceiling, and come crashing down on my head. But I wasn't dead yet!

"Okay! One kidney from you. But we need two more."

Breathless from his sudden display of heroics, Rastin was left under the scrutiny of the reservoir dwellers. Well aware that our discussion concerned them closely, they listened as hard as they could in hopes of catching familiar words in the dialogue whizzing back and forth over their heads. But they understood nothing, and because of this their patience was melting like soap. The son of the old man couldn't take it any longer and began to talk. Surely he wanted to know what I was saying. But Gaza must be saying something like, "Wait a minute, I'll tell you later!"

The man who felt like his whole family tree had been insulted because his father wasn't chosen for leader of the reservoir wanted some answers. Now! I was going to provide him with the facts he wanted. It wasn't going to be in Pashto.

"Rastin, listen to me."

Rastin, now trying to ward off the guy with a hand on his chest, who had now come up to him and was elaborately jawing into his ear, was saying, "Tell, Gaza!"

"I'm going to open the lid now. I'm going to toss in a key. In the partition in the back, on the wall, there's a ring with a lock. Open the ring with the key, then put it over the guy's wrist and lock it."

Still trying to fend off the man, Rastin shouted over the voices that were once again talking over one another, "Not necessary!"

"If you say so . . ."

My attempt at sending the first inmate to the cell I'd built specially for the reservoir state was thwarted. Rastin, taking account of both the man and the others around him, must be saying that for now, everyone should keep calm and that an important issue was being discussed. But the old man's son was talking without pausing for breath, as if he was reciting a story by heart. Without a single halt. But then Rastin said something that caused him to stop and freeze with his mouth open as though his final sentence was lodged there. Rastin said a few more words and the reservoir stilled entirely! He must be relating the kidney business. The $66,000 shortage! If it had been me I couldn't even have held out for so long. I'd have blabbed right away. But Rastin was cut from the cloth of a leader. He knew about crisis management! When he was finished, the man quietly went to sit down beside his father. And Rastin, looking up at the nearest camera, said, "Okay! No problem."

"Did you tell them everything?"

"No."

"So how'd that guy shut up?"

"I say, boy father dead. Boy, I say, crazy! We are trap here! I talk to boy, I say, I save us. Understands?"

Now, I hadn't expected that. Rastin wasn't only a leader but a true lawyer! I had no idea if he had graduated, but he definitely didn't need a diploma. For making up a story about my father being dead and their being locked up inside a reservoir at the mercy of a crazy boy within those mere seconds would have been harder than writing a complete dissertation on Roman Law!

"Gaza?"

"Yes?"

"Don't open door!"

"Okay!"

"You are open door, they attack!"

"Okay, Rastin."

"Now sing . . ."

"What?"

"A melody!"

"What?"

"Song! Song!"

"Song?"

"You crazy! For be crazy!"

I laughed. There was a calendar on the wall facing me. On it, the ten stanzas of Mehmet Akif Ersoy. The Independence March[3] was a song after all! I began to sing. In that moment the tens of faces on the screen turned in my direction. Thirty-two people, including the old man, looked at the cameras, and I really did feel like a crazy person. I believed that I was crazy at least as much as they did. Only Rastin among them didn't think this. That was why he was the only one not looking up at the cameras.

---

3   The Turkish national anthem, based on the poem by Mehmet Akif Ersoy, a poet, academic, and champion of the Turkish War of Liberty.

Dragging his left foot back and forth through the sawdust on the ground, he was probably pondering over who would provide the two other kidneys. When I finished singing the second stanza of the march, Rastin murmured something. It was a short sentence. Maybe only a word. And they all began to applaud me! We really *were* a democracy now. The leader thought himself to lead through the lies he told, the people believed the laws it deferred to really existed for its own good, and all the radio announcer could do as the sole news media of the country was pretend to be crazy.

I didn't talk to Rastin again that day. I only watched. One by one he visited the small groups clustered at various corners of the reservoir and talked to each of them. Then at some point he got up and approached one of the cameras and said, "Gaza?" four times over. I didn't answer. He hung his head and retreated. He was so overwhelmed by responsibility that he sank down into the first available spot and went to sleep. Or pretended to sleep so no one would bother him. The others were probably trying to figure out a way to escape from the hole they thought themselves to be imprisoned in. The women wept. The old man and his companions stared ahead silently, while the others submerged themselves in the rise and fall of deliberation. Meanwhile the sole child in the reservoir hummed the melody of the Independence March from the remnants stuck in his head.

First thing next day, I took my place at my table and turned on the microphone.

"Rastin!"

Rastin, long desperate for the sound of my voice, stood up immediately and said, "Yes?" The others looked up at the cameras and smiled in hopes of endearing themselves to the boy who held their fate in his hands.

"So this is what we're going to do: my father has talked with the guys. It looks like one kidney is enough. So there's no need for you to arrange two more. It's been taken care of. I don't know where they'll perform the operation, but it's probably somewhere in Greece. I think it's okay for you to tell the others now. You can tell them I fooled you by saying my father was dead . . . I'm going to talk a bit more now and pretend I'm telling you what I told you yesterday, and you can pretend it's the first you've heard about this sixty-six thousand business . . . all right? I'm going to keep talking . . . but you ask me some questions too."

But Rastin said nothing. He only looked at the camera. There was a crack in the right side of his glasses. I hadn't noticed it before. Maybe it had happened during the night. The glass hadn't been able to withstand the exhaustion coming off his eyes and had cracked. Or it had happened during one of the fights of the day before. As I was contemplating all this, Rastin turned around and walked away. He sat back down in the spot he had been sitting. The first wave of the day shook the reservoir afresh, and everyone fell on top of him. They had him surrounded, and the world's most dissident chorale was abusing his ears when Rastin cried out in a tone of voice I had never heard up till then. I had no idea what he was doing. Not just me, the others had no idea, either. Rastin had let out such a cry that it had put an end to that horrible concert in its first curtain. Then Rastin shut his eyes and put his head between his hands. The ones around him slowly backed away and retreated to their spots. I still couldn't tell what he was trying to do.

"Rastin!" I called, but he didn't raise his head.

That day, although I attempted to talk countless times, Rastin wouldn't answer. When the others brought out their rations to eat, he wouldn't accept anything that was offered to him. He merely observed those around him. The people surrounding him. The eating, talking, pacing, praying people. He would have given his kidney so they could make it to where they were going. Perhaps Rastin imagined every bite that went into their mouths as morsels of his kidney . . . Is it worth it, he must have been wondering. The leader contemplated his people and asked: is it worth it for these people?

The others, seeing that Rastin was silent and had been mostly useless at negotiating with the crazy boy, approached the cameras one by one to ramble and cry. One group had started to try to force the lid open. But dear Ahad must have had these days in mind when he had installed it, not really a lid but a safe door. They didn't have a chance.

Especially not the woman who kept waving her child at the camera and yelling. Who knows what she was saying to me? To persuade me . . . I even thought at some point that she was trying to tell me that she'd break the child's neck if I didn't open the lid. But I was wrong. Most probably, by holding the child by the neck and shaking it, she was trying to show me how weak and sick he was. That must have been it, because no sooner had she picked him up and buried him between her breasts, she walked away from the camera.

On the television channel especially tailored for me, a series called *threats* followed the documentary on *begging*. The old man's son was especially good at that. He got so worked up I began to think he should be locked in a reservoir for the rest of his life. First, every part of his face began quivering. Especially when he was yelling. His eyebrows, his cheeks, his beard, everything. His fists, which he practically stuck under my nose in the attempt to brandish them to me, kept dropping in and out of sight of the camera. He appeared to be punching the wall. But since this tantrum exhibit also fell short, he would then go over to his father and put his hand on the old man's shoulder while he continued his yelling from there. The only person not approaching the cameras was Rastin. He was the only one not talking to me. My task, as it happened, was to watch. I didn't want to be involved. I just waited for Rastin to take action.

Toward the evening something strange happened, and Rastin asked the man next to him for his canned meal. The man refused. So Rastin grabbed the can out of the man's hand in a single lunge. He did it so quickly and with such assurance that the man was left speechless. All he could do was get up and walk away from Rastin. Consuming the contents of the can, Rastin then yanked a bottle of water out of the hand of the woman sitting on the other side of him. The woman first stared at Rastin nonchalantly knocking it back, then at the others. They in turn gestured as if to tell her, "Let it go." Having drained the bottle, Rastin wiped his mouth on the back of his hand, looked straight at the camera across from him, and without bothering to stand, shouted:

"Gaza! You are there?"

"Yes!"

"You? This light. Turn off?"

"Are you asking whether I can turn them off from here?"

"Yes."

"Shall I?"

"No."

And Rastin got up to say something to those around him. He was pointing at the fluorescent lights on the ceiling. Then he turned to the camera and said, "Turn off! Turn on!"

I stood and walked in the direction of the reservoir to flip on and off the light switch on the wall. I had no idea what the hell Rastin was trying to do. But at least it passed the time . . .

When I went back to the desk, I saw smiles on people's faces. They tapped Rastin amiably on his shoulder and seemed to be praising him. That was when I understood. He had been showing them that he had me under control. That he could communicate with me . . . He was in fact proving that he was the only person in that reservoir that could communicate with me. I laughed. I leaned toward the microphone and asked, "Is there anything else you want me to do?"

"No," he said. "Talk to me."

"Talk? What shall I say?"

"Talk."

"All right . . . where'd you learn Turkish?"

"Kabul University. I was come Istanbul University. For *master degree*. Understand?"

"So why didn't you?"

"Fate!"

"You speak it pretty well anyway!"

"Thank." He went over to the old man's son, pulled him to his feet, and said, "Watch."

"I'm watching, Rastin."

Then he pulled another man from the same group to his feet and talked to both of them. At first the men shook their heads and started to sit back down. But then almost everyone in the reservoir began shouting at the men at once. At that, darting glances at one another and then the cameras, both men began taking off their shirts.

Right then Rastin cried, "Gaza, for you!"

And now the two men, naked from the waist up, began wrestling . . . Yes, it was clear! By making me talk, Rastin had told the men that I had given the weird order of wanting to see them wrestle, an absurdity they hadn't much hesitated to engage in simply because they would have done anything to get out of the reservoir. Not counting the social pressure a minute ago, of course! Fine, but why was Rastin doing this? Actually, I think I already knew the answer to that. His answer to the question of whether these people were worth it was: they aren't! But he had already agreed to give up the kidney that would carry the thirty-three people, including himself and a child, to their dreams. Now was the time for revenge! Or more precisely, the time to fill the imminent space of his relinquished kidney . . .

The two men wrestled as if they would tear each other apart while Rastin looked on, his face devoid of expression. It was like a dog fight. Two dogs biting at each other in a pit of the earth and coming up with nothing more than grease and sweat . . . The others watched the wrestlers and the cameras in equal shares and cheered and clapped as if they were slapping themselves.

**Do you realize what a revolting thing this is to do?**
Huh?
**Look at these people! Look at the state they're in!**
Don't you think it's funny?
**Funny? Don't you see how depraved it is?**
But I didn't do anything! It's all that Rastin's doing.
**You told the man he'd have to give up a kidney.**
Yeah, but I never told him to start a wresting match. Plus it's too late now. I can't do anything until Rastin tells them the truth. These people would kill me.
**Then tell him to tell them! Is this what you call creating a country?**
I think it may be exactly that, you know? Because the whole idea is never to get your hands dirty . . .
**Great job! Exploiting people's conditions to put them in this situation is a huge achievement, kudos!**
Cuma!
**What?**
Remember when I didn't turn on that air conditioner? I hadn't actually forgotten to. I didn't feel like it. I couldn't be bothered to get out of the house and walk all the way to the shed. Just to spite my father, actually! "There's one left in the

back," he had said. "Get up early tomorrow so you can turn on the air conditioner!" Of course I got up. In the morning, early . . . but I didn't get out of bed. I just lay there and stared at the ceiling. At that snow-white ceiling. Believe me, Cuma, there's nothing as revolting as that ceiling! Not what those people are doing to one another, not what I've been doing to them. Nothing is more disgusting than that ceiling.

**There's one more thing that's not disgusting, though, Gaza!**
What would that be?
**That Rastin agreed to give up his kidney!**
So what? He just thought himself to be a good person for a minute, that's all. I thought the same, once . . . no big deal.

In their third day in the reservoir, Rastin lost all stability and increased the intensity of the commands that were supposedly coming from me. He picked at random two people and, seating them opposite each other in front of one of the cameras, told them to start slapping each other. After watching for a bit, he made a third person join them. A few minutes later he added twelve more people. Eventually a fifteen-person ring was formed, and in a row they all slapped one another, from left to right . . .

Naturally some of them objected to taking part in something so ridiculous, and Rastin didn't even have to chide them. Each time the others instantly replaced the *rebels* with someone willing to perform the dictated task. In a sense, those expelled from the ring were also expelled from the public. No one talked to them or shared their rations with them as they had failed to perform their social duty. And in a rage they would sulk in a corner, but after a while, seeing the reddened cheeks that should have been theirs, could no longer resist and began begging to take their rightful places. This time the ones receiving slaps in their place would make a case of martyrdom and resisted against giving up their spot.

"Rastin!"

He was in the middle of the ring, watching the slaps delivered from cheek to cheek, when he heard his name and looked up.

"What?"

"How long are you going to keep this up?"

"When are we go?"

"I don't know. I haven't received word yet . . ."

I wasn't going to ask, but I did:

"Rastin, do you have to punish these people to get back at them for your sacrifice?"

He answered without a beat. As if he'd been waiting for me to ask.

"No. I give kidney. For me. For them. To go. No problem. I do this for them. Because I leave home. Because of them. Understanding? I leave Afghanistan. Because of Afghanis. Afghanis, this people. Home, hell. Me, Kabul, always struggle for these. War! For this people! But for nothing! How you say, population? *People?* Afghanistan, public, population?"

"The people?"

"Yes, always I struggle for people. But when I go prison, no people! Many friends die. Prison. You ask, why not Istanbul University. Because I go prison! You understand? It's all for people! For *this* people! But when you need, no people! Don't be sad, this small punishment is for them. My friends die. Understanding?"

I think I did. But there was still something I didn't understand.

"But these people aren't the same as the ones who killed your friends and put you in prison, are they?"

"Is worse!" said Rastin. "This people say nothing!"

Right then a participant in the ring hesitated, and noticing this, Rastin went over to lean in and yell into his ear. The hand in the air then landed on the cheek it was meant for, and the slap ring commenced. It was then that I recognized the beehive I'd stuck my nose into for what it was. I watched a university student, who had been ready to give up everything he had for his people, penalize people with the crime of leaving him so helpless he had to flee his homeland. I watched people punished with the crime of going about their daily lives and neglecting to see or hear what was going on while Rastin and his friends went to prison and gave their lives.

Then I left Rastin to his quite futile revenge and rose from my desk. He would never have retribution because no one had actually asked him to go to prison or die for them. That was the point Rastin was missing. Heroes came up with their own missions; the public didn't do it for them. Heroes didn't get to demand explanations of the public. Heroes were of the brave and stupid variety. The public was cowardly and sneaky. There was no way for them to see eye to eye. But since Rastin presumed to pass judgment on the public, he couldn't be that stupid. He was a true leader. As much a leader, and as much of the people, as was adequate. That made him brave *and* sneaky—the most dangerous of all types.

On the evening of the third day, Rastin arranged for the other thirty-two to stand in the farthest corner of the reservoir, bade me to open the lid, and replaced the used buckets with empty ones. He had led his public to believe that I was armed. I was supposed to have a gun in my hand. But that hadn't stopped him from taking the sandwiches I had prepared and giving them to the reservoir dwellers. They had just run out of food and, in shows of gratefulness, kissed the timely sandwiches.

At the very last, they received word from Rastin: he had convinced the crazy boy upstairs to get in touch with his father's friends! That meant that they'd be setting out soon. With this news Rastin became irrefutable god of the reservoir. The old man, his son, and the others had forgotten all the disputes of the past and become Rastin's most eager supporters. Everyone worshiped him. At some point, while the others slept, I even saw one of the young women kneel in front of Rastin in the partition I had made for the toilet, before opening his zipper and her mouth. I was watching the woman while Rastin watched the camera. He was grinning . . .

A day later we found out that another woman in the group was four months pregnant. She announced that if it was a boy, she'd name it Rastin. So, if Rastin was god, what did that make me? Was there a theological term for god of gods?

In light of all these transformations, Rastin was also changing. He seemed to have let go of the fury he had the first few days. His communication with his public had become more mechanical, and he had reduced the frequency of tormenting people on my behalf. There was one morning, though, that for some reason he had one of them whipped with a belt. Maybe it was meant as a reminder of his authority. There really was a small country in the reservoir now. A living, breathing, and working country. Rastin gave his people a variety of assignments. For starters he made them clean the reservoir. At least three times a day. Then there were exercises. Every morning and evening. He let the one who had broken the biggest sweat shower with a bucket of water that he got from me. He read parts out loud from the only book in his possession and started debates on the topics he pinpointed. A fight, even if small, ensued after every debate, and Rastin watched smilingly from a corner. As the reservoir people chewed one another out over presumably pointless topics, Rastin took yet another woman to the toilet and told her what to do with her mouth.

What he was really doing was shifting the source of the violence. The violence no longer came directly from the crazy boy, but from the people, and was returned to the people. So Rastin was always able to find some way to set them off against one another. Under so-called orders from me, he would declare, "Either the lights stay on, or the fans!" and withdraw, leaving the choice to them. Consequently those who wanted to read the Koran all night and those about to lose it from the heat would lay into one another. But he never discriminated between the Tajiks and Pashtuns. Because he must have known that a fight that arose between those two could only end with a murder or two, if not worse. So he would keep clear of ethnic issues and, by focusing on common problems, made sure that each discussion shuffled the persons comprising the opposing groups.

For example, he would adapt the enforcement about the lights and the heat to food and water, claiming that one would have to decrease if the other increased and of course, once again, the choice was up to the people. This way the people got the impression that they were consulted about everything and didn't question Rastin in the slightest. They were divided into those that wanted more water and those that wanted more food, and occupied themselves only with the other.

Rastin was actually merely imposing the standard method that circumvented questioning of the administration. Millions of people were being ruled over out in real life with a similar method. They too were asked questions. They were asked to vote and handed questionnaires or forms to fill out. "Where would you like to be right now?" they were asked. Or, "Who were you in a past life?" Or, "Who is the most beautiful woman of the city?" Or, "Diet or regular?" or, "How would you like your steak?" Of course, those millions of people were as oblivious as the reservoir dwellers. *They* were the steak! They were being asked how well done they preferred *themselves*.

But since they couldn't see this for the reality, they leaned back with the self-satisfaction of having the capacity to choose and said, "Well done!"

Then again some said, "Make it rare!" And it was done as they said. Bloody . . .

In addition to this method, Rastin had also begun taking another approach that could be considered a breakthrough in political science. Once his biggest enemy, the old man's son was now his chief assistant. Rastin whispered into his ear the orders supposedly received from me, and he then told his own assistant. The orders moved from ear to ear, and Rastin didn't have to directly engage with anyone. In this way the hierarchy in the reservoir was able to take on not a pyramidal, but more like a *spiraling* form.

First of all, in the center was Rastin. Directly to his right, the chief assistant. Next to him was the deputy assistant, then *his* assistant, and so on the chain went. Starting at Rastin and following a circular, widening curve, the orders moved along from ear to ear. At the end of the outermost ring of the spiral would be the reservoir's only child or a middle-aged man that was almost as weak as the child, alternately . . . women, naturally, weren't included in the spiral, because they weren't included in anything. Even the champion screamer that was the child's mother was a huge nothing. In the case that an issue concerned them, the order departed from the outermost ring of the spiral and was delivered to the women clustered some distance away.

In truth, it was evident that the reservoir people's political venture had started with a democratic election but turned into a dictatorship in days. But this went even beyond the pyramidal ruling scheme of a regular dictatorship. Each individual was bound to the one person that was more powerful. The one on top, that is to say center, was the leader. Since their seating and dwelling situation constituted a spiral shape, they had to face one another, but could communicate with only the ones on either side of them and one each on the lower or upper rung of power. Whereas a pyramidal hierarchy would have power classes formed of people leveled equally. Classes that could be of a thousand or of three. But in a spiral hierarchy every individual was a class unto himself. Maybe this structure needed to be named something else. Like ultradictatorship or something. Because every individual was a dictator to the person below them. With the exception of the boy or that weak man, everyone was a dictator on varying levels. Yet they were all part of the same spiral, that is to say the same line. Hence it seemed that there was no hierarchy at all between them.

Perhaps that was why Rastin sustained this spiral scheme of seating. This way the people remained unaware that they were part of an ultradictatorship. After all, they were almost face-to-face with their leader, certainly on the same level. It was like their leader was *one of the people*! Plus when you looked from a distance, they appeared to be a closely connected group, gathered together, with no trace of a hierarchy to be seen. If Rastin had asked me for a stool, for instance, that would have been different. Rastin could have sat on the stool while everyone else sat on the ground and the thirty-centimeter discrepancy in height would have exposed the dictatorship to the naked eye. Instead Rastin insisted on the spiral dictatorship that was entirely his invention and inserted this innovative ruling scheme into political science as a class that could conceivably be taken at least four hours a week, although it was now unknown.

Of course, as with any structure, this too had its drawbacks. For instance, the context of the demands issuing from the outer rungs of the spiral deteriorated or altered by the time they reached the center. Or an order issuing from the center would have been modified completely by time it made it to the end of the spiral. But ultimately we were talking ultradictatorship. Due to the Chinese whispers mode of communication, it was completely natural and acceptable for such divergences to occur in the leader's orders or the public's demands. Compared to the level of communication my father and I had, the transmission of information in the shed was practically telepathy! In the meantime Ahad had returned and right away asked:

"They give you any trouble?"

"No," I had said. What else could I say? He wouldn't have understood anyhow. Or, I wouldn't have been able to make him understand, anyhow . . .

The morning of the twelve-day anniversary of our reservoirland, I took my place in front of the monitor to see the women gathered in a corner facing the wall, eyes closed. It didn't take me long to figure out what was going on. For at the other end of the reservoir, the weakling that usually assumed the tail end of the spiral was totally nude and under barrage of tens of fists and feet. All of this was happening so fast I couldn't think of anything to do. I looked at Rastin. He was just watching. As always.

Several times I cried, "Stop it!" but he wouldn't listen.

It was like he couldn't hear me. I, on the other hand, didn't want to lose any goods. What I was watching wasn't one of the shows involving people whipping or slapping each other or doing push-ups until they were out of breath. They had the man shoved up against the corner where the wall met the ground and were kicking him like they meant to bury him in that very spot. I had to find a way to stop it immediately. The first thing I could think of was to kill the power in the reservoir.

And only then did Rastin pull himself together and shout, "Okay, Gaza! It is finished!"

When I turned the power back on, I saw the weakling on the ground in his own blood, trying to breathe, and yelled at Rastin, "Why'd you do that?" But he was unruffled.

"Not me!" he said and gestured to the people around him. "They did it!"

"They wouldn't do anything unless you told them to!"

He shook his head several times first, slowly, then, "They would," he said. "They would . . ."

Then he ordered the owners of the fists and kicks that were flying around a moment ago to help the man, who shuddered with every breath, to stand and to clean the blood off him. They did so, listlessly as though they were gathering up pieces of a broken machine.

"Tell me!" I shouted at Rastin. "What happened?"

"Nothing," he demurred at first, but then told me what that nothing was . . .

It had all begun with the weakling claiming that he could sneak up and disarm me next time I opened the lid of the reservoir. "I'll take care of the kid, take the gun from him, and this whole ordeal can finally end!" he had said.

But the others countered that such action was highly risky, that everything was under Rastin's control and that surely someone would come fetch them soon and send them on their way. At that the weakling accused them of cowardice. Accusing the public of cowardice, the ultimate taboo in ultradictatorship, had earned him the punishment he had deserved!

There wasn't much I could say to that. I just stared. I watched the people. I watched the man they dressed and dropped in a corner like a sack, the women who weren't the least bit surprised by what they saw when they opened their eyes and turned around, Rastin who sat in the center of the reservoir, and the spiral that formed around him. Then I looked back at the weakling. I think he also looked at me. Or I was imagining things. I printed out the article I was writing about reservoirland and shut down the computer. The screen went dark and buried the ultradictatorship below ground . . .

I spent the next two days penning corrections onto the article. Perhaps only to keep myself from going to the shed. But on the third day when I could no longer help myself, and turned on the monitor, the first thing I saw was the motionless body of the weakling. They had covered his face with his jacket and laid him down in front of a camera so I could see him. I had turned on the microphone and expelled the first syllable of, "Is he asleep?" when Rastin's broken-spectacled face covered one-sixth of the monitor and spoke:

"Dead!"

For a second I wanted to ask, "Are you sure?" Another second later I changed my mind. It occurred to me to say, "Fuck!" but I didn't say that either. I wanted to talk about coming forty-third place in all of Turkey or my mother wanting to bury me as soon as I was born, but that didn't happen, either. At some point I even wanted to ask, "Where's Felat?" That definitely didn't happen.

Left at a loss for words by all these things that didn't happen, I got up and went over to the reservoir lid. I went down on my knees and opened the lock with the key in my pocket. Instead of the world's most beautiful girl, a thin man came out of the reservoir. And his exit was exactly as he'd described to the others! I brought out his body from underneath the lid that I opened two hand spans' width and went to call my father. He was drinking beer.

"What?" he said.

Not knowing the real words for anything that happened aboveground, I said, "Something's happened. Come!"

He stood and began walking to the shed. He was a step ahead of me. I was on his left, looking at his swinging left hand. Once upon a time, I used to play a game on the pavement of the town's only main street. I'd come up about a step's length away to women walking ahead of me and try to catch their swinging hands with my dick. It wasn't hard at all. In fact, it would be such a casual collision that some women would apologize. And I, flustered by the momentary contact, would say, "That's all right!" and keep walking. What I wanted to bump into my father's hand as we passed through the garden was my right hand. Perhaps our hands would collide and hold on. We might even walk into the shed hand in hand. No matter who I was, what I was, he wouldn't let go of my hand, he would hang on. But none of that happened.

Upon his first step into the shed, he saw that the dark purple lips that left no space for anything else on the man's face and cursed. First at the body that lay at his feet, then at me! After all it had been my task to watch the goods. To boot, it had been my idea to place cameras in every corner of the reservoir! That left me as the sole culprit. I had put us out for nothing! Suddenly I thought of Dordor:

"Whatever I owe, I'll pay!" I said. That shut Ahad up. He inhaled and exhaled a few times and scratched his head. Possibly he was calculating for how long he would have to suspend my pay. He had made it to the week's worth of growth on his neck when he abruptly stopped. He must be done with the calculation. We were into the month of March. That was why his voice was cold. Not because he was a monster.

"Go, bury it!" he said, and pointed in the direction of the arbor.

It took me two hours to bury the weakling. One hour to dig the hole, another to cover it. My father had buried Cuma the same way years ago. I had even asked, "What if someone comes?" and he had replied, "We're burying a hole here, not a corpse, don't worry!"

Turns out that really was the case. Digging a hole and filling it was a matter of two hours. Burying a hole. If it had been a matter of burying a corpse, if I had stopped to consider for a single moment that what I was burying was a person, it probably would have taken ages. Especially when the person initiated into the earth was one that had died by my hand . . .

Perhaps that was how my father had stayed calm when he had buried Cuma. Because he hadn't killed him personally.

Although he was directly responsible for the death, but not the hand that killed him . . . like me. I wasn't the one that killed the weakling. No matter that I was utterly responsible for his death, I was neither one of the ones who beat him nor one of the ones that watched the beating in silence. I was the same thing that had sent Rastin to prison instead of master's studies at Istanbul University: fate! I was fate! I was the sum of the living conditions of those people. And that sum came out to zero. A colossal zero, large enough to swallow us all! A zero as large as the rings of Saturn!

That was why I wouldn't be the one to hear that weak man's voice in my ear for the rest of my life. It was Rastin! He now had a Cuma of his own. A scrawny man that would come to life for all the times he died and make all the deserted islands of the world hell for Rastin. For the ones that beat him were deaf! Their eardrums and their consciences were long perforated. The weakling's voice would bounce off all those deaf ears and sooner or later find a way into Rastin's mind. I knew all this because I remembered killing Cuma. I hadn't gotten out of bed just because I was mad at father, and so I hadn't turned on the air conditioner. Rastin wasn't any different. He hadn't intervened in the brutal beating of the weakling because he hated his people. So he could scoop up all his people in one move and toss them into a bottomless pit of guilt.

But Rastin had miscalculated. Because that reservoir had had no room for any guilt except his. If there had been, they wouldn't have kept their peace back when Rastin and his friends were going to prison and dying for them. Even if they were unable to make anything resembling a sound, they could have at least opened their mouths and puked on the streets that a handcuffed Rastin was being dragged over! At the very least they could have done that. But I couldn't recall any news of collective puking in Afghanistan. Therefore the dead voice of the weakling would follow only Rastin. Because it had nowhere else to go. In the end, ghosts knew it all. They knew who was a wall of flesh and who was human. Some they passed through, and into some ears, they whispered everything they knew.

**The Power of Power [1st draft]**

Crisis as a Source of Power [Crisis: A Political Socket?? Fuck that! Not scientific at all!]

**INTRODUCTION**
There are two types of information in the world: information you seek to find and information that finds you. If information seeks to find one, it has without doubt been produced for marketing something. Either a political lie is being hustled [not scientific! Find another word!] as truth or a new cell phone needs selling. Furthermore, information that finds one is soiled from all the slithering it has done and stinks of shit [take that out not scientific!]. Consequently, the only information of value is the information that is sought to be found. This is what should be trusted.

The information gathered from the experiment in the reservoir may, by exactly this reasoning, be accepted for fact. Because the Researcher has invested extraordinary [don't flatter yourself! Flatter yourself with scientific terms!] effort in gathering said information. Fluctuating information [you said there were two kinds of information? Say this is a subtype!] is information of which the truth and validity constantly varies with time. For example, information pertaining to humanity is fluctuating information. [A person is fluctuating information for another!] Especially information pertaining to close relations. Meaning friends, relatives, etc. . . . [redundant, cut this bit!] Therefore, the Researcher has taken the route of considering fluctuating bits of information on a different level and comparing them with information from other sources to test their validity. The other sources are the tools of mass communication.

Among the sources for this research, besides the tools of mass communication, is the newspaper called *From Kandalı to the World*. In addition are hundreds [don't be lazy, list them all!] of websites and TV channels. Lastly, the Researcher, believing that a scientific study must be imbursed by personal observations, has done his part and has had no reservations about reflecting his thoughts on the paper.

[Pile of shit! Rewrite the whole foreword!]

**ARTICLE**
Bulleted for scientificness. [Take this out!]

1. A leader who in ordinary times is in communication with his public, retreats into himself in times of crisis and begins withholding information from the people he leads for the sake of avoiding scrutiny later. Another reason for this behavior is to prevent panic and uphold social order, and by extension his authority.
2. Due to his withdrawal and the strain of crisis, the leader who in ordinary times believes himself to be part of a

corporate effort, begins regarding leadership as a personal responsibility. As a result, he begins to consider the time and effort he has extended for his people as a sacrifice. As the crisis is prolonged, the sacrificial feeling brewing inside the leader begins turning into an inflamed indignation against the people. Due to this, the smallest disharmony he experiences with the people he would once "give up a kidney for" causes the inflammation to leap into his realm of thought. This in turn results in the exacting of spontaneous revenges on his "thankless" public.

3.  However, since crisis is still in effect, the public overlooks the leader's rising authoritarianism and reactions verging on the vengeful, due to its viewing him as its sole savior.

4.  Hence the crisis takes the form of a psychotherapy session where the public suffers the consequences of the leader's whining, yelling, and defamations.

5.  During the crisis, the dealings with his people are based in self-satisfaction and sexuality. The people's regard of the leader, on the other hand, is centered on the father figure, bearing a familial aspect. Hence in times of crisis, the leader-public relationship is incestuous. By nature, it is a scandal.

6.  In legitimizing the over-authoritarianism of the leader, the crisis becomes an alternative source of power. It's imperative that the leader stabilizes his country on the level of "sustainable crisis" so he can profit from this source to the maximum. For this, it's essential to devise small inner conflicts. The fine line between civil war and inner conflict is the boundary of the crisis's sustainability. The leader that engenders hundreds of inner conflicts without ever setting off a civil war holds extraordinary

power as long as he is able to keep his country walking that fine line.

7. A leader's power is measurable by the number of airports, universities, stadiums, squares, boulevards, dams, bridges, and newborns that are named after him while he is still alive.

8. The leader's fear of death, which is the meaning of his life, is balanced out by his assurance that his legacy will outlive him, and the psychotherapy session ends on a positive note.

**Appendix 1:**

As can be derived from the aforementioned, the principal task of the people is to treat every leader that reigns over it and enable him to die a peaceful death. This is called the People's Hospital. In return the leader erects Public Hospitals in service of the people. The branding of those that don't fulfill the task of treating the leader as traitors may be presented as a new topic for inner conflict put to use in prolonging crisis.

**Appendix 2:**

A country's entire defense mechanism is formed around the objective that in the case of mass deaths, its only remaining citizen in the world be the leader. According to this, the human race is to be perpetuated by the mating of said world leaders. [??? No observation no experimentation not scientific! Don't be presumptuous!] Therefore leaders do not say, "It's either me or him!" They say, "Either you all or me!"

**Sources:**

*From Kandalı to the World*

Hundreds of websites [list them! don't forget the municipality webpage]

Tens of TV channels
The reservoir
Thirty-three Afghanistan citizens
Fifteen-year-old Gaza [you don't get to be both researcher and source!]

[Spiral scheme of leadership]
[The weakling or the child]

[COMMAND →
DEMAND ← ]

I sat in the arbor, lost in thought. I stared at the spot where I had buried the weakling and asked myself if he might have had a family. Inasmuch I knew the answer! Because he had come from such a place that he must have had at least nine siblings, six children, three grandchildren, and forty-six nephews and nieces. So it didn't do much good to assume that his parents were no longer alive. He had grown up in a land where people were born in heaps and died by the dozen. And all that he had wished for was to go to a land where people were born alone and died alone. But his journey had ended in Kandalı. And in Kandalı, people were buried as soon as they were born. At least people like me were . . . then some were stillborn. Such as the weakling . . . out of the womb of the reservoir he had been delivered stillborn, to be buried and eradicated the same second.

"Gaza!"

I turned my head to see my father step into the arbor.

"Did you talk to them, Dad?"

"We're good, it's all right. We pay up and the deal is done."

What was I supposed to say? I should thank him obviously! Obviously!

"Thanks, Dad."

"That's all right and all but . . . that makes two, son! What's your beef with the Afghanis?" he said, laughing.

I hadn't misheard. That was exactly what he had said: with Cuma, that makes two! He didn't know what he was talking about. Son of a bitch! All I had to do was lean over and grab the shovel under my feet. Then in a single move, bash in his face! There was nothing and no one to stop me! A humming began in my ears as I reached for the shovel.

**Don't, Gaza! Leave it . . . don't.**
Cuma?
**Don't!**

I could have killed my father then, in that garden, in that arbor, with the shovel still bearing traces of dead earth. But I didn't. Instead I just stared at him. The way I had looked at the images transmitted all the way from the cameras in the reservoir to my monitor. Without feeling anything. Because Ahad was there too. With all that was under the earth, there. Among all the corpse-eating insects. Among all the Afghanis who had lynched the weakling. With Rastin, even! With all those that had exhibited their women to me, all of them! I stared him in the face. So he might understand how deep down he was in the earth! But there was no possibility of that, of course. He just kept grinning. For whatever reason his fury had left him. Maybe he'd received some good news from Aruz. But what good news could Aruz possibly have? Could the Grim Reaper come bearing glad tidings?

"We're going to Derç tomorrow, in the morning. To pick up goods. Two hundred heads! Well, aren't you in luck! No need to cut your pay now. Man, if this isn't turning out to be one bountiful winter!"

So it was! Two hundred heads had cleared up the whole mess. Neither the weakling nor his corpse in the garden were the wiser. Two hundred heads of sawdust would suffice to cover ourselves in. We should be glad, shouldn't we?

"Stop sulking already! What's done is done! Fuck it!" He was about to leave but stopped. "Tell you what! This bunch is leaving tonight."

To elaborate on *this bunch,* he had gestured at the spot I had buried the weakling in and continued.

"We're heading out. Get them all in the trailer by eleven p.m. We'll set off around midnight."

"Okay, Dad," I said. Then I turned my head away. So I wouldn't have to look at the spot he was pointing at any longer . . .

So apparently the time had come for Rastin's bunch to head out . . . Fine, but how? Surely they had seen my father's face on the way off the eighteen-wheeler into the truck or from the back of the truck to the reservoir. They would see it again tonight when they got off the truck and onboard the boats and were sure to remember. There was nothing I could do about that. More importantly, though, what would they do when they saw me? Once I opened the lid and they filed past me one by one and climbed into the cab . . . could they possibly walk past the crazy boy that had made their lives hell for the past few days as if nothing had happened? What about Rastin? Would he want to depart on a journey that ended with him giving up his kidney? Maybe this was just the time to run away from home! The time to leave everything as it was and get the fuck out! But predictably I didn't . . . Instead I went to the shed and turned on the monitor and the microphone. For a while I just watched reservoirland. I watched the reservoir people sit and debate among themselves as usual while their utterly indifferent leader leafed through his book.

"Rastin! You leave tonight!"

Although he had been waiting for more than two weeks for this news, it didn't seem to affect him at all. All he did was to close his book and stare into the camera across from where he was sitting.

"Rastin, you're leaving! I'm going to open the lid at ten p.m. Then you'll get on the truck and set off around midnight."

By way of reflex, Rastin turned his head to look at the clock on the wall.

"Don't look at that, it's broken."

"I knows!"

"Excuse me?"

"Clock is too slow! Broken!"

So he had that figured out . . . Whatever, it didn't matter.

"You are lie!"

"What are you talking about, Rastin?"

"You real crazy!"

"Knock it off, Rastin, I said you're leaving. What are we going to do about it? They'll see my father. They'll see that he's not dead!"

"You were say, clock is right. But is wrong. You are lie!"

What was it with him and the clock? Yes, I might have confiscated the watches of all the reservoir dwellers and left them alone with that clock, but who cared?

"All right, fine, I lied! I admit it! The clock is broken! Are you happy? Now tell me what we're going to do!"

"Come night. Open lid."

"What are you going to tell *them*?"

"Kidney!"

"What?"

"I say I not give kidney. Is all. Because you are liar."

"What's that got to do with it?"

"I thinks . . . men want kidney, want organs. Man die here, no one comes. You not send news! So no one want kidney. No one want two thousand dollar. You are liar! Why? Why, Gaza? Do not tell, forget it . . . because I am also liar, Gaza. I, worse than you. Because I want that man should die. I want that these people kill him. You take his kidney. I keep kidney . . . but no one comes . . . understanding? But let this be secret. You, me, secret between! Do not tell to anyone. I do not tell you either."

And I burst into tears. All at once! The reservoir dwellers exchanged looks and then looked around at the cameras as if they might see me. My sobs must have been bouncing off the walls. A reservoir filled with my weeping! It had all started like an attack. Like a heart attack! But as I cried, it wore off. I even began to observe myself from a distance. Gaza observing weeping Gaza! So maybe I could have calmed down if I wanted to. But if I stopped crying, I would have had to speak, and now that knowledge made me unable to stop. I had to answer to Rastin, but I had no idea where to find the answer. I was completely empty inside. I didn't have the answers to anything. Anything! If had I tried, I might have been able to rattle off technical excuses such as not knowing about the weakling's death until it was too late to take his kidney. And in the medical sense, I would have been justified. But I was tired of justifying myself through lies! I didn't have a single lie left to tell. I didn't have the strength to explain, either. But it looked like Rastin was stronger than me. Strong enough to admit that he had let the weakling die and so weak that he could let another die to save his own kidney . . . There was nothing left to say. Both Rastin and I were done for! The reservoir had been the death of us.

"Okay," said Rastin. "Okay . . . come evening. Open lid. Then go. We go truck. You come. Father not important. No one look . . ."

I could only push out two syllables from between my lips.

"Okay . . ."

I was just leaving when I heard Rastin again.

"Tell me something, Gaza!"

"What?"

He shot at me the three questions that had been brewing in his mouth. Even despite all the concrete separating us, he tried.

"Men do not want money, right? I keep kidney? I assume correct?"

I did open my mouth, but . . . I swear, it wasn't me who spoke:

"No, Rastin. When you go to Greece, they'll take your kidney! Sorry!"

"Liar!" he yelled. "Why then you are cry?"

This time it was me who spoke. It wasn't exactly talking, but it was my voice.

*"Fear not, the crimson banner that proudly ripples in the dawn, shall not fade . . ."*

And I was accompanied by another: the child in the reservoir! He clapped, laughed, and oscillated between mumbling and hollering. Then another joined our choir: a leader by the name of Rastin. Though only one word came out of his mouth over and over:

"Liar!"

Shouting hard enough to bust his vocal cords out of his nostrils, he proved that a single word can be strung into very long sentences indeed:

"Liar! Liar! Liar!"

In his fury he even swung a bucket he happened to get his hands on and broke one of the cameras. He was so far gone it hadn't occurred to him that the bucket might be full. As it was, the only child in the reservoir had just gotten off it, but it was too late. A fountain of shit had hit the fan and splattered the walls and the people before giving anyone a chance to even scream. Stained hands came off faces, and still Rastin couldn't figure out what he had just showered upon them. Breathlessly he turned this way and that, as if nailed into place, and was still unable to face the bucketful of facts. Even though it was all there in front of him. In the brown dots on his spectacles! He would have found what he was looking for if only he had taken a few deep breaths to steady himself, because it was everywhere he looked: shit.

Neither the child nor I paid any heed. And to the tune of the Independence March, we abolished the reservoirland I had erected to the tune of the Independence March.

The headlights of the truck lit up the narrow, tree-lined road as we moved through the night. The light we emanated swept the asphalt fanning out in front of us. The dark tree trunks melted into one another while others, whitewashed below the waist, danced in and out of sight like ghosts. Now and then those ghosts reached out as if to grab and stop us. I could hear it. The sounds of the branches swept over the truck in waves and abated. But none of those branches were strong enough to catch us and deter us from our path. Even the thickest of them were left broken like matchsticks in our wake, and we slipped through their leafless hands. Besides us, there was no life in the forest that had given its last breath back in March. Sure it would be resurrected by April, but until that day, the forest was just a big corpse. And every corpse had its worms. That would be the road we were traveling on. We rode on its back as it slithered through. We were inside a monster that spewed fire from its two eyes and scorched everything it beheld on its way. It roared so loudly every time we shifted gears that we couldn't even hear the radio. So my father lit a cigarette and turned it off. Then he turned to me and asked:

"Do you smoke?"

Right then a thousand voices inside me shouted "Yes!" in unison, but I didn't listen to any of them.

"*Smoke*, Dad? No."

Just that morning, I had buried a body in our garden right in front of my father. Yet it was out of the question to smoke a cigarette in front of him. There wasn't any logic to be found here. I'd buried logic along with that body. Not that it wasn't already dead for years . . .

"Take one, go on!" he said, holding out the pack. I looked up at him. He was smiling. Was it a trick? Would he pull over as soon as I made for the pack and break my reaching fingers? Seeing my hesitation he spoke.

"I know you smoke. Go on, take one."

He knew everything! He always knew! That was his job: knowing me. Watching me! Constantly stalking me! AHAD was the name of a secret service with the one occupation of gathering information about me. A secret organization! Absolutely! I would find out years later, in equal parts amusement and brooding, that my paranoid theory wasn't all that far-fetched. In a history book I'd read, it was said that the Arab officers of the Ottoman army who were stationed in what is Iraq and Syria today united and created a secret organization to give name to their dreams of independence. The name of this intelligence organization—the goal of which was to spill the military secrets of the Ottoman army, the uniforms its members wore, etc., to the British in order to start the Arabic revolution—was *El-Ahad*! So I mustn't have been that insane, on that night, to think that all my father ever did was spy on me. Not *that* insane.

So I pulled a cigarette from the pack and lit it. My hand shook a bit at first, but then I got it together. As I put the lighter in the pack the way my father did and was about to hand it back, he said, "Keep it."

Goes without saying that I didn't reply, "I already have a pack on me." I took it and put it in my pocket. I waited for my father every time before raising the cigarette to my lips. We drew in the smoke and let it out in unison. Rolled down the windows in unison and tossed the butts out in unison. Then I watched the ghosts fly past on the road. Thinking about the ghosts in the back . . .

Things hadn't turned out like I'd feared. In the evening at exactly ten, I'd gone to the warehouse and opened first the doors of the vault and then the reservoir. I'd left the six wristwatches by the lid of the reservoir and, like Rastin had said to, left the warehouse and hidden behind the door I'd left ajar. In this way, without being glimpsed by any of them, I'd been able to watch them leave the reservoir one by one, and the owners unite once again with their watches, before they climbed into the back of the truck in pairs. I'd even counted them so there wouldn't be some kind of screw-up! The thirty-one illegal immigrants got into the vault and then Rastin, who was last, paused and glanced around. I was sure that it was me those eyes sought, but I was in no mood for confrontation.

In any case I'd had to hear Rastin. Because he yelled, "Liar!" Although this time the word sounded hesitant leaving his lips. As much as he didn't believe he'd have to give up his kidney, he just couldn't be sure. Because he, just like me, knew that all you never wanted to believe was real.

For example, he hadn't wanted to believe that the people for whom he'd once fought would abandon him, but that was what happened. I hadn't wanted to believe that my mother would bury me alive, but that had happened too. We were aware how much bigger the possibility of hell was compared to the possibility of heaven. So Rastin didn't wait long before looking down and spitting into the sawdust beneath his feet, adjusting his glasses, and hopping into the vault, pulling its doors shut behind him.

But there was something he didn't know. For perhaps the first time in his life, his worries wouldn't come to fruition and his kidney would stay in its place. And that was the only gift I'd be able to give Rastin. Rastin himself had given the others a similar gift. For days he'd convinced those people that they were imprisoned in that reservoir and then falsely proclaimed their emancipation. In the end, our circumstances were so shitty that the only thing we could do was point at hell and beg for purgatory. For ourselves and for those around us . . .

Now the only thing left to do was get to the shore where the boat would moor and take the thirty-two people out of the back and onboard that boat. I was thinking of stopping my father before he could get out of the truck and saying, "I'll take care of it." How I'd say it exactly was: "Now don't come out in the cold. I'll go take care of it!"

At first he'd say, "Absolutely not," and then, thinking that I felt guilty over losing the goods, give me a chance to atone for my mistake.

At least that's what I hoped. Actually I think I didn't care all that much. Even if one of them happened to see and recognize my father on their way from the vault to the boat, in the heat of the moment they wouldn't be able to do anything about it. I'd watched the changeovers onto the boat dozens of times. They'd get so excited it was like they thought the boat they were getting on was taking them to Mars. Perhaps in a way, the journey about to be taken was really tantamount to going to space for those people. Still, in my eyes, they seemed more like the monkeys sent into space than people. Yes, perhaps they would breach the atmosphere and make it into space, but they'd forever remain monkeys!

For whatever reason, ultimately, in those few moments that their blood pressure was a roller coaster, that is, one of the most important instants in their lives, I doubted any one of them would pounce on my father and cry, "I thought you were supposed to be dead!"

Later Rastin could very well find a way and tell them that he'd been duped by me. I'd had the opportunity to quite closely examine how well he lied to people. He was cool as a corpse when it came to that. In fact he was such a competent liar that he could have convinced anyone who remembered my father, in a few words, that they'd seen a ghost.

So none of this was a problem. There was something that resembled a problem, although small: we'd never before gone to the meeting place described to my father by the captain. It was in an area we'd never delivered goods to before. As far as I'd been able to tell, it was a small cove. A small cove where the forest ended and the trees tapered off until the reef plunged into the sea. At least that's what it looked like on my father's drawing. After every bend in the road, he peered at the piece of paper he held against the steering wheel and tried to make sure he was driving the truck on the right itinerary.

It was two in the morning and I was about to close my eyes so I didn't have to stare out into the darkness any longer when rain started falling. For the following few minutes, I watched the drops. Drops hitting the windshield like flies and shattering. And I lowered my eyelids. The roaring of the truck faded out first, then real life . . . All that was left was a dream, and my mother.

For the first time in my life I dreamed of my mother. Wearing a green dress with a print of purple flowers, she was on a beach I didn't recognize, and pregnant. Behind her was the enormous sea and small clouds. Her shoes in her right hand, she stood straight and stared at me. Her legs were together and her bare feet were buried in the sand to the ankles. She was like a tree with purple flowers that only grew in the sand. With her left hand she was trying to gather up her long black hair tousled by the wind and, I think, smiling. That's how I was seeing my mother in the dream. Because that's how she'd looked in that one photo at home. I looked into her eyes to see if I could tell whether or not she was happy. Only her eyes. But it didn't work at all. Whatever she'd been feeling in that second the photo was taken, none of it had overflowed physically. All she'd been doing was standing, being pregnant and looking into the lens. My father must have taken the photo. In an early hour of the morning, he'd stood with the sun behind him and, probably without intending to, gotten his own shadow in the frame as well. My father was a shadow reaching all the way to my mother. She appeared to rise out of the sand, from the point the shadow ended. I was in a dream. Maybe if I asked her, she'd tell me. She'd stir to life inside that photo and talk to me.

"Why, Mother? Why'd you want to kill me? Please tell me . . ."

I waited . . . but neither did her lips move, nor any sound come out between them. Then my eyes slid over to the shadow, and I thought of my father. I tried to understand why he would keep this photo. Why'd he have a photo of the woman who tried to kill his son in the drawer of his bedside table? I have to wake up, I said. I have to wake up right away and ask him that. And my eyes opened . . .

The rain had picked up, and we'd cleared the forest. To one side was an abyss, to the other were crags. We were ascending Kandağ. Slowly . . . I saw the telltale lights of a distant village and turned my head to ask.

"Why do you keep that photo of my mother?"

The windshield wipers bent and straightened like two doped-up marathon runners doing sit-ups, while my father didn't take his eyes off the road.

"Why, Dad?"

He turned to look at me for a second and then turned his face back to road, saying, "As a memory!"

"A memory? Memory of what? My mother was going to kill me! Then she was going to leave you! A woman like that, and you're keeping her photo as a memory?"

He didn't speak until we were over a bend so narrow that the rear wheels practically swung over into space. When the road again became a long rise that stretched out in front of us, I heard my father's voice.

"Where'd this come from, you twat? Why would you think about this now?"

I could have said, "My dream!" but I didn't. Instead, I started rattling off the things I was starting to see as the fog dissipated in my now alert mind.

"Why would a person keep a photo of someone? Because he still thinks about her, I'd say. Right? In fact, because he still loves her . . . and that's why you keep that photo. In fact you love my mother so much you never fell in love with anyone else. That's why you never married. Right?"

And Ahad laughed! He looked like a fool that laughed because he couldn't think of anything to say. Like he would laugh himself to death so he wouldn't have to speak! But how long could a person keep on grinning to himself? He couldn't hold it out very long, naturally.

"Don't be stupid!"

Yes . . . I had Ahad figured. I had everything figured . . . My mother may not have spoken to me in the dream, but really she'd told me everything I needed to know. With that stance and those eyes and her feet plunged into the sand. She'd told me the whole story by not telling me anything. When that photo was taken and when she was pregnant with me, my mother hadn't felt anything. That was why there wasn't a shred of emotion on her face. Or on her hands . . . In that photo, my mother was a tree. Or a grain of sand. She was the sun behind my father. She was an entire sea . . . My mother was nature, who felt nothing.

She couldn't have loved my father even if she wanted to. She couldn't have held me in her lap and called me her son even if she wanted to.

"Then tell me!" I said to my father. "Tell me! What'd you do to my mother that was so bad she wanted to run away? What could you have done? Imagine, she hated you so much she'd even have done me in!"

He was going to hit me, I knew. He was going to hold the steering wheel with his left hand and whack me across the face with the back of his right hand. I was expecting it. But he didn't. He didn't do anything. In fact, that's what he said.

"I didn't do anything! I didn't do anything to your mother."

"Then why? Why'd she want to get rid of us? Why'd she try to go give birth to me in that graveyard? She could've gotten a divorce! Right? She could've divorced you and then left me to you? Or I don't know, maybe taken me with her! But why'd she go and do a thing like that?"

The wipers fell behind the rain now. The more the rain picked up, the more my father slowed, though he still kept going. And Ahad cried:

"She did say that! She did! She said, let's get a divorce! I asked what she'd do with the baby. She said she'd get an abortion! Why, I asked! Because I want to leave, she said! I want to leave and see other places, she said! I want to see it all, I want to know it all, she said! Just like you used to say, huh? That's why you went and took that exam? Do you get it now?"

My father was really talking to me for perhaps the first time ever. Or I was hallucinating and Ahad was actually talking to himself. The words poured from his mouth so fast they'd drown us before the drilling rain could. But I pushed my luck. In case he could hear me, too.

"So what'd you do? You told her she wasn't going anywhere, didn't you! You said she had to stay! You forced her!"

172

And I thought of the reservoir. And I thought of the separate cell in that reservoir. And I thought of the iron ring I'd hammered into that cell. And I thought of how I'd thought of chaining people to that ring! And lastly, I thought that what I'd thought of, my father might very well have thought of as well!

"Isn't that what you did? You kept her by force! You chained her somewhere and she had to stay there, didn't she? Then one night she ran away! And you ran after her! You chained her, didn't you! You chained your wife like she was an animal! You tied my mother up like a dog! Didn't you?"

He turned to look at me and said nothing. Only accelerated. Staring at me as he did it, too! I think he was smiling . . . like my mother in the photo . . .

"Mind the road!" I yelled. "Mind the road!"

But he just stared at me.

Father and son, eye to eye, we fell into the void. A void as deep as an abyss . . . a void the size of Kandağ . . .

I could never be sure. Never! Was it an accident, or suicide?

## CANGIANTE

One of the four basic techniques of Renaissance painting. Signifies the transition to another color when grading into lighter or darker tones of a color is unattainable or unreasonable. Is a sudden change in color.

My face came to first. I felt small drops hitting my cheeks, eye-lids, temples, and forehead. Then my ears came to life. They too had awakened to the sound of rain and waited for my eyes to open. But my mouth opened before they did. To let out a scream in case there was one trapped inside. But all that came out from between my lips was hot silence. That heat most probably was blood. It must be warming the ground it fell on more than it was warming me, because I started shaking where I lay. And my eyes juddered open. They rolled in their sockets to find some-thing to see. The first thing they saw was darkness and to this they adjusted first. Picking the visible out of the invisible, they gave meaning to the darkness, and a stone surface materialized in front of my eyes. A boulder. It hovered above me like the low wall of a cave. I could reach out and touch it if I still had a hand. I tried. I saw my right arm. At its end, a hand that still had five fingers. It slowly rose and stopped. This way I knew that the wet ceiling was at an arm's length.

I hadn't moved my head yet, but it was time. I was left-handed. I first rested my left cheek on the earth and saw the night. Open air, trees, bushes, and raindrops that splashed off where they fell and onto my face . . . then I turned my head to the right and saw the same thing. This time I raised my left arm, extended it to the back, and my hand hit a stone wall at least as wet as the ceiling. I trailed my fingers over the wall, feeling its dents and protuberances. When my hand entered my field of vision once more, it was on the ceiling above me that was attached to the wall. I wasn't in a cave. I was underneath an overhang open on either side. Underneath a tarp of stone . . .

The palms of my hands could feel the mud I was lying on top of. I was stretched out on the soil, on my back. Clearly there'd been nowhere better to fall. I was at the bottom of the world and I had everything figured out. I could conjure up everything that had happened up until that instant the truck hovered over the void. My father looking at me and me yelling at him, "Mind the road!" But I couldn't remember the rest. And I didn't care. All I wanted to dwell on was myself. On myself and my situation. Who knows how many trees or rocks I'd hit on my way down until I arrived at that rock? Who knows how I'd been flung about to end up underneath that overhang?

Rising up on my elbows, I unstuck my back from the earth, raised my head, and for the first time in my life felt glad to see my feet. I even moved them in my gladness, not stopping to think that they might hurt. The piece of rock half a meter above me stopped at my knees and everything below was getting doused in rain. Night and shadow surrounded me on three sides and stared. My face and everything else hurt like my skin had been grated, but I didn't feel severe pain. I could get up. At the very least I could sit up.

I pressed my palms against the ground and pulled my knees toward myself. I bent my head so I wouldn't bump it against the stone ceiling and rested my back against the wall behind me.

The sharp bumps on its surface surely poked into my back, but I didn't feel it. The gloom made the colors of my hands, shirt, and trousers so dark that I couldn't tell the blood from the mud. I just brought my hands to my face, stomach, shoulders and assumed that whatever damage had been done to my body, I could feel it out. Clutching at myself I searched for breaks. A broken bone or a severed piece . . . but it seemed that everything was in its place. Same as the day my mother gave birth to me. . . elbows, ears, and eyes, in the total that they should be. I wasn't sure about my teeth, though. I thought I could tell by my voice. In any case it was as good a time as any to start talking to myself. As good a time as any to see if I still had a voice . . .

I said, "You're alive," and something spilled onto my chest. It must be a thread of saliva and blood that stretched from my jaw to my chest. I broke the wet thread like I was swatting a fly.

Then I glanced around. Thinking maybe I'd see my father. He might have taken the same route and been lying somewhere near me. But there was no one to be seen. I had to get up as soon as possible and find him, wherever he was. For if I was to kill him for putting my mother in chains, perhaps for her entire pregnancy, I had to do it now and immediately. There are some nights . . . nights like sawdust . . . that suck in all kinds of crime and redeem all kinds of criminals in the morning . . . That was the kind of night I was in. A night one could get away with killing his father!

I could stand beside him with a large stone in my hand as he lay expiring underneath a tree and let gravity do the rest. I'd crush that skull of his, inside which I was now sure once circulated the thought of imprisoning the woman who wanted to leave him, and end it at that. This way he'd even have a gravestone. If someone asked how he'd died, I could reply, "By a gravestone falling on his head!" But first I needed to gather myself. To get it together a bit more . . .

I raised both arms and stretched them out to my sides. I collected some rainwater in my hands that reached past the piece of rock above me. Then I tried to use the water in my palms to wash the blood and mud off my face. I don't know if I managed, but at least I felt better. I was ready now. I could crawl out from underneath the piece of rock and stand. Just as I'd bent my head and leaned forward, something struck the ground at my feet. Something large. Something the size of a person! It had happened so quickly that I was frozen. I hadn't yet let out the breath I was holding in when another person fell! Onto the same spot, right in front of me. On top of the other one. All I'd been able to do was pull my feet back. I pulled them back underneath the overhang and froze. Seconds later another person fell. Not right in front of me, where I'd been expecting it to, but to my left, so I started and reflexively raised my head, bumping it against the rock. As I stared in horror at that person's outstretched hand, near enough to almost touch me, another one fell. To my right this time! And another! Then another! It was raining people! I couldn't make sense of it all. I wanted to dash out of there immediately but couldn't muster up the courage. I had no idea where they were falling from. But wherever it was, must be very high up. Because they struck the mud like meteors. It was like they were being fired out of a giant pistol in the sky! In fact, it was as if that pistol were trying to shoot me. It riddled the ground around me with holes as it sent those human-bullets flying at me.

They made such a sound when they hit the ground that I felt punched in the heart each time! My bones broke and my ears filled with blood with each one that fell. They didn't cry out or contort or try to get up. They were already dead and simply raining on me. At times I heard a deep thud but didn't see anyone fall. Those must be the ones falling onto my stone ceiling. And the others, to my right, my left, and right in front of me! I recoiled in the opposite direction of wherever they fell but, being unable to get out from under the rock, couldn't move more than a few centimeters.

Knees to my chest, arms pressed to my sides, I tried to shrink as much as I could. I saw hands, feet, and faces. Some touched me, others lay like rag dolls at most a meter away from me. Their legs bent from the knee not backward but to the sides and their arms vanished underneath their torsos. They crumpled shapelessly like puppets with severed strings. I knew who they were. They were the Afghanis in the vault. It was like they'd all climbed to the top of a building to jump off one by one.

I couldn't make sense of it! From where and why were they falling? How was it that they rained down on me like birds afflicted by death in flight? As all these questions faded my mind and eyes into darkness, they kept on falling. Their limbs tangled together as they piled up on top of and underneath and next to one another. The big mud pile they accumulated into kept growing larger. Two rains fell simultaneously and merged together. Human flesh collided with water and turned into muck. In that brief duration during which I breathed at most four times, a wall of flesh rose up around me. A wall that enveloped my entire field of vision! In front of my very eyes, those dozens of corpses came between me and the night and trapped me underneath that piece of rock. Now I was inside a cell made of three human walls, a dirt floor, and stone. At the very bottom of a mass grave . . .

I was fifteen at the time I got trapped underneath all that human debris. Sooner or later my mother had gotten her way. I was buried alive.

I sat there shaking. And as I did, I felt fine hairs touching my ears. Who knows whose hair or beard or eyelashes or eyebrows they were? It was dark. I could see nothing. But they were all there. All over me! I was so terrified of touching them that I couldn't even flinch. They touched me, however. I just sat there, shoulders stuck between two walls of flesh. My hands rested on my knees that were pressed together. I could feel my palms sweating where I pressed them fast against my knees so I wouldn't touch anything.

I began moving my feet forward inch by inch. My knees had to unbend only slightly before I touched them. Those people. There wasn't even enough space in front of me to extend my legs completely. My hands still on my knees, I did the only thing I could. I screamed.

"Dad!" I hollered. "Rastin!" I howled. But my voice didn't go anywhere. It circled round and round inside my cave. As it did it went in one of my ears and out the other. I'd either go deaf or hoarse. My vocal cords were the first to give up.

I didn't have a phone. Even if I did, I don't know if it could clear human flesh. All I had on me were a paper frog, two packs of cigarettes, and two lighters. The latter were the most likely to help. I was so scared of seeing the bodies, however, that I could never have lit one of the lighters. Yet I couldn't keep on sitting there like that any longer, either. I had no choice but to touch those enmeshed bodies. At the very least I could try pushing them with my feet. I thought I might have a chance if I could create even the tiniest gap. Without taking my hands off my knees, I started kicking out with both feet. I couldn't even tell what exactly I was hitting, but I pumped my knees and tried to shove whatever the soles of my feet happened to land on. But it wasn't working. I just kept on striking a soft wall that wouldn't budge, over and over.

Perhaps if I leaned forward slightly and also used my hands I could do other things. But there was such pressure on both my shoulders that I was sure I would lose what space I had if I were to lean forward. The many kilos of flesh on either side of me would immediately fill the space I left behind and I'd be even more stuck. Still, I decided to use my hands.

Trying to square my shoulders, I leaned my hands against the walls on either side. My right hand touched some fabric. My left hand bounced right off, as four fingers had hit a brow, while the thumb coincided with an eye socket. I needed some fabric for my left hand as well. But all my palm kept landing on was some-one's nose or mouth. The mouth had been the worst because my fingers pushed past the lips and touched a pair of teeth and part of their gums.

Hopelessly I went back to where I started, which was the brow. Trying to keep my thumb as far as possible from the eye socket, I put my hand against that brow and pushed as hard as I could. But nothing happened. The head that I grasped by the brow didn't even budge.

So I gave up on my left hand and banked on the right. I could feel each individual rib underneath the fabric. I pushed as hard as I could, but the wall on my right was at least as sturdy as the one on my left. I didn't give up, however. I tried over and over. The more I tried, the more panic replaced my fear. In my panic I started not caring what I touched. Whatever I could grab with both hands, I shoved. My left hand even went in the mouth and out again. In the meantime I also kept on hitting the wall across from me with my feet. I was like a thrashing worm. I continued to kick and shove from where I sat until I was short of breath. But it was no use! No use at all . . .

That's when I started to cry. I shed tears and sobbed loudly, breathlessly. I hadn't cried much in my life, but had burst into sobs for the second time this week. Of course the situation I was in was multiple times more horrifying than Rastin seeing through my lie. As was my crying. Multiple times louder! I opened my mouth as if I'd tear it right open and in my voice that had long gone hoarse, howled like some strange animal. After all, there was no one to see. There were dozens of people around me but none of them could see my unsightly weeping. I cried so hard my eyes hurt from squeezing them shut. I was like a baby who'd started crying in his mother's womb. A baby who cried because he knew he wouldn't get to leave his mother's womb. A baby who cried not to take his first breath, but to release his last . . .

My weeping juddered to a stop a few minutes later, like a train braking. My tears petered out and eventually dried. I was like a dead body now. A corpse sitting motionless, hands on knees just like before. I was one of them. Like one of the people surrounding me. The only difference was that I was still breathing. All of this seemed like a mistake in calculation. Me being the only survivor in a pile of corpses where all should be dead had to be some sort of mistake. But in that tiny void, I was the only one capable of making mistakes. If there had been another, he was dead now. So all of this was my fault. Everything . . . and this fault must be corrected . . .

I was sure no one would be able to find me. That road we'd been riding on must have been out of use for years. And we didn't matter the tiniest bit to the captain waiting for us at that dark cove! He, like us, like the Afghanis, was illegal. Even our existence was illegal! I highly doubted he'd try to track us down. He'd never take that kind of risk. Right then I thought of Yadigar. Our legit partner in crime!

*Maybe he knows*, I thought. What road we'd take and where we'd go to deliver the goods . . . but then I realized he wouldn't care, either. It would have been unseemly for him to coincidentally find us, so far away from the patrolling area of the gendarmerie. He had no reason to put himself in danger. No one would come to save me. I was the only one that could.

Suicide had ceased to be an option in my mind. It was more of a sensation like a thousand knives stabbing me all over at the same time. It was like hate! That was the instant I ceased to think of suicide but to feel it. My sixth sense was suicide! If everyone around me was dead, then so would I be! My lighters would be good for something when I burned myself to death. I'd set us all on fire. First I'd set alight the ones around me, then myself.

I was such a fool I really thought I could do it. I was such a fool I even pulled the pack out of my pocket to try. I was such a coward, however, that I couldn't do a thing. I was afraid not of dying, but of burning. Plus how was I supposed to go around setting fires with that meager flame and all the wetness around me? Lighter in hand, I just froze there . . . and it suddenly made more sense to set alight a cigarette rather than myself.

When the flame from the lighter lit up that tiny hole, it was too late. I struck the lighter, forgetting for a brief unwitting moment how much I feared the light and the things I could see in it. But I was able to neither bring the flame up to the cigarette that was between my lips, nor even move. For in its light, I saw hell itself. And in that hell, the only fire was the one in my hand. That would mean that I was the devil and this was my home.

But I wasn't able to regard for too long the walls of my home and, vomiting, flicked off the lighter. With my hands I wiped what I could off my jaw. And just as I tried to dry my palms by rubbing them against my trousers, twelve small, glowing dots I hadn't noticed until then caught my eye. They glowed on my wrist along with the minute hand, the hour hand, and the stick that indicated seconds. The face of the watch, the governor's gift, showed quarter past three. Like in that photo in *From Kandalı to the World*. But this time, it was night. The darkest night of the world, in fact. For no one was burning and not a single flame was rising in hell. When really it was what lit up the Earth, not the sun: hellfire . . . and maybe some morphine sulfate.

I'd taken the watch off my wrist and gripped it in both hands. Elbows resting on my knees, I sat motionless. For exactly two hours I'd watched the seconds indicator revolving. Or this was all some autohypnosis and I just didn't know it. In the glow of the stick that indicated seconds, I tried to forget the hell I'd seen in the light of the lighter flame. At a quarter past five, something happened.

"More . . . more . . . more . . . more . . ."

Who was speaking? Whose voice was it? Where was it coming from?

"More . . . more . . . more . . ."

Was I hallucinating? But no, I could really hear that voice. It was coming from afar and sounded strangled, but I could hear it. I hollered.

"I'm here! In here! I'm in here! Can you hear me?"

Going silent, I waited.

"More!"

Whoever it was, they were replying to me. Just as I wondered why they kept saying the same thing, my question collided with its answer like a pair of accelerated particles. Because that's how much Turkish they spoke, that was why! As well as "More!" Because it was one of the Afghanis from the back of the truck! So where were they?

I wished I could ask, but I didn't know any Pashto. Throughout the years, perhaps a thousand people had passed through the reservoir speaking Pashto, but I'd never cared what they were saying. There wasn't a single Pashto word in my mind. My ears had heard thousands of words in Pashto but withheld none. My hearsay mechanism, which always and everywhere worked like an obstinate butterfly trap, hadn't turned a hair in that reservoir. Because it had been sure that Pashto wouldn't have any use in real life! When really real life was everything that fell outside human perception! I was learning . . . and hearing:

"More . . . more. . ."

I couldn't figure out where exactly the voice was coming from. It seemed to be shattering into a thousand pieces and coming at me from every direction. Or reaching me through the thousands of holes in between the bodies around me. I didn't know where it was coming from, but it was always at the same volume. Or at the same low volume, I should say, because it was very faint by the time it got to me. It was as if one of the bodies was speaking from its stomach! Apparently the distance between me and the owner of the voice never changed.

"I'm here!" I'd shout. "I'm here!"

Then I'd fall silent and wait and they would reply, "More!"

That was all. That was the extent of our communication. We repeated this dialogue over and over. We repeated it so many times that it eventually turned into a single sentence, "I'm heremore!"

The hour, for that matter, eventually turned into six in the morning. But still I couldn't spot a single stirring in the bodies around me. If it wasn't someone who'd survived the accident and was standing by the pile of bodies, wondering how to get me out, I didn't even want to think about what it might be. For that scenario would involve someone stuck somewhere else in the wreck just like me. A while later, I had to believe that this was the case. My reluctance was the reason it took so long . . .

The voice also mustn't have wanted to believe, for it had yelled, "More!" hundreds of times. Goodness knows where it was trapped, waiting for help from me. For forty-five minutes we'd begged for help from each other in vain. What's more, they had had it tougher, having had to do it in Turkish, saying the only word they knew.

In the meantime, the vomit that had left me when I saw the walls of hell had long dried up, and I'd vowed not to use the lighter again. But the place that I was at in the world and in my life made me well aware that I could fuck away with any vow within a matter of seconds. Neither my loyalty to my vows nor my spine had been left intact by the boulder I was bent double under! In fact, I hadn't just lost my loyalty to my vows, but to everyone else as well! I had lost it so much that what little consolation I could give myself came from imagining that my father was dead.

*At least he's done for*, I thought. Then it'd abruptly occur to me that he might not be dead. Maybe he too was lying injured somewhere. But I'd shake this thought out of my head and yell, "No, no! Ahad's check is cashed! Ahad is no more!"

I'd receive as a reply, "More!"

To which I'd call, "Get it already! I'm stuck in this fucking hole just like you! There's no point in yelling!"

Yet again it would say, "More!"

. . . Which one of them could it be? Which of the ones from the reservoir? Which of them could have learned the magic word because they knew they would be passing through Turkey? Who could this person be who'd obviously asked around before even setting out in order to ask for more water, more food, more air, more this, more that, and more of everything? With another group I'd have known for sure. But this time a man by the name of Rastin had come between us. They'd had no need to look me in the face with expressions like those of starving children and beg, "More!" as they usually did, instead begging to Rastin in their native language . . .

The voice was so low I couldn't even tell if it was a woman or a man. Maybe it was that kid who'd sung the March of Independence with me! His body the size of a leaf, surrounded by corpses on all four sides, trying to make his voice heard . . .

"Who cares who it is?" I said. "What do I care? What difference does it make? It's not like he's going to be able to come rescue me!"

But they didn't think so and kept repeating, "More!"

So, in order to ignore all else and forget about the enormous disillusionment I was experiencing, I began to stare at the hand indicating seconds. With each tick rightward, I imagined that the sun would rise soon and that surely someone would see the truck or the human pile over me and come for help. I imagined this sixty times per second and 3,600 per hour. I stared at that indicator as though I were counting prayer beads . . .

It was now seven. I was sure that the sun had risen, but no one was coming to rescue me. I was still in the dark, too. The dead were lightproof. They'd embraced one another so tightly that nothing could penetrate them. Except rainwater and oxygen. No matter how thirsty I became, there was no way I'd ever gather the water droplets in my hands to drink. The water, trickling over the bodies and dripping onto my legs from the edges of the rock over me, repulsed me. Who knows what pathways it took and what it mixed with? Whose blood and saliva? It made me so nauseated that I kept moving my hands around so I wouldn't touch it.

But it was different with oxygen. I couldn't avoid that. It entered me even when I sealed my lips shut. It overcame all obstacles in its way just to keep me alive in that hell and found some way to barge into my nostrils. In that very place and time where I thought no one was coming and I was feeling suicide afresh, it would keep me alive to death! I fucking hated oxygen. For not getting off my tail and tracking me down in that hole! Maybe it was a curse! No matter where I went, I wouldn't be rid of oxygen! I was cursed! Tutankhamen the child pharaoh of the reservoir had finally been cursed! After all, I had a pyramid of my own now! An actual pyramid of human flesh rose above me. In fact, dozens of people had died in the name of erecting it. When I was the first person that should have died! Because this pyramid was mine! I was buried under it, just like I was supposed to be. But a curse put upon me by all those deaths caused me to survive. I'd been buried in my own pyramid along with the curse. Oxygen was the curse I was doomed to breathe in. Such a curse it was, it kept me, the pharaoh, alive in my own grave.

By eight I couldn't hold it in any longer. I let go of all the urine pooled inside me and straining my groin to get out. My trousers and the ground I sat on grew warmer. For a moment, in the cold, I felt slightly better. I even felt angry for not going for so long. What did it matter what I looked like when I got out of that human trap hole? What would it matter if I puked or pissed or shit on myself? Though of course I'd only been in there for five hours. That wasn't long enough to leave civilized habits behind. Maybe in a few more hours . . . say, ten or fifteen hours later, I might turn into a real subterranean animal and start eating my own crap. But five hours were useless. At most one pissed on oneself and thought it embarrassing, then finally arriving at, "Fuck it! Who's gonna know?"

Really, it all came down to hope. I was kept civilized by believing that the moment I'd mix with humankind again was very near. My suicidal thoughts had evaporated with the sun, which I knew was rising though I couldn't see it. Once again I was having the dream in which someone found me and lifted the bodies off me, rescuing me. In the hole, pessimism and optimism switched places so often that one would take over my mind before my emotions could adapt to the other. For instance, in the moment I was in what ruled me and everything else was the thought of liberation. It was having its stint, and though I might be in the dark, it was lighting up every corner of my mind. I'd sunk into the lowest depths of the earth, but I still wanted to live. Though I'd practically have to rip my mouth open to breathe, though I'd have to expand my nostrils like craters, I wanted to live. Oxygen was no longer a curse but a hero with superpowers! A superhero that could infiltrate the wall of human flesh to reach me! I wanted to survive!

I wanted it so badly, in fact, that I hollered, "Until everyone dies! If this world has shutters, I'll be the one to close them!"

The voice, which I hadn't heard in the past half hour, replied, "More!"

"I'm going to live!" I said and in return came another "More!" I laughed.

All this would pass! Pass and be through! Once I was out of here, I'd go back to school! Everything would be different. Ahad would be dead. I'd start life afresh. I was only fifteen. It wasn't too late for anything. I could pretend I'd emerged from my mother's womb after fifteen years and be a completely new Gaza! I wouldn't repeat any of my mistakes. All that I'd lived through until then would have been a test drive of sorts! A test life or something! A rehearsal that had been bequeathed me so I could see potential traps and mistakes and take precautions before real life started. My head had turned into a volcano and erupted, spilling optimistic lava all over me. It was hot, but it didn't burn. I was warmed by optimism. My skull had burst open so wide it bloomed like a flower out of my hair. It resembled the crown of a king. A crown made of bone, looming over my brow and ears! Encased in the crown, my velvety brain! No one knew it, but I was king of the world. All I had to do was sit and wait, until I could declare my kingship in a whisper into the ear of my savior. I wanted to be reborn as soon as possible. Born again! I'd been buried a fool but I'd be born again as king. I just needed to be patient. And survive, of course! For that, I had to have some water. No matter what it was, I had to drink the corpse water dripping onto me. All I had to do was reach out my hand.

I did and opened up my palm. The first drop fell and the second came thirteen seconds later. I filled the cup of my palm in two minutes and twenty-nine seconds, checking it against the watch on my other wrist. Then I brought it to my mouth and spilled half the water down my chin and the other half between my lips. In the instant I swallowed, however, the four pieces of my skull, agape like the four corners of an envelope, locked together and my crown disappeared.

For I'd been reminded of the face of the weak man I'd buried in the garden. For after he'd been beaten and tossed aside, no one had given him water and he'd laboriously raised his hand and reached for the wall near him. He'd intersected one of the trails of water formed on the wall due to the dampness in the reservoir, wetting his fingers first and then his lips. When I collected water in my open palm, we'd resembled each other so much that it hadn't taken long for that image of him to spring to my mind. But far from coming alone, that image of his gaunt face had also brought with it the expression he had after he died. And with that image marched in all the dead faces surrounding me, and together they wrenched my kingdom away from me.

The heat of optimism abruptly vanished and left in its place a spiky March chill that bit into me from every direction. I was shaking. I gripped my jaw to stop my teeth from chattering. My hand, however, was also shaking. From both fear and the cold. I knew that if no one came to save me very soon, I'd have to watch all those faces decay. With the exception of the boulder that I leaned my back against and which covered me, allowing me to survive, everything around me would rot sooner or later. My whole world would be infused with decay. Who knew what kinds of insects had already formed an army and started marching toward the foot of Kandalı to feast on the giant cake waiting for them? Maybe they were already coming up through the earth. Right in the spot I was sitting! They would beeline between my legs to gnaw on whatever dead thing was in their path. What was I supposed to do then? Was I going to have to eat them to survive? I didn't know the first thing about how bodies decayed. My expertise was elsewhere. It had to do with another kind of decay.

The decay I could tell from a glance was the one that happened aboveground. I knew all about the decay that began when a person was still breathing, with mold forming over the heart or brain. That was as far as I'd been able to progress in the classes life had thrust me into by the scruff of my neck. I didn't know anything further.

What's more, the last class I'd had was on burying the dead. That was as far as I knew. Burying and moving on. Nothing beyond. Beyond that was a huge mystery. Wasn't it the same for everyone anyway? Who cared what happened to his mother, his father, his lover, his brother, after they'd been buried? Once they were in the ground, who cared what became of those bodies he'd loved and even worshiped? All the ordinary people of the world and I, all we knew about was the part up to the burial. Maybe we even sometimes said, "Now the insects will eat them."

Really, everyone should be cremated! That was what should be done! At least then we'd know what happened after death. "One becomes ash and scatters," we'd say, and no one would contradict us.

But below ground was at least as complicated as above. It was at least as colossal a mystery as above. I hated nature! Everything eating everything else! I hated that the entire cycle was sustained by everything eating everything else. Wasn't there some other way? Any other choice? Was this the almighty and faultless nature everyone spoke of? Whatever or whomever it was that had created this nature, what kind of a sadist did you have to be to say, "I'm going to set up such a system that everyone will go bumping one another off just to stay alive!" All those animals eating one another, all those people eating everything, all those bugs eating the bodies, all the other bugs eating those bugs . . .

"Fuck them all!" I was yelling. "Fuck whoever it is that dreamed up this world, and fuck to hell everyone that ever regarded all this flesh-eating and blood-drinking as a miracle and gave thanks!"

I was so furious that had I had a pen and paper, I'd immediately have written a petition. Seeing as all those faiths had been penned and made into books, that was obviously the most sensible mode of communication. I'd write a letter of complaint and toss it into the air, or wherever Allah or God or this or that was! As the Quran started with "Read!" I'd start that letter with, "Why don't *you* read *this*!"

"Just you wait until I leave this hole, I'll do it all!" I said, and in answer, I kept hearing the voice, "More!"

But now more than before it seemed to be asking, "More?"

In reply I said, "No more! That's it, for fuck's sake!" and wept. And also checked the time.

I was numb. I was numb all over. My legs, my arms, every muscle, and even my tongue and lips were numb. Once again it was a quarter past three, and I'd been sitting there for exactly twelve hours. I was pretty sure that the thing pressing against my shoulder was someone's head. In fact, whoever it was, I'd felt their ribs when I'd tried to shove them hours before now. Maybe that had been someone else's body, I couldn't know for sure. At my right shoulder was someone presumably folded up jaw to knees. At least I thought so. Just beyond was the face, the mouth of which I'd inserted my fingers into in the dark. Where the rest of the face was, I had absolutely no idea. I could no longer remember the scenery I'd glimpsed for a few seconds in the lighter flame.

Really, if not for the watch in my hand, I'd have been able to remember very few things. Everything blended together. First of all, it felt like the accident was years ago. Yet when I drank the rainwater dribbling off the bodies, it was as if it had only been minutes. Apparently I was losing my mind and that terrified me. So being rescued wasn't enough, but I had to be rescued before I lost it. I was so afraid of spending the rest of my life as a loony that I now prayed to all the divine powers I'd cursed at and knew by name a few hours ago that I would die before I could go mad. That was all I wanted: to die before I could go mad.

But nothing helped me remember the chronological order of events. Neither incessantly following the seconds indicator, nor counting the seconds out loud at the top of my lungs, even. I always started to mess up after a while. I'd count seventeen after five or zone out staring at the seconds indicator and panic when I came back around, not being able to figure out how much time had passed.

Then I'd hold my breath and shut my eyes, waiting for the face of a clock that read a quarter past three to appear in my mind. A clock face that read a quarter past three was, for me, the beginning of everything. It was a milestone. It was like history's propelling clock or some such thing. If I lost it, everything would go up in the air. It would go up in the air in a jumble, and I'd never be able to add up the time I'd spent in that hole. If I couldn't add it up, surely I'd go mad. There was no time in there. Even if there were, I wouldn't know it. Because there were schools you needed to go to in order to know. Schools people went to who could tell, from just a glance, the time of death of a body . . . All I had was an onset hour and that was all. It was my past and everything I had. If I forgot it, I'd be obliterated. I'd be nothing more than a grain of sand hurtling around in empty space. And if I really were a grain of sand, I could only be one inside an hourglass.

So I tried to ingrain the clock face showing quarter past three inside my mind as much as I could and held my breath until it loomed behind my closed eyes. Though my heart picked up speed and it was a strain, I didn't let go of my breath until I saw that clock face. It both calmed me and helped me remember the time. Calmed me, because I felt like holding my breath severed all my ties to the world. No more transactions took place between us. My body still sat there and I still sat inside my body, but in a sense, I evaporated. I evaporated into thin air and felt myself exempt from everything. That was my solution to the panic attacks. But I still had to find a way to write down, someplace or other, the clock face showing quarter past three.

What was more, since the clock face in my hand was to point to a quarter past three every twelve hours, I had to mark those as well. I had to put a nick in a certain spot every twelve hours. Of course, thinking about all this drove me into deeper panic. All of this preparation meant accepting that I wouldn't be rescued on this day. So, I'd again hold my breath and wait for the panic washing over me to recede. The worst part was that I'd have to light the lighter again in order to make the marks. Besides, where and how was I supposed to write these numbers down? They might be washed away if I wrote them in the mud.

I'd started glancing around as if I could see anything. I wasn't able to, of course, but when I raised my head, I came up with a solution. I could write on the boulder above me with soot from the lighter flame. But then I'd use up too much of the lighter fluid. I had to make a choice. I'd either be left without light sooner than I should or there would come a time that I'd forget everything I knew in relation to time and go mad.

It wasn't really that hard to make a decision. After all, I was too afraid to light the lighter. I even had a spare. The lighter inside the pack my father had given me. So it seemed to be decided. The date and time would be inscribed on the rock above me in soot.

But now I was wondering how I could avoid seeing the things that would come to light along with the flame. How could one avoid seeing hell? Was there a way? Of course there was! To think of all the autopsy specialists in the world! Who knows how many people's utterly cold gazes, right in that moment I was fearful of seeing all those corpses piled on top of one another, were studying the bodies they tore apart with their steady hands, the bloody spectacle in front of their eyes? If they could do it, so could I. At the very least I could light the lighter and ignore the bodies as I went about my business. I could raise my head and fix my eyes on the rock. In the end we were all flesh, me included. We could very well be on sale by the pound in another planet's butchers!

With sudden determination I leaped into the future like a first-time skydiver. I raised my head and flicked on the lighter. Yes, I could feel the bodies, and my eyes knew they were there, but I stubbornly stared at the boulder. Yet though I held the flame to a single spot in hopes of seeing a soot stain appear, there was no change in color, or none that I could see. The rock was wet. Maybe that was why it didn't work. As my hand started to burn, I couldn't hold out any more and was about to put it out when I looked down and saw a pair of breasts. A woman's breasts . . . then I took my thumb off the lever.

I was in the dark again but the breasts hovered in front of my eyes. The woman's neck and head, caught between the legs of another body, had been out of sight. The part below her waist also extended over the pair of legs of another and disappeared into the darkness. She stretched forward and up like one of those wooden female torsos on the front of pirate ships. Her back arched backward like a bow. All I could see was the part between her neck and her slightly distended belly. There was no rest of her. The buttons of her shirt had popped off, causing it to sag open to either side, and her breasts spilled out from inside a white bra.

I was so aroused by this vision I'd glimpsed for only a second that I wanted to flick on the lighter again to gaze at it, and even find some way to touch those breasts. But they were out of my reach. To do that I'd have to lean forward. That would cause the two masses of flesh on either side of me to instantly fall and fill the space between my back and the rock behind me.

Maybe I could remove my shoes and touch them with my toes. Or I could lunge forward with no regard to the possibility that the load on my shoulders might fall when I was out of the way. What did I have to lose anyway? If anything, a gap of thirty centimeters. I didn't think the body on my right could move much anyhow. After all, it was folded up between the boulder and other bodies as though it had no bones. But I was sure that the body on my left would fall, if only its head.

I was so frenzied that I disregarded everything and flicked on the lighter so I could stare at those breasts, and only them. There was a face right next to them. I was trying to avoid looking at it at all costs.

And I did! I leaned forward to slide my finger underneath the band in the middle of the bra to pull it up. Both breasts were left exposed when the bra was lifted. The bra itself slid up to rest somewhere above the breasts, near the woman's vanishing neck. At the same time there was an earthquake behind me! The corpse on my left dropped behind me, not just the head but the entire body, filling the space between me and the boulder.

Now my knees were near enough I could rest my elbows on them. I'd lost a space of not thirty centimeters but at least half a meter! I would never be able to stretch my legs any more than this. For a second I thought I might be able to sit on the body behind me to make room for my legs, but the boulder above me wouldn't allow that. It wasn't high enough. What was all this for, then? I was about to find out!

First I put down the lighter and then unbuttoned my trousers. I was in such a hurry my hands shook, and I couldn't open my zipper. Finally, with my feet against the body opposite me and my back against the body behind me, I was able to raise myself momentarily and unzip my trousers to pull them down.

Then, in the dark, I began to caress the breasts, the locations of which I'd committed to memory, while with my other hand I began touching myself inside my underpants. It was all very cold. Colder than my hands. And nothing was happening. The blood inside me wasn't pooling where it was supposed to, and I couldn't feel the breasts I was touching to be the pieces of meat I'd been aroused by a minute ago. Nothing was real! Nothing at all! Me being there, caressing the breasts of a corpse, what I was doing to myself, none of it!

So, eyes filling with tears, I struggled for the unachievable. All was gone. All my hopes had disappeared into such a black hole that not a single trace was left behind. There was no way I could ever get them back out. I'd found myself sitting on that ice-cold piece of earth, kneading a piece of clay that would never harden. I was wringing, releasing, and caressing a dead pair of breasts and feeling nothing.

But I had no intention of surrendering to all the lifelessness. Everything was dead enough as it was, but I wasn't! Despite some difficulty, I bent my head to tuck my feet underneath me and gripped the breasts to pull myself forward. I took my left hand off the chest to lean my forehead against it, and slowly coasted my face over it. My eyebrows, eyes, cheekbones, nose, and cheeks. I wanted every part of my face to touch the chest that was cold and hard as marble.

Then I kissed the spot I imagined the veins of the marble to knit together. My lips parted and the two tips met. The tip of my tongue drifted over and around the nipple.

I was doing all this so ponderously that it felt like every movement took hours. I started sucking. Eyes shut, I knelt on my knees. One hand clutched the breast while the other clutched at me. As I sucked on the nipple with my lips and tongue, so I touched myself with five fingers. Neither faster nor slower. My fist moved back and forth as though sharpening a knife, the heat rising inside it. As it rose it became bigger than my fist and forced my fingers apart.

I was thinking of the world's most beautiful girl. And of the others . . . I'd completely forgotten where and who I was. My eyes shut tight, I waited for that one moment. That moment would bring an end to everything, suffusing my harrowed body and mind with such pleasure that it would all cease to matter. Pain and pleasure would become so level that life would be stretched like a line between them and I, tightrope walker, would do cartwheels on it. I could feel it. I could feel the last drop roiling inside me before it made the glass overflow. A river was about to flow out of my loins, I just knew it.

Just as I was poised to meet that instant with all my cells opening like floodgates, breath held, a bitter taste filled my mouth! A sticky, viscous, bitter fluid! At first I thought it was blood! What else could it be in the midst of all those bodies? Surely it was blood! Who knows what part of the woman it had come from all the way to her nipple? Who knows how much of it I'd sucked in, even swallowed?

I jerked backward. Sailing like a spring toy on my knees, I knocked my head against the boulder before falling on my back onto the body stretched out behind me.

With a scream I sat back on my heels and immediately began spitting and wiping my mouth with the back of my hand. But it was too late. I'd already swallowed at least a few drops! I wasn't about to go looking for the lighter I'd left on the ground. I took the pack out of my pocket, pulled out the other lighter, and lit it.

First I examined my hands. There was nothing on them that resembled blood. There was only a yellow-tinged clear fluid forming fine bridges between my fingers. The fluid I was after was more or less the same color, but it was clear what I was seeing hadn't come from me! I looked up quickly and looked at the woman's breast. There it was! It oozed out of the nipple like a fat teardrop and dribbled onto the earth.

The drop I'd seen must have been the last as nothing came after it, and everything dried up. I couldn't make sense of it at all. Why, I was asking. How could it be? What is this stuff? Some kind of disease? An infection? Why would a woman's breast leak that kind of . . .

I stopped! I'd hit such a wall that I had no chance but to stop. I'd come to such an understanding that my shoulders collapsed under its weight. The breast I'd been sucking on belonged to the pregnant woman. The woman who'd have named her child Rastin if it were a boy. She'd said she was four months pregnant. Her body had long prepared itself for the baby but hadn't been any the wiser when it died halfway. What I'd sucked on had gathered in that breast for someone who'd never be born. I'd tasted mother's milk for the first time in my life. My own mother hadn't done it, but in the end somebody had nursed me.

I didn't know what to think. Or what to feel . . . I wasn't even sure I felt shame. The lighter remained in my grip, lighting up everything like a torch, but I hung my head and saw nothing. My trousers were around my ankles, and I was sitting on them. I flicked the lighter off and put it between my teeth. Then I sat up slightly to stretch my legs in front of me, despite some difficulty, and gave my back to the body behind me. Extending my legs as much as I could, I pulled up my trousers and zipped and buttoned them. Sitting up again, I folded my legs underneath me and dropped onto my heels. I took the lighter from between my teeth to put in my pocket, shut my eyes, and held my breath.

I started to wait. I waited for the clock face to appear in my mind's eye . . . but it didn't. I was unable to conjure up the picture in my pitch-black mind. No matter how long I held my breath, the clock face appeared neither in front nor behind my eyes. That was when I descended one level lower into hell. For I realized that I was unable to remember the hour of my arrival in it. What had just transpired left my mind so ravaged that nothing was left behind but pain. The pain took up so much space that my mind had dispensed with all else to make room for it. The hour of arrival, naturally, was part of that and it had been cast out with everything else.

Now I could go mad and I did. I started hitting myself. Slapping at myself! Then I hit the bodies. Anything that came across my fists, I punched. I hit legs, bellies, chests, and other things I could guess at but didn't want to think about. I'd lost it. I just howled as I played the skin-covered drums surrounding me. I rose and fell on my feet, striking my legs, my bent knees, and my groin! I struck the piece of flesh I'd desperately embraced in hopes of the pleasure it would give me to abate my pain. I flailed at the entire world given to me in that tiny space. I'd no longer be sure of anything. Neither the passing of time, nor anything else!

"You may've been here for days!" I started to scream. "How would you know?"

How would anyone know, really? Who could tell me this when even I didn't know? Maybe I'd been here for weeks. Yes, only that would explain everything! Would I have lost myself enough to consider making love to a corpse if I hadn't been here for weeks? Of course not! But then shouldn't everything have rotted?

I yanked the lighter out with such force that I tore my pocket. I don't know what I hoped to see when I lit it. Was it more preferable that they had rotted, or that I'd gone so insane that I'd wanted to fuck a corpse before they even had a chance to? Which was it? When the lighter was lit, everything would come to light. I'd either have to see the decay or accept that I was decayed on the inside!

Taking a breath, I struck the lighter and opened my eyes. I looked at them all. At everything! Into their dulled eyes! At their discolored lips! Their bloody noses! Their shredded skin! The bones poking out of their flesh! Whatever it was life offered me, I looked at it all, one by one. There was no decay at all. So it seemed that I was the one who was decayed. My history of being buried preceded all theirs. My decay had begun the night my mother tried to bury me like a rock. I'd been rotting for fifteen years!

I hated my mother so much then that brought the lighter flame to the nipple I'd just sucked milk out of and waited for it to burn. As I waited I hated my mother that much more and covered both breasts in burns.

Since there was no more initial hour in my mind to write in soot, I sucked in all the smoke. As I expelled the smoke after it had traveled every possible place under my skin, I studied the reservoirful of people around me. Then I thought of the others. The other people that had come through the reservoir on Dust Street . . . I saw the world's most beautiful girl in the smoke coming out of my nose. Then the other girls . . . though none of it had felt like rape, all the girls I really had raped . . .

"Now," I said, "that's how you take revenge!"

For now I understood. They were the ones who'd presented me with those breasts, knowing I'd go after them, making my coffin even narrower and causing me to forget what I should never forget. They'd done this so they could have their revenge on me!

"See?" they said. "You wanted to touch us. And we accepted either out of fear or because we were dead. But in the end it's you, not us, who's gone mad! You!"

And I said, "Not enough! This much suffering is not enough! Give me some more! More, more!"

But now there was no reply. Whoever it was that had said, "More!" was no longer speaking to me.

Perhaps that was because, through a gap the size of a keyhole, it had seen all I'd done and me for the monster I was. It wouldn't even say that one word anymore. Or it had already croaked! It had drowned in its own blood inside its confinement to become another brick in the flesh building over me. I wasn't interested. Whether it was dead or alive, I didn't care one bit. After all, I could yell enough for us both. I could stare at those dead faces flickering to life in the lighter flame and say, "More!" As many times as I wished! "More!" Until my throat cracked! "More! Come on! Isn't there any more? Is this all there is? More, come on! Whatever it is you have to give, give me more! Whatever will happen, let there be more of it! More! More! More!"

Gaza! Calm down and flick off that lighter. Then close your eyes and hold your breath. The numbers you're looking for are three and fifteen. When you came here, it was a quarter past three and that was twelve hours ago. This is the last time I help you. It looks like you won't be hearing my voice again. Because you don't deserve it. Now, let go of your breath. Good-bye.

Really? You're going to leave me here alone? Fine. Go. Do what you want! So I don't deserve to hear your voice! All right. Leave me here! Fuck off! I don't need anything! I can very well survive without you! I might go mad, but I'll live! I won't just check out like you! I'll live a long time yet, Cuma . . . Cuma! Was it you? Was it you all along who said, "More"? Cuma . . . Cuma!

I kept thinking of Dordor and Harmin trapped below the earth, unable to step onto it. Or I was hallucinating. Or I was sleeping and watching dreams revolve around my head, holding one another by the tail. I couldn't tell if I was awake or not. I burned a mark into a leg, owner unknown, every twelve hours, keeping track of the passing time that way. On another's back, again with the lighter, I'd written *03:15* in a burned shade. So I had no problem concerning the time and date.

I even hollered at the top of my lungs once every hour for at least five minutes, just in case someone heard me. I'd found an unopened pack of biscuits in the pocket of one of the bodies. Every four hours I put one in my mouth and let it melt on my tongue in a five-minute long ritual, believing myself to be full. I also continued to drink the rainwater distilled by human flesh . . .

Though I wasn't sure how much of this I did awake and how much asleep, I was leading a more or less orderly life. The slave merchant, finally stranded on his deserted island, was already accustomed to it! Moreover, aside from all that, when I lit the lighter, I was able to witness something no one could get accustomed to! True, at times I'd been able to assist myself by picturing autopsy specialists, but this time it wasn't working. After all, no autopsy specialist had ever had to climb into the refrigerator in the morgue to sleep with the cadavers. But I did! And this way I could closely observe the way they swelled up. Their faces and especially their bellies inflated, their skin distended, and tiny flies buzzed around me. Slightly disappointed that I wasn't dead like the others, they soon vanished back into the darkness they'd emerged from. I lived there, too, really. I hid in the dark because I had nowhere to escape.

Everything, everywhere, and everyone stank so badly that I sat there with two pieces of fabric I tried to keep wet shoved as far as possible into my nostrils. My lips dried because I breathed through my mouth. Though that wasn't an issue. The issue was that the flies, exercised in flying into gaping mouths, could also visit me and my tonsils. So I lived with a shawl wrapped around my face, covering my mouth and nose. I'm not sure that it stopped the awful stink, but I felt that it did. Finding fabric wasn't a problem. Clothes were all around me. Shoes, shirts . . . there was even a coat. It was all a matter of fabric! Whenever I wanted to, I could grab some and tear it all off. But the three sweaters I was wearing were sufficient. I'd spread a coat and a thick woolen vest underneath me. All in all, it was clear I wouldn't freeze to death.

Though staring at the bodies changing colors as they became more and more naked with every piece of clothing I pulled off, now that could be deadly! So my eyes were mostly shut. Despite the fact that life had scribbled over us in its inability to undo us, and left us in such pitch darkness . . .

I'd been there for 107 hours. My legs were a pair of logs. The blood coursing through them was no longer a river but merely sludge. It'd sat for so long it'd turned into muck. My legs were pulled into the quicksand, making my flesh heavier. No matter how much I rubbed or struck them, my blood wouldn't move.

If the world's ugliest lake was a river cut off on both ends, the deadest legs of that hole were my own. My last resort was to lean my weight against the body behind me, raise my feet into the air and stretch my legs as much as I could to pedal an invisible bicycle. This exercise proved to be somewhat useful, and my legs belonged to me again if only for a few minutes.

Even in that tiny space, all that I possessed was so ready to leave me that I had to fight great battles to keep them intact and with me. For my mind, legs, life, and all that I had were just poised to leave me there at any moment! I knew they were! They were waiting for me to become too weak to fight. As if we hadn't spent all those years together, shared all we had! They were looking for a chance to betray me and were practically yelling, "We were never loyal to you!"

What was there to trust in this world if even your mind was after the chance to betray you? The minds of others? Never! That was how the body behind me had spent his life in the reservoir. By putting his trust in the mind of another . . . I'd wrapped him up in clothes and turned him into a mummy. While doing that, I'd seen his face, recognizing him as the old man's son. He'd first put his trust in his father's mind and then Rastin's. He'd become a dog! I'd seen with my own eyes how easily a man like that, making decisions based on the minds of others, could switch sides and captivities. And how well had that fared him, trusting others? What benefit could come from that? Had he made fewer mistakes? Absolutely not! Perhaps he'd only had to own up to fewer mistakes, had never really felt any responsibility during those days he'd spent at the reservoir.

The bizarre tranquility of his face, as I wrapped it up in a thin vest, really said it all. He had the expression of one who'd never had to make a decision based on his own mind in his entire life. A face untouched by responsibility and facial muscles unstrained by free will . . . there! Putting his trust in the minds of others had worked for this man! A weight the size of all decisions to be made during a lifetime had been lifted, in a sense even liberating him, on the day he'd decided to stop making his own decisions and let others make them for him. Like all people, he'd been born under siege by the obligation to make decisions but had shown the courage to give up his will, even at the cost of becoming a machine, to break through that siege. Where he'd emerged was beyond responsibility! In trusting the minds of others rather than his own, he'd kept his mind unsoiled by life, and through constant obedience he'd kept himself from being questioned by anyone. Especially by his own conscience! His exemption from all questioning was thanks to this exact obedience.

For one who'd given up his will, obedience was the freedom to make all the mistakes in the world! Obedience was an awesome way of committing all the crimes one would never dare commit on one's own! Obedience was a dream you woke up to as a different person each day! Such a dream it was that one constantly dreamed doing things that one knew in reality one hadn't done. Obedience was a miracle! It would make an ordinary person launch the atom bomb and then convince the whole world that that person was innocent. Obedience was the antidote to guilt and consciousness! Everyone should obey! We should all find someone to obey and blame *them*! Whether we were the leader of a country or the leader of a children's gang, we should find someone to obey.

Above all, it was essential to keeping one's sanity. Even if we were an utterly lonely emperor, with no one around to command, we would do well to find someone to obey. That was what God was for! So all the kings, emperors, dictators, and presidents of the world could obey! So they could wash their consciousnesses with the bleach of obedience and say, "He who giveth!" to have a peaceful night's sleep!

In fact, only leaders were allowed to obey God. All the other people carried out the orders of both the leader and God. The whole issue lay in deciding whom to obey. A single choice, and then you were exempt from all ensuing choices! Kind of like a horse race, all this business was! You had to place your will in the right person. It should be the kind of leader that would, in a time of crisis, never tell his people, "All this is your fault!" He should take and spend all the willpower entrusted him and entrust his own will in a god that would never question him. That way, he could send into space the responsibility for all the crimes committed in that nation like some industrial waste. The condition for not going insane from remorse and staying pure as a community was chain obedience.

I myself had obeyed my father. I'd trusted in his mind and given up my own. But later, by bits, the pest of free will had reared its head and led me to make some decisions. So what good had it done me, trusting my own mind? Had I made fewer mistakes? Absolutely not! In fact, I was in such a state I was even responsible for the breath I took! I'd taken over steering my own world and sunk it so deep that it was crushed underneath other people. I was drowned by all the minds I hadn't put my trust in. My free will imprisoned me inside a cell made of flesh.

The son of the old man was probably laughing at me beneath the vest covering his face! I was sure he was taunting me! Though maybe he felt sorry for me. That was why he didn't mind me leaning my back against him. I didn't mind him, either. I wasn't angry.

Actually, I wasn't anything. I didn't feel anything. I was in a fantasy world. Something like a world of memories . . . I tried to think of the good ones. The good memories. They were few, but they made an appearance anyhow. Mostly they drifted into my mind like leaves from my times with Dordor and Harmin. In fact, right then, I was thinking of Maxime. I recalled how much I'd laughed . . .

One day, Harmin had found a spy camera on one of the immigrants he'd taken onboard his boat. At first he suspected that it was a spy astronaut sent from a rival crime planet but, figuring out that the man was a journalist, soon calmed down.

He was a French journalist named Maxime researching illegal immigration routes and trying to figure out how you could go in one hole in the East and come out another in the West. He'd landed in Baghdad in a passenger plane from Paris, mailed his passport back to Paris, and then introduced himself to the first illegal immigrant he'd come across as a Georgian hoping to get to Paris.

Seeing the sheaf of cash waving in front of his face, that idiot in his turn didn't suspect a thing and said, "Okay!"

That was how Maxime's journey, which he embarked on under the delusion that he would unlock the world's biggest secret, had started. He'd been included in a group of five and sent directly on the boat without coming by us. Harmin's attentive eyes, however, had sensed that there was something off about Maxime and found the minute offness hidden in the strap of his backpack as if he'd put it there himself.

Maxine had been so terrified at being discovered that he'd somehow gotten away from Harmin to leap off the boat adrift in the middle of the sea and begun swimming without knowing where to. Harmin had then rolled and lit a joint to watch the Frenchman's hopeless strokes through the open sea. A while later, when the journalist was almost depleted with exhaustion, Harmin grabbed and pulled him aboard, effectively saving his life.

Despite thinking he'd be killed on the spot, Maxine got away with a perfectly tolerable beating that gave him a pair of identically black eyes before being presented with a completely unexpected proposal.

"It's okay!" Harmin said. "I understand, it's no problem. Naturally you want to know how this thing works . . . but that's not something you do with a spy camera or whatnot! Here's what we do: you pay us, and then you shoot a documentary about us. You can ask anything you want and we'll answer. Then at least you won't have to think about where to insert that stupid camera!"

At first Maxine was unable to believe his ears, but then said that he needed a cameraman and a sound guy and asked to call a TV channel in France that he thought he could sell the documentary to.

At that, Harmin replied, "There's no need. We'll take care of that. You find the money," and locked Maxine in the bow locker.

A few days later, all the technical gear including a professional camera and a mike that resembled a dead cat on the end of a spear had been delivered to Harmin, as per the order placed with his burglar friends in the city. In the meantime Maxine had gone into town accompanied by Dordor to withdraw the desired cash, and so the preparations were complete.

Of course, familiarizing himself with the subtleties of the trade of trafficking wasn't Maxine's sole objective. More than that, he wanted human drama! A hefty news report of human drama! A piece of news about humanity that would fill his hands with a few awards and, if possible, his pockets with a few stacks of money, at the same time clear some European consciences! This documentary was a dream come true for Maxime! He'd come to the right place. We had it all. Humanity, drama, all of it! The children denied nourishment on the way, the women raped, the elderly people deposited into the sea because they'd died of heart attacks . . . We were a gigantic human circus!

Yes, the Frenchman was definitely in the right place. At the wrong time, though. Because it was my birthday and although he hadn't an inkling, Maxime was part of my present. Naturally I didn't have an inkling about any of this, either. I didn't find out about it until much later. All Dordor and Harmin told me was: "Come to Fox Cove tomorrow and don't you laugh!"

212

When I went to the cove in question the next morning, I was greeted with this sight: Dordor and Harmin sat on the rocks wearing ski masks while a blond man with a camera on his shoulder, whom I later found out was Maxime, stood in front of them. With them were two dark men whom I also later found out were the procurers of the stolen goods. One wore headphones and had a gigantic mic in his hands while the other examined the reflector he was holding.

As soon as Dordor and Harmin saw me, they quickly stood and ran to me, bowing and kissing my hands, hulking bodies and all. At the same time they cried, "Don't laugh! Look really tough! Yell at us even!"

I did so even as I had no idea why. Watching all this with his eyebrows raised so high they almost merged with his hair, Maxime ran toward us at Harmin's command. They spoke in English. Whatever it was Harmin said, Maxime was also soon bowing down in front of me and kissing my hands. When they later explained, I laughed so hard I almost fell out of my seat.

It was really very simple. Nothing to be confused about. I, twelve years old at the time, was a child shaman who was the spiritual guide to every trafficker in the Aegean! That entire criminal network saw me as a demigod and never set sail without receiving my blessings.

When Maxime asked, "Fine, but how'd he know we would be at this cove?" Harmin went as far as to reply, "He knows everything! His eyes see all."

At that, thinking he'd fallen into a paradise of *deranged criminals* just like the one he'd imagined, Maxine bowed down with great reverence and kissed my hands . . . but there was a problem. The child shaman wasn't going to allow filming. Nothing could be done if he didn't allow it. Maxine desperately asked if there was anything that could be done to persuade me. Dordor turned to me and asked:

"Do you remember that story you wrote?"

I could, since I'd only ever written one in my life!

"Yeah?"

"There, that's what we're gonna shoot now!"

"How?"

"We're making a movie! We'll adapt your story! And you'll be in it!"

Dordor's voice was all around me in that pitch-black hole. My eyes filled with tears as I heard it and I kept on remembering.

"It's your birthday, kiddo!" Harmin was saying. "This is your present! You're gonna have a movie! Now how do you like that?"

I liked it a lot, of course! I was ecstatic!

"Don't let on, now, stop grinning!" said Harmin.

I frowned, but I couldn't keep still. The only way to convince the child shaman to allow filming was to shoot a film for him! When Maxime heard this, he was momentarily at a loss for words, but then must have pictured himself on stage at a large hall being applauded because he said, "Okay!"

Actually, this whole thing about a present, that is, making a film for me, had occurred to Harmin as he'd watched Maxime . . . the exact instant he'd puffed on his weed, watching Maxime thrashing around in the sea in hopes of being able to swim away . . . this is what Harmin had thought: "So if Gaza likes stories so much, why not give him one? In fact, why not film it and let this guy do it? If he's as well acquainted with cameras as he appears to be, that is!" Then he'd made up that lie about the documentary to find out if Maxime really could use all the equipment needed for shooting, and then said, "All right! Fantastic!" In the time it takes to smoke one joint, he'd come up with both the idea for the film as a present and decided who would direct it. The sea air really did clear one's mind!

214

But there was a problem with my story. A location problem . . . My story was so simple that we could actually start shooting right away. In fact, it was so silly that Maxine could have taken it for contemporary art and marketed it as video art elsewhere. But unfortunately the story took place in Cappadocia. A boy rented a hot air balloon and took a tour of the area like an ordinary tourist. But soon he accosted the man who operated the balloon by a knife to his throat, saying, "Let's go!" Basically the boy hijacked the balloon.

But then of course the man said, "Where are we going?"

And the boy looked pensively into the distance and said, "I don't know . . . wherever it is we'll happen to fall!" and the story ended. I'd never seen Cappadocia. All I'd seen was a picture in the paper. A photo in which dozens of balloons hovered over the fairy chimneys[4] . . . but we weren't in Cappadocia and there was no way of getting our hands on a balloon!

So Harmin said, "Write the rest! Think!"

"Okay," I said. "Here's what we do then . . . The boy travels all the way here, and the balloon falls somewhere around here! You can be the balloon guy! Let's say the boy and the balloon guy befriended each other on the way."

"Nice!" said Harmin. "Then?"

For a while I thought with my hand on my chin and then blurted out all the nonsense brewing in my head.

"Then Dordor shows up! He's the owner of the balloon! He has a guy with him, maybe. They followed us and want their balloon back. They're searching for us in the woods. Then one day . . ."

I was out of batteries.

"What, one day?" asked Harmin. "What happens one day?"

---

4  Naturally formed volcanic rock pillars in central Anatolia, used as cave dwellings in 7 AD by persecuted Christians, a major tourist attraction in present-day Turkey.

Right then I thought of Harmin's boat. And all those illegal immigrants . . .

"One day, they run into each other in the woods and start talking. So the two parties sit down and talk. The owner of the balloon figures out that the balloon is no longer, that it's damaged. He's really upset. The boy says that he shouldn't be upset because if they pick up the journey where it was left off, all together, he'll forget everything and all his troubles will be over. The man is so impressed that the four of them join forces and hijack a boat to set out to sea. How's that?"

"Incredible!" said Harmin. "Perfect!"

But of course I was just getting started!

"Then they meet other people and persuade them to join the journey. And all together they hijack a plane. Then they find a bunch of other people and join them as well. In fact, they keep joining everyone they run into so finally they're millions and they keep moving. The journey never ends! No one stops! They just keep going. Then everyone in the world joins them, and billions of people carry on with the journey side by side. There's no problem because they're all going in the same direction. And since they all have one goal, just to keep going, they don't even fight or war among themselves! Just think of it, billions of people, side by side, walking in the same direction!"

Harmin, for whom all this was conjured up as much as it was for me, asked:

"So where are they going?"

"They're all going somewhere else!"

"I thought they were all side by side, going in the same direction?"

"They are! They're all walking side by side! But of course in the end they die. Because they're traveling all their lives. That's why they're all going to a different place. Wherever they're supposed to die, that's where they're going!"

Laughing, Harmin hugged me . . . then, saying, "Okay, for now, let's just shoot the part up to the boat. The rest you can do when you're grown!" he'd called Maxine.

And so we shot the film . . . We shot in a single day the forest confrontation and boat hijacking scenes of that story of a colossal journey starting with a boy's leaving and going on to encompass all humankind. At the end Maxime handed me a tape and said the only Turkish word he'd learned all day:

"*Tamam?*"

"*Tamam!*" I said.

And Maxime turned to look at Harmin. It was time to start the documentary. Harmin nodded at him and turned to me.

"Go on," he said, "straight home! Dordor will drop you off. Happy birthday!"

On the way back, I couldn't get an answer out of Dordor about what was to happen to Maxime no matter how many times I asked. Some months later, however, I found out from Harmin as he was ranting at the stars: they'd sent Maxime back where he'd come from. Not to France but to Iraq. They'd tied the man up and stuck him in a sixteen-wheeler and never seen him again. When I asked if that meant he'd been killed, Harmin had replied, "No. He's probably been *traded off* . . ."

"What does that mean?" I'd asked and he'd told me.

The ones who had an estimable citizenship and profession, such as Maxime, were taken to the hostage market in the Middle East to be sold. The place referred to as the tradeoff hostage market was probably a reservoir somewhere off the map, just like ours. In that reservoir would have been people from all the capes stuck into the Middle East like noses. Germans, Brits, Frenchmen, and Americans were the most popular, needless to say. Then some organization would show up and buy someone from the hostage market to blackmail whatever state the hostage was a citizen of.

This way, an organization that had a beef with say, France, would declare that they held a French citizen and journalist and start reeling off their demands. In a market that was set up to supply hostages for this kind of tradeoff, journalists in particular were extremely valuable. As a matter of fact, rates in the hostage market were in constant flux just like they were in the stock market in relation to changes in international politics, but some citizenships' worth never decreased. Such as American citizenship . . .

However, the one thing that could really turn this market on its head was an Israeli hostage! Now that was an extraordinarily valuable tradeoff! A true gem! In fact, it was such a gem that in return for a single Israeli citizen—and even more preferable if it was a soldier—it would be possible to have fifteen hundred Palestinian captives returned. Fifteen hundred lives in return for one! But then it was the Israelis' problem what to do with that life, of course. For once his life had such a high value, he had foregone his right to go into depression or become a pacifist!

Just as a boy, and it could have been me, who had been sent to the city for an education by an entire eagerly expectant town that had raised money for that purpose no longer had the right to play hooky, so the Israeli no longer had the luxury of becoming an alcoholic, becoming sick because he didn't take care of himself, protesting against a single governmental decision, or in broader terms, wasting his life away. After all, if your life equaled 1,500 lives, you couldn't even consider suicide.

Though he was no Israeli soldier, as a journalist whose market worth was nothing you could turn your nose up at, who knows where Maxime was now? Maybe no buyer had yet showed up, and he was still waiting at the hostage market. Maybe the French state had already conducted a clandestine bargain and pulled their citizen out to Paris . . . I'd never know. I hope he's fine, I thought.

Then I opened my eyes and rewatched my film . . . not the one on tape. For at first I wasn't able watch the film that was on tape, although I'd been squirming with curiosity. Nor had I been able to go into the city or ask someone to help. Dordor and Harmin were staying in Greece for a while. So they weren't able to help, either. Then I'd discovered something. The existence of another film!

Whenever I picked the tape up, the day of the shooting would unravel in front of my eyes, and I was able to watch everything we did frame by frame, even to pause or rewind or fast forward it. It got so that after a while, I didn't even have to touch or look at the tape. Lowering my eyelids like a pair of tiny silver screens, I could watch the movie whenever I wanted. The more time that passed, the less I cared about what was on the tape. I even thought that maybe not seeing it would be for the best. After all, the movie that circled around in my head didn't have a single flaw. That was the way I preferred to remember it. And every time I did, I thanked them all. Dordor, Harmin, Maxime, the burglars, all of them . . .

Neither movie on the tape nor the one in my head had titles. Even my story didn't have a title. Well, now seemed like a good time to find one. But right then I felt something rubbing against my left hand.

I was so startled that I tore off the shawl wrapped around my face and flicked the lighter to see what was touching me. And saw them . . . hundreds of larvae packed inside a hole they'd carved into a bare back just to my left. Gathered into a mass, they were tearing into that back. Some of them slid off and rolled toward me.

Then I looked to my right. And saw that a leg there was in the same state. I started to scream. I tried to lift the body to my back and place it to my left. However, since its legs were wedged between the rock and other bodies, it wouldn't budge. There was nothing I could do. I started to grab up as many clothes and as much fabric as I could. I yanked off everything I could grab hold of. The same larvae emerged from underneath every piece of fabric. They were eating holes into every body they could get at and squirming around as they feasted.

I began wrapping myself up. My feet, legs, torso, arms, neck . . . I assumed that was the only way I'd be able to protect myself. Maybe they wouldn't touch me but eat through all the bodies around me, clearing my way to escape. But I wasn't in any state to think about that now. I was so horrified by what I'd seen that my only defense was wrapping myself in fabrics like a mummy. Screaming as I did! The only parts left exposed were my hands and face. I left a sliver open in the shawl near my eyes and mouth as I wrapped it tightly around my head, and then stopped. I had to do something about my hands. So that nothing could get at me. Neither those larvae, nor anything else. At that moment, if I could have, I'd have chopped off my hands just because they were exposed. For there wasn't a single shred of fabric left behind that I could use.

I wept. With every thought of the possibility of something, dead or alive, touching me, my heart tried to climb out of my mouth and, being unable, lodged in my throat and choked me. All I could do was flail my hands. So that not a single fly could land on them, nor anything touch them.

I couldn't stay in the dark any longer. I had to see everything so I could shield myself. But that was impossible. I had to quit flailing and flick the lighter to be able to do that. I couldn't. I just kept flailing. A while later I sensed that I was able to see into the darkness. For now I knew everything. I could see where the larvae accumulated and carved holes on each body and hear the sounds they made as they did. I could hear and see every single thing. Neither the darkness nor the fabric stuffed up my nose could prevent it.

220

Because I could smell them too. All five senses had opened like floodgates, drenching me in life. I could also see my hands that I held at chest level, waving at the ends of my wrists like five-fingered corpses. There was nowhere to run. Even the darkness was no longer safe because I could see everything I shouldn't have to see as sharply as though I were some nocturnal animal. I could see them with my eyes closed. It was as if my eyelids had been punctured!

I held my breath in final desperation. So that maybe I might calm down. That didn't work either. So I tried again. Perhaps I just needed to hold it longer. At least that's what I thought. I started counting the seconds. Not being able to hold out longer, I released my breath, then took another and held that in. I counted! Then released again. Held it. Counted. Repeated for maybe an hour. At the same time I kept flailing continuously. Finally, a white spot appeared in front of my eyes. And it all happened at once. First the spot expanded into a snow-white screen, engulfing me like a fishnet thrown on top of me, trapping me.

That was when my pulse slowed down, and I opened my eyes. I was in a tunnel. A tunnel with brownish-pink walls. I was inside my bowels! Then everything was white again, and I opened my eyes on a million lines.

They were reminiscent of the white lines appearing on a pitch-black sky when lightning struck. A thousand of them flashed out of the same kernel and into a thousand other kernels. A thousand lines in turn flashed out of those kernels and scattered to other kernels. I was watching a gigantic cobweb that contained a million centers. What was more, it was three-dimensional. I was inside my brain. Inside a nerve cell . . . I didn't have to put this into words to be aware of it. I just knew that I was there. I could go anywhere inside my body. It wasn't actually moving. I was already inside the body. All I had to do was focus on a part of it and open my eyes, and whichever part of my body it was I wished to see materialized in front of me. It didn't surprise me one bit. It felt natural that I should be able to see inside my body. As if it were something every creature on the face of the Earth was able to do at will, to watch the blood flow through their veins . . .

On that day, I wanted so badly to get away from the bodies around me and the larvae tearing them apart that I hid inside my body for lack of anywhere else to run and could see everything when I opened my eyes. It wasn't a hallucination. For up until that day, I hadn't even known that the tissues and organs I saw inside my body even existed. I knew neither their names nor their functions nor their forms. It couldn't have been my imagination because I didn't know about them. Still I was able to see them all. In fact, years later when I got interested in human anatomy, the first images I looked at weren't unfamiliar to me at all. Because that day, I closed my eyes to the outside world and opened them on the inside. I was the biggest proof that one could have complete awareness of oneself and one's body. It was all a matter of breathing. My prize from a breathing game I'd discovered by chance. A prize that enabled me to feel and see every corner of my body from my internal organs to my very cells . . . and I hadn't had to look at the watch. I could hear the seconds go by like my second pulse and count the minutes and hours with no difficulty at all. Neither I nor my story nor my movie needed a title. I *was* time . . .

I was inside my body for approximately two hundred hours. I spent those thousands of minutes studying my liver, bones, stomach acids, and everything else that was underneath my skin. I flowed through my bloodstream, pounded inside my heart, and dissolved along with my fat and then my muscles because I hadn't had anything to eat.

In my 317th hour underneath the bodies, I felt hands roaming over me and only then came outside of my skin. I was on a stretcher when they undid the shawl wrapped around my face. It was the first time I had seen daylight in thirteen days and five hours.

Admittedly with difficulty, I managed to mumble that someone else might be alive under the wreck. Though I hadn't heard the voice in a long time, I tried to explain how I'd heard someone yell, "More!" for hours, maybe days.

"Get him out as well," I said. "Get *More* out as well!"

But they didn't listen to me. The faces, which I couldn't make out because they blended into the crystalline rays of the sun, would not answer. They merely carried me. Still, I obstinately repeated the one word that was on my mind, "More!" until I passed out. But they just wouldn't get it . . . Neither whispering nor hollering it did any good. My bearers remained forever silent. But I tried! I said the word any way it was possible to say it. I even said it backward in case the world had turned upside down in my absence: "*Ahad!*"[5]

---

5   *Ahad* is *daha* backward, Turkish for *more*.

I heard voices. One smooth, the other hoarse. One young, the other old. The younger was asking:

"What do we do about the chief of police?"

"We need him. Don't get him involved. Let the mayor handle it. The gendarmerie, too. Tell the prosecutor, we don't need anyone implicated in this."

"They've sent in journalists from all over. The entire lawn is filled with cameras . . . We have to make a statement."

"Just say that an inquiry is under way and get on with it. Try to focus more on the kid instead. They won't touch the rest with him in the picture. All that time, without food or water . . . a miracle. That's what you say. Say it's God's miracle. Give their faith a kick."

I opened my eyes slightly, and from what I could see between my eyelashes, I was in a hospital room. There was an IV in my right arm. I counted four fat drops falling out of a glass bottle into a small, transparent box and from there into a slim pipe to mix into my blood. Then I turned my head in the direction of the voices and saw, through an open door, into the neighboring room. The owner of the elderly voice sat on the bed while his younger counterpart stood by. I could also see their faces. And I knew I'd seen them somewhere. I shut my eyes again just as the one standing turned his head to look at me. I let my eyelids drop and looked into the darkness and the photo that developed there. I'd figured out who they were: the governor and his errand boy . . . as sure as I was that I didn't resemble anyone that could hear, lying there, they lowered their voices and started to whisper. I could no longer hear them.

I once again watched them with my eyes open a sliver, just enough that my eyelashes were still touching, when I felt that something was off. The old man and the young man seemed to have switched places. As if they'd traded identities. The errand boy had become the governor and the governor was committing orders to memory just as though he were an errand boy . . . but I remembered them both so clearly. I even remembered their exact stances, and even who was looking at whom, in that picture in the newspaper *From Kandalı to the World*. Yet what I was looking at from that hospital bed was telling me the exact opposite. Was it possible that I was this confused? I didn't think so. Still it was enough to make me doubt everything I knew.

The young man stooped in front of the old one, nodding as he listened. Was it possible that I was misremembering my whole life? Even worse than that, did I seem to have everything backward inside my head? Could there be a world in which the errand boy was really the governor? If there were, did that mean Ender was Yadigar's father? Or was it me who was Ahad? My heart picked up speed as I started to sweat.

It can't be, I said to myself. I can't be this far gone! But what if it is? No, no! I told myself I remembered correctly. I was just about to persuade myself when I saw the young man whom I knew to be the governor kiss the old man's hand. There wasn't a *bayram*[6] coming up anytime soon. I was sure it wasn't the morning of one, either. I no longer had any cause for doubt. Spending 317 hours in that hellhole had caused me to lose my mind. I started to weep. To scream . . . I started to swing my head this way and that and into whatever I could. A nurse, then an aide, came running. One held my shoulder while the other gave me a shot. Everything went dark as my voice went silent. I still didn't stop screaming. Inside the darkness that enveloped me, I screamed and threw myself against walls, but everyone thought I was asleep.

When I opened my eyes again, Ender was sitting next to me. Or someone whom I thought was Ender. I reached over to grab his arm and yelled:

"Ender! Is that you? You're Ender, right?"

He laughed. "Are you nuts, man, it's me!"

"But the governor?"

"What about the governor?"

I told him. The things I'd seen and heard. When I got to the part about his father with the "let the gendarmerie handle it," I skipped it.

But the more I told, the more Ender laughed. Then he said, "What's not to get?" and this time the more he told me, the more I laughed.

Indeed, the more assured I was that I hadn't gone crazy, the more I laughed! It was actually all very simple. Yadigar had told his son and that's how he knew. The governor and the errand boy belonged to the same cult. A cult formed by former members of the cult we all knew as Hakeem. It was called Tanzim. The old man was Tanzim's Kandalı chapter. That is, the cult's

---

6  A religious holiday or feast, on the first day of which relatives and officials alike visit each other and pay their respects to their elders in the form of hand-kissing and pleasantries.

regional executive. Be it a town or a city, Tanzim had a chapter in every region it was able to reach. As it was, it was perfectly natural that the young governor, a regular disciple, would show deference to the Kandalı chapter. He was at the service of that old man before the governor or anyone else. I could see now. Especially why the old man hadn't moved a muscle during the watch ceremony in the government office. It wasn't as if Tanzim's Kandalı chapter was going to go around dusting furniture or serving tea. He was a general in a private's uniform. It had all come to light.

More importantly, I definitely wasn't crazy. More accurately, I wasn't the one who was! Hearing that Kandalı was run not by the civil administrator in chief but his janitor had an elating effect on me. I almost got up to hug Ender.

Right then a nurse checked my IV and asked, "How are you feeling?"

I almost blurted out, "Perfect!" I said instead, "I don't know . . . OK, I guess."

The nurse smiled and left the room. It seemed as though she had other patients to check on right away. Was there another survivor? Was I just confused, as I was wont to be? Right then I thought of Ahad. Or more precisely, it was as if one of those bodies fell right onto my forehead and crushed everything underneath. Could it be that he wasn't dead? I had to find out as soon as I could. I had to be sure I'd never see his face again for as long as I lived.

"Ender . . . my father?"

"I'm sorry," he said. "They found him in the truck . . ."

I closed my eyes, and my temples moistened. Two enormous teardrops rolled through my hair and behind my ears into the pillow my head was resting on. For the first time in my life, I was weeping with joy. In fact, right then, I pictured myself walking into a courtroom the day I turned eighteen and changing my year of birth. With this piece of news, I knew I was born again.

Meanwhile Ender, cheating off similar scenes in the movies he'd seen, grimly gripped my arm.

When I opened my eyes once more, so many questions crowded my mind that I didn't know how to begin. Above all else, what was to become of me? Would I be thrown in jail for smuggling? How was it that those bodies had rained on me and how was I rescued? I opened my mouth to start with whichever one, and the governor came into the room with the mayor. Yadigar followed them. The former smiled, while Yadigar showed his clenched teeth in the pretense of smiling.

The governor put his hand on my shoulder and said, "May you have a swift recovery! Allah has bestowed you to us."

Though I was sure I hadn't been bestowed to *them*, I thanked him anyway.

Right then I noticed Ender and Yadigar looking at each other and appearing to try to communicate with their eyes. Perhaps Yadigar had told his son everything and hoped to pry the facts out of me through Ender. After all, Ender was the closest likeness to a friend out of everyone I knew. That was the title by which he'd been able to come into my room and wait by my bedside so he could find out everything I knew as soon as I woke. I was Ahad's son, after all, and what I knew could have dangerous repercussions for Yadigar in particular. Still, none of this held any importance for me at that stage. It wouldn't be very smart to bring up prison, though. No one was looking at me as if I was going to jail anyway. Quite the contrary, it seemed more like they were looking at an earthquake survivor rescued from rubble weeks later. For the moment I could make do with just hearing about my rescue. And so the governor recounted.

A shepherd had been the first to see the truck and the pile of bodies on the slope. He'd gone to the gendarmerie as soon as he'd seen it. I could imagine the rest. Yadigar, who had called us for days in vain after finding out through Aruz that the goods were never delivered, must have rushed to the site of the accident. Seeing that we were too much of a scandal to sweep under the rug, he'd had to inform everybody. In a short period of time, all of Kandalı, from public prosecutors to the mayor, were gathered around the bodies. So how was it that I'd been pelted by them?

The governor glanced at Yadigar and reluctantly took over. There wasn't actually much he could say. Judging by the tracks on the slope, he and the prosecutor had worked on an analogous chain of events for the report. According to that, the truck had veered off the road over the edge and turned over almost completely when it crashed into a large crag to its right. That was when my door sprang open, flinging me out. As the truck tumbled down the hillside, I'd tumbled down similarly to end up underneath the rock. Where they'd found me, in the end, was about fifty meters below the road. It had been due to sheer luck that I hadn't hit any rocks on my way down, just trees and patches of mud. I'd come away from a fall that should have broken all my bones with only the hundreds of scratches all over me.

Meanwhile the truck had been sliding along like a turtle on its back, coming to a stop about twenty meters from where I'd fallen, suspended over the trees and crags. According to Yadigar, the cab was pointing in the direction of the road its tires had just parted from, that is to say, the summit of Kandağ. My father, his chest crushed by the wheel he was wedged behind, died on the spot. It wasn't hard to guess the rest. In the back, suspended at almost forty-five degrees inside the truck anchored parallel to the slope, the immigrants, dead from crashing into the steel walls and one another, slipped out through the slide below them and piled up against the doors. The lock holding the two wings together was unable to withstand the pressure, setting forth the hail of people that pelted me. They rained on me from twenty meters up and trapped me in them. A final particular was that there'd been no skid marks on the road.

"The rain must have washed them away," said Yadigar.

I added inwardly, "*If* he actually stepped on the brakes . . ."

Right then the prosecutor came in and told the governor that he'd like to get my statement. The governor, however, replied, "Not now. Let the child rest. You can take care of it later. We should be going too . . ." As he herded everyone out and pulled the door shut, he winked at me.

Did he mean to tell me something? Quite possibly. Did I know what he meant to tell me? No. But how bad could the implications of a wink be? This is it, I said to myself. This is it! It's all over. No one is holding me responsible. Ahad is the only criminal here. And perhaps also Yadigar. None of this has anything to do with me. I'm the wretched fifteen-year-old son of a villainous, criminal father. The subtext of my defense hadn't really changed much since that holding cell Yadigar had shut me up in. I was a victim, and no one could say otherwise. In fact, I was so much a victim that I could get away with murdering anyone that dared say otherwise!

Everything was fine . . . I even had a TV! I must be in the most luxurious room of the hospital. I turned the TV on with the remote I took off the bedside table. Everything was fantastic . . . I flipped through the channels. That was when I saw an explosion. A huge explosion! I saw two gigantic statues carved into the almost yellow, wall-like side of an enormous crag, crumble into a cloud of dust. I knew those statues. I knew them well. As soon as I saw it, I knew! I'd carried them around in my pocket for years. Carried on the back of my paper frog . . . I turned up the volume and listened.

"A week has passed since the Taliban forces gained control of the Hazarajat region of Afghanistan and dynamited the giant statues known as the Buddhas of Bamiyan. The United Nations . . ."

I can't say why, but I thought I might drown in what I'd seen and heard. My thumb sought the button on the remote. When I couldn't find it, I grabbed it with both hands and pressed all the buttons at once, turning off the TV. Everything stopped. Even the drops coming through my IV stopped! First I thought of Cuma. Before all else, him . . . then I thought of how unfair I'd been when he'd shown me the picture he'd made and I hadn't believed him, thinking he was just making fun of me. Maybe that was why I turned the TV off. Because I didn't want to have to look the truth in the eye any longer . . . because I was ashamed of myself . . . but there they were! Just like Cuma had drawn them! Those two gigantic statues had really existed and that meant Cuma's home had been there too. But I'd missed out on the statues. They'd been blown up and become property of the past via a cloud of dust. I hadn't made it there in time! Could they have torn down Cuma's home as well? I thought of myself and the bodies that had fastened me onto the earth's surface. Those two statues had been demolished during the very days I'd been crushed underneath them. Me and those two Buddhas, we'd crumbled into the earth together. So far apart, yet simultaneously . . . If it was still standing, that was where Cuma's home was! Somewhere there!

"I'm sorry," I said. Thinking he might be able to hear. "I'm sorry I didn't believe you!"

But Cuma wouldn't speak to me. Instead, in the place where I should have been hearing his voice, inside my very head, an ache rose like a black sun. It suddenly rose over all my horizons! It filled my head in a deluge and swept down my neck to spread over my shoulders first, then my chest. I was having the first of the many pain spells I would never stop having. I screamed and screamed! Instead of Cuma's voice, my own came out.

The nurse came and saw me shaking. The bulb she broke to draw into the syringe in her hand read *Diazem*. But I needed something else! The only thing that could stop the downpour of pain suffocating me. The only thing that could fill the void left by Cuma's absent voice and help me take enough of a breath to be able to pass out. Just as those two statues had been dynamited, so it was the only thing that could destroy the pain inside me. We hadn't met yet, but the day would come . . . first letter morphine, last letter sulfate. We had the same birthplace: pain. For I was born not of my mother, but of labor pains. I'd been born not because I was wanted, but because I was in pain. I'd moved past spasms and aches to take my first breath. It had all left its mark on me. All those pangs and aches . . . I was covered in birthmarks all over. My insides, my outside, all over. As soon as I felt the morphine sulfate through my veins, I'd comprehend it all. I wasn't the son of a woman who birthed me by way of her own pain, no! I'd see that my real mother was the morphine sulfate that drew into itself all the pain I had. It wasn't long before I was adopted by an angel that came with a red prescription! When she came, I'd finally have a family too! And what a family:

The two Buddha statues that no longer existed,
Their shadows Dordor and Harmin, long dead before the statues,
An opiate known as morphine sulfate,
Cuma's voice, which I didn't know if I would hear again,
The void left by Felat, forever gone from my life, which he'd entered like a fifth season,
And me!

An extraordinary family! A perfect family! We even had a pet. It was a paper frog, but there it was!

The next day the prosecutor came into the room to collect my statement. Pulling up a chair to sit next to me, he eased into the conversation by saying, "My condolences. We've buried your father," then adding, "Those dead immigrants . . . We're working on identification . . . Is there anything you'd be able to tell us? I mean . . . maybe there was some list your father kept . . ."

"I don't know," I said. "I don't know anything. My father never told me anything. I wasn't allowed to go into a lot of parts of the house. Like I couldn't go into the shed. If there's anything, that's where it would be."

"We already looked there," he said. "We checked it out. We found the reservoir too . . . He was clearly keeping the people in there . . . We also found his computer."

A knot looped in my throat.

"Computer?"

"Yes . . . your father apparently monitored everything on it. He had cameras installed in the reservoir. Took a whole bunch of notes . . ."

Another knot looped over the other one. I swallowed but it didn't go away. In fact, it got even bigger. Right then the prosecutor asked, suddenly as though he'd just thought of it:

"You're that whatsit, aren't you? The kid who made top scores in the high school entrance exams? That was you, right?"

He wasn't a Kandalı local, after all. So he could remember facts correctly!

"Yes, but my father didn't send me anywhere," I said. "Anyway, he asked me to drop out of school as well. So I did. So my father had a computer, huh . . ."

Smiling, the prosecutor leaned in close and whispered.

"You're a very clever boy . . . but it's a nasty habit you've got. Underestimating other people's intelligence!"

The second he saw me draw a breath to reply, he touched my forehead with his index finger and continued, still whispering.

"You were found in a truck filled to the gills with illegal immigrants, do you realize that? So don't you dare tell me you don't know anything! I know that that prick Yadigar is in on this . . . Now a man is going to come in here. He's going to write down everything you say, and you know what you say? You say that your father was conspiring with Yadigar. You say that you saw the mayor coming to the house. You say that your father bribed them. Do you understand me?"

All the knots in my throat had come undone, and I was ready to rat everyone out.

"I'll say whatever you want me to!"

The prosecutor smiled again. "That you will. I've no doubt about it. What I'm actually interested in is what else *you* want to say!"

Could he have figured out that the files on the computer belonged to me and was just egging me on? The files were brimming with the evidence of the torture I'd inflicted on the reservoir dwellers! I didn't know what I was supposed to say. Would it to any good if I told the lie about my father putting out cigarettes on me? Or should I talk about Aruz?

"Well?" said the prosecutor. "Is there anything you want to say to me? Something I don't know?"

I couldn't hold it back any longer. I had to cry. I did cry.

"My father killed someone . . . Actually, he killed two people. One he buried in our backyard. The other, in the forest over near Derçisu. He said if I told, he would kill me too! So I couldn't tell anyone! I couldn't say a thing to anyone!"

Now that wasn't what the prosecutor expected! As a matter of fact, I existed to underestimate people's intelligence! Because I didn't care about anything and I was the secret champion of the fast chess tournament. And I had just returned from hell, too! No prosecutor on the face of the earth stood a chance against me. I wasn't the devil's advocate, I was the devil himself!

The prosecutor was only able to say, "Calm down," while at the same time shouting, "Nurse!"

Because I was shaking and crying and, with my remaining breaths, hollering, "Dad!" I was a local hero having a meltdown. I was sure my voice carried out the window of the room to the reporters on the lawn. I was the most interesting story to come out of Kandalı since the day it was established. In fact, even the largest news agencies of the world would take my story at face value. A boy emerging alive out of a pile of bodies! What prosecutor could presume to whisper me into a corner? I'd come from a place even worse than the Auschwitz I'd read about in books. Who cared if I was guilty or not? Even if I were guilty, a thirteen-day inferno had washed me clean of my sins. Nobody could touch me. Like that old man had said, I was a miracle! They'd covered up my mother with my father, but they wouldn't do the same to me. I'd have the last word in everything for as long as I lived!

They dug up the weakling first. I didn't feel anything. I only thought of Rastin and what he'd done. Then we went to Derçisu, and they dug up the spot I pointed to through my tears. It had been on my mind so often that I found the spot my father had dug years ago in one guess. How was I supposed to feel about remembering the site of a grave so accurately without a gravestone? Was there an emotion reserved for this type of situation? Or did one have to invent one? I could neither smell lavender nor see the trees around me. I merely waited as though it was my grave being dug and my body that would emerge shortly. I was a type of non-matter. And I had no intention of becoming matter . . . The remains of Cuma were take out piece by piece and put in a body bag. The sound of the zipper plunged into my stomach like a knife . . .

The next phase was the autopsies. They would be carried out on both the bodies. The Ankara embassy of Afghanistan, ailing from a form of cancer known as civil war, was in no state to deal with the problems of its dead citizens. It therefore looked like they would be buried in the cemetery at Kandalı after everything was over. That would mean that Cuma was to be buried in the place I was born. So what did that mean? Was there meaning to be found in these types of situations? Or did one have to invent one?

The prosecutor kept scratching his head and staring at me while all this went down. There was nothing he could say. He was aware of staring savagery in the face. More importantly, he'd grasped that this savagery was part of my daily life and was apparently starting to feel sorry for me. That was why the man who'd interrogated me in the hospital as if he would bite my face off was now replaced by someone I could almost call affectionate. He even finished off his questions with "that's OK if you don't remember." But I did!

"The one that you dug up from the yard, he beat to death. He suffocated the other one with a bag over his head."

When asked, "Do you know why he did it?" I'd reply, "Because of the women."

"If there was a woman he fancied, he'd forcibly take her out of the group and rape her. Naturally there were times someone would object . . . That's why he killed these two . . . At least as far as I know . . ."

I was talking about all that I did for years as though it had been my father who'd done it. It was true in a way. I couldn't be that far from Ahad genetically, right?

The prosecutor's eyes opened wide as he listened, his stomach rising and falling. "We can stop if you're tired," he'd say. But I knew it was he who was tired. I'd been let off from the hospital for the day. You could say I was all better. The mysterious ache hadn't stopped by again since then, and I didn't feel so bad at all.

On the way back, I saw the latest issue of *From Kandalı to the World* in the prosecutor's car and couldn't help laughing. On the front page was the photo of that watch ceremony in the governor's office. Yes, it was the same photograph, with only a small difference. There was a black strip over my eyes. I was mentioned only in my initials. The headline was "Villains!" The heads of the villains were circled in white so they wouldn't be confused with the others. Although there wasn't yet a ruling made in their case, in the paper's opinion the mayor, my father, and Sergeant Gendarme Yadigar, once a hero, were definitely guilty. The white circles around their heads resembled halos. It wasn't for nothing that that photograph had evoked *The Last Supper* for me! The bureaucratic and political world of Kandalı was quaking. It was highly probable that the newspaper archive didn't have another photo in which we were all together. So it must also have been due to a lack of means that the photo had been recycled. After all, the piece featured a paragraph on everyone in the frame, with the exception of the janitor. A statement from the governor, the opinion of the District Gendarmerie General, the Chief of Police's placations of, "Those responsible will be duly punished, lest anyone have any doubts!"; allegations of mistreatment at the gendarmerie headquarters concerning Yadigar, some dramatic words about me, curses circling around my father, and evidence, item by item, about why the mayor was the most incompetent local official in the world!

In fact, I only understood why they would involve the mayor when I read those lines. With the help of the old janitor's asides, I put two and two together and figured it all out. The mayor was not of the party that the sect named Tanzim supported, was all. Therefore there was no reason why he shouldn't be banished down to the core of the earth. Aside from that, had he really committed a crime? Possibly . . . in fact, if you ask me, everyone in the photo had everyone else's number. Some were guilty of keeping quiet, while others were guilty of being singularly involved. All in all, no one in that photo was really innocent. That photo had been taken after we'd had Jesus for supper! There the dogs were, lined up in the hospital lawn brandishing mikes and waiting eagerly to scrape the bones clean.

Passing through them, the prosecutor's car ground to a halt in front of the building when one of the dogs pounced at the window I was resting my head against. An aide came to open my door, and I climbed out. Right then a wave of pain the size of Kandağ poured on the back of my neck like glue and I collapsed onto my knees and one hand at the hospital entrance.

Cameras encircled me and the word spilled from my mouth, along with a lot of saliva, "Saliva!" I'd gone rabid instead of the dogs!

As the aide took my arm and pulled me to my feet, I glimpsed the eyes and raised eyebrows. The murmuring lips and the way they withdrew the mikes extended at me . . . There were no questions they could ask me. They could tell this wasn't anybody that could give them answers. All I'd done was trip and look at the saliva spilling into my hands before saying, "Saliva!" but that was sufficient in itself.

I was like a child raised by wolves to become one myself. I'd lived with corpses for thirteen days and become one too. Those corpses really had looked after me! They'd kept me from freezing, even fed me with the milk I'd suckled out of a dead tit. Now I had the look of one who was one of them. I had such a look the dogs all bowed their heads and their cameras and pulled away. I didn't quite have the *third-page news* vibe I was supposed to. I was nothing like what they were familiar with.

The news agencies, papers, and TV channels had sent all the wrong people to that hospital lawn. Only a war correspondent could hope to talk to me! I *was* a war and dead people came out of me! *The Physics of Living 101* . . . and not just any old war correspondent, I needed a civil war correspondent! Only they could take the annihilation of the two gigantic Buddha statues and the things I had to tell. None of the others could stomach it.

And they didn't! They shut off either their gaze or their cameras. Because they knew! I was a piece of news that had hell between the lines. Something readers would turn the page and TV audiences would change the channel at. So I needed to stay as merely a headline! Hell was only a word and needed to stay that way. The devil did not *hide* in the details! He lived there. The detail was his home. His address! It was hell! No one wanted to go there if they could help it. So the details were hidden away. We, all the news, were all just digests for one another, nothing more. A news digest! Someday someone would have to write a digest of this whole world to avoid boring anyone with unnecessary details.

"Good evening, ladies and gentlemen. According to a newsflash, people were born, lived, and died on a planet known as the Earth. Now, on to the next piece of news . . ."

I was to be placed in an orphanage in Istanbul and resume my studies. That was the governor's plan. As an orphaned boy who was supposed to be dead but had survived, he didn't want me living anywhere remotely near Kandalı. He thought I should be cast away. The sooner I, along with all the horrible things associated with me, was erased from memory, the better. Well, I'd be happy to be! It was no trouble at all. He kept glancing at the prosecutor next to him and then turning his head to address me.

"Put this all behind you!" he said. "There's a brand-new life awaiting you . . . and don't you neglect your studies. We believe in you! You'll grow up to be someone important, Gaza . . . If you ever need anything, we'll be right here . . ."

We were in the state office. Across from me, the prosecutor kept nodding in assent to all that was said. My statement had been in condemnation against Yadigar and the mayor just like he'd asked. Ender would've killed me if he knew, but the prosecutor promised me that the court would keep my identity confidential. Because I'd told him I was afraid. "I'm afraid they'd do me harm!" I didn't actually care . . . all I wanted to do was go home to collect my things and get on the bus that would take me to Istanbul. The governor stood first, then the prosecutor. Lastly, I did . . . We were done with one another. I had nothing more to ask of them, or they of me. I extended my hand. They preferred to draw me toward themselves and bump their temples against mine.[7] That was how the state and I parted ways. In a cloud of still-steaming-fresh negotiation and temples bumping . . .

When we left the room, I saw the Kandalı chapter sitting in an old chair. The old man had his eyes closed again. So not only photos but real life captured him that way too . . . Then I was introduced to a middle-aged man. He was a driver working for the governorship.

"This is Faik Bey . . . He'll take you to Istanbul."

Faik, not knowing what to say, was only able to blurt out his get-well wishes. He didn't look like he was looking forward to a long trip with the boy who'd been dug up from underneath corpses. But I was pretty sure he was getting expenses. The thought of that travel allowance must be keeping Faik sane. After all, working for the government was an art of survival. The only problem officials had was that they never knew what to do with the life they clung to with tooth and payroll. The memo on that had yet to come in . . .

The bus would depart in four hours. We left the building, and I climbed in the white car Faik pointed out. Rolling the window down, I took a last look at the Kandalı Government Office. I thought of the day I'd climbed up its front steps with my father and gone in, then left again with a watch on my wrist. A few seconds sufficed to run through the whole day. As for my whole life, I was finished recalling it by the time we turned into Dust Street.

---

7   Greeting Turkish nationalists prefer to the widespread greeting of kissing both cheeks.

I felt as if I'd been away for a century. In reality I'd stayed in the hospital for only eight days. The doctors had told me, "You're much better! Totally fine!" and discharged me that morning. So I'd only been away from the street, signpost erected by my own hands, for twenty-one days . . .

We ground to a stop in front of the house.

"I'll wait here," said Faik.

I got out of the car and, as I walked, took from my pocket the key the prosecutor had given me. I opened the door of the house and entered. I knew where we kept our only suitcase. Underneath my father's bed. Pulling it out, I carried it to my room and put it on my bed. I opened my closet and started to place my clothes in the suitcase. I was finally leaving! I was getting the fuck out of there! It was all over! No more Ahad, no more immigrants, and no more Kandalı! I was packing a suitcase for the first time in my life . . . It wasn't as hard as I expected, I thought. Neither leaving, not running away, nor disappearing, none of it . . .

My suitcase was ready. I went back in Ahad's room and opened the drawer of his bedside table. I found my mother's necklace and photograph as quickly as if I'd put them there myself. There was some money with them . . . I took it all and put it in my pockets.

I didn't wish to stay in the house any longer than that. Taking the suitcase, I walked to the door. Drawing my last breath within that house, I opened the door and saw Ender. He was standing next to the car, talking to Faik. Seeing me, he went silent and started walking toward me. I took the time to shut and lock the door. As I did I tried to calm myself by thinking that if he'd found out about my statement about his father, he'd run, not walk.

Ender walked right up to me and stopped an inch away from my nose, and something unexpected happened. Without a word, he wrapped his arms around me. I did not remember the last time someone hugged me. I didn't know what to do.

First I met Faik's eyes as he stood watching us. Then I looked away, but didn't have much of a choice of things to look at, as I couldn't move my head. My jaw planted on a foreign shoulder, I stood rooted in place. I'd inadvertently put the suitcase down to raise my head and hug Ender back. But standing silently poised like that felt so pointless I just wished more than anything that it would stop. More accurately, I was afraid my inhumane sentiments would be deciphered. I was especially wary of Faik being able to tell that I felt nothing in the face of such a friendly hug from another person. I don't know why, but I was wary. Maybe I was ashamed. So what was Ender doing right then? What was he looking at? I wished I could see his face. At least then I could imitate him! I met Faik's eyes again, and this time I had to lower my eyelids to avoid his gaze. Yes, this was better! Shutting your eyes during an embrace ought to make one look more genuine. But then I thought my tightly shut eyes made me look as if I were beside myself! As if I were being overly dramatic . . .

Those few minutes' worth of hugging seemed to stretch on for never-ending weeks. Finally Ender relaxed his arms, removed them from my back, and spoke.

"They've laid my father off . . . He's going on trial . . ."

What was I supposed to say?

"I know . . . The prosecutor threatened me. To get me to incriminate everyone . . ."

"Son of a bitch!" said Ender.

"But I didn't say a thing . . . He'd have put me in prison too if he could!"

"Son of a bitch," he said. Again . . .

"Yeah!" I said. "A total son of a bitch!"

Then Ender abruptly embraced me again to whisper this time. "I mean you're the son of a bitch, retard! I know you told them everything! I'm going to fuck you up!"

I tried to disentangle, but Ender held tight and continued to hiss into my ear:

"You're done! I'm going to do you in!"

He lowered his arms and stepped back.

"I swear I didn't tell them, Ender!"

Right then we heard Faik calling. "Kids, come on!"

"Hold on a minute!" I called. Then I whispered back at Ender, who was breathless with fury. "You can believe whatever you want to! But I never said anything to anyone!"

At this Ender licked his chapped lips before speaking. "Fine, if you say so . . . but don't you think about coming back here! I'm going to burn this house into the ground!"

"Be my fucking guest," I replied.

Then I walked off . . . I knew Ender watched me from where I'd left him on the front stoop. I could feel the weight of his glare on the nape of my neck and my back. Faik opened the trunk, and I put the suitcase inside. I got in the car.

"I can give your friend a ride if you'd like," said Faik.

"No," I said. "He has stuff to do . . ."

The car started and pointed in the direction of Dust Street. We were riding over that dust-covered fragment of a road my father had never bothered to have tarred. I saw Ender in the rearview mirror. Fists clenched, he stood like a scarecrow and his stance alone looked like it might blow the car up. He could burn the house all he wanted! I was never coming back to Kandalı. Never ever! Only the trees and a bit of sky were left in the mirror as Ender vanished. I never saw my childhood friend's face again.

Actually, no one saw Ender after the age of nineteen. He went to do his military duty and never returned. He was blown to pieces by a PKK landmine on the Süphan flatlands, somewhere near Felat's village. The land he stepped on let forth death . . . You could say he had his revenge on me, though. Just a week after

246

that seemingly endless embrace, I received word from Kandalı. It was the prosecutor.

"Someone burned your house down," he said. Then he asked: "Who do you think might have done it?"

"I don't know," I said. I'd made a principle of not turning in two members of the same family. It might very well be the only principle I had in life . . .

I could surmise that Ender never forgave me. He hated me until his last breath. Of course he knew I was one of the people that put his father in prison. It was Kandalı! Privacy wasn't a court order there, it was a tale. And I'm sure that for as long as he lived, Ender dreamed of killing me at first sight. But he'd gotten mixed up in another tale. In that tale Felat, who'd been turned over to the mountain guerrillas of the PKK by his father, put a landmine in Ender's path in order to save my life . . . As I said to Ender, believe whatever you want! In the end no one can fool you except for yourself. In the circumstances of the twenty-first century, that's better than nothing, right?

I was sixteen and Istanbul was excellent. My school was excellent. My dorm was excellent. My grades were excellent. Time was excellent. Life was excellent. The only trouble was with the word *excellent*. It was insufficient in conveying just how good I felt. Other than that, everything was excellent.

I was so used to the dorm Faik had delivered me to in person a year ago, it was like I'd spent my whole life there. Two floors had been arranged as the dorms, and two other floors had been designated for the common areas. Really, that was what every room without a bed was called: common area! The computer room, the TV room, study hall, hobby room, and other rooms . . . On a sign nailed to the wall next to door of each room was its respective name. In that building, every spot I happened to be in had a name. Even Istanbul had names: weekdays, weekends, and day trips. All this certainty and order enthralled me. There was no way of getting lost in this building. Even the toilets and showers were numbered. The space had been conquered by man and doled out evenly.

I was sharing with others for the first time in my life. This was quite a novelty for someone who'd spent years deciding the living conditions for strangers. Just a few seasons ago, I was the one dispensing while others shared. Now the dorm principal Azim did the dispensing, and I shared the dispensed with the other kids. Although I'd grown up on the *dispensing* end of this practice, it was an arrangement I was no stranger to. The only thing one had to do was to form good relations with the person with dispensing power. In fact, the stronger the relationship, the more advantageous the transaction! The dorm was a kind of reservoir after all. You had to keep close to the one running the reservoir . . .

Next to all this, time had also been split up into fastidious portions and turned into a volume of weekly programs. Every action had a starting and end time. On a board in the entrance floor were marked breakfast times, study hall, times allotted for the use of each common area, dinnertime, lights out, waking-up time, exit times, return times, and times for everything else, and on our wrists were watches with black plastic straps courtesy of Azim. Yes, I'd left the governor's time frame and entered Azim's. Time here was like a tamed predator. We were its only owners and it was magnificent! Neither space nor time had the smallest fissure or hole. Neither leaked a single drop to be lost in nothingness. They'd been designed with the utmost functionality, turning us, ages ranging from thirteen to eighteen, into life machines. We led a life as precise as a flawlessly manufactured time bomb.

Azim was highly impressed by my file that was forwarded to him by my school in Kandalı. As soon as Faik left, he'd said, "We're going to do great things, you and I!"

I completely misunderstood him at the time. It was also out of habit. After all, most of the adults I'd known until then had been absolute frauds. I thought Azim was looking for a partner in crime, just like my father had once. What Azim really meant was university. I was to finish high school with a top average after all! There was no need to go into it. The real concern was which university to go to and what kind of academic education I was to receive. I was in complete agreement with Azim! Our meeting was that of a naturally born champion and the trainer who'd waited for that athlete his whole life. It was ambition at first sight!

Unfortunately I'd arrived midterm and wouldn't be able to start school right away. It would be unacceptable, however, for me to do nothing. Azim immediately found a sponsor to help pay for language courses for me, saying, "You're to learn English!"

Just when I started going to the classes, fourteen hours a week, he turned up with a retired high school teacher, this time saying, "You're to study mathematics." In the meantime he enrolled me in chess club and said, "I'm expecting you to place at worst third in the first tournament!"

And I did everything Azim said. It was all so soothing and kept me so occupied that I thought neither of the darkness I'd come out of or those bodies. It didn't even enter my mind. It was forgotten. Actually, it had been wiped clean the moment I stepped in the dormitory. I never even dreamed of those faces. I dreamed of other things. Dreams about the future. Dreams about chess, about college, about books and the Gaza I would become . . .

There was just the one night when rather than all this, I dreamed of myself coughing. Then a key appeared in the palm of my hand. A small black key. I recognized the damp key in my hand.

"This is the key to a safe," I said in the dream. "The key to the safe in my mind. Everything about my past is in that safe. It's all locked up in there. That's why I remember none of it. And since I don't happen to have a sea inside to toss this key into, I threw it up . . . Nothing to worry about . . . go back to sleep . . ."

It was actually a dream of reason. It was an attempt at rationalizing my being able to avoid remembering a hundred times a day all the hells I'd traveled through. I didn't remember because I didn't want to remember. I didn't remember because I was strong enough not to. It was the kind of strength that made my past and memories subordinate to only me. Most importantly, the horrendous ache that had assailed me several times in the hospital seemed to have left me for good. It, too, appeared to be subordinate to me. I'd banished the ache and it had fucked off. That was as it should be! Because in just the same way, I would bring my future to its knees before me and do whatever I asked of myself! With the support of Azim, naturally. I couldn't do it without him. My only link with the external world was Azim. At the moment, he was the navigator of the gondola that would take me into the future.

He worked me so hard during the period until school started that my rebirth, which started the moment I found out my father was dead, continued prodigiously thanks to my ever-learning, ever-expanding mind. I no longer attacked the pages of every book I came across the way I used to. I only attended to the ones I needed to read, to preserve time. Azim made me the library attendant. Actually, since the other kids went to school, leaving me by myself in the building, I'd become responsible for everything.

My days passed in a flurry of cleaning, tidying up, going to English class, and following the study schedule Azim prepared for me. For instance, I washed the toilets and showers for an hour, then studied math for an hour. Or I sorted and labeled the books donated to the library, then read up on history or philosophy. Azim thought I ought to especially read Plato. I was reading the Dialogues he'd given me as a present. I also had to finish at least two novels per week and write summaries to leave on Azim's desk. I had almost no free time at all. I worked all the time. I was either reading or writing or attending to the building.

One of the rare intervals I was able to give my mind was after lunch. I sat with Azim after I brought his coffee to his office and played chess with him. He wasn't as good at it as I was. So I was able to think of other things or look around the room as I waited for his move. Photos of his kids and wife, awards in a glass cabinet, certificates on the wall, and more photos of his kids . . . He had two daughters. They were both students at the university. But Azim never talked about his family. He never brought it up, as though those were mock photos he'd bought along with the frames. Azim and I talked of other things. We conversed about the future, about knowledge, the books I read, life, and discipline. After all, Azim was a discipline counter. A *discipline-o-meter* . . . Sometimes I got the impression that he even knew the number of words that came out of his mouth. Discipline, rather than his spine, was what kept him upright. Discipline, a selection of words and most often silence . . . the distance between us was both far and close. We were intimate as father and son and complete strangers at the same time . . . Sometimes we didn't talk at all . . . I'd merely enter and exit his room. Sometimes Azim called after me as I was leaving:

"Gaza?"

"Yes, sir," I'd say.

"Are you alright?"

"I'm fine . . ."

"Are you sure?"

"Yes."

"Good . . ."

I started school nearly seven months after my arrival at the dormitory. It was a mediocre school with utterly incompetent teachers and a bunch of idiots for students. Even so it was perfect for me, since it was clear from day one that I'd be top of my class. Azim even said, "Just bear it for the year and then we can arrange a scholarship." He was true to his word. The following year I was enrolled on scholarship in a private school with a tuition that could take at least eight illegal immigrants from Dushanbe to London.

And so at seventeen I found myself in a place the children of the wealthiest families of my country of birth were schooled. The kids here were even stupider. I had no difficulty surpassing them all to become the pride of the school, the crest of which I carried on my uniform. To boot, I had neither mother nor father. This made me an even more touching spectacle in the eyes of my teachers. Moreover, I had nothing more in my pockets than a meager allowance from Azim and a paper frog. I could neither go skiing in Kitzbühel in the winter, like the other kids, nor be grudgingly dragged into the New York Metropolitan Museum by my parents in the summer. The indisputable reality was that my existence in the school raised the average intelligence and perception curve. We, myself and everyone else, expected much from Gaza! Azim most of all . . .

I saw less of him now that I was in my second year in the dorm. Our chess sessions had waned to once per week. On Friday evenings, right before Azim departed from the dorm to go home, we'd meet in his room and make up for all that was left unfinished in that one hour. Most of the kids in the dormitory were deathly jealous of me, but there was nothing they could do about it. There was nothing I could do for them, either. I just helped them out twice a week in study hall with the classes they struggled with, hoping that would atone me for the discrepancy in privilege between us. They were all worrying about what they would do once they turned eighteen and had to leave the dorm to face real life. Actually they could submit a plea to the administration and stay in the dorm until the age of twenty-five, given that they got into university. However, none of them had such plans. All they wanted was that their current lives freeze into a chunk of ice and stay that way forever. Some of them even lost sleep over this and secretly cried at night.

I'd been staying in a four-person room since I'd arrived in the dorm. I'd been with the same boys for the past two years:

Rauf, Derman, and Ömer. Like their peers, the three of them had common interests: girls. Before bedtime they always wove shared fantasies concerning sexuality before they could close their eyes. None of them had ever touched a woman and eagerly waited for that day to arrive while at the same time hoping they would never grow up. For them, becoming adults meant a full sack of loneliness and disaster. Of course I never told them anything about my past. I definitely didn't mention my various sexual encounters with the dead and the living. For them I was nothing more than a roommate they could trust because I didn't steal their money or blab their secrets. I didn't wish to be anything more anyway.

All my relationships with the people I knew from the dorm or school consisted of temporary engagements much like the wheels of a clockwork with one another. Everything about my life was merely functional. All those people I greeted, who knew me by name, were no more significant to me than my shoelaces. Everything had a function, that was all. And mostly the same function at that. I made small talk with them and they left me alone. I knew that not communicating at all would raise question marks and only make my life more difficult. I was fixated on the future. Unlike my roommates, the things I feared were behind me, not ahead. My relations with my schoolmates weren't much different.

Although up to a point the vague devilishness and pair of pale blue eyes I inherited from Ahad made me piquant for the girls in my grade, I knew they mostly thought I was just an irritating asshole. I was pretty sure their families compared them to me with each low grade they brought home. "You have everything, and look at Gaza! The boy is all alone in the world! Yet look how successful he is!" They must be hearing this all the time.

In turn, as they nodded at their parents, they were surely imploring inwardly, "I wish you would just die so I could be an orphan like Gaza!"

Actually, I thought they were assholes too. At least technically. Although every once in a while, I did see their mothers. And their fathers. They would come by the school. What could it be that enabled the ugliest animal of the forest to mate with the most beautiful, except for money? Many other things aside, money also helped make every generation more beautiful. So it appeared that the mothers of most of the students had sold themselves at least once. Beauty was a contagious stock. I could see it. I wasn't that dumb. Not all that dumb . . .

Thanks to the scholarship Azim had got me through his efforts as almost a one-man Ministry of Education, everything was coming along the way it should. But now Azim was also changing. He thought I wasn't spending enough time with him, insisting I go to university in Istanbul. But I'd already done my research. This was during the years when the Internet was actually useful. I'd looked at all the universities in the world that seemed interesting and made my decision. I wanted to go to England. To Cambridge University, to be exact. Despite the fact that Azim thought I should study international relations in Boğaziçi University, I really wanted to study social anthropology. A department devoted to indoctrinating the rules of interpersonal exploitation held no interest for me. I would rather be where those rules were unearthed and recorded.

After all, I'd spent my whole life thoroughly studying the individual-society relationship. Neither Cambridge nor any other school could hope for a student that knew humanity as well as I did. What other student enrolled in or about to enroll in social anthropology in Cambridge had conducted social experiments on people at fifteen, as I had? If there was to be a user manual on the creature known as man, then I was the person to write it. Azim's little dreams, trapped inside the walls of the dorm he ran, didn't matter to me. I couldn't conceivably limit myself to them. If Azim wouldn't help me get into Cambridge, then I had no more use for him. His function in my life went out like the light of a dying sun. He himself was unaware of this, however. He thought that he still lit up my world as though he were Socrates. In reality he was just a cooling rock that had no more use. In fact, I could sense that he would do everything in his power to keep me from going to Cambridge. It was time for me to recover the freedom I'd traded in in the name of my interests . . .

Toward the end of the year, on a Friday evening, we sat playing chess in Azim's room as usual. Azim's eyes would ordinarily be fixed on the checkered board and its sixty-four squares, calculating his next move. Now, however, like me, he was glancing around and not really paying attention to the game. Our gazes met as they roamed around the room. He took a breath and said:

"Have I ever told you that I'm proud of you?"

He hadn't. Now he didn't have to.

"Thank you."

"Really!" he said. "Excelling at your studies after all the things you went through . . . helping me out around here so much . . ."

I gave another thanks . . .

"Well, how do you do it?"

"Excuse me?"

"How do you manage to do it?"

"I don't know . . ."

"Because I can't . . ."

We were no longer playing chess. We'd moved over into a different game. That's why I stayed silent. But Aziz went on.

"I'm fifty-one years old. I've spent my whole life with children like you. Of course none of them were quite like you, that has to be said! But . . . I've always been surrounded by children, do you understand? I did everything I could for them . . . and what came of it? What good did it do? It's really all in vain, you know? All in vain!"

"How could it be?" I said. "Who knows how many children's lives you've changed?"

"That's right," he said. "I did . . ."

He leaned back in his chair and took an envelope out of the inside pocket of his jacket.

"I found this on my desk this morning. Someone wrote me a letter. Look . . . it even has a stamp. How odd . . . it must have been years since I've received a letter . . . You know what it says? That I've been molesting you. In fact, that I have some sort of relation with you . . . and that I'll be reported to the institution if I don't resign . . ."

I laughed. "Who'd write that sort of nonsense?"

"I don't know . . . It isn't signed."

"It must surely be someone from here. I know all of their handwritings. If you'll allow me . . ." I said, extending my hand.

Azim, however, put the envelope back in his pocket, saying, "It's typed." Then he shook his head and continued. "I'm so sorry, Gaza . . . so sorry . . ."

"Don't be," I said. "Don't you be sorry . . . you and I know what went on. We know the truth. You never molested me, and we never had any relationship of that sort . . . We fell in love as two men, that's all!"

"But you weren't the way I am . . . I pressured you."

"No! No one in this life can ever pressure me into doing anything! Now, don't think about it anymore . . . Also, it's your turn . . . If you don't figure something out, it's checkmate for you in four moves."

All my relationships had a function, and I wasn't really that different from my classmates' mothers. Azim had done all he could for me, and now all he was good for was playing chess. He was hopeless at it too, and worse than that, he couldn't imagine a life without me. I left Azim alone in his room with the walls closing in on him and headed to the stairs. I leafed through the pages of a newly purchased book of poems as I slowly ascended. They were written by some guy named Rimbaud. I don't know why, but every line I read felt familiar. Although I'd never written any poetry, I somehow recognized the stories in his words . . . Does reincarnation, I wondered, only happen for the Dalai Lama? Or does Rimbaud keep dropping by because he has unfinished business in the world? I was dwelling on these things and chuckling as I went into my room.

I cared neither for Azim nor for that guy called Verlaine whose poems I'd read a few months ago. It was so awful I couldn't enjoy a single word. His only contribution had been to introduce me to Rimbaud. Or should I say, to myself?

Azim left and was replaced by one Bedri, every bit a clerk as Faik the governor's driver had been. He'd also been raised in a dormitory. Every time he opened his mouth, he'd begin with, "I was just like you."

I laughed inwardly every time I looked at this man who claimed to be just like me. The moment he arrived, he picked up on the fact that I was a meticulously operated goldmine. After all, for a government worker, an accomplishment that he hadn't had to waste office hours on falling into his lap was a stroke of great luck. He could flaunt me all he wanted, even take me with him on visits to ministries and parade me around like a circus animal. For I looked so good I could be the logo for the Foundation of Social Services and Children's Welfare! I was living proof of how well the system worked!

He kept saying, "Absolutely!" as he listened to my plans about Cambridge! "We must absolutely make this happen! You have to become a man of science! Don't worry, I'll do everything in my power!"

I no longer had any need for the little games I had resorted to with Azim to secure myself. In Bedri's book, it was enough that I be a star who could dazzle the minister responsible for social policy. On his path to counsellorship, I had the capacity to catapult Bedri into the kind of position he ordinarily could never have attained. For that I needed to finish high school as top of my grade and be patient. Although I was to turn eighteen in the final year of high school, Bedri would assure me, "Of course you're going to stay with us, I'll see to it." And it was as he said . . .

In the meantime I parted with my roommates one by one and waved them all off to their new lives. Rauf left first, then Ömer . . . Derman was the last one to go . . . Who knows where they are now? Who knows what they're up to? Those people who never did me a wrong turn and who accepted me as their oldest friend from the first day, who knows where in the world they exist as the finished sentences they are?

Rauf had never known his parents. Ömer, on the other hand, was in the dorm due to his mother having killed his father. Derman's situation was completely different, being Bosnian . . . As a very young child, he'd miraculously survived as his parents were murdered right in front of his eyes. From what he told, the Serbians had come into their home, shooting at everything that moved and then left, taking the horror-struck Derman for dead. With his grandmother who had found him frozen like that, he'd gone on a long journey all the way to Istanbul. He was placed in the dormitory when his grandmother died and so came to live in Azim's building.

I was quite sure no other kid besides me had had inappropriate relations with Azim, but did have my doubts about Derman. Derman did everything he could to avoid running into Azim inside that tiny building. When he did, he'd freeze like in that story of his. As if he hoped Azim would take him for dead . . . In fact, during Azim's farewell speech, I thought that Derman must be the only one among us who was truly glad. Since Azim's departure didn't come as a surprise to me, being the author of the blackmailing letter, I felt nothing that day. So Derman's eyes that were at least as blue as mine were the only bright things in that crowd. Or it was just my imagination . . .

In the end those three boys left my life, and three strange voices filled our four-person room. The voices of others . . .

If I hadn't been too busy building a life for myself, I'd have paid more attention to the boys I'd shared a room with for three years, reciprocating the friendship they extended to me. But I couldn't. I was never able to have real feelings toward those boys with their acceptance of me as I was. It was all due to my bleakness. Loud on the outside but feeble on the inside, unable to partake in any honest relationship or bond with anything, I used everyone in that dorm to their very dregs and threw them all in the trash just like I did with Azim. They spoke to me, but I never listened. The only reason I kept their secrets was because I forgot them as soon as they told me. They were fond of me but never knew what it was they were fond of. I never let them. All their fondness for me went into my chest and out my back, flowing into dross . . . Later, many times, they tried to get in touch. I never returned their calls. I never cared to receive any of their news. For they were each just one of the paving stones I'd laid underfoot. I didn't do anything other than walk all over them . . .

I hope that they're all right . . . I hope that they met people with real feelings who loved them for real. I hope they've forgotten about me. I hope that I haven't caused them to lose their faith in friendship. I hope that Azim hasn't committed suicide. And I hope I never see any of them ever again! Although I've changed much in the many years that have passed, I'm not a better person. Whatever I was in those days, I'm that and more! More cruel, more murderous, more of a liar, more of a monster, and more and more of more of everything . . . Today, I'm a full-blooded corpse. Nothing more . . . or perhaps a bit of morphine sulfate.

We got off the bus and Bedri asked:

"Are you all right?"

"I'm fine," I said.

"Are you sure?"

"Yes."

"Good . . ."

We'd just finished an eight-hour trip, with only the streets of Ankara left to travel. We got in a cab, and Bedri recited the address of our destination as he put on his tie with the help of the mirror on the sunshade he pulled down. I was in the backseat. We left the bus station and entered streets that appeared identical. I was wearing my school uniform. That was Bedri's preference, as I looked more studious in the suit . . .

I watched the cars passing us by. Inside were bleary-eyed men and women. Ankara was long awake and already seemed sorry to be. At every red light, I watched the tens of people on opposite pavements walk toward one another to merge together. Their faces were pale and vacant. Ankara was an abdominal cavity and we were passing through it.

We got out of the cab in front of the ministry building, and Bedri checked his watch. There was still an hour and a half until our appointment. Bedri glanced around and must have spotted what he was looking for as he said, "Come, let's have a bite to eat here. I have business at the bank. We can take care of that after."

We had breakfast among people in uniforms like mine and suits like Bedri's. Asking the waiter to refill his tea, Bedri turned to me and asked:

"Are you excited?"

"Not really," I said.

In reality I hadn't slept for two days. For two days I'd been thinking about my meeting with the minister. It might take a few minutes or an hour, but by the time I left the building in front of which we'd just gotten out of the cab, my life would have changed completely. Every step I took afterward would bring me closer to England. I was in one of the most important phases of my rebirth. I should have been excited, but I wasn't. Instead I felt something else. A restlessness, the cause of which I couldn't identify . . . Maybe it was due to the night trip, I thought, and brushed it aside. After all, the darkness that the bus had slipped through for hours had evoked another kind of darkness for me. It had even rained intermittently throughout the night, and I'd watched as the raindrops hit and shattered on the windowpane my head rested against . . . but now wasn't the time to remember. It really wasn't.

"All right then, come on," said Bedri and we rose . . .

We crossed a wide avenue and entered the bank he'd mentioned. "You sit," said Bedri.

It was crowded inside despite the fact that it was so early in the day. Maybe it was for the same reason that most of them were old. It was the hour of the elderly who'd lost sleep over work all their lives who, now that they had nothing to do, could no longer sleep. We were surrounded by people who knew the opening times for banks and all other buildings. The world of elderly butterflies who didn't want to be late for anything because they didn't have much time left, and fluttered off ahead of time to every destination . . . Gripping their queue tickets from the vendor in the entrance, they were sunk into the waiting seats, quietly observing their surroundings. From where I stood, I could see that the seats were brand new. Though the plastic coverings had been torn off them, transparent remnants straggled off the edges. No one had bothered to take them off completely. Maybe they hadn't felt any need to. After all, the people sitting on them had lost their sight long ago.

"No one cares about anything!" I muttered. Then I took a few steps and sat in the only empty seat in the waiting area. I stared first at my knees, and then the knees next to me. I raised and turned my head to glimpse the owner of those knees. I'd never have been able to guess his age, but everywhere I looked were wrinkles. On the old man's face was a pair of glasses with a brown frame. Just like Rastin, he'd taped together the part of it that went over the bridge of his nose. I shook my head and murmured, "No one cares!"

Totally unaware that I was watching him, the old man sat with his eyes fixed on the digital screen where the queue and teller numbers appeared. The small and crumpled piece of paper inside his palm read 82. For a second I took that for the guy's age. He had on a worn coat. He watched the flashing numbers in the digital screen attentively and kept glancing back at the 82 in his hand. Then finally it was time. The bright red dots on the screen spelled out 82. I waited for the man to rise but he didn't. He first looked right, then at me. Our eyes met, but he looked away, sticking his trembling hand, along with the ticket, in his coat pocket. He was sure no one knew it was his turn, including me. One of the tellers called "82!" twice. But the old man did nothing and just waited. When the screen finally went over into 83, he rose and crept toward the exit.

As I was wondering what it was he wanted to do and why he changed his mind, I saw the old man get a new ticket from the automat. He crept back toward me and sat back down. Glancing at the ticket in his hand before turning to smile at me, he said, "Looks like I got a ticket for the wrong line."

I neither replied to his lie nor smiled. But he continued:

"I have a grandson just like you . . . What grade are you in?"

I might just be able to answer this one . . . I might say something that wouldn't upset anybody. I have no idea why, but I was feeling restless. I wanted to infect everyone else, so I bent over and whispered:

"You're so lonely you make me sick!"

The governmental office of the Minister of Education was almost the size of our shed. Entering it after a long wait, we saw that the minister was on the phone, sitting in a chair taller than him. His secretary gestured for us to sit, but we chose to remain standing until he finished the call. Finally getting off the phone, the minister shook our hands and said, "Please sit." So we did and right away began listening to Bedri.

As a true government officer, Bedri managed to relay in the most carefully chosen words that as he'd mentioned in writing before, I'd been top of my class in the final year of high school and in the current semester, and that I'd scored full points in both the TOEFL and the IELTS.

As he went through all this in bullet points, the minister watched me, several times exclaiming, "Bless him!" and I watched the cut-glass ashtray on the coffee table in front of me. This was during one of those glorious years when you could still smoke inside . . .

As Bedri began to say, "Honorable Minister, we would like to ask your excellency for—" The minister cut him off with a single, "Let's make a doctor out of you!" He stared fixedly at me and smiled. I think he resembled Yadigar slightly.

Not knowing what to say, I smiled meekly. Seeing that I wasn't replying, Bedri completed his own sentence and wrapped up by saying that I'd need a yearly bursary of about twenty-five thousand pounds to be able to study in the social anthropology department of Cambridge. Then he interrupted the temporary silence once more to mention that my high school was willing to cover half of said expenses.

During all this I'd once again fixed my gaze on the ashtray. I watched a ray of daylight coming in through the large windows to shatter into pieces inside the cut glass. The light traveled all the way from the sun to get crushed inside the ashtray like a butt. I myself had considered studying to be a doctor. It had occurred to me. That way I'd be able to do research on the Korsakoff Syndrome, manifesting in people during prolonged periods of hunger. But then I'd thought, "Human health isn't worth the effort!" Then, "Maybe I should be a biologist," I'd said. I'd get a degree in biology and then specialize in entomology. This way I'd be able to pinpoint a body's time of death by examining the bacteria or insects on it. But a while later I also changed my mind about that, thinking, "Who gives a flying fuck who kicked the bucket and when!" I was still interested in biology, however. It was the appropriate branch to gather information about the buildup of fluid, colostrum, in women's breasts during pregnancy. As a matter of fact, the taste of that milk remained on my tongue years later. It never went away no matter how much I swallowed.

"You'll come back later though, right, Gaza effendi? Let's settle on that first!"

Was this being said to me? I raised my head to look at Bedri.

"Don't you decide to settle down over there! The motherland needs men like you, son!"

Since Bedri's lips remained unmoving, it must be the minister talking. I turned to look at him and once again meekly smiled. At this, Bedri said, "He's a little flustered, sir, if you'll excuse him . . ."

But there was no change in my pulse. I was sure of that because I could see my heart. I beat inside it and listened to its deep, rhythmic sound. Maybe that's why I could no longer hear what was being said. I listened to my heartbeat surrounding me on all sides as though it were coming from four enormous speakers in all four corners of the enormous government office and watched the mouths moving in the faces staring at me. And as one of those mouths opened slightly wider, the voice coming out drowned out my heartbeat.

"Son, are you all right?"

It was the minister talking. I think I could talk as well. At least I could last I checked.

"Yes," I said. "I'm fine. How are you?"

The minister laughed. Bedri didn't.

"Gaza is a little overworked, is he now?" the minister asked Bedri. But his eyes were still on me.

"Sir," Bedri said, "as you can surmise . . ."

"Okay!" The minister cut him off again. "We'll take care of it . . . but now, if you'll excuse me, I have a meeting . . . I'll have a word with the counsellorship, they'll get in touch . . . and, Gaza *bey*, as for you, I wish you the best of luck, son. Go, attend your studies, and return. Deal?"

Having said his last word, the minister stood and extended his hand to me. Bedri also rose, but I remained sitting. Bedri grabbed the minister's hovering hand and said, "Sir, thank you so much, believe me when I say that our boy Gaza will not let you down," and glared at me.

I only stood up then. Bedri had withdrawn his hand, and it was my turn to shake. But there was a problem. A big problem . . . I didn't want to touch the minister. Not just the minister, anyone. If I just lifted my right hand and shook the minister's hand, I would walk out of there with a bursary that would be the culmination of my rebirth. I knew that. But neither my body would hear me, nor my mind obey. On the outside someone resembling Gaza was clearly there, but that wasn't me. I was lost inside myself.

Leaving the minister's hand hanging in midair, I turned around and walked. Bedri and the minister were surely saying something, maybe shouting. But I could only hear my heartbeat. And walking in step with that rhythm gave me much pleasure. I'd regrettably gone mad at the wrong time. Though not necessarily the wrong place, for that government office was definitely the same size as our shed.

"My mother brought me a cake last week. For my birthday. But I didn't eat it. You know what I did? I ate the candles!"

Şeref, who constantly spoke to me just like Ender had once done even though I never replied, was in the neighboring bed. In the thirty-four-person ward, I was between a wall and Şeref. No matter how hard I buried my head in my pillow, I couldn't avoid hearing that cracked voice of his.

After the small scandal in the minister's office, my unresponsiveness and ghostlike gait had made Bedri decide not to kill me, and flag down a cab for the hospital instead. Since I screamed every time he touched me, however, he'd been at a loss for what to do, and finally got me into the cab by force.

The doctor in the ER, unable to get a reply out of me and observing that I screamed whenever I was touched, scratched his head and said I should be transferred three floors up to the psychiatry clinic. But there was a problem. The first time the elevator arrived, it was vacant and that meant I'd have to be alone with Bedri in there, which I couldn't do. After several tries we were able to get into another elevator with two people already inside.

I could actually see and hear everything. I was actually aware of everything, but my body and my reactions weren't mine. They would absolutely not listen to me. For instance, I knew Bedri and I could ride that vacant elevator together, but I couldn't bring myself to step inside. The part of my mind that was self-aware was trapped in the dark somewhere, observing events from there. It was like it sat in a box in a theater, watching a show it couldn't participate in. Meanwhile it learned. One of the things it learned was that I could only ride in an elevator if I was alone or if there were at least three people in it besides me. This didn't surprise the part of my mind that was still aware. It merely accepted it as a newly discovered law of physics and said, "That's the right way!"

When we got to the third floor, the less I wanted to be touched, the more people tried to touch me. As a result my screams rang all through the hallways and they decided to put me to sleep. I had to be grabbed from all four sides by four aides and wrestled facedown onto a bed so my pants could be pulled down.

When I came back around, Bedri was beside me. I could see him, but I couldn't talk, because my mouth was full . . . and anyway, Bedri didn't appear to want to talk. He stared at me like a poor fool whose house had fallen down around his ears. After all, there was nothing more the little genius he'd invested so much in could do for him. I was a machine he'd never figured out the mechanics of and I'd gone bust when he needed me the most. So I was pretty sure he wanted to stay with me a while longer so he could distance himself from his fury, or at least the urge to break one of my arms. Considering the humiliation I'd caused him in the minister's presence, you could even say he was being overly generous. He could have just abandoned me in the ministry's lawn and no one would have been the wiser. He could've said, for instance, "He assaulted me and then ran!" But he'd done nothing of the sort. Maybe he still had hope. All of this might just be a minor breakdown. I might revert back to the

270

Gaza he knew any moment, and we could go back to the minister's to try our luck at an apology. We could start all over again and race hand in hand toward success. However, that meant I'd first have to take my hands out of my mouth. I'd shoved all ten fingers in there as soon as I'd woken up. So they wouldn't touch anything. "That's the right way," said a voice inside me, "that's the way it should be!"

So neither Bedri nor I could avoid the situation we were in. We were brought to this point by circumstance and stuck there. I was like a taxidermy animal, stuffed up by life before I was even dead. He, in turn, like the owner of a racehorse he knew he'd have to shoot because it was crippled . . .

There wasn't much we could do. Bedri stood slowly and started to put his hand on my shoulder. Then he recalled how I'd reacted to anyone who tried to lay a hand on me all day, withdrew his hand, and walked out of the room.

From what I could see from where I lay, he talked to a doctor in the hallway, sneaking glances at me, and then undid his tie and put it in his pocket. He took a step to return to my side, but the doctor stopped him with a hand on his arm. He looked at me a final time before turning around and disappearing down the hallway. There were other children he needed to bring up and a dorm he had to run.

That was the last I saw of Bedri. Our partnership was over. After this, the only thing he could do was keep an eye on my condition from a distance and make sure that I at least received treatment.

"Don't worry," said the doctor who came to my side, "You're going to get better. Then we'll send you off to Istanbul. I gave my word to Bedri Bey."

But the doctor wouldn't be able to keep his word. I never went back to Istanbul, let alone got better. For a person without a family, his city of residence no longer held much significance for the state. Social Services were ubiquitous, and no one thought I should go back anywhere. I'd also unfortunately survived long enough to turn eighteen. With myself . . . there was no space left for anyone else in my life of eighteen years.

A suitcase with my things arrived from Istanbul a few days later, and I was put on a white van. My destination was decided. A hospital in Gölbaşı. A bed in a thirty-four-person ward, next to Şeref . . . I'd been there four months and Şeref was still talking:

"So when exactly is it never too late to turn back? I mean, where exactly is that? Because not turning back is also fun up to a point, right? Don't you think?"

## CHIAROSCURO

One of the four basic techniques of Renaissance painting. Signifies the maximal emphasis of light and dark to separate them sharply from each other. The prominence of the clash between light and shadow results in deeper perception of depth and gives dimension to form.

I'd hidden myself away from everyone and locked all my doors from the inside. The 317 hours I'd spent in hell had been dormant for three years to surface again in that government office and suck me back in. It really was odd that all the commas of my life, that is, its turning points, had to come about in government offices. Maybe I had some sort of allergy to governmental chambers, I really don't know. All I knew was that I'd really assumed that I had left that black hole behind and been under the delusion that I could go on living as though nothing had happened. When in fact life for me had ended among those rotting corpses and I hadn't known it. My efforts to go on breathing along with other people had only lasted three years. No matter how much I tried, I hadn't been able to race fast enough toward the future, and the past caught up with me. In the end I found myself being repulsed by people and stealing Şeref's capsules of morphine sulfate.

Unlike me, madness wasn't the only one of Şeref's problems. He also had brain cancer that he deemed "meant to be!" He had three delightful tumors playing patty-cake with metastasis. These masses, blinding Şeref's eyes with the light they released into his brain, were sure to kill him. But they wanted to make sure he suffered enough before they did. That was why they flooded twenty-one-year-old Şeref's body with pains of unendurable weight. The pains would turn Şeref into a submarine, and together they would sink into the depths of his bed. Şeref was given thirty-milligram capsules of morphine sulfate every twelve hours to keep him afloat, but then I butted in. I'd seen what those little blue capsules did to Şeref, and I wanted the same.

When I met morphine sulfate, it was addiction at first sight! All I had to do was look into Şeref's eyes from where I lay as though I was listening to him. In a brief time, our transaction turned into routine. The nurse who brought Şeref's capsules didn't check underneath his tongue, so I could retrieve my share of morphine sulfate after she left. Despite the fact that it was covered with Şeref's saliva, a *second mouth* capsule was no less effective. Naturally it took a while for him to understand that he was supposed to put the capsule on the stand between us, instead giving it to me directly, but we were all partaking in the initiation period. Şeref had been initiated to me too. He talked to me but didn't try to touch. In return for the capsules he deposited on the stand, he got a constant listener who stared fixedly at his face as though he were listening. Having someone to listen to him mattered more to Şeref than suppressing the pain flooding out of his skull. In the end each got what he wanted. That meant that we weren't all that insane. Not all that insane . . .

The reason it wasn't thought a medical necessity to give me a single one of the morphine sulfate capsules produced on earth in multitudes was because Emre, the young psychiatrist appointed me, didn't believe I had any aches. He was absolutely certain that I had no chronic pain. But I was really chronic all over!

Thanks to Azim the archive freak, who'd included my hospital records from Kandalı in my files and painstakingly passed on this official legacy to Bedri, Emre had the majority of information about my condition. Bedri, whom I'm sure must have felt like a betrayed lover, short of hurling my things out of the window of my room on the third floor of the dorm, had been quick to mail every document concerning me to the hospital in a rage of similar vein. So neither Emre nor his young colleagues, despite being informed of my little adventure with the dead at the foot of Kandağ, thought it possible that such an experience could cause maddening pain. That was predictable really, since they'd never been confronted with someone rescued from underneath a bunch of corpses. So to them I was more like someone rescued from underneath rubble after an earthquake.

Emre's diagnosis, for instance, was definitive:

"Post-traumatic stress disorder, for sure!"

That was what he told his colleagues. In my presence too! And they would at first nod and then rest index finger against jaw in pretense of thought. And the most impatient would start the show named *Contradiction Just for Kicks*:

"But the symptoms have acute properties, no? It's been three years since the occurrence, but it still seems to be in the acute phase..."

Another would up and start relaying his own dream:

"I believe it can be approached as a subtype of trauma-related social anxiety disorder..."

But no one liked this argument and the chorus kicked in.

"Hmm..." they said, in unison.

Then there was a solo. By a different voice...

"We're going to Chez Le Bof when work lets out, just so you know. Emre has a crush on the waitress, looks like he's buying!"

Since the chain was complete, it was Emre's turn again:

"I don't have a crush, I just like the way she takes that cloth napkin and puts it in my lap."

Chorus:

"Hmm!"

The one with the invalidated dream gave one last attempt: "You have social masculinity disorder!"

But no one cared for or laughed at his little joke and dispersed to different corners of the ward in a figure out of a synchronized dance. After all, there were the ones waiting for a chance to bash their skulls against the wall so they could break it open. True lunatics! Although as a case I was interesting enough, I was no study anyone would spend hours on.

In truth, whatever disorder it was I had, its symptoms were very clear: I could touch no one, let no one touch me, and be alone with no one. I had to either be all by myself or in a crowd. Otherwise I'd start to shake and scream before being suffused by pain that clogged every one of my pores. Aside from that, there was another significant detail: I didn't speak.

But that was more of a preference. I could talk if I wanted, I might even never shut up, but I had no more interest in expressing myself. Anyway, how many more times was I supposed to? How many more times was I supposed to part my lips to say the same old things like a politician attending rally after rally or a beggar boy imploring with the same words a thousand times a day?

For three years I'd spoken mouthfuls and in the end found myself in a loony bin. It would appear that loquaciousness hadn't done me much good. It didn't have any other use than to tire out my tongue. Plus you couldn't pick a fight if you never talked. Because every word meant a fight. Those who claimed "In the beginning was the Word" were right, because I was sure at this point that fighting came before everything in this world. As many words as there were fights! The ward was filled with savage boxers trying to land punches made of curses from where they lay. A whole bunch of crazies who'd split their brains to hold one lobe in their left hand and the other in their right woke, pretended to be alive, and slept inside one circle.

But you couldn't say we were that badly off. The psychiatrists' gang that surrounded us, who were yet of insufficient age to have reached the budget for opening one's own practice, tried to be as creative as possible in the treatments and discharge us as soon as they could. For instance, my treatment in Gölbaşı went as far as to entail making me observe a birth. Emre, who hadn't covered much ground with his PTSD theory, had decided to go with the flow completely, crossing over to the world's most scientific method, trial and error. Of course having me watch a birth had been Emre's idea, but there was a problem with the application. It wasn't very easy to find a pregnant woman who'd volunteer for something like that. Since there wasn't someone around dying to have some lunatics watch her as she gave birth, I had to make do with recorded images. Maybe it was in everyone's best interests that this technicality kept me from witnessing any births. I was sure I might feel an irresistible urge to shove the newborn right back where he came from.

Emre, however, was stubborn. With a single-mindedness that took even me by surprise, he'd relayed the matter to the administration of the zoo in Ankara and asked them for help, as he thought it absolutely imperative that I observe a birth. And so I started setting out on tours of the zoo to watch wild boars or llamas giving birth. All this effort was spent, in Emre's words, to reintroduce me to the *vitality* I'd become detached from. And to figure out whichever point it was where *vitality* and I had become detached, even if I was unable to, and glue us back together . . .

Alongside all that I was also on meds, of course. Antidepressants heavy enough to numb most of my brain and turn me into a voodoo doll . . . My days, in fact, worked exactly according to the workings of a voodoo doll. Of course it wasn't as if someone else felt pain when I was pricked. My curse was of a different kind. My right hand, for example, hurt all day, and in the evening something bad inevitably happened to it. I'd either punch the wall until it bled all over or skin it with my teeth. Sometimes it was the back of my neck that hurt all night until, in the morning, I was either bitten in that spot by a mosquito or slapped on my way to the toilet by some dickwad who couldn't control himself. Ultimately it appeared that my body, with the help of the meds, saw the future and sent me signals in the form of those aches. Yet I could also see Emre's efforts to solve the matter through actual therapy, not just chemicals. I could see everything. In any case Emre was also starting to see the light. Especially since my blood test results started showing traces of Şeref's capsules, he'd had a mind that I might not be as sick as I looked. After that he switched Şeref's station to get him as far away from me as possible. But Şeref could still find a way to give his most loyal audience the payment for listening . . .

I wasn't off the hook for my thieving of drugs, however. Declaring that we were on to the next step in my treatment, Emre ordered me to scoop up my own excrement with my hands and study it. Its stink wasn't all that different from those of the rotting corpses. Although I wasn't quite sure what my excrement was supposed to reintroduce me to, I was trying to do as I was told. Either that or I was hallucinating and doing this in secret by myself in a toilet cabin. Then I'd wash my hands and go to the hospital library.

I actually spent the majority of my days there. I read all the time. But it never seemed enough, as my eyes never went bad. The library had been founded with books donated by all the psychiatrists who passed through that building. Most of it was on art, the rest on politics and philosophy. Perhaps for the sake of doing archeological excavations in the pit that was humanity, the psychiatrists had abandoned, along with their books, their dreams of becoming politicians or philosophers.

I saw Da Vinci's *The Last Supper* in one of those books and read the whole story. Since I was crazy, it reminded me of the photograph in *From Kandalı to the World*. This was actually a benefit to being crazy. Because for the sane, the life passing by in front of their very eyes didn't evoke shit. They only believed what they saw. Whatever it was they saw, that was life to them. It was what it was . . .

Then one day, I came across *them* in a book I was riffling through: the Buddhas of Bamiyan . . . Almost the entirety of the sculpture-related book was dedicated to Buddhism and those two Buddha statues. I'm sure no one who'd read that book to this day could have shed as many tears as I did as I turned its pages. I carried those two gigantic statues in my pocket, Dordor and Harmin in my dreams, and Cuma inside my very bones . . .

I should admit I went a bit far in my relationship with that book. I tore out its pages and spread them underneath my bed-sheets to spend a few nights with those two statues, thinking of Cuma . . . Unfortunately, the nurse noticed them when she was changing the sheets. Then she went and ratted me out to Emre. He in turn told me to eat the pages featuring photographs of the Buddha statues. I couldn't disobey Emre. I ate twelve pages and so, in my next shit-monitoring session, was able to witness the statues rising up out of my palms.

So you couldn't say my life wasn't entertaining. For instance, there was this pair of compasses in the pen box in Emre's room where I saw him for forty minutes every Monday, which, in my opinion, was extremely interesting. Although there was an aide with us in every session, since in the first months I couldn't be alone in the room with Emre, I could now manage with just the open door. I could see the people in the hallway from where I sat and relax, remembering that I was among people. But what interested me most was that mysterious pair of compasses in that pen box. Perhaps Emre was a *secret child* that liked drawing cir-cles in his time off or had some circular theory he was developing in the psychiatry field, I can't say. Those pair of compasses sat there and waited to be used by me.

On yet another Monday, the second I sat down in front of Emre, I just plucked the pair of compasses out of the pen box. Fearing I might harm myself or him, Emre stood up immediately, but by the time he walked around the table to reach me, I'd gotten hold of a piece of paper and started drawing the image I'd visualized the first time I'd seen the compasses. Becoming aware that I had no desire to stab the compasses into anything other than the paper, Emre stopped and watched.

The first thing I did was close the legs of the compasses all the way and draw three quarters of the smallest circle possible. Without moving the sharp end I'd fixed right in the middle of the sheet, I cranked the compass slightly wider to draw another circle made of broken lines. After I'd rotated it fully I opened it a bit more and drew a third circle, again broken. After that came the fragments of a fourth and a fifth circle, each wider than the preceding one. Understanding that the outcome was a circular labyrinth, Emre sat in his seat and shook his head in wonder. Our eyes met for a moment, and we smiled at each other. Then I drew the sixth circle and moved on to the outer wall of the labyrinth. I left a narrow gap in the seventh circle that became the exit of my labyrinth. Finally I joined the integrated circles with short lines in order to form corridors. Only then did I remove the sharp end of the compasses from the sheet to proudly contemplate my work. I wasn't selfish. I wished to make Emre proud too and spoke for the first time since I'd come to the hospital:

"Go on, solve it!"

Pretending that hearing me utter a coherent sentence hadn't taken him aback, he took the piece of paper from me and pulled a pen from his breast pocket to start working on entering through the single door of the labyrinth to get to the small circle in the center. I, on the other hand, glanced around the room to dwell on other things and saw Rastin everywhere I looked. And also the spiral hierarchy scheme . . .

"There!" said Emre and showed me the paper. He'd figured out the labyrinth, although not without some difficulty.

I still said "congratulations," so I wouldn't get him down. He was so pleased to finally have a modicum of communication with me that he went as far as to say, "Thanks," and extend his hand to shake.

And although I did my very best not to stab him in his extended hand with the compasses, I wasn't successful. Then I did what I should and apologized.

Though Emre said "That's OK!" as he clutched his bleeding hand, this move on my part got me locked in the isolation room for two days. That was how I was able to understand that the duration Yadigar had kept me in that holding cell for had a standing in the science of psychiatry! Forty-eight hours of isolation was the cure for any ailment.

For me, the isolation room was more appealing than anywhere and anything because its isolation enabled me to close my eyes and return into my body. Becoming an astronaut inside myself, doing the cellwalk, not the moonwalk, was amazing! I even thanked Emre when I got out. What I said exactly was:

"Thank you for sending me to myself . . . By the way, I have a recommendation. I propose that, rather than public restrooms, public cells be placed in the streets. Anyone who wishes should be able to go inside and close himself off. Just like in restroom cabins, there'd be a red sign in the lock signaling that it's occupied. Then other people could leave things like food or water through a hole in the door to show their support for the person who wants to be alone. Wouldn't that be great? I think it would be fantastic!"

Through Emre didn't consider my proposal, he smiled with contentment at hearing me speak fluently and attempted another handshake with his bandaged hand.

At that I asked, "Do you have some gloves?" After a short search through the hospital, I was presented a pair of leather gloves and was able to shake hands with those on. It really was a grand day! I'd made a tremendous leap in the fifth month of my treatment and was able to touch a person, even if through fabric!

When I entered the ward with a smile on my face, however, the first piece of news I received made it freeze. While I was in the isolation room, Şeref, my supplier of morphine sulfate, had died. The first thing I thought then was that no one else in the ward had cancer. I wished someone did, but they didn't! No one else other than Şeref was on morphine sulfate. So as I walked from the door of the ward to my bed, at the sixteenth step if I remember correctly, I made up my mind: I was going to leave that hospital as soon as I could. That way, I'd rob the first pharmacy I came across and wouldn't have to start all over again.

In the hospital, no one would shut up about it: starting all over! I had absolutely no intention of doing that. All I wanted was to pick up my relationship with morphine sulfate where I'd left off. I must also do this inside a cell where I could run the fuck into myself. There was no life for me outside my skin. Another person in the same situation would surely think, "Fine, but where'd I find a cell?" but I was in luck. I was so lucky, out of the billions of men on Earth I'd had Ahad to call dad. Now he was dead, leaving me with an inheritance of a cell. Now I had an isolation room of my own, and it was in Kandalı. I pictured myself lying in that reservoir in the dark, surrounded by capsules of morphine sulfate. I smiled to picture it. If I'd had a pair of compasses, I could have drawn the picture of paradise without ever moving the sharp edge propped against the paper! For I knew what it looked like. I'd furnished it with Ahad's money. So it could be hell for others . . . but it turned out to be paradise. For me at least! As the biggest sinner on Earth, my plan for redemption was laid out: going to paradise and dying there. Never through suicide . . . but through time.

I had to either be discharged or escape as soon as possible! And since this was no adventure novel, I had to go for the former first. How hard could it be to fake recovery? After all, my insanity wasn't the kind to show up in X-rays or blood tests! I carried a disease no X-ray could identify! I could even travel around the world without anyone knowing. But first I had to get out of that hospital. For that, unfortunately, I had to touch someone bare-handed. What was more, I had to do it without screaming or my face crumpling under the weight of the ache flooding my insides. I thought that I should perhaps start with a few exercises. A few experiments . . .

Naturally there was the whole history of medicine at hand, and I had to carry out my tests on animals like all scientists of conscience. I'd touch them first. The rest would surely come. How much of a difference could there be between touching a chimp and touching a human? Weren't they both descended from the same primate? A primate named Adam . . . Sure, one was smarter than the other, it's true! It had followed its instincts to go the way of the chimp and continued to evolve in harmony with nature.

The other, on the other hand, with all its idiocy, turned to a creature hell-bent on dissatisfaction and found itself excluded from nature.

But I didn't care about any of that because it didn't matter if the flesh I touched could count or bring about the end of the world. Flesh was flesh in the end! It was gross, but I had to touch it. Then I'd have to go one step forward and be able to touch humans. I tried to console myself by thinking that if I was in another place and time, a cannibalistic tribe in the seventeenth century for example, I might even have to eat humans, much less touch them. That was also a type of culture, after all, and the chances of being born into it were purely mathematics. Just as the Buddhas of Bamiyan were products of a culture, so was the Taliban that blew them up. In fact, the people that built those statues 1,400 years ago were of the same Buddhist culture as the people who kill Muslims in Burma today. One ought to not make a big deal of the concept of culture. After all, culture was the concern of obsessive maniacs who piled up their die-hard habits by passing them from generation to generation, effectively turning the world into the house of a hoarder! Sure, it was also collective memory, but was under high risk of Alzheimer's! Plus if a presentation were made today introducing everyone to all the cultures of the Earth, telling them, "Go ahead, pick one! Free transportation. Whichever culture you like we'll drop you off in, so you can live there forever," I wonder what esteemed high-culture areas of the world would be deserted in about three seconds? I thought of all this, but of course none of it was any use to me.

When I told him I'd start touching animals and move up in levels, Emre hesitated at first. After all, it wasn't his idea. People needed a certain period of time before they could accept thoughts from the minds of others. They needed to take the idea presented to them and, in that period, personalize it by making some changes. This made it possible for them to own up to an idea as if it had been theirs. For Emre this period of self-deception took about four hours. He came to the ward to lean against my bed frame and say:

"All right . . . we'll do as you say . . . but I'm going to ask you to assist in the labor of an animal!"

Assist in the labor of an animal? I loathed this guy's obsession with birth! Maybe he didn't even care about the births that much but was just making up random treatments on the go just so he'd have something to add to my idea. I still had no choice but to accept. I was in a hurry.

"When?"

"Let me have a word with the zoo, and then I'll let you know. Maybe we'll find a farm instead . . . let's just see . . ."

He left . . . and the second he did, my stomach started aching. The image of a different animal rose up in my mind every time I blinked, and I could feel their jelly-like placentas in my hands. The ache was becoming more violent and I shook. I sat in bed and looked around desperately. Right then I thought of the most harmless animal I knew. I took it out of my pocket and started touching it. I rubbed it against my face. Against my neck . . . Like a balm, I rubbed it into all the aching spots . . . and the pain began to fade. I must confess it was Cuma's paper frog that saved me that day.

Three days later, accompanied by a driver, Emre and I headed to a farm near Polatlı so I could kneel in front of a cow going through a difficult labor. As the farmer took the pair of hooves poking out of the cow and pulled on them, I asked, "What can I do?"

"Stroke her," he said. "Just stroke her . . ."

I glanced first at Emre and then at the gigantic animal lying flat against the wall of the barn, took a breath bigger than myself, and touched its hot back. I yanked my hand back as though it would burn, but then took another breath and touched it again.

The animal turned its head and said, "Don't be afraid." It was Emre who'd spoken, but I didn't care. I stroked her . . . and stroked her . . .

The pair of hooves became a pair of spindly legs and the calf's head emerged between them. The instant it was tugged out into life and separated completely from its mother, I started to weep. My tears soaked my temples that should have already started throbbing with pain, and I wept as if it were me who was born. Then I took the farmer's hands to say, "Bless you! Thank you . . ."

Emre was so happy on the way back that he told me several times that he was proud of me. After all, we'd killed a bunch of birds with one stone. I'd been able to touch both the animal *and* the farmer. I even went to extremes and touched Emre's arm by way of reply the whole way back. A bunch of times, even . . .

"Just stoke her!" we said in imitation of the farmer, laughing at each other. "Just stroke her . . ."

When we returned to the hospital, Emre and I parted ways, and I went in the bathroom. Standing in front of one of the sinks, I turned on the tap and began removing the dried egg whites adhered to the palms of my hands like a second skin. I wasn't that dumb. Not all that dumb . . . The surest way to avoid touching a person or placenta was to cover my palms and the insides of my fingers with *another* placenta. For this method I actually owed Ahad for wasting me by pressing down on the cigarette burn on my wrist on the day I left Yadigar's holding cell. It was when he'd finished his spiel and taken his hand off my wrist that he'd told me, "Go break two eggs . . . separate the whites, and whip them good, put them on there! It's good for your burns!" I'd done what he said but it didn't do a damn. The only thing I'd observed was those egg whites coating my hands like a pair of clear gloves.

Thus the only thing I needed for my performance at the farm was a couple of eggs, and there were plenty of those in the hospital kitchen. The rest was acting. And I'd been acting since I was born. For Gaza was not the name of a person, but of a part. A character. That's how it was supposed to be. I'd have long killed myself otherwise. Had Gaza really been a person, there'd be no tolerating his existence. Loving him, even less of a possibility! Therefore Gaza was really just a double. A double specialized in action scenes! That was exactly how he'd been able to utter that sentence so naturally: "Just stroke her!" He'd repeated it over and over . . . stroke the cow, love yourself, love people, love life . . . just love them. Is that so? Fuck you! You've ever known a Gaza in your life? Why don't you try and love him if it's so fucking easy? In the end, I was probably a nutcase . . . but not so much of one as to go touching people.

We stood in front of the entrance of the building and watched the snowflakes drift around us and melt as soon as they landed on our shoulders. Or I did. Emre wanted to shake hands. I first looked at his hand, then smiled and embraced him in a way he didn't expect at all. The same way Ender apprehended me years ago, so I did Emre. This time around I wasn't the one who had to worry about where to look during the embrace! Emre was the one trapped and bewildered between my clasped arms. I held that pose for as long as possible so he wouldn't be able to tell that my intention was to touch the fabrics covering him rather than his hands.

I even whispered in his ear, "Thanks for everything." Then as abruptly as I'd embraced him, I withdrew.

Slightly shaken by such a heartfelt farewell and at a loss for words, Emre took out of his pocket the piece of paper on which I'd drawn the labyrinth and showed it to me, saying, "See, I've been keeping this . . ." Then he added, "You're a very smart guy, Gaza!"

I remembered that from somewhere. Hadn't the prosecutor said something of the like? He'd said "kid" instead, I think, but now I was grown up. At least that's how I appeared on the outside.

Though I tried not to look at the dried blood on the paper, my gaze slid to it and I raised my head, saying, "I'm really sorry."

"Don't worry about it! It was my fault," Emre said, about to put the paper back in his pocket when I spoke again:

"That's not the real solution to the labyrinth, though."

"It isn't?" he asked, peering at the paper in his hand.

"Give it some more thought." I smiled.

"Okay," said Emre. "I will. Good-bye, Gaza."

I left the hospital in Gölbaşı in a van similar to the one that brought me there. I'd entered the building as a nutcase and left as a nutcase *and* an addict. All I had in my pocket was Cuma's frog and some money raised by Emre and his colleagues. It was cold. Everything was covered in a merciful layer of white. But the tires and I were fitted with snow chains. Neither mercy nor the snow could stop us. We weren't stranded and never looked back . . .

I got off the hospital van to board a public bus to Ankara, thrusting into the crowd like a reluctant fist. There wasn't much I could do. The bus was so crammed I had to either make either shoulder or elbow contact. Human flesh surrounded me, and I had a long way to go. The best I could do was keep my eyes shut as much as I could and grit my teeth. As I brushed past all that meat and fabric, I felt like the real solution to the labyrinth that I'd mentioned to Emre. For Emre to get to the solution, he'd have to erase the labyrinth completely. That would just leave the trail he'd drawn with his pen. That trail was my secret I'd built the labyrinth around. When the labyrinth was erased only the letter G would be left on the paper. Not for Gaza, of course, but for *khat*![8] I felt like a hunk of khat on that bus to Ankara. Just the

---

8    Spelled *gat* in Turkish.

same as always . . . as though I was being chewed up . . . to finally be spit out of the bus.

I was at the terminal. Nineteen years old and on the trail for morphine sulfate . . . I walked past the two pharmacies in the building dozens of times until it was time to board the bus that would take me to Kandalı. The place was crawling with cops, however. Or I was hallucinating. That's why I wasn't able to enter either one of the pharmacies and threaten, "Give me the morphine sulfate or I kill you with my invisible gun!" Anyway, how was I supposed to rob a pharmacy without a weapon? I knew then that I had no choice but to make do with the Tolvon in my backpack. I'd just sleep on the matter . . .

I boarded the bus that pulled up to the platform an hour before departure, took a near-overdose of Tolvon, closed my eyes, and promised myself not to open them again until I reached Kandalı. By a miracle I was able to keep my promise. I'd skipped over the hours-long trip in a single slumbering step. Had I not been able to, I would likely have been out of my seat before the bus had traveled a hundred kilometers, gone over to the driver, and grabbed the wheel to swerve off road. Had I not been able to sleep, I'd be the first one to sail through the windshield . . . but sleep I did!

That was the way in which I set foot in Kandalı, which I'd left at fifteen, four years ago, claiming I'd never come back. A different person might have felt an emotional turmoil or three, but I felt nothing. I just walked on the paving stones. First I walked past the gendarmerie station, then the restaurants where I'd placed orders for the world's most beautiful girl. None of it mattered to me. My home wasn't Kandalı as much as the reservoir at the end of Dust Street.

After a half-hour hike, I passed the sign reading "good-bye" and saw my own. It was still there. Although slightly changed . . . there were four bullet holes and rust on it. Someone had shot my

292

sign. Though it had died on its feet. I brushed it with my finger-tips as I passed and entered Dust Street.

I inadvertently sped up with every step until I encountered a pitch-black wreck. I laughed. Ender really was some arsonist. He must've known what he was doing. It was like he'd used lightning bolts instead of gas. He'd burned the single-story house right down to the ground, leaving behind only its skeleton. Its walls resembled the rib cage of a dinosaur. Half the roof had fallen in, leaving the building, once a stately abode to Ahad, like a rotted tooth. Really, Ender couldn't have done me a bigger favor. Not even all the hate within me could have enabled me to start such a flawless fire.

The arbor and shed remained as I'd left them. Even the hole where they'd dug out the weakling's body was still there . . . I opened the door to the shed and saw that everything was gone. Looters from Kandalı had taken all that they could get their hands on. I wouldn't have minded if they'd looted the shed itself piece by piece! The only thing that interested me was the reser-voir. Police had most likely smashed the lock on its lid. The man-hole lid was still there, however. It was interesting that the looters hadn't hauled it off to sell as scraps. Maybe they'd been too afraid and tried to stay out of the reservoir to evade Ahad's curse.

I lifted the lid with both hands and set foot onto the first step leading down to the reservoir. I descended the stairs slowly and flicked on a lighter. I'd been mistaken about the looters. They'd cleared out the reservoir too. They'd taken the fans and the cam-eras. Only the camera that Rastin had broken with the metal bucket had been left behind. They'd taken the clock off the wall as well. Of course, they wouldn't have known that I'd messed with its mechanism. Who knew whose wall it hung on now, making time lag?

I smiled. Home at last . . . I put out the lighter and sat down right where I was. Then I lay facedown onto the cold floor. I don't remember which one had taken the first blow of my life, but I turned my left cheek to rest against the ground. I stretched out my arms as far as I could on either side of me and pressed down on the sawdust with the palms of my hands. I was cold but absolutely did not care. I was embracing my home! My eyes watered, though I was smiling. I rolled over onto my back and raised my hands, running them through the darkness all around me so I could touch it. I was overcome with laughter. I stroked the air of my paradise and filled it with mirth that bounced and echoed off its four walls. "I've arrived!" I hollered.

"I've arrived at last! I've returned to you! I have nowhere else to go, that's why! You're the only home I've ever known! You're the only thing I know . . ."

I wept. As much as I pleased, at that. This was true freedom: weeping as much as one pleased. And perhaps also, weeping about whatever one pleased.

I had so little money that I was going to have to make some decisions. Like the decisions Rastin once forced his people to make . . . I would either drink or eat. I would either have warmth or light . . . I picked the bottle and candles.

Then came turn for another decision that had nothing to do with the amount of money in my pocket. A decision concerning the amount of sickness in my cells: I'd either have to rob a pharmacy or shut myself up in the reservoir to try to forget about morphine sulfate completely. Both were tough. Really tough . . . especially robbing a pharmacy! There was no way I could be alone in a tiny shop with a pharmacist. With customers inside, however, I'd definitely be caught. I didn't know what to do. I'd left the hospital so I could have access to morphine sulfate. At least that's what I thought up until the moment I went inside the reservoir. Maybe *it* had been calling to me all along: the reservoir . . . and morphine sulfate merely the backdrop for my paradise. I can make it, I thought. I can seal myself off from everything and leave the morphine sulfate outside.

I tried . . . but neither the antidepressants in my backpack nor my attempts at holding my breath to get underneath my skin were any use. Morphine sulfate withdrawal was blindness at first sight! No matter how hard I shut my eyes, a blinding light remained behind. Nothing was dark enough. And I was definitely not isolated enough! Who knew what was drifting through the air? What kind of bacteria? What microscopic monsters raining down over me? I might not be able to see any of them, but I knew for sure that I was swallowing a thousand every time I opened my mouth. Even if I pressed my lips together and pressed my palms over them, I knew they were inside the breath I drew in through my nose!

It was barely a week since I'd arrived at the reservoir, and I felt more chewed up than ever. I'd gone outside only twice, for a few bottles, a few loaves of bread, and some candles. The first time was uneventful, but I regretted my second time going to Kandalı. Just as I stood in front of the pharmacy, someone butted in between me and the display window. One of the kids once herded by Ender. He recognized me. Though I pretended not to recognize him.

In any case my lie fell short and he launched into a story beginning with, "Have you heard?" The protagonist was Ender and he died at the end! In it, he joined the military before his time and took his last step onto a landmine while walking in the Süphan plains. I hadn't been able to say a word and turned to run back to my cave, leaving the kid standing there.

"I'm screwed!" I kept saying as I paced around inside. I was sure that kid would go around telling everyone that I was back in Kandalı. Then they'd all come flocking to see me. To talk to me, to touch me! I couldn't have that. No one could!

Days and nights passed with me cowering in a corner of the reservoir, shaking. Crammed between two walls, I waited for all of Kandalı to come together and march at me. They would come and tear me apart! It was only a matter of time! I did not sleep. I kept raising the lid to listen in on any footsteps. As much as leaving the reservoir was out of the question, I knew that as long as I stayed there, I was no different than a rat in a cage. The place I picked to hide from the world was the best place to be caught by the world! They'd find me as surely as if they'd put me there themselves, and bury me with those same hands! All of Kandalı's people would besiege me and puncture my skin with their stares. The only thing I could do in defense against all this was to hold my breath. To cut off all contact with the living. But that was no use either. In reality I was so fearful that I couldn't return within and go underneath my skin. I tried over and over. Perhaps for hours on end. Nothing happened. I could neither beat inside my heart nor go with the flow of my blood. And I started to weep. In a corner of the reservoir, shrunk into a tiny ball, I couldn't do any more than weep. Then I brought my palms to my face to wipe away my tears and in raising my head saw him:

My past, standing some way off in the darkness. He stood in front of me like some malformed animal, staring. He had hooves. Just like those of the calf whose birth I'd observed. Standing up straight on very slim, black-haired legs, he was dripping with clear slime resembling a placenta. His body was of earth. And I could see the hands, noses, and teeth of dozens of bodies engorged inside that earth. The only thing he lacked was a face. There was only a pair of red dots in the place his eyes should be, glowing in the dark. Exactly like the dots on the digital screen I'd seen in that bank in Ankara! He had no mouth or nose, though every time he exhaled a cloud of mist appeared underneath his red eyes. The beat of his decomposing heart was heard intermittently, like the clock I'd set to lag. When I couldn't stand it anymore, I screamed "No!" from my enclosure between the two walls.

"No! You are not my past! My past is nothing like this! It's nowhere near as horrific! You don't fool me! Do you understand? Because I know what I've been through! I haven't gone that insane yet! Not *that* insane! I remember everything! In fact I'm the only one who remembers! You want to hear it too? Huh? But it's the last time! I won't tell it again. You know why? Because I'll believe in whatever I choose to tell! Not you or anyone else! I'll only believe in the story *I* tell! Do you understand me?"

And I rose and marched at the monster purporting to be my past. I didn't stop. I walked right through him and started to trumpet my tale. It was clear where I would begin:

"If my father weren't a killer, I wouldn't have been born . . ."

It was hours, maybe days, in the darkness until I finished recounting my own story to myself. I talked until I collapsed. Until I got back on my feet. I lost my voice but still wouldn't quit. I relayed every single thing I knew about my past. And now, it was all over . . . all that was left was the future.

I left the reservoir and headed to the shed to open its door. I warmed in my lungs the icy breath I drew in through my mouth before exhaling through my nose. I spoke.

"You're going to do whatever you want to! You worry people might show up here. Okay! You don't feel as safe as you should. All right! What we're going to do, then, is make sure no one can ever set foot in here! Remember those books you read as a child? Remember the fortresses in those tales? With moats around them? That right there is what we need. We don't have an alligator to toss in, but that's all right! We can make do with a moat!"

I had to find a shovel. I turned into the road leading to town and walked. I was searching for a construction site. Kandalı, however, had vowed to never change. That meant having to walk for hours to find a construction anywhere around it. Finally, near the town's other entrance, I came across an active construction site. I didn't hesitate for a second. I simply walked on and entered the area. Judging by the sign at the entrance, a prison was being built. Just what Kandalı needs, I thought. A prison. Construction actually happened to be my area of expertise. I could seek out the architect to make a few suggestions but I was in a hurry. That's why I hurried on. The workers passed by on either side of me and no one asked me any questions. My clothes were so filthy that possibly I'd become invisible. In the end, after circling once around the future prison with currently only two stories rising, I found what I was looking for. There was even a pickaxe next to the shovel. I took both and walked to the exit. As I passed through the gate, I heard a voice:

"Where're you taking that to?"

I could've stopped. But I didn't. I happened to have some experience in these matters. Years before, Yadigar had also stopped his car next to me and asked me a bunch of questions. Then he'd hauled me off and stuck me into that hole. I didn't want to go through that again. I kept on walking. But the voice was intent on following:

"Look here! Guy, I'm talking to you!"

At this I stopped and turned. There was a distance of about fifty meters between the man and me. I shouted:

"We have a funeral! I'll bring it back after we bury our deceased!"

Naturally he didn't know what to say. This was the chance I was hoping for. I turned and walked. When I heard his voice again, it was unintelligible. He might have been offering his condolences, he might have been cursing. It didn't make any difference.

I felt a heaviness descend on me as I passed through the shopping street and immediately understood why: everyone was staring at me. Especially at my clothes and hair. Who knows

300

how long it had been since I bathed? They must be wondering where I'd come crawling out of. They must either be asking one another, "Who the hell is this guy?" or complaining about the state of the world, "Is this place infested by bums lately! What an eyesore!" I didn't pay attention to any of it. I just walked on. At some point, walking past the pharmacy, I slowed down. I quickly sped up again, though, as I couldn't perform a robbery with a shovel or a pickaxe. I left Kandalı behind, entered Dust Street, and stopped.

I looked around and pictured a circle encompassing the shed. But right after, I thought I would have to enlarge its circumference to include the house too. There might not have been anything left there to loot, but I knew firsthand that children were always intrigued by *wreckage*. More importantly, whores who had been driven out from all over the area showed up in Kandalı every spring and went seeking a place they could sell their goods on the go. I was sure that they must have been using the circumference of the house or the shed itself. I'd seen drink bottles and used condoms strewn around. It appeared that I'd have to include the house in the circle for immaculate isolation. The moat that would protect me from the people of the world would, therefore, go across the very spot I was standing, where Dust Street merged with the garden of the house. Digging the moat would take months but I didn't care. What were a few months in comparison to my decades of nausea?

I threw down the shovel and raised the pickaxe over my head, landing the first blow . . . at the fifth, I was reminded of the pit I'd dug to bury the weakling in, and picked up speed to forget. I crashed through the soil and the more I did, the less I was aware of anything else besides it. The weakling vanished and so did my aches . . .

I bulldozed through three meters of the four-meter width of Dust Street. My moat had to be two meters wide, same as its depth. Later I would pave the bottom and find some water to fill it up with. I thought that stealing a fire truck would be suitable for that task, before remembering that I was incapable of even robbing a pharmacy.

"That's OK!" I said. "I'll get the water somehow. I'll even get a tarp. I can pave the inside with that instead of stones. But now you must get some rest. Go home, lie down . . . You *are* hungry though, aren't you? Just follow me!"

The day I'd paced in front of the restaurants because I couldn't decide what the world's most beautiful girl would prefer to eat was still vivid in my mind. I even remembered which restaurant it was that a waiter stood in the doorway saying, "Come have some soup." . . . I ran straight up to it and went inside. I saw that waiter right away. Before I could get a word out, he lunged at me, saying, "Get out! Get out! Get out! Out! Go on!" I recoiled so his reaching hand wouldn't touch me and left the restaurant. The waiter remained standing in the doorway, still staring me in the eye.

"What?" he said. "What do you want?"

"I'm hungry!"

"Got any money?"

"No!"

"Then get walking!" he said. "Get out of here!"

First I looked into his eyes. Then I turned, crossed the street, and sat on the opposite pavement. The waiter, whose pity was apparently reserved for children, still stood in the doorway of the restaurant and stared at me. There was no soil underneath my hands. I would have eaten that. But there was sawdust. So I scooped up the sawdust on the pavement with my hands and, staring at the waiter, stuffed them in my mouth. At that he disappeared inside as though something sucked him in. Since the show was over, I spit the sawdust out.

Two minutes later I was sitting on the pavement with half a loaf of bread in one hand and a spoon in the other, eating soup.

My life would definitely straighten out if I could just hold out a bit longer. I could sense that I wasn't far from becoming *the idiot of Kandalı*. As far as I could tell, Kandalı had an open position for town idiot. That office could be mine if I tried hard enough. After all, providing food for town idiots was somewhat like feeding pigeons in the city. Besides, the folk of Kandalı owed me! They owed me something around the amount they had promised to raise among themselves some time back to support my education! For now, though, soup would suffice . . . As I dwelled on all this, I heard two women talking as they walked past. One asked the other:

"Isn't that Ahad's boy?"

I was unfortunately too well known to evade correct recognition! The other woman's reply was another question:

"Who on earth is Ahad?"

To *that* question, I replied as I looked up at the waiter who had come back to collect the empty bowl:

"More!"

I had another bowl of soup. I handed the empty bowl back to the waiter and swatted my pants. As the sawdust stuck to them fell away, I paid absolutely no attention to the stares. There was a moat between us. Even the thought of it was enough!

Now it was time to collect some things Kandalı folk would be unable to give me, even if I was an idiot. Sticking my hands in my pockets, I started walking along the pavement. To two children whom I suspected of trailing me, I turned and said, "Mind that you don't fall!" Indeed, if they took another step, they would fall into the moat that surrounded me and drown. This was lost on the kids, however, blind as they were. Though they did stop following me.

I walked a little farther and entered the jeweler's. I sold my mother's necklace and bought a carton of cigarettes. In this way the smoke of my mother's guardian spirit traveled through me.

Then I walked some more and entered the pharmacy. I asked for Band-Aids. My hands were blistered from grappling with the shovel and pickaxe. "Anything else?" asked the pharmacist. It was on the tip of my tongue as my searching gaze roamed over the glass cabinets behind him, but I couldn't bring myself to say it.

Then I walked some more and fell over . . . I got up and walked some more. Then I fell over again. I got up once more, walked. Fell down again. That was how I finished off what remained of the money. Stumbling on, vodka bottle in hand . . . my mother's guardian spirit had only held up to this point: tobacco, medication, and intoxication. But they definitely proved more useful than her!

Then I walked some more and entered the graveyard. I looked for Cuma's grave even though I knew I wouldn't find it. I even implored him to speak to me even though I knew he wouldn't. Ultimately nothing else happened than night. So I went to the reservoir and shut myself in. Or the other way around. I shut the reservoir into myself.

It was the second day of my construction of the moat. I struggled to dig through Dust Street. Done with the pickaxe, I now had to shovel out the soil I'd razed. But my hands shook. Possibly due to fatigue, or maybe the cold . . . I could barely hold on to the shovel. Still, this was no time to quit. After all, I could rest forever once the moat was finished.

Wiping the sweat off my brow with the back of my hand, I looked up at the sky, but there was no beauty to be seen. And so I took a deep breath and plunged the shovel into the earth. Bracing my knees to carry the weight, I hoisted up a thick layer of soil and tossed it over the side of the pit I was in. *I'm going to need a wheelbarrow*, I thought.

Then when I looked down to plunge the shovel into the earth again, I glimpsed a bottle at my feet, half-buried with its lid on. I bent down. It suddenly occurred to me that this could be a trap. I stood up straight immediately and looked around. It could be that someone from Kandalı had come and buried this bottle here while I was in the reservoir. If that was the case, they must be nearby watching me. In fact, there might be something underneath the bottle that could do me harm! I thought of Ender. About the landmine he stepped on! Now this, this could be *my* landmine! Perhaps Ender himself had put it there years ago! I'd pull out the bottle and blow up! I don't know why, but dying right then seemed very reasonable. Possibly because I'd looked up at the sky earlier and saw nothing that was beautiful . . .

I grabbed the bottle by the neck and pulled. Expecting to be blown to pieces, I found myself just standing there with the bottle in my hand. I noticed that there was a piece of paper inside. I held it up to the sunlight. On it were lines of some kind. If all this was taking place near the sea, the bottle and the paper inside would be from the victim of a shipwreck. Like in the books . . . but I was on land. Where no survivor ever had a chance . . . I tried unsuccessfully to unscrew the lid and take the paper out. Consequently, I climbed out of the moat, threw down the bottle, and smashed it with the shovel. I recognized Ahad's handwriting as soon as I'd pulled the piece of paper free of the shards:

*My God . . . I just can't forget. Forgive me. Even if you don't, make sure someone finds this paper. I beg you.*

That was all. I didn't know what to think. Ahad's drunkenness was no secret, but I'd never heard him beg God for forgiveness. I turned the paper over. On the back of it was a plan. Ahad had roughly sketched out the plot and marked a spot on Dust Street as X. Next to it he'd written *tree*. I laughed. He must've been really drunk when he drew this plan. Only the two of us would know which tree that was. In between the sycamores lining Dust Street on both sides was a single olive tree. We used to ignore the sycamores and refer to just the one as *tree*.

Ahad must've written it out of habit. No one else could've made any sense out of this plan but I, unfortunately, could. In fact, I was the only person in the world who could make anything out of looking at this picture . . . but there was one thing I couldn't figure out. To take a piece of paper and write such things, to put it into a bottle and bury it . . . it wasn't like Ahad at all.

"No way!" I said. "There's no way!"

I thought maybe I was imagining it. It really didn't seem possible. Ahad, standing here, digging into the soil with his hands, and then burying this bottle! There was absolutely no way! After all—then an image flashed in my mind! The image of Ahad, years ago, when I rose early and left the house to get food for the world's most beautiful girl, passed out on the chair . . . sitting right in the spot I was standing now, appearing to have watched the dirt road all night long. I closed my eyes and tried to visualize it down to the last detail. I was looking for something, but I didn't find it. There was no bottle to be found in that picture. He'd passed out and there was no bottle around him. Because the bottle he'd imbibed till morning to then toss the paper into was no other than this one! It was the bottle I'd smashed with the shovel just now! It lay in the dirt in three pieces . . . the note and the plan really did belong to Ahad! And I really had never known my father.

I had to make a decision at this point. I could either let Ahad back into my life or crumple up and throw away the note. Which was for the best? It didn't take me long to make up my mind. After all, I'd spent my childhood with two pirates named Dordor and Harmin!

Peering at the piece of paper in my hand, I walked until I was in line with the olive tree. The cross on the plan was quite close to the tree. The edge of the dirt road. I was standing over the spot Ahad had marked. I looked around. There was nothing that seemed out of the ordinary. Whatever it was that had my father begging for forgiveness appeared to be right underneath me. Whatever it was he couldn't forget was below the ground . . .

Putting the piece of paper in my pocket next to Cuma's frog, I started to dig. As I dug I was wondering what I would find.

There was no possibility of guessing what it was Ahad was hiding, however. He would've buried the world if he could find a hole big enough to bury it in. So I was prepared for anything. I just kept on digging. Breathlessly . . . all the breath I'd taken up till then was enough. I thought about every remorseful letter of those sentences and sweated. At the same time, I wondered if there was any way of kicking the shit out of the stroke of luck that brought me to that bottle! But then I'd think of the moat. I felt annoyed that I was wasting my energy when I should be working on that. What could it be that Ahad couldn't forget, anyway? Could such a thing even exist? The Ahad I knew had absolutely no conscience whatsoever. If he had, I'd been spared it. I didn't know what I felt or what my life would look like from now on. I just plunged the shovel into the earth. Then I heard a sound. The sound of metal against metal!

I kneeled down to part the earth with my hands and saw it: a metal cabinet with two doors. It just lay in the earth on its back like that. It looked like an ordinary filing cabinet. It was a least a meter high. I lunged at its likewise metal handles and tried to open its doors, but it was locked. Standing up, I grabbed the shovel and swung it as hard as I could. Nothing happened. I swung again and this time one of the doors caved inward. That made a gap, admittedly small, between the two doors, and all I had to do was put the shovel in there and crank. There was a sound like bones breaking, and I tossed aside the shovel.

Kneeling again, I reached into the hole and pulled the doors open. Then I started laughing. I'd never found any treasure before in my life! All the money Ahad had ever made from smuggling migrants was at the tips of my fingers. They were stacked inside clear bags just staring at me. I pulled out one of the bags and raised it into the air to peer at it. As I laughed I spoke to Ahad:

"This is what you couldn't forget? The money you made off all those poor souls? This is what you were begging God to forgive you for?"

Then suddenly I felt my face changing. My lips came together first, and then my eyes filled with tears. I was no longer laughing. I was thinking of Ahad. Maybe he really had lived in remorse. He might even have been ashamed of the life he was leading. He hadn't touched the money he made off those people's desperation but instead hidden it away. He hadn't wanted to spend it. He'd even felt so bad on a night of intoxication that he'd hoped someone might find the money and relieve him of his burden. Perhaps I'd never met the real Ahad. So, would I be touching the money? Absolutely yes, as I was just Gaza as usual!

I started taking out the bags one by one. But there were so many that I thought it would be easier to just pull the cabinet out. Instead of walking back and forth a dozen times, I could just drag all the money to the shed inside the cabinet . . . I took the shovel and began digging around it again.

Half an hour later I'd managed to make a short incline on one side of the hole. I'd latch on to and haul out the cabinet. I leaned over and pulled, gripping the gaping cabinet with both hands. Although with difficulty, I was able to budge it. Taking small steps backward, I maneuvered it from its spot and tried to move it up the incline. The only thing I saw was the inside of the cabinet. I kept my eyes on the bags of cash that moved slightly every time I pulled. Then my gaze slid to the hole the cabinet came out of. The space left over from the cabinet . . . I could see inside ever so slightly. And I suddenly stopped and looked up. I looked up at the sky. I saw clouds merging with one another. I still hadn't let go of the cabinet. I could sense its weight throughout my entire body, but couldn't move. I only looked at the clouds. I didn't want to see anything else. But then I became unable to see them either, for tears were filling my eyes. The sky shook as I looked up at it.

"Of course . . ." I said. "Of course . . . of course . . . could it be any other way?"

No matter that I didn't want to at all; I bent down my head again to look into that pit and the bones inside. Bones merging into one another like the clouds in the sky. I started to scream.

"Aaahhhhhhh!"

And started yanking on the cabinet.

"Aaahhhhh!"

And I tried to haul the cabinet up the incline.

"Aaahhhhh!"

Maneuvering the cabinet onto the dirt road, I shut up. I took a single step toward the pit and saw everything. Then I immediately stepped back and closed my eyes. But unfortunately, being a chess player, everything I saw engraved on itself on my mind even if didn't want it to. I thought, *So it turns out this money is a prize for whoever finds what's underneath.*

Two bodies broiled by the soil, stripped to the bones . . . two skeletons curled up lying side by side. They still had clothes on. They were covered in dust and disintegrating with time but they were there. Around what was left of their wrists and ankles were chains. Clearly they'd been tied up before being killed and buried. Ahad had been the one to do it. I felt nothing.

Eyes shut, I simply nodded. "Of course!" I said. "Of course! What were you expecting? To see something pleasant? You looked at the sky a minute earlier, see anything pleasant there? Couldn't forget the money he made off the poor fools, could he? You idiot. There, that's what he wasn't able to forget. Open your eyes, just open them!"

I sank to my knees and opened my eyes. Dust covered me. Eyes on the cabinet and the hole, I listened to Ahad. I heard his voice saying there was no need to lay asphalt over Dust Street . . . I always nodded. "Yes, Dad, that's right," I said. "You're right, who needs it?" Here I was, nodding again. Not much had changed since then.

We had one olive tree. Only that one we called *tree*. Because I called it that. Because I'd planted it. That's the spot the piece of shit had pointed out to me! "Plant it here!" he'd said. It was all floating past my eyes and around my ears. Everything! I sat there in the dirt road, watching us. Watching a boy plant an olive tree with his father's hand on his shoulder. Back then, I'd loved Ahad! I had no one but him! That's what he used to say: "We have no one but each other!" and I would nod.

Now I was nodding again. I was also weeping a little, I think. But only a little! "Don't cry!" he used to say. "You're not to cry!" I'd immediately wipe away my tears. That must have been why the word *freedom* always made me think of crying as much as one liked.

My hands shook. I was sure by now that it wasn't due to the cold or fatigue! Had I frolicked over these corpses all those years? What about my mother? Had she known about these deaths? Maybe that was the reason she'd tried to run away from Ahad! She'd wanted to flee her husband whom she'd found out to be a murderer . . . yet she'd wanted to get rid of me too, hadn't she? She was just as cruel as Ahad! In fact, maybe it was my mother who had killed these people! Why not? For someone who considered burying her own child alive, how hard could it be to kill a random stranger?

"No!" I was hollering. "No! I'm not going to end up like them!" Whatever the truth, it had to surface! Who knew how long these people's families had been searching for them? It all needed to come to light! "Enough!" I yelled. "I've had enough!"

I would go to the police. To the gendarmerie! To a prosecutor! Find out who these people are and track down their families, I would tell them. I don't need any more corpses in my life, I would say. I don't need any more darkness! I'd even go to the governor!

He'd said, "If there's anything you need, we'll be here." Yes, there was something I needed! I did now! There were to be no more secrets on this plot of land! What I needed was the truth! I'd even touch people if I had to! I'd touch them and beg! "Help me!" I'd say. "There, these are the bodies! Now tell me what happened! What happened to me? What happened to my life?"

I stood and walked to the pit. "Wait here! I'm coming! I'm going to get you out of there! It'll be all over soon!" I was saying at the same time . . . but suddenly I was silent. For I'd glimpsed something that choked me up. I stood rooted in my spot. It was something I perhaps should never have seen. But it was too late now. I'd come too close to the pit and seen the piece of fabric wrapped around one of the skeletons. It was green . . . with a purple flower print . . . it was the same dress as the one in the only photograph of my mother!

"Why would you want to know that?" Ahad used to say. "So you find out where her grave is, what then?" When I insisted, he'd say, "At a village. Just some village . . . I wouldn't know where to look now if I wanted to find it!"

The night I was born, he'd caught my mother at the cemetery and scooped me up before running to the hospital. Then he'd told the first white coat he came across that his wife was at the cemetery, dying. An ambulance went and returned, and Ahad, had said, staring at the body of his wife, "Take care of my son!" Without even waiting for dawn, he took my mother away to bury her. Neither the mosque in Kandalı nor the cemetery occurred to him as he senselessly drove in the truck for hours. Then he'd gone into a village, had had the funereal prayers carried out, and buried her there. That was Ahad's story!

"No one heard!" he'd say. "No one found out about your mother trying to kill you. Don't you tell anyone, either! This is our secret. Do you understand me? It's enough that you know!"

It was enough that I knew! It was enough that I knew that my mother tried to kill me, was that so? I was yelling:

"Is that so, Ahad! No one can know except me, is that it? Then who is this woman? Isn't she my mother?"

My voice bounced off trees, jarring their trunks and causing the last leaves on their dry branches to fall off. They crumbled as they drifted about and landed on the woman in the green dress.

"Ahad's story!" I was shouting. "How did I ever believe it? How could I?"

My tears trickled into my mouth, and I gulped each one down like a morphine sulfate capsule. I didn't want to know or see anything any more. Going down on my knees, I began to drive forward the dirt on the edge of the pit. To push it in by the handful! Hollering and weeping as I did!

"We're burying holes here, not the dead!" I said. "Mother!" I said. "Ahad!" I said. I shook my head. I turned to the skeleton lying beside my mother and asked, "Who're *you*?"

I saw the trousers it was wearing. Its shirt . . . I could tell it was a male but tried to avoid thinking. I shook my head so I wouldn't understand. I pulled my mother's photograph from my pocket and tossed it into the pit as well, covering it. All I wanted was to bury and forget it all. To pull an earthen quilt over it all and end the matter. I wasn't seeing them anymore. Neither the chains around their wrists, nor the clothes, nor my mother's photograph, nor the bones nor the skulls! I piled the clumps of dirt over them so fast I'd lose my balance and fall over onto my face. I'd get dirt all over. Under my nails, in the roots of my hair, between my teeth, everywhere!

I kept it up until Dust Street was restored to its previous state and closed the hole. There was one last thing I had to do. Pulling Ahad's note out of my pocket, I stuck it into my mouth, weeping, and ground it up as much as I could between my teeth before swallowing. I was breathless . . .

I wiped the sweat off my brow with the back of my hand and looked up at the sky. But I saw nothing that was beautiful . . . truthfully . . . I saw nothing that was ugly either.

I sat in a bank, peering at the number on the small slip in my hand, waiting for my turn. I had two large bags with me. They were filled with Ahad's money. I'd thought the most reasonable thing to do would be to open an account to deposit all the money.

In reality I was constantly dwelling on something so I could forget what I'd seen in that hole on Dust Street. On other things . . . at least, I was trying. I had no intention of facing the fact that my father had killed my mother and some other person I didn't know. If I were to go down that kind of acceptance lane, I might find myself at the dead-end possibility that the man with my mother had been her lover. I might even hit a wall built of the likelihood that he was my real father.

For this likelihood would have been perfect explanation for the mercurial way Ahad had treated me for as long as he was alive. After all, the way Ahad looked at me had forever been loaded with the question, "Do I love you or kill you?" With those pale blue eyes of his! Just like mine! But what if my mother had found another pair of blue eyes to fall in love with? There, once again, I'd been unable to stop myself from dwelling. When there was enough morphine sulfate in my bloodstream I wouldn't have to think about any of it. But clearly there wasn't enough.

I'd first carried the bags of money to the shed before going down to Kandalı at rabid-dog speed to return with the biggest bags I was able to buy. Then I'd dragged the two bags over Dust Street to the main road where I'd waited. After a half-hour wait, I'd flagged down a cab passing by and, when the driver asked where to, said the word that caused his eyes spring wide open: "Izmir!"

After a two-and-a-half hour trip, I paid the driver for the most lucrative run of his life and got out of the car. The spot I got off was in front of the biggest hotel of the city, which up until now I'd only heard of. The man at the entrance, dressed like the general of a nonexistent army, declined to let me in due to my appearance, but the bills I handed him had a pacifying effect. The real issue wasn't how I looked. I stank so badly the cab driver had had the windows down for the whole ride.

After the mandatory chat at reception, and a down payment sufficient to convince them I could stay there, I was able to go up to my room. The only thing that enabled me to struggle through all this was the dream of the morphine sulfate I would unite with soon. Such a dream it was that it had given me the strength to endure being in the cramped space of a cab with another person . . .

Up in the room I took as quick a shower as was possible and left with the bags once more. To the driver of the cab I caught, I said, "I need to find a pharmacy," adding, "I'm kind of in a hurry!" I really was because I couldn't take it anymore. Thinking about the incident on Dust Street while also being alone with another person was obliterating me. I was trembling. I was aching all over. Even in my eyes . . .

I kept telling the driver, "They don't have the medicine I need here either!" as I went through seven pharmacies. None of them would sell me the morphine sulfate without a prescription. But finally, the eighth pharmacist said, "We don't have M-Eslon but we do have Skenan LP, which is the same. We ordered it online for a customer, but he never came to pick it up. Of course it *is* rather expensive . . ."

I laughed angrily. Glaring at the pharmacist who had to talk in such run-on sentences just to do illegal business . . . I bought a total of eight boxes of Skenan LP. One for each pharmacy I'd asked! For three times the market price of M-Eslon . . .

I'd clawed through one of the boxes by the first step I took on the narrow stretch of pavement between the pharmacy and the cab, torn through the plastic casing to pull out the capsule by the second, gulped down the capsule dry on the third, and on the fourth step, got into the car as a brand-new person.

But now I was thinking that that single capsule hadn't been enough. Just as I was reaching for the packet in my pocket for another, I heard someone call out the number written on the slip in my hand. I was being called from the cash desk. Right then I thought of the old man at that bank I'd gone to with Bedri. And I did the same thing as he had. I waited quietly. I wasn't ready to talk to anyone. When my number on the digital screen was replaced by the next, I got up and went to the ticket vendor to get a new queue number. Then I returned to my seat and sat down.

That old man had gotten a new number and continued to wait so he could stay in the crowd. His only concern was to stall his return to the home where he was slowly dying of loneliness, even if for a little while. To talk to someone as he waited at that bank, if he could . . . when he asked me what grade I was in, that was maybe the first he'd spoken all day. He was so alone that the entire day had passed in silence and he'd wanted to hear the voice of a person speaking to him. But I was so sick that I didn't want anyone speaking to me. Unlike that old man, I didn't want to hear anyone's voice. For I knew I'd have plenty of conversation in a bit when I would stick two bags of money in the cashier's face! Perhaps if I shut myself up in the reservoir again, I could avoid talking to anyone and await death in silence. But that was also out of the question now! I couldn't go back to Dust Street as long as those human remains were there. That plot of land in Kandalı was finished for me. Its soil was so tainted that even I couldn't live on it. Or maybe only I couldn't live on it. In the whole world, only I . . .

I was unable to escape this time when a security guard, having glimpsed the number in my hand, said, "They're calling you. Your number's come up."

What happened next was a spectacle that enveloped me. Once he heard the figure I wanted to deposit at the account I would open, the officer immediately took me to the office of the branch director. Thinking he'd stumbled upon a goldmine, the branch director gave an impromptu speech on ways to invest the money but, seeing that I wasn't interested, he'd said, "We'll take care of it, don't you worry," before shutting up. I signed dozens of documents, and every signature was different than the rest. The branch director even noticed and said, "Just sign your initials, that might be easier." I felt good about living in times in which people weren't interrogated over the hefty quantities of money they deposited in banks. I gave silent thanks to all past and present politicians who'd done their best to carve a niche for dirty money, as well as money of dubious origin, in the national economy.

When I left the bank I had nothing more to do. I had to return to my room right away and lock the door. The life on the streets was too personal. You had to face and talk to people for even the most minor things. The world could keep turning without me. So I flagged down a cab and got in . . .

It didn't take much time or effort to turn my hotel room into an isolation chamber. Meals were left on my doorstep on a tray so I didn't have to interact with bellboys. Then I'd leave the empty plates and trays on the doorstep and pull the door shut before anyone saw me. The only problem was the housekeepers who insisted to cleaning the room. The solution I came up with was to limit the cleaning sessions to once per week and on that day, wait in the hallway until the whole thing was over.

Initially I had as much interest in turning on the TV as I had for opening the curtains. But slowly I started doing both, watching the life outside and on TV although I couldn't touch them. Neither life could do me any harm, since they were both behind glass.

At the end of the thirteenth day I didn't leave the room, I thought I might need books and a computer. Though my body was accustomed to being inert, my mind wasn't. My brain had always run at a faster pace than my heart. Therefore I needed to keep it busy at all times. If I didn't, it screamed like a child who'd discovered his mother's corpse, and irritated me constantly. I dreamed of a life in which I could take care of everything over the phone. That was how it should be! I had to start with the pharmacy. Its number was in the small plastic bag with the boxes of morphine sulfate. I called and placed my order. However, though I introduced and described myself to him, the pharmacist hung up on me. There was nothing to be done. I knew I'd have to go outside if only for once.

I'd take care of all my business in the same day. I inserted my daily dose of morphine sulfate into my blood and the cash I'd set aside for myself in my pocket and went down to the reception. I told the woman with her name on her chest that I'd like to stay at the hotel another month.

"Sure," she said at first before curiosity got the better of her and she tried to find out my reasons for staying at such an expensive hotel for so long. To do that, she rambled some indirect queries like every ordinary fraud. But her efforts were fruitless. For every question she asked, I replied with another. So our conversation went something along the lines of:

"Your business has been delayed, I assume?"

"Where's the nearest bookstore?"

"Go down the main street, to the right two hundred meters away. Is this your first time in Izmir?"

"Where can I find somewhere that sells computers?"

Her chin dropping down level to her name on her chest at not being able to get anything out of me, she was obliged to check the monitor in front of her, saying, "Right, the room is available," take the money I handed her, and bid me a good day.

As I left the hotel, I was thinking that the woman had been eyeing my clothes the whole time and that I would need new ones so as not to attract any more attention. It was going to be a long and extremely tedious shopping day . . . just as it turned out to be.

When I returned to my room, however, I had everything I needed. What was more, I'd be able to conduct my whole life on the phone. Most importantly, paying the money for my next order of morphine sulfate up front had convinced the pharmacist that he should never hang up on me again. I was basking in contentment at having minimized the amount of contact I'd have to have with people to go about my daily life.

"Maybe I'll buy a house," I'd say, closing my eyes. "I'll have a house of my own, and I'll shut the door and leave everyone outside!" Really though, that was a bit tricky. I'd need to be alone with too many people if I were to buy a house. "Maybe later," I said.

"When I up the dose of the morphine sulfate a bit more. Or a bit later than that. When I have to mainline the morphine sulfate with a needle because swallowing doesn't cut it. Or maybe a bit later than that. When my veins are too riddled with clots and become useless . . ."

I could go buy myself a house then. And then I could overdose and die in it! Being found dead in a hotel would be humiliating. They'd find my corpse as soon as it started to smell. Then tens of strange, insolent hands would touch my body. I had to die in such a house that no one could find any flesh on me to touch. I had to find the most remote house in the world. Like that lighthouse in the novel by Jules Verne. I needed to find the house at the edge of the world. I had to decay long before anyone realized I was dead. That's how they ought to find me. Rotting! I ought to make them sick when they laid eyes on me! It had to be fear at first sight! At least then we'd be even . . .

I'd been in the hotel for seven months and lived in a state of absolute discipline. My loneliness was at the exact degree it should be. The Internet, books, and me . . . and maybe, also, the mirrors . . . All the hotel employees, including the manager, had gotten used to me. No one ever bothered me, even though my presence there remained a mystery. After all, the most important thing was that I pay for the room. I could continue to enjoy my immaculate isolation as long as I kept that up.

As rare as it was, however, I did feel the lack of people around me. I even had moments when I wondered what my life could be like if I were able to touch them or have real relationships with them. Such fear would come over me then that I'd immediately immerse myself in morphine sulfate. At least then I'd be shielded from the panic that threatened to tear me apart. Panic was a cannon covered with poison spikes! It roamed inside me, leaving everything bloody and riddled with holes. But there'd been different effects ever since I'd started shooting up the Skenan LP. I experienced memory loss, though briefly. I'd sit in bed and get my fix, then open my eyes to find myself in the bathroom. I had no idea how long I'd been or how I'd gotten there. Like a sleepwalker, I simply acted without realizing . . .

I didn't like this effect. I was especially anxious that I might leave the room when I was in that state. The more anxious I was, though, the more morphine sulfate I needed. I had a sense of being in a true catch-22. I could count only on discipline to overcome the feeling. If I was going to end up in a catch-22, it had to be my own! Every one of my actions had to take place at the same time every day, and I had to be the boss. I had no tolerance for flyaway minutes. Perhaps it was a leftover habit from the dorm . . . a leftover habit from Azim, to be exact . . .

I exercised in order to tire out my body. There was a limit to what I could do inside the room. Even so I managed to bring in a treadmill from the hotel's gym. I thought that by exhausting my body I could prevent myself from leaving the room while under the influence of morphine sulfate. Because I'd realized that locking the door wasn't enough. Once I even opened my eyes to find myself in the hallway. When I came to, I found myself just standing there on the burgundy carpet of the hallway, a little ways down from the door to my room. Like a statue . . . and even worse, I was facing the elevator at the end of the hall.

Who knows what I'd do if I went out on the street? I didn't even want to dwell on it. I hadn't gone outside in months and didn't intend to for several more. I'd just hurry to an ATM near the hotel to withdraw cash and back. But that didn't count as going outside, since I never met anyone's eyes or touched anyone.

Something was brewing in me, however, and it apparently had to wait for me to sync with the morphine sulfate before it could dart out. I'm not sure who was keeping watch over whom.

All I could tell was that both sides lay in wait. At least I did. I ran on the treadmill for hours so I could control the dark side that wanted to take my body outside among the people. Until I collapsed . . . Aside from that, my life was perfect! Or I was just imagining it, as usual.

In my ninth month at the hotel, I decided I would no longer resist the intoxicating effects of morphine sulfate. I took a great leap and started taking walks in the morning. Going down to the shore, I weaved my way through the people. It really was a great enough leap to make me weak in the knees. I had to put up with people bumping into me as they passed by or saying, "Good morning!" In truth I intended these excursions to prevent me from doing something worse while on morphine sulfate. There was no limit to the things I might do in that state. I might even solicit a prostitute and find myself having sex with her. Anything could happen! So if I possessed even the smallest spark in the way of getting well, *I* had to be the one to turn it into a forest fire, not the person I was under the influence of morphine sulfate.

I started lightly experimenting with this. I'd go sit in a café and eavesdrop on the conversation at the next table. Next-table conversations were completely harmless. I wasn't being spoken to or addressed, but I was somehow involved in the communication. I was trying to reintroduce myself to people . . .

A while later, I figured out what types of conversations took place at which café or bar and started scheduling my daily tours to correspond. For instance, I'd go to one place to listen to middle-aged women, another place to listen to girls my own age, and yet another place if I wanted to listen to men of all ages talking about those girls. Eavesdropping on next-table conversations was really like gazing at the fireplace. It was one of the safest types of socializing because there was no responsibility. It was like those times I'd get out of my seat and stand over the waste basket in the corner of my class in grade school to sharpen my pencil. I felt invisible as the whole class went on right next to me. Unfortunately you couldn't sharpen a pencil forever. Likewise the conversations didn't last either . . .

Then I took a further leap and joined an Internet chat room to communicate with people, no matter that it was only writing. That, however, was a total disappointment. I knew as soon as I'd joined that I was fooling myself. I could converse to death over the Internet on any and every subject imaginable, but this wouldn't help me utter even as much as my name in real life. So I realized that the Internet wasn't really all that different from morphine sulfate. It was like reading the minds of the completely unfamiliar people I passed by in the street. And that wasn't what I needed. There was enough noise in my head as it was . . .

Aside from this I also joined guided tours a few times. I followed the rambling guides through ancient ruins and on hikes. Soon I also gave up on that, however, because someone would always try to talk to me on snack breaks and I'd clam up. When anyone turned to me and asked me something, I'd feel dizzy, my heart would constrict. I'd forget everything I knew and stammer, turning into a complete imbecile. I was starting to believe that my people allergy was biological rather than psychological. Because whenever I was near them, my neck itched, my face burned, my palms sweated, and my temples throbbed with pain . . .

I recalled the words of the young psychiatrist at the hospital in Gölbaşı whose diagnosis Emre and the others hadn't taken seriously: "A subtype of trauma-related social anxiety disorder . . ." He had been right. In light of my more recent situation, at least, the correct diagnosis for me was this: social phobia or anxiety or worry or whatever the hell it was! I'd been able to pass Emre's test of reconciling me with vitality, even if only through self-deception. It was time to become ordinary. To perform the social endeavors ordinary people undertake in their ordinary lives without even thinking about it . . . yet no matter how hard I tried to convince myself, I never felt safe among people and could never believe them. I thought they would surely harm me and close in on me on all sides and suffocate me. I was afraid they would bury me inside themselves. I was afraid of being crushed under their emotions and thoughts, of the weight of their bodies breaking my bones. I was threatened by their constantly moving lips, their restless hands, and their teeth that flickered in and out of sight. Those thirteen days and five hours of hell had ruined me. My sickness was too severe for any amount of recovery to help! At least that's how I felt. No matter how much progress I made, I was sure I'd never have any real relationship with anyone.

As a young boy, I used to say, "When I grow up, I'm going to be all by myself!" Well, here I was, all by myself! But now I was trapped by my loneliness. I'd merely wanted an isolation pocket I could go in and out of whenever I wished. So I could get away from Ahad and the immigrants . . . an isolation pocket with a door . . . but now there was no such door. All those corpses had walled off the entrance, leaving me alone with my breathing. Inasmuch as my body had departed the reservoir in Kandalı, I was still gazing at the walls of that dark cell. The reservoir followed me everywhere like the imaginary moat that once surrounded me. That was the reason my loneliness was a snare. I'd been hunted down by life and waited for the hunter to come collect me. Just like morphine sulfate, loneliness also came in doses and that was where I lived . . . but the human inside me, the survivor against all odds, searched for a way to go among his own, that is, other people. But I resembled a haystack on the inside, and the chances of a needle finding a way out of there were very slim. So my days were either drenched in a waterfall of morphine sulfate or found me drenched in sweat on the treadmill.

Aside from that, I read. I only read. I read about the world, the people, and the time that I was missing out on. There was nothing else I could do. Perhaps I could also kill myself, but I left myself no time for that. I always nodded off before I could hang myself.

I lived in that hotel for ten months. Due to the speed at which I was depleting my money, however, I was compelled to move. Not to an apartment, but to another hotel . . . it was named the Ship. That's why I picked it. In memory of Dordor and Harmin . . . One of its two stars had been scratched into the wall of the elevator, probably with a key.

I spent at first months, and then years, on that Ship. In the beginning I became even more reclusive, never mind getting better. I became so introverted I turned into a whirlpool. I started to suck myself into a vortex and everything got mixed up. My past resurfaced, and it was more horrifying than it had been in the reservoir. Because it was invisible! It was only aural. It resembled Ahad's voice. It was muffled as though it was coming up through the earth. My only resort was to emerge from my whirlpool to scream, "Enough!" and add:

"You are not my past! My past isn't anything like this! I'll tell you what my past is! Listen to me good because this is the last time I'll tell it! And whatever it is I choose to tell, I'll believe in from this moment on!"

Where I should begin was evident:

"If my father hadn't been a killer, I wouldn't have been born . . ."

When I finally finished the story and was silent, I was no longer a whirlpool but a calm expanse of water. Then I picked up living from where I'd left off . . .

My single-serving life, as usual, was a disciplinary sentence. I did every single thing with a precision to the millimeter that I perfected over time. I knew how much dirt I would get under my nails due to which activities throughout the day, how many times I would consequently need to scrub them with the nail-brush until they were completely clean, the number of words I could memorize in one reading, and how long I could stand on one foot, left and right respectively. I knew how many people's birth and death dates I could reel off and how many Renaissance artists I could name while doing sit-ups without my back or heels touching the floor.

My memory was a code of conduct for discipline, and I was discipline itself. After all, there was nothing to keep me busy except myself. So years passed by in the service of upgrading myself as if I were a piece of technology. In a laboratory I'd laid the bricks to surround me, since after all the only information I needed to produce me was myself, but of course it always fell short at one point. Naturally it was the fact that I'd never had a chance to test the final product, myself.

Needless to say, my attempts at quality control didn't count, as my sickness would start smothering my consciousness as soon as I went out among people. I couldn't repeat something with someone else present even though I was perfectly capable of it on my own. My potential capabilities, which blossomed in a controlled test environment, chemically reacted with the carbon dioxide expelled by random strangers and were rendered nonfunctional.

As stupid as I was when surrounded by human flesh, I was that much more intelligent when on my own. A mortal when everyone else on the streets was god, I was the god of gods between the walls I shut myself up in . . . Really it was all a matter of putting in the hours. I had the time to be the god of gods, was all. Others, however, were subjected to all the side effects of living together and put the majority of their resources into it. But they didn't even know it and thought they were supposed to live together. And now I also wanted to believe.

Whenever I went out, however, I'd hit the wire mesh called reality and start to shake. I talked to myself constantly and couldn't stop. I sat on a bench and talked about whatever I felt like. People glanced at me and walked away, unsettled. I tried to shut up but couldn't.

Then it occurred to me to write. "If I write, I might stop talking!" I thought. I started going down to the shore with a notebook and pen. I tried to write everything that went through my mind in the book to keep from talking. But after a while I found myself writing letters to the people around me. In truth they weren't letters but cries for help. Similar to my cries when I was beneath those corpses . . . I may not have been able to touch these people or talk to them, but I tried to make some sort of sound in writing at least.

An old man would sit next to me on the bench and I'd write in the book:

*Hello . . . my name is Gaza.*

But no one could hear what I was writing. Then I wrote in capital letters. Letters that shouted! But they were still inaudible! The old man got up and left, and a young woman sat in his place. I turned a page in my book and tried again:

*Hello . . . my name is Gaza.*

My first three years in the Ship passed by like this, as I could do nothing but improve myself and look for ways to escape from my prison of loneliness. I made hundreds of plans for escape and used them all. I was caught every time, but I never gave up. It was hard to escape from a prison guarded by one's own self! But sooner or later I'd make it.

By my fourth year at the hotel, I was on the streets all the time. Every day! I was in front of, behind, and next to people constantly. I got on elevators with them, pressed the same buttons they pressed, and retrieved the bottles they threw in the trash to bring to my lips. I drew up close to women from behind the way I used to as a boy and got their hands to bump against me. I got on buses at rush hour and let people brush against me. Felat would have been proud! Each invention I made in the service of approaching people was a true gem! I did everything I could! Everything!

And on my fourth year at the Ship, a miracle happened! I experienced extraordinary intimacy of a different kind, one that hadn't occurred to me until that day. I was finally compensated for all the time I spent on the streets in a transformative moment I stumbled upon by coincidence. It changed everything!

It was October. The sun shone as though in announcement of the miracle that was about to take place. It was the afternoon and it happened all at once:

I joined complete strangers in the lynching of a complete stranger.

I stood there, just staring at the sun. It stared back from its perch over the most elaborate building in the square, the watchtower. The haggling over trinkets had long been cut off by the back-to-your-rooms gong, the frequency of which was only audible by tourists such as myself, sweeping most of the crowd under hotel towels. Those remaining in the square before dinner kept opening their shopping bags to try to subtract the weight of their finds from the degree they'd been ripped off. For this they would stop every three steps, the sunlight spilling over their shoulders like golden capes each time.

I'd also heard the gong, but I didn't want to leave my spot. From where I stood, I saw everyone silhouetted against the sun. They neither had mouths to talk about me behind my back with, nor eyebrows to rise and fall or eyes to ignore me with. The people were between the sun and me, and they'd all gone dark. I couldn't make out any of their faces or read any of their thoughts and savored the self-deception. Their shadows, as dark as their bodies, stretched out around them and made a world of giants of the square's pavement.

From where I stood, I watched them pass by underneath my feet and crushed their heads. I didn't have to take a single step. They were the ones extending their arms, legs, and bodies under my soles to be smashed to pieces. I may have been standing on the shadows and not on the actual people, but for the moment it was enough. It was more than enough for someone who felt his only viable chance at being close to anyone was an organ transplant . . .

Right then I felt a humming in my ears. Then suddenly the earth started shaking. I saw the giants run from their land and immediately looked up to scan my surroundings.

The people had suddenly vanished. A child whose mother tried to drag him away by the hand was pointing an ice cream at something behind me. I'd started to turn around when something dashed by me. It was so fast I had to blink twice to see that it was a person. At first I thought it was a pickpocket. But it was more like the guy was running from a tsunami than the police. Not for freedom, but for his life. Spinning around on my heels, I saw said tsunami. After all, two-thirds of the human bodies rushing at me like lava from an erupting volcano were water. In fact, the water flowed from their mouths in the form of foam, while their arms, which they swung to run faster, undulated like the gears of a harvester ready to chop down everything in its way. I was either going to get trampled by them, or start running, or throw up my hands and cry, "Stop!"

I didn't have much of a choice because I had the courage to neither be trampled nor talk. So I was going to run. But how? The smallest miscalculation in timing would mean being trampled by the racing crowd or, if I got too close to the man, contaminate me with whatever crime it was he'd committed. I had to run in such a way I could blend into the crowd without any damage.

It was too important a decision to be left up to me. So I unconditionally turned over the command of my body and mind to fear. The tyrant known as fear readied me like a relay race runner so I made a perfect start as soon as I felt the breath of the crowd on the back of my neck. If all the trapeze artists of the world, who made a living hurling themselves into thin air at the right time so they could catch a pair of hands, could witness me setting out, they would have envied me; so flawless was my timing. And I didn't even have a net below me. Only dusty concrete with feet wearing it out, waiting for someone to fall so it could scrape off their skin.

I was so merged into the mob that I felt as if we'd been together since whenever it was they'd started running. As if we'd been running shoulder-to-shoulder since we were born, even. I was no longer in the front lines but some way off in the back. In the midst of the people. Fear had picked me up like a baby and swathed me in numbers. It was no longer my tyrant but my god. And just like any other god, it needed a sacrifice. I didn't have to look too hard, since the sacrifice was some distance ahead, screaming as he ran. A few more steps and our voices caught his ears first, and then our hands his shoulders. Though he tried to shake free one last time, our numbers quickly swallowed him. It was as though he was losing not a finger or an arm, but his entire body, to a bench saw. I'd shoved past the two necks in my way to see him up close when something struck the inner corner of my eye.

At first I thought it was a small pebble or the finger of one of the people near me. I was still running, though with one eye closed. It was as if my eyelids were glued together and sealed closed with red wax. I knew I had the color of the wax correct when I looked at the finger I reflexively rubbed my eye with. My fingerprint was red. But what sealed my eyelids together was blood, not melted wax. The first blood of the sacrificial victim had sailed through the air like a fishing line and struck me in the eye with its hook. I was seeing blood.

I realized right then that I was now ruled by something other than fear. Fear had assumed god form to rise to the heavens and so excitement had gotten hold of my body and reason. The excitement of moving as one with and in the same direction as the people I hadn't been able to be near in years. The excitement of chasing the same ideals as people I'd have difficulty looking in the eye on a regular day, let alone touch! Just a few minutes ago, I'd been taking pleasure in crushing their shadows and now they had me by the hand, inviting me to crush someone else.

I felt freer than I'd ever been. The walls of my prison of loneliness were demolished! No one judged me or thought I was crazy. I was the society and its influence, and I was drunk on it. The mob and me, as I blissfully melted into it, we were magnificent. Like a gigantic stingray undulating in the air. A perfect leviathan. Our feet left the ground and our hands tangled. We collided, tripped, held on to one another. We rose and descended, fell and got up and ran without a glance behind. Breathless, elbow-to-elbow, we traversed walls of dust, our sweat spilling onto one another's shoulders. We didn't blink or ever stop shouting. It didn't matter what we were saying or where we were going, because we were after him. That precious bloodied body. The body that was redder every time it rose above the sea of hands and emerged more naked every time it sank into the crowd below.

If they could, his ravaged nostrils would've inhaled us into his lungs instead of oxygen. His eyelids, if there were any left to open, could only close by rubbing against us. For we were all around him. There were a hundred of us, perhaps a thousand! Who knows how many nails we had, how many teeth? How many of us had eaten, how many shared a name? None of it mattered because we were now one.

He was our soul and we were his flesh. And like all souls he was ahead of the flesh. A kick would send his head flying just as it got ahold of his hair; his body would be dragged away just as it was about to crush his torso. We shook off the hair wrapped around our fingers, still attached to their roots, as our soles beat the ground. We couldn't hold on to him. From hand to hand and foot to foot he flitted like a butterfly, its wings open in appeal. We couldn't reach him. Billowing bonelessly above our heads like a flag, his body, in a split second, turned into a deflated ball and bounced off our toes. He was a tree trunk being carried off by the current, and we were the current itself. He vacillated between existing and not existing, bobbed up and down on the waves. And there was just one thing we desired: to get to him before he died. To douse our ears with his final scream, our faces with his final breath. Don't let it end, I screamed inwardly. Whatever it is that's called *now*, don't let it end! Because I didn't know what I'd do when it did . . . but it did end.

First we were surrounded by mist and we started coughing. Then our eyes watered, and there was a barrage of police batons. Every drop went in through the backs of our necks to spill out of our mouths. Down the corners of our lips, leaving broken teeth. We dissipated like smoke under lashes from pressurized water. Everyone ran or hobbled back to where they'd come from, the undulating stingray vanishing. Leviathan was dead.

I watched the rest on TV. On the evening news. Police had found the soul we'd abandoned in the square, drenched in blood. I found out his identity from the anchor: B dot F dot.[9] He was a retired literature teacher. A rapist that filled a fourteen-year-old student with himself instead of with poetry. He'd spent eight years in the cell he'd been put into as a protection from the other inmates and was assaulted by a person, and then God knows how many people, on the day he'd been released.

---

9   The names of victims or alleged criminals are disclosed by the Turkish media in initials.

"Incredible!" said the anchorwoman, whose shade of blond looked like it would require serious surgery to obtain. "It's incredible that he escaped unharmed from the assault of a mob of such magnitude! Yes, ladies and gentlemen, as you can s—"

The power went out, and I found myself staring at my own reflection on the dark screen a few inches away. I sat on the foot of my bed in the narrowest room of the Ship. The most valuable piece of furniture in the darkness was now the light that emanated from the glass onto the wall, which in turn came from a streetlamp. It and its halo stared at me like St. Giraffe of the streets. The perpetual hum of the air conditioner, usually running at maximum so as not to leave guests any room to grumble, was silent. Though it had kept me warm ever since it had gotten colder, or at least that's what it had felt like . . .

Time stood still first. Then cold filled the room in a flood, and I started shivering so hard I thought I'd drown. So hard that it made me nauseated. I could neither stop my jaw nor my hands. Even my eyes must have been shivering. If someone took a photo, I'd definitely come out blurred. The room was so narrow there was nowhere to throw up except on myself. Difficult as it was, I clamped my lips shut to hold back the remnants of the last meal I'd had, which now came up all the way to my teeth. I didn't know what to do. I couldn't have caught something. Yet perhaps!

Had I by any chance contracted a virus from the crowd I'd been a part of? Why not? That much hate was bound to infect me. A really peculiar disease with a name I'd have to ask the doctor to repeat at least three times before I got it! Arms wrapped around myself as though in an invisible straitjacket, I shivered as I tried to pinpoint the reason. It didn't take long. It found me: fear. It struck me on the brow like a hammer from the heavens. I fell backward. As I writhed on the bed like a living person inside a body bag, I saw the room turn into fear. First, the white-maned horses in the shitty hotel painting above my head took on the form of fear and trampled me into the ground. Then the wall across from me took on the form of fear to collapse onto my legs and the ceiling took on the form of fear to collapse on top of me. Finally, the power, in the form of fear, came back on.

I got off the bed so fast my head spun. "Right away!" I said.

"Right away! Right now! I have to go, I've got to run! They'll discover what I've done! They'll discover that I was there today! There, in that crowd! Did I hit him? Was I able to hit that man? Does it matter? Isn't it enough that I was there with them? They'll put me in prison! I'm screwed!"

My voice, rising in volume, had started to echo within me and then off the walls when someone knocked twice on the wall I'd braced myself against to keep from falling. I shut up and held my breath. Who was in the next room? Would he turn me in? Had he heard me yelling? Would he call the police? Then there was another knock. And another. And another. And another. And another and another. It ended on a groan. A violin wrapped up the drum solos. The panic, the shivering, the fear, and everything else . . . were ejaculated into oblivion.

No one was looking for me! No one would call the police! No one cared! The people in the next room, the people next to them, and the people underneath and above them, and all those who'd climbed over one another in that square to kill a person and seemingly failed, they were, every one of them, screwing, or had screwed and were busy digging tunnels to dreams. Life went on so hard I was embarrassed at being scared. I laughed. When in Rome, do as the Romans do! Wasn't that how the saying went? But I was a Spartan in Rome! So I screwed neither myself nor anyone else.

Instead, I broke open two morphine capsules on a piece of paper, crushed the miniature bubbles with a lighter, and patiently dissolved the dusty powder in cold water before drawing it into a filtered syringe. Then I sent it into my bloodstream through the space between the peace-sign fingers on my right hand like I was boss of the motherfucking world.

Two days went by without anyone knocking on my door. I wasn't arrested, nor did anyone come nosing around. In the meantime I recalled Baudelaire, his famous quote: *My heart is lost; the beasts have eaten it.* I myself was one of the beasts now. To boot, there was no penalty to eating hearts if there were enough of the beasts. If there'd been, Baudelaire would have added: *Then the day came and holes riddled each of their hides!* But there was no such line in any of his poems. So it would seem that the lynching kitchen had one principal rule: no matter how much dirt you get on your hands, you'll be clean when you leave! So that's what I did, washed up and left the room. It was clear where I was headed.

I returned to the square where it all began. It was at least as clean as I was. There was neither a bloodstain nor a molar in sight. One more battlefield had been wiped clean from history by a firefighter's hose, allowing tourists to replace the killers and the bodies. Fine, but could the act of lynching be counted as battle? I was dwelling on this question when I spied a couple taking turns photographing each other. This reminded me of the homework

I'd presently assigned myself. I now gave myself simple assignments and tried to complete them no matter how hard. I'd progressed from pen and paper to vocal cords. I managed to talk to people even if only slightly.

"I can take your picture if you'd like."

They were so absorbed in taking up the frame that it took them a few seconds to process my words. The young woman, smiling, acted before the man.

"Thank you so much. If you could please snap us in front of the tower . . ."

Her boyfriend was taken aback by her abrupt acquiescence. He hadn't had the chance to look me over to determine whether I looked like I'd run with the camera. He might have handed it over with more assurance if he'd had five more seconds. Since he couldn't very well say to a stranger, "I'm worried you might be a thief. Would you promise you're not a thief?" he was obliged to point out the shutter release. I took the camera and took four steps back. I brought it up to my face and squinted into the viewfinder with my left eye.

First he put his hand on her shoulder. Then she turned and flattened the length of her body against him and put her hand on his chest. They bared their teeth in unison. The moment they'd been waiting for had arrived. They probably looked like a pair of dumbasses in the majority of the photos they'd taken that day. They'd cut the forehead off one or the nose off the other trying to include in the frame, not counting themselves, buildings, statues, fountains, horse carriages, horses, and other horseshit. Anyhow, it was really none of my business. What concerned me was my treatment, and I'd faultlessly completed the first step, the offer to take a picture.

The second half of the assignment, however, was more difficult. In no way could I let myself be intimidated by these two people as they struck the pose of their lives in front of me and held it for at least thirty seconds, in spite of the discomfort behind their frozen smiles. And I'd only been able to inwardly count to six.

The woman was the first to react. After all, the responsibility for letting me into their lives rested on her. Without her smile wavering, a very impressive feat, she asked, "Isn't it working?"

I didn't reply. This was a medical condition. It was a cleansing process. Pressing that shutter within thirty seconds was like an addict taking up heroin once again. Resistance was excruciating. These people standing in front of me like taxidermied pets weighed so hard on me that it was as if their stares pierced my throat and their teeth—between lips I suspected must be getting numb—tore off my ears. Or that was just how I felt. All they did was stand there and stare at me. Or at the camera in between us, to be accurate. Now the man asked:

"Isn't it working?"

Once again I didn't reply. That they asked this, really, was proof of their goodwill. Instead of saying "Why aren't you taking the photo?" they placed the blame on the camera by asking, "Isn't it working?" I couldn't do this to them any longer. But I was a dam that must remain standing until the very end, straining under the pressure of human existence. Just as he started to take his hand off her shoulder to move toward me, I cried:

"All right, here I go!"

It was a kind of hurrah. He resumed his pose, and I pressed the shutter. Thirty-three seconds exactly! It was an extraordinary achievement! We'd all passed the test of forbearance! They'd shown me how civil they could be while I'd assured myself that I wasn't afraid of them. Two steps each brought us together, and they looked first at the photo on the camera's screen and then at me. All three of us were smiling now.

"It's come out great, thank you so much," said the woman, obliging me to complete the next level of my assignment.

"You're welcome. Two liras."

Both their smiles vanished.

"Excuse me?" said the man.

"The charge," I said, "is two liras."

It was the woman's turn to speak: "You charge for taking photos?"

"Obviously."

"But you never told us!" he said.

"You never asked," I replied. "I thought you knew, so . . ."

"How were we supposed to?" they grumbled, before the woman, not wanting such a ridiculous episode to stain their memory of the day, silenced him and thrust her hand into her bag:

"All right, all right, whatever!"

My treatment session seemed to be nearing its end as she dug into her sack-like bag for her wallet. As such, as the search practically stretched out over ten years all the way into a black hole, I had no idea where to hide. In the meantime the man shook his head as he probably cursed his mortgage, health insurance, education, and love for the woman—in short, all that he had—for standing in the way of his wasting a cheat like me on the spot. It was, of course, not the two liras that caused his loathing but rather my brash disregard of common courtesy that reminded him that he should trust no one. He was probably fuming about how he'd never have a moment's peace in this world, and how everyone was lined up for the chance to screw him. In any case, we all stared at the same thing. The gaping mouth of the bag that was resolutely unwilling to wield the wallet. Then she suddenly looked up at the man. Naturally, so did I.

"You don't have it?"

"No!" he said, since he couldn't say, "No, for fuck's sake!" And again in silence we watched the mouth of the bag. Standing there apprehensively was so embarrassing that I almost ran off at some point. But I had to endure. I'd been running for years. I wasn't going anywhere this time. I had to calm down. I had to think of something to take me out of the moment. The lynching was the first thing to come to mind. I thought of the lynching. How good I'd felt engulfed in that crowd. The ease with which I'd touched people, fearlessly . . .

"There you go!"

The woman slapped the two liras into the palm of my hand like it was a ruler, before linking her arm with her boyfriend's, saying, "Come on." They walked off, quickly at first, then more slowly. I felt great watching them shrink. It wasn't long, however, before my stomach was spinning like a drill pin. This time I was in an open enough space that I wouldn't puke on myself. Still, out of habit, I cupped my hands. When I threw up, part of it landed on the two liras and part on the dusty paving stones of the square. Glancing around, I tried to holler but could only whisper:

"Someone call the fire brigade!"

I returned to the hotel and locked myself in. But that was no good. I still wasn't safe. The attendant I'd walked past just now had greeted me in such a way that I'd known he meant, "I can go into your room any time I want!" I grabbed the chair with one short leg that betrayed me every time I sat down just like the stool in the shed, and propped it against the door. Then it dawned on me that this was no good either, since the door opened outward. There was only one remaining solution: locking myself in the bathroom.

The cramped bathroom I'd constantly complained about since moving into the hotel, though always inwardly and never to reception, was finally to be of use. It was as big as a telephone booth, its door and three walls all within reach of the occupier. This time, however, I also noticed there was no key in the door. But I had no other choice if I wished to slow down my pulse.

In one step I entered the bathroom and shut the door but couldn't let go of the knob. Anyone could open it from the outside at any time. So I had one hand clutching the doorknob as though someone were trying to force it open and one hand against the mirror, not knowing where else to put it. Ten breaths later, when I was calm enough to look up, I met my own eyes. And just like I had for some time whenever I saw myself in the mirror, I started talking:

"You want to get better? Do you really want to get better? What was it, your sickness? Inability to go out among people, is that it? Socializing, isn't that what it's called? Not being able to do that! Don't you see it's not something that'll go away with something as stupid as you just did? You know what the real cure is? Let me tell you: socializing to the extreme! That's the only way you can save yourself. So you have a sickness that makes you squirm like a worm in the depths of the earth, then what you do is you learn to fly! That's the only way you can find middle ground! You have to balance your sickness! The only treatment for you is to lynch! There is no socializing on this planet more extreme than that! Are you listening? Don't mention any of this to anyone. Now go out and find yourself a woman! Just kidding, you freak, don't worry. Go inside and do some push-ups. Or wait, brush your teeth first. But don't you let go of the door!"

The lynching wouldn't stop occupying my mind. I thought of and read about only it. As I did I became only more aware that it wasn't just any old violent act. Lynching was more than the sum of a random multitude's fists. It was a social fact! It was an act that had a role in social anthropology! In fact, it was formative! It was formative in the relationship between society and the individual, between the majority and the minority. It was a collective right! It was what Rousseau had referred to as *direct democracy*! It was everything! The American known as Charles Lynch, who made it possible to put a name to all this, was a genius! He may be remembered today as a barbarian, but the United States of America ruled the world by his law: the Law of Lynch!

When I tired of reading, I'd train my eyes on the ceiling and contemplate . . . My room and I, we were inside a tiny glass sphere that the lynching had shaken up, dispatching fragments of thought off the floor. Inside the glass sphere, I watched my thoughts drift down like snow. After some time the whiteness engulfed me and a landscape emerged . . . a landscape at least as scientific as my article, *The Power of Power*.

Ancestor of man, the first primate to stand upright had, as he did so, given himself a concussion knocking his head on the thick branch of the tree next to him. Said concussion was genetically handed down from generation to generation and had two consequences that changed the course of humanity's history.

First of all, a large portion of the brain was rendered useless. Therefore man, as the descendants of that primate, had to make do with the remainder of the brain. The second consequence was: *fear of environment*, offset by his eating of a fruit he picked off the branch of a tree, forming the backbone of human existence.

Naturally if this primate could have carried on on four feet like other animals, it would all be different. Since getting from one point to another on four feet increased the risk of getting raped on the way, however, it had no choice but to stand. It would still have been nice if he had looked up before doing so. Anyhow, thanks to this ancestor of ours, we were either idiots or cowards. In any case we couldn't be blamed for anything. You could even say we'd made quite a bit of progress in a sense. After all, we could finally define the common fear that was a quintessential part of our identity.

In truth, this fear was nothing more than a self-composed mayhem scenario cultivated by experience. It needed a name and Latin was required for credibility: *Bellum omnium contra omnes*. The omnipresent state of war! It was the worst possible scenario. It was therefore our true source of fear! Such it was that we scrambled to defend our lives with weapons, our virtue with clothing, and our property with walls . . . and if possible, to be born, live, and die without being seen or caught. For omnipresent war meant an apocalypse that would spare no one, and we knew this.

Who would stop our neighbors, whose eyes never strayed from our wives and our money? Was there any reason they wouldn't just assault us some night? On the other hand, how were we to ignore our neighbors' wives and money just pleading with us to claim them? Who could put an end to our envy and prevent us from declaring war on everyone, and everyone from declaring war on us?

As it contemplated such questions, testaments to the fact that it had lost none of its animal savagery despite its ability to walk upright, humankind received a holy signal: the concept of singularity.

It was actually not that holy a signal. It basically had to do with the number of stars that gave us life. The day we realized that the sun and the moon were each a separate celestial body and that the yellow thing that brought spring was one and the same, our minds immediately overflowed with the concept of singularity, being at least as skilled in mimicry as chimpanzees.

Ultimately we toiled to make everything singular. Because that was the right way! One god, one leader, one state, one nation . . . but above all, one enemy!

Singularity was a breakthrough, a miracle. By advocating the necessity of war against a single entity, we were able to banish the possibility of omnipresent war forever.

Yes, lynching was a kind of battle. A battle the majority pitched against the minority. A battle against the singular. Like all else, this too was summed up in Latin: *Bellum omnium contra unum.*

In any case, the war against one enemy brought families together first, then tribes, and then communities. And so it was that society, the lack of which was felt until its advent, was finally created.

So who was the one enemy that would bring all these people together? What did it matter! Who cared! In war, the enemy was nameless! The enemy was the enemy! Once you knew the enemy's name, you might also remember that he was human too and no longer be so cool-headed about venturing into war. History was rife with soldiers who didn't know the names of the people, organizations, or nations they fought against! When all was said and done, the name of the singular enemy didn't matter a bit. What mattered were the rewards to be reaped from the lynching of the enemy:

Lynching meant unity. Unity meant no chaos. If there was no chaos, there could be commerce. With commerce came progress. And if there was progress, there could be more commerce! And then more progress! We could progress ourselves to death! We hadn't stood upright in vain after all. We were ready to take huge leaps into the future, and that was awesome!

A society on the trail of a common enemy never manifested divergence, inner conflict, or restlessness. It was so comforting to hate the same person or thing as the neighbor and his neighbor and his neighbor and the entire population! It was so assuring people could spill blood more harmoniously than ever before. The harmonious spilling of blood was what made a society. In fact, it was testament to the advancement and peacefulness of a society.

For these reasons, developed countries of the present were those who'd been able to singularize their enemies long ago. In this way they were able to do away with their inner conflicts and unite against the common enemy. They also did everything they could to prevent regions they'd made a habit of exploiting from reaching a similar phase. They kept such regions in a state of perpetual, all-inclusive war so they would remain weak.

As a result regions such as the Middle East, where a lynch culture had never developed properly, surfaced. Since unity in lynching never developed, a different lynching took place on every street. If they'd been able to open their eyes, they would have seen lynching for the uniting aspect it was in their religious culture in particular. Wasn't the unified Stoning of the Devil of thousands in Mecca a perfect example of a lynch mob?

Come, whoever you are,[10] come and stone the devil! All they had to do was stop warring with one another and unite against a common enemy! To stop the pointless stoning of one another and come together for the one true great lynching! Just like the developed countries! Still, the people of the Middle East did the best they could . . . Lynching dictators when they managed, Western diplomats when they could get their hands on one, they strove to sow the seeds of a modern nation even if only on a local level.

In the end lynching was in humankind's blood. By nature it was everywhere: in the family, in the neighborhood, in society, in international relations, everywhere. Dozens of nations even came together daily to declare a common enemy. Thanks to this common enemy state, they had at least one thing to agree on and settled their daily negotiations with more ease.

I dwelled on all this and could see everything. I could see especially clearly why it was a dozen men against one person in the legal method of execution that was the firing squad. In fact now, in the words of Martin Luther King: I had a dream!

In that dream, beings from outer space came to our planet and all the world's nations united in alien lynching to live in peace and kinship!

And if lynching could bring about world peace, it could definitely cure my sickness! All I had to do was switch sides. I'd felt like the one being lynched all these years! Now I'd cease being targeted by the mob and join it instead. I would cease to be the common enemy and instead become a rabid, esteemed member of the society that foamed in the exultation of hunting the common enemy down.

---

10 Quote by Rumi. "Come, come, whoever you are. Wanderer, worshiper, lover of leaving. It doesn't matter. Ours is not a caravan of despair."

All these thoughts got me so worked up that I bolted from the bed, knocking my head against the painting on the wall. It hurt but I paid it no heed. What did I have to lose except my cowardice and the tiny usable portion of my brain?

However, looming before me almost as large as the room was a problem that needed solving. Yes, my redemption lay in lynching, but where to find it?

According to the anchorwoman who must've been resurrected after death by bleach, this had been the biggest assault of its kind in years. It looked like there was no point in remaining in this city. I couldn't wait years for another lynching to take place. I couldn't expect to luck out the same way twice in a row. So, since the lynching wasn't coming to me, I'd go to it. How, then? How did one catch up with a lynching before it even happened? They didn't abide by a schedule! Or did they? Maybe they did.

After all, I'd spent my whole life seeing various mouths on TV utter the words, "These are pre-organized acts by obscure dark forces," in reference to the lynchings that took place in various parts of the country. If that were true, it meant that someone went around organizing lynchings as if they were concerts, setting up a whole show. So how could I get to those dark forces? Could I myself even conceivably become a dark force someday? Was there hope for me in that regard?

First I had to make a list. The probable lynch list. I must spread out a world map and mark all the places where lynching was a probability. For that I had to study the lynch histories of nations and cities and find out if the societal conflicts that gave rise to lynchings still prevailed or not.

The incident three days ago that had brought a city back to the Middle Ages, even if only for half an hour, was exceptional. The assault of an ex-convict was too specific a situation to be able to foresee in advance. Since I couldn't very well keep track of the release dates of all the child rapists on Earth, the lynchings I had to concern myself with were of the political kind. The enlightening ground for all the world's ignoramuses, the Internet, held all the information I needed.

I spent the following week studying the political conflicts still prevalent in the world. But figuring out which one was a potential ground for a lynching was impossible. Still, something worth mentioning did take place that week when I watched this piece of news on TV: a few hundred Americans, gathered in their town's largest avenue to welcome home soldiers returning from Afghanistan, attempted to lynch four Afghanis who wanted to protest the procession. This gave me an idea.

Really, the person or group that was targeted in a lynching was always the most hated one. Only the tiniest spark was needed to set the lynch mob going. In the end, Americans assaulted Afghanis every day with their accusing stares, on the street, in the store, but waited for the right moment to actually try to lynch them. What I had to focus on, therefore, was hate.

If I could figure out who hated whom, I'd also figure out where to go to lie in wait for the lynching. But it had to be hatred of a magnitude at which one took the mere existence of the other as an insult. So, who hated whom for merely existing? Why, racists and bigots, of course!

When I researched the regions where these two types of discrimination were at their most prevalent, I was presented with a most fantastic world tour. I'd struck a goldmine. The only things I needed were a passport and a few visas. I was going to be the world's first lynch-tourism agency and customer. The world's first lynch-tourist! It wasn't too shabby for someone who hadn't amounted to anything up till now. After all, just ten days ago, I'd been trying to seek solace in crushing people's shadows. In fact, twenty-four years, five months, and thirteen days ago, I'd been crying just because I'd been born.

A month had passed since the lynching incident, and I didn't feel great at all. My condition had so declined that I had to write down the lines I'd have to utter throughout the day and memorize them. This way, when I said to the bellboy that brought my breakfast to the room, "Can I get another orange juice?" or the housekeeper, "You don't have to clean the room today," I avoided partaking in the exchange by reeling off sentences I'd committed to memory. Reciting words from heart protected me from having to make any decision during communication. It wasn't me who spoke but rather my memory and vocal cords. Thanks to this method, I was able to feel somewhat as if I wasn't present, which eased the pressure. When my lines were predetermined, I didn't get flustered thinking about them and tried to exist without drawing any attention.

It was actually quite similar to how a soldier crawls on the ground to advance under fire. In reality I'd never seen a soldier crawl except on TV. Speaking of which, due to the hotel owner's cooperation with the district municipality, the Turkish Armed

Forces showed up on my doorstep,[11] but for whatever reason assumed my depravity was contagious. With a certificate of disability proving that I singlehandedly posed a threat to the entire army, I had them tell me, "Go putrefy on your own!" I was all the more assured I could crawl more discreetly than any soldier in any army in the world. In every sense of the word . . .

As much as it was referred to as *daily*, life was anything but, always finding ways to surprise me. Events always took turns that caused me to forget my lines, screwing up the communication guidelines I'd prepared. I didn't matter to any of the people I had to talk to. My skits or I weren't included in their interests. They had no qualms about complicating even the simplest of dialogues, always had new questions, and practically competed in taking me by surprise. Needless to say, such situations rendered my memorized sentences useless.

Since the basis of law lay in overlooking the identities of those one encountered, that is, taking every person, including me, as equals, I had been on quite amiable terms with the law in recent years. When the sentences I used were out of line with life, or I felt bad, I'd take the Turkish Criminal Law booklet out of my pocket to read. The juridical texts in that book carried no names, surnames, or personal information. Instead, there was some guy in a state of constant dismay that kept oscillating between winning and being sentenced, and he was referred to as *one*. One whose right to expression had no importance, mute or blind, one-legged or five-eared as one may be!

In reality the anonymity of law was, of course, just a fantasy. Nothing on this planet could be anonymous. No king was ever tried on the same terms as a pauper, nor would he ever be. Still, whenever I felt like my throat was being constricted by the

---

11  Referring to recruiters for military duty, mandatory for every male citizen of Turkey over the age of eighteen.

identities of those around me, thinking in juridical terms gave me somewhat of a relief.

One of those terms was *act of God*[12] . . . *vis major*! It was the lawful correspondent of an excuse that was acceptable in the event one didn't come through with any number of one's responsibilities. Act of God! It could be an earthquake, or it could be a heart attack. In my case, it was the sum of life. Life itself was an act of God! I was in a never-ending earthquake with a case of perpetual heart attack. So I tried to calm myself by pretending to be exempt from any kind of action. That, however, was also no longer working . . .

I was aware of being mercilessly judged by people even though they didn't know me! I was worse off than a pauper caught in the web of the legal system. At least paupers could talk. In fact, their special beggar powers enabled them to instantaneously pick someone out in a crowded sidewalk that couldn't resist their demands, that is to say, me, to materialize near me with their upturned palms. Their mercy-dars must also be receptive to weakness, since they could always find me, even in a crowd of thousands.

I had no such powers and could find no traces of game in my radar other than myself. So I could neither prove my innocence in the makeshift courts of the everyday nor escape the wrongful sentences.

No sooner would the police officer in the passport department ask, "Your job, what do you do?" while waving in my face the form on which I'd left the box for profession blank, before tending to the person in line behind me, than the security guards would see the sweat accumulating on my brow and search me like I was a live bomb, and the visa attendants, skeptical of

---

12 In Turkish law, closer in meaning to French law from which it's derived, *force majeure*.

everything I told them, would check all my information three times and keep me waiting two hours for procedures that should take five minutes.

Yet as one whose whole life was an act of God, reciting from memory was the best defense I could come up with for now. Every time I went back to the room, I patched up my tattered shield by writing alternative scripts and implored the people I would meet the next day to fall in line with the reality of life, though they didn't know it. Naturally none of them heard me. Not when I implored them from my bed, not when I stood in front of them and asked when I could have my passport back . . .

During this period of doubting my personal recovery, I was roused by an unexpected incident. On my final visit to the consulate for the visa needed for my World Lynch Tour, I saw a crowd gathered in front of the building. Holding banners, shouting slogans, kicking the walls.

At first I hesitated, but then recalled the lynching in the square. The ease with which that crowd had accepted me . . . You didn't need an invitation to a lynching because everyone was invited! Though timidly, I approached the intoxicated people, and one of them spoke to me even though he didn't know me at all. In fact, he looked into my eyes and yelled:

"God is one!"

Though I enthusiastically opened my mouth, the same enthusiasm choked me up, but no one noticed. For right then the others roared in unison like a well-rehearsed choir. It made my innards tremble. It lifted me to a high only attainable by cocaine and at similar velocity. Inside the moment I was freed to be myself!

By the time the police showed up to personally define the limits of savagery, I'd torn up four pavement stones, two waste bins, and one banner stick and hurled them at the building, screaming incoherently. I felt like such a part of humanity in that brief interval that when I got in line in front of the building again the next day, I was much more at ease. More importantly, I wasn't repeating my lines to myself over and over again. I didn't feel the need any more. Sure enough, I didn't suffer the slightest communication problem in any step of the visa procedures that day. What's more, I improvised each one. After all, I'd had my lynching fix! Though rather inadequate, something resembling a lynching was running through my veins. A kind of methadone that could be substituted for a lynching. A situation the law might define as a social incident. A social substance that could take similar effect in the absence of lynching itself. Though of course I'd gotten my start on lynching, the most potent stimulant there was. So I knew lynching was the real medicine necessary for my treatment. Protests or similar demonstrations had no importance for me. That's when I thought of football games.

I attended six games, three weekends in a row, at which I dissolved into tens of thousands of people, in bleachers where it didn't matter a bit where anyone was from, this time as part of a Mexican wave instead of a tsunami. In these games, the effects of which were ephemeral but violent enough to enable me to be ordinary for a few days, I cursed at the top of my lungs with complete strangers, at complete strangers. Naturally each time I joined the larger group of supporters. I'd lived long enough as Don Quixote and it was time to become a windmill. And that was easy. All you had to do was buy a few accessories. A few uniforms and scarves that I alternated depending on the game sufficed to make me invisible. The crowd was such a magical thing that once part of it, neither name nor body remained. The masses swallowed them both and provided release from the responsibility of having an identity. The crowd was a spectacular suit of armor shielding one from oneself and everything else. It didn't look anything like the piece of tinny shit Don Quixote wore. It was so sturdy that I could sling the worst curses at people I wouldn't have dared even look at slantwise anywhere else.

Yet once the game was over and it was time to queue up and leave the stadium, I noticed that the people I'd cursed in unison with just a while ago felt at least as uneasy as I did. Just like me, they were also dying to get onto a bus, a cab, or into their car and hightail it out of there. Alone, no one wanted to encounter the people they'd collectively hurled insults with up until a half hour ago. That was why we pushed against and cowered behind one another like a herd as we walked out of games. None of us wanted to wander away from the herd until we felt safe. Though some among them were deranged enough to have joined the lynch mob in the square, most resembled me. But I didn't want a mob made up of ten thousand copies of me. I wanted a lynch mob. Not a mob pretending to be lynch mob!

So before I set out, I followed the news constantly and slept only four hours a day in the hopes of catching a lynching somewhere in the country. But not much loomed on the horizon. So I started to watch footage of old lynchings and fantasized. Some of them were extraordinary. Especially the Sivas massacre[13] or the Rostock riots. True lynchings, each one! Torching buildings, vandalism, killings, the whole deal. Or: the social *purification* movement that surfaced in France as soon as WWII was over! Those black-and-white images of French women believed to be colluding with the Germans as their hair was shaved and they were dragged through the streets until they turned into pulp! It was all so magnificent! But those kinds of things didn't happen every day!

Still, in purblind hope, I did leave my room to go to the airport and board the first plane I could find. I boarded seven more

---

13 The attack on Madımak Hotel in Sivas, Turkey, on July 2, 1993, which resulted in the killing of thirty-five mostly Alawi intellectuals and journalists by an anti-Alawi, pro-sharia mob.

planes in twelve days and covered more than four thousand kilometers within the country. Shoulders hunched in hotel rooms bruised by humidity, I waited for hate to dawn. But nothing happened.

There was just the once when, completely by chance, I ducked into a small crowd to rail and curse at two people I later found out were members of parliament. But that lasted for mere seconds because police surrounded us like tentacles and we were outnumbered three to one. All you had to do was to look at one of the people sprawled on the crowd. There were three cops per each one of us. I'd ended up being the lynchee instead of the lyncher and almost got arrested. Of course what I thought right then was that I should be a cop. I had to be on whichever side was bigger mob! I'd never stand by the weak and the few! I wished to be a thousand against one! Ten thousand! A hundred thousand! A million! I wanted a mob! I wanted a bigger mob! And to holler: "Which religion doesn't have déjà vu? I'll take that one!"

The second I entered the Ship, the receptionist handed me an envelope and said:

"Your passport arrived. You gave the shipping people my name. Don't do that!"

"Don't worry, it won't happen again," I should have said, but I'd memorized something else:

"Is there an envelope for me?"

Naturally I didn't wait for an answer, leaving the man gaping at me and walking to the elevator. Then I went up to my room. Then I collected my things. Then I left the building known as the Ship. Then the building known as the Ship sank. Because I said so.

## UNIONE

One of the four basic techniques of Renaissance painting. As in Sfumato, colors and tones dissolve into one another. However, unlike Sfumato, the colors and tones used are always saturated and vivid.

Bearded, at least 1.80 meters in height, the middle-aged man wore only a white piece of cloth over his loins. It was cold, but he didn't care about that. His eyes were closed, feet just as bare as his torso and legs. Hands joined at his chest, he manipulated his breath in order to slow down his pulse. For that moment, out of everything the world offered him, he accepted into his mind only those he needed. He didn't need to be cold, so he didn't feel the cold. Right next to him was a large table. And on the table was a glass cube, the sides of which measured at most forty centimeters. One of its surfaces was removable, providing the cube with an entrance no bigger than itself.

We were on a street. A crowded street. On the pedestrian walkway of a district where people jostled one another to shop harder and faster. They talked. They haggled and burst out laughing. The sound of motor vehicles from the surrounding avenues pervaded the air. Engines were gunned, brakes slammed on, and windows rolled down to dump out music like butts from an ashtray. All the sounds merged and vied with one another to bore into our ears. The noise of the city was crushing us all. But the man stood up straight and heard nothing else but his heartbeat. I was sure of this because the unhearing expression on his face was somehow familiar. Only the face of a man who had started to beat along with his heart would bear those lines, I knew . . .

He opened his eyes and gazed at life. To be more accurate, he opened the gates of his eyes and we gazed into his life . . . He spun on his heel to face the table next to him. Slowly he lifted his right knee and placed his foot on the table. His legs were as long and flexible as a frog's. He leaned against the table with his fingertips and hoisted himself onto the table in a single move. Now he looked much taller. Focusing on his breathing once more, he inserted his right foot into the cube and set it on the bottom. Bending down, he placed his right knee against the far corner of the cube. Meanwhile he had one hand on the cube and the other on the table for balance. He remained like that for a few seconds before putting his hips inside the cube and seating them on the bottom. He lifted his right hand he had been gripping the cube with up till then and touched his face with his fingers as he drew it toward himself. First his elbow, then his right shoulder, went into the cube. He stopped . . . So did we. Then slowly he bent his head down and into the cube. Moving his right leg inch by inch, he was able to make some room for himself, however small. With the fingers of his right hand, he gripped the tip of his left foot and started to pull it toward himself. This way his left foot went over his right shin and his legs, from the knees down, formed an X, pressing against the glass surface of the cube. Raising himself slightly on his right hand against the narrow base, he brought his hip slightly farther away from the door of the cube. Only his left arm and left knee remained outside. He raised his arm and thrust his knee in the cube first. Then he slowly lowered his left hand. With his entire body inside a tiny cube, the man's left hand hovered over the table, palm exposed, as though it weren't real. Then the hand fluttered down like a piece of cloth to gracefully fold over his right foot.

A young man whom I'd taken to be one of the spectators up till then immediately approached the table, picked up the glass lid of the cube, and paused. After a few beats, he sealed the cube with the glass surface. The only things we could see now were fragments of a pair of legs, crossed, and the hairless head bent forward between them. He was wedged inside a cube as high as his knee. We were observing a man become so small so as to cease existing. Or maybe so as to come into being . . .

I wept. And not just because the man in front of me, folded into himself, reminded me of being under the corpses. I had another reason: an incident I'd played a part in three months ago . . . I just couldn't forget. Because it had changed everything. Everything!

I was nearing the end of the second year of my lynch tour. I'd been veering from one country to the next for the past two years. I honestly hadn't expected this much. On the first plane I'd boarded to start off the tour, trying to imagine what awaited me, I hadn't really had high expectations. The world, however, was very quick to verify the savagery of the hate it was loaded with. In the space of two years, I attended more lynchings than I could ever begin to count. It was like everyone had been waiting for me to show up before they could start chewing one another out. They'd waited for me to join them all this time and would tear apart one of their own only when I did. Or I was just imagining things and the world had always been this way. It was a cradle of lynchings before I came along, and would be after I passed. It was rooted not in soil but in hate. And all I did was walk over it.

The Middle East, North Africa, the Balkans, mainland Europe, Britain . . . there was sure to be a lynching going on in every one. You didn't even have to be at the right place at the right time. Lynching was ubiquitous and constant. It sufficed to read a few newspapers in various languages and smell the air. The creature called man thrived on lynching, this much I could see . . .

I saw hundreds flock to a single child like a school of piranhas to tear its flesh apart, and likewise drag a woman around by her hair and rape her for hours . . . I saw it all, because I was there and one of them. I watched dozens of bodies burying people instantaneously. I even willingly became part of these flesh structures frenziedly crushing them. The more I saw of those we buried, the more I saw of myself. Our mere presence covered and suffocated them every time in the form of a heap of bodies. I really had been able to change sides. I was no longer the one under the rubble. I was one of the bodies forming the rubble.

I saw kids . . . lynching one another in front of school buildings . . . kids who, not content with only that, documented everything with cell phones and dispensed them online like flyers to ensure lifelong humiliation for the lynchee. I saw the happy slappers too. Kids who sneaked up on random, unsuspecting people on the street, struck them, and ran. Whose friends in turn documented the deed to publish online . . . I saw the suicide bombers of the Middle East. People who exploded. Who lynched in reverse! I saw the lone bombs who, rather than being lynched *by* the mob, lynched *the* mob. Then I fantasized about a British kid who was killed when he chanced upon a suicide bomber on his happy slapping spree, which made me laugh. I saw that there were countries where some games were impossible.

I witnessed the constant effusiveness of the mob. The perpetual cries and bellows . . . Every word was a piece of coal. To spur on the fire. It distracted me. So I listened to Nasenbluten to block it out. Ears hidden behind my turned-up collar, I heard only the music. For two years it was all I saw and heard.

And I tried to get better. I tried to make peace with people through my lynching of them. If in a rare, lynch-free locale, I used cash to provoke them. I assaulted derelicts with people I coaxed off the street. That's how I came to realize that being a foreign power wasn't that much of a challenge. Cash solved everything, period . . .

When all was said and done, however, I didn't improve a bit! I was every bit as gravely sick as I had been in my days at the Ship. Aside from lynch-related negotiations or relations, I couldn't communicate with people. That wall between us never came down. I couldn't feel anything anymore. The effects of the lynchings I'd attended eventually wore off and disappeared. Like morphine sulfate, lynching turned into a burden I couldn't relinquish. It became no different than the births Emre made me watch. Lynch mobs killed or maimed people with the same ease with which those babies were born, as though it were the world's most mundane feat.

The lynchers, on the other hand, were the same everywhere. The concept of crowd dynamics was for real. The mob's shepherd was the mob itself. The individual's fate rested in the hands of the mob he was in. This was the state of things regardless of whether the instigator was a group of provocateurs or simply the willpower of each separate individual. In fact, everything that ever went wrong in the world was caused by a silent agreement between billions of people. A person who witnessed a rape on the streets could be charged with complicity for not helping the victim. When societies displayed the same behavior, however, there was no charge, because it wasn't even considered as a crime then. The characteristics of lynch mobs all over the world boiled down to the same thing. Whichever language they spoke, whatever appearance they had . . . all individuals that came together to form the mob thought the same thing when, chasing the victim around, they saw one another:

"This is what I'm doing now. Because you're doing it too. You lynch, therefore I lynch!"

Meanwhile the complete stranger running with him thought the same:

"I'm here because you're here!"

They meant nothing to me. Neither the people, nor the births or the deaths. Man, sentenced to a prison walled by birth on two sides and death on the other two! Once he was born, though, all four walls of his prison were made of death. That explained, in fact, why fear of death came as the only bonus meaning to life, as Harmin had said. And lynching was the name given to the instant that fear became tangible as a rock.

"Maybe that's why I'm not getting better," I told myself. Because the only meaning to my life was the fear of death! And because I still spent my days among others' fear of death!

Then, one night, I saw that boy . . . He walked by himself. He must have been fifteen or sixteen. His hands were in his pockets. Head bent, he looked nowhere but at the pavement he walked on. He was an Arab . . .

From a pub frequented by English Defense League fans whose sole enemies were Muslims, I'd lured several kids by stuffing a few notes into their hands. They'd asked me who I was and I'd replied, "What does it matter! I've at least as much hate as you!" They tagged along without even caring to ask who it was that I hated. They were hammered, but I wasn't. Still I joined in their ruckus and walked with them as I surveyed the surroundings. We were looking to find ourselves an Arab. Anyone who looked Muslim. They didn't even have to really be Muslim. Looking like one would suffice. That was when we came across the kid. A kid whose only concern was to avoid the chill as he walked with his head buried between his shoulders.

My entourage and I exchanged glances and said, "All right! This is it!"

We were on an avenue where the glow from the streetlamps didn't quite reach one another, leaving dark areas in between.

The occupants of the houses on either side of the avenue seemed to be long asleep. Either that or they must be sitting in the dark, because no lights emanated from the windows. Most importantly, there were no cops in sight.

We were on the left-hand pavement of the avenue. The boy, glancing over at us in an instant of apprehension, was on the opposite side. I intentionally kept my companions chatting. So the boy wouldn't get suspicious. My experiences over the years dictated that in hunts like this, silence always caused the game to pick up speed and escape. Appearing to be a horde of drunks was always a surefire way of camouflage. Of course, in this instance, the members of the horde I was in really were drunk. That was why, unable to contain themselves much longer, they bolted across the street and toward the boy. Naturally I darted too!

Our footsteps, ringing in the silence of the night, alerted him like an alarm in his ears, and he started running as well. There were nine of us nocturnal animals. For a moment, among those kids, I felt all right again. Like in the old days! Perhaps that's why I failed to realize . . . because I was seeing red once more . . .

The avenue was interjected by an alley and the boy, running as fast as he could, was heading into that narrow road. I'd advanced ahead of the horde without realizing it. The only thing we did was run. My brothers-in-lynch weren't sober enough to curse and run at the same time. We were fast all the same. We followed the boy into the narrow street. In spite of all the morphine sulfate I'd imbibed over the years, I was running fast enough to impress myself. A few hundred meters later, houses gave way to walls and streetlamps became infrequent.

Staring at the boy's back as it weaved in and out of the darkness, I hissed through my teeth, "You've gone down the wrong street!" Growling, "No one will ever know! No one will hear your screams!"

In the end it was as I'd predicted. The street was a dead end! I was worn out, but it had been worth it! He had nowhere to run. I could see the tall wall at the end of the street. I could see the boy too. He was searching for a door in the walls on either side. Or some hole he could squeeze through . . . but it was all walls! There were more than thirty meters between us, and despite the darkness I could see him dart this way and that like a little squirrel, and then pause to look at me. Once he knew everywhere he touched was brick, I saw no more necessity in running and slowed to a walk. The boy was crying. I was laughing. I spread my arms to remind him that there was nowhere to run. Now there were at most ten meters between us. Turning my head, I said, "Let's finish this!" But there was no one with me! I stopped and turned around. The street was deserted. My horde had disbanded to goodness knows where. The sons of bitches had abandoned me! I'd been too bloodthirsty to notice.

On that narrow street, I was alone with the Arab boy . . . He was shouting. But I couldn't understand him. He was speaking in Arabic. He was shaking, walking backward into the wall behind him, and then, startled, stepping forward, only to walk backward again because he couldn't approach me, either! He rambled and seemed scared nearly to death. He wept, even as he hollered at me and smacked his tears away. He put his hands in his pockets and turned them inside out to show me that they were empty. Two small, white pieces of fabric dangled on either side of his pants as he continued to weep. I didn't know what to do. I wanted to turn and run but was frozen in place. What could I possibly do to someone on my lonesome? Those drunks had been my skin! Now I felt like I'd been flayed! In all the lynchings I'd taken part in over two years, I'd never been left alone with the victim! So I was frozen in place and beside myself, and I cried out. Actually, I just thought aloud. Very loudly:

"I'm scared too! Do you understand me? I'm scared too!"

But the boy understood nothing. In fact, my yelling scared him even more. Right then I felt moisture on my lips as I parted them to say something. It wasn't sweat. I was weeping. I was also weeping, now. Reaching out my hands, I started walking toward the boy. "Don't be afraid!" I was saying. "Don't be afraid!" Perhaps I was talking to myself and not him.

When I advanced upon him, he stepped back, tripped and fell. He sat up but remained on his knees. Hands raised, he shook his head and talked through tears. "Don't!" I knew he was saying. "Don't come near me!"

I couldn't understand him, but I could guess! Yet I was crying at least as hard as he was and wished only that no one on that street had to remain afraid. I grabbed the boy's hand that was raised to shield himself from me and went down on my knees to try to embrace him. At the same time I raved.

"Don't be afraid anymore! Don't be! Please, don't be afraid! I beg you, don't be afraid!"

The boy shoved at me with both hands to try to get away. But I wanted to hug him harder, have him lay his head on my bosom and to tell him, "There's nothing to be afraid of any more!" I wanted him to believe me! For the first time after many years, I was really touching someone . . .

Then abruptly he shoved me away, squirmed out of my grasp, and got up, taking off with all his might. Like the man who'd run past me in that square at the first lynching . . . the boy darted past me like a ghost and his footfalls faded like a dream. I remained on my knees, weeping as I stared at the wall at the end of that alley . . . weeping for Felat . . . for Cuma . . . for all those dead Afghanis . . . for my mother . . . for Dordor and Harmin . . . for myself . . . and even for Ahad . . .

Now I stood on that noisy street and wept as I watched the man in front of me. He'd been folded into the glass cube for minutes. People surrounded him, applauding, whereas I wanted to take a hammer and smash it . . . the cube, and my past . . . to free us both. Him, and myself . . .

I had three hours till my plane took off. Holding a ticket to Rio de Janeiro I'd bought months in advance, I circled the airport. According to the plans I'd once made, the World Lynch Tour would continue on the continent known as America. But for whatever reason, I didn't feel like entering the building. Instead I got on a cab and said, "To the nearest pub!" I had time after all.

We halted in a district whose residents, judging by their looks and gaits, were at least as dark as the walls they leaned against, and I got out. I was about to step inside the pub when one of the shadowy figure approached me. He was a pro. He'd figured out my addiction at a glance. We went to a nearby playground instead of the pub. That was where he kept his stash. But he had one shortcoming: I was sure he sampled everything he was selling! He asked me where I was from.

"I'm Turkish," I said.

"Why didn't you say so, brother!" he said and we started afresh. "Here I'm thinking, is this guy *Albanian*? Russian? What's your name?"

"Gaza. Yours?"

"Edip . . . but around here they call me Oedipus! Oedipus *the Motherfucker*! You dig? Meaning I jump your mom!"

"But that's when it's your own moth—"

"*Wha?*"

"Forget it! How much for the stuff then?"

"Hold on, brother! Let's have a chat! Not everyday a guy comes from the motherland . . . Want me to roll you something?"

"No thanks! Is this Subutex?"

"Yes! Made in France! Hip shit! I have Buprenex, too, that stuff's British! Oedipus the Motherfucker! You dig? I do your mom! How many?"

"I'll tell you how many when you tell me how much it is!"

"OK! Cool! Don't be mad! What team you on?"

"What?"

"Football! What team?"

"All of them!"

"Come on! I do your mom! How can that be?"

"It can! I've been to all their games. How much for the Buprenex?"

"Oedipus the Motherfucker! You dig?"

There were kids right there next to us . . . on the slide, the swings, the seesaw . . . especially the slide . . .

"What?" I said.

Oedipus rambled and swaggered at the same time. In the meantime kids slid off the slide like corpses.

"*The Motherfucker!* You dig?"

"I don't."

"*Wha?* Edip! Oedipus! Edip! Oedipus! You dig?"

The kids continued to fall. They laughed, collided with one another, slid. Then one kid started climbing up the slide as soon as it was empty, clutching the sides. The slide was so tall, however, I wasn't sure he'd make it to the top. Right then I thought of the game Dordor and Harmin used to play where they would wave at the boats carrying tourists. And I also played a game. I put everything I had on the kid making it to the top. All my attention was on him now.

"You buying or not?"

"What? Give me a minute!"

"Want me to roll something?"

As hard as he tried, the kid's feet kept slipping so he couldn't go more than halfway up the slide.

"No thanks!"

"I do your mom! You dig?"

And the kid fell down for the last time before giving up. Then he walked towards the ladder like the rest. The slide was empty. I looked at Oedipus *the Motherfucker*. Then I put down my bag and ran. If the kid couldn't do it, I would! I slipped with my first step onto the slide and fell on the ground. Oedipus was yelling:

"What're you doing? You fool! Forget the Buprenex, no good for you!"

I laughed where I lay . . . That was all I could do: laugh. And it felt good . . . As I got up and dusted myself off, I turned to Oedipus and said, "Keep it!"

"*Wha?* I do your mom!"

"I quit!"

"What?"

"Everything!"

Then I grabbed my bag and ran. Oedipus was still yelling in my wake and, I'm sure, swaggering!

I got in the first cab I saw and said, "Heathrow Airport!" Then I closed my eyes to conjure up once more the frog pictures that had covered that playground.

I was reading a news item I'd been on the lookout for. It was about a Kurd in Switzerland who was murdered by his family for being homosexual. There was a photo underneath the item. The photo of a wedding ceremony. The urn holding the murdered young man's remains and the blond, bespectacled man carrying it stood before an applauding crowd. The man had a smile on his lips and tears in his eyes. So they'd been able to get married after all.

Looking at the urn, I asked quietly, "Felat, could this be you?" I folded the newspaper shut, trapping my whispered question between its pages. I got to my feet. I opened the carriage lid and retrieved my bag. Taking a few steps down the narrow corridor, I waited for the airplane hatch to open. The entire way, I'd leaned my head against the window and watched the cotton field of clouds and the sunlight irrigating it. "I really have to skydive one day and fall through the clouds," I'd thought. To fall down to Earth like a raindrop . . . then, to trickle into the soil like a raindrop and rise again to merge into those clouds . . . Really, a piece of me was already in those clouds. In fact, they carried pieces from every person who'd ever passed through the world. For every one of them had cried. Even the toughest among them had shed tears at birth. They were in the water circulating within the atmosphere: all the tears of the world . . . I'd imagined parachuting through my own tears . . .

The hatch opened and I inched forward. When it was my turn to exit through the hatch, I paused in the threshold and drew the warm air into my lungs. I might not be in Rio de Janeiro, but in a short while I would be setting foot in a land at least as hot.

The Pakistani border guard stamped my passport when he saw my Schengen and USA visas. I was able to enter Pakistan, the pro-Turkey country I descended on without a visa, only thanks to Europe and the USA's collateral. No surprise there, I thought. No surprise there . . .

Out of the dozens of cab drivers that swooped down on me on my way out of the airport, I tried to pick the crookedest one. What I really sought was an illegal glint in the eyes. My years in Kandalı had taught me to recognize that glint. I'd grown up under the gaze of illegally glinting eyes. And now, a pair was in front of me once more. Two little devils sat cross-legged in an angelic face and stared at me. As soon as our eyes met, he bolted toward me and spoke in English as he took my bag:

"Welcome to Islamabad!"

"What's your name?" I asked.

"Babar," he said.

I allowed Babar to lead me past the crowd of one-armed beggars, three-way pickpockets, and quadruple-tongued touters, moving through the path he cleared. We walked until we halted in front of a thirty-year-old Mercedes, and Babar said, "There, that's my palace! Mobile-palace!"

Except one of the palace's gates was jammed shut. We tried the other one. I ended up in the backseat listening to Babar talk at me in the rearview mirror.

"There's this hotel," he said. "A very good hotel! My uncle's hotel. An absolute palace!"

Babar was a palace freak.

"All right," I said. "Let's go."

The car, with a webbed crack spreading over its windshield, started up, and we were on our way. Babar chattered ceaselessly and likely speculated about the things he could sell me. Was it a woman I wanted? Or a boy? Drugs? An antique carpet? I decided I'd save Babar the trouble. I knew for sure what I wanted:

"I want to go to Afghanistan."

He laughed and said:

"Then I'd say you've gotten off at the wrong stop!"

"You're right," I said. "There's been a mistake . . . Can you fix it?"

He didn't reply straight away. He considered. Asked the first thing that came to his mind:

"You're a soldier?"

"No," I said. "I'm a tourist."

He laughed again.

"If you're not a warrior, you'll be bored in Afghanistan. War all day long! Nothing else! Even the journalists don't go there anymore. They're all here. They hang around in Islamabad to write about the war in Afghanistan. Because it's all the same!"

"Maybe I'll find something to do," I said. "But I have to get past the border first . . . preferably without showing my passport . . ."

"If it's heroin you want, I'll get it for you!"

He assumed I was here to get my share of Afghanistan's notorious heroin. It was my turn to laugh.

"No thank you . . . I just quit!"

"Then get a visa!" he said. "I can get it for you . . . I can take care of it!"

The profit margin of crossing the border illegally must be so small he was trying to point me toward other transactions. But I knew what I wanted. Grasping both seats, I pulled myself forward and bent toward Babar's right ear to say:

"I have a friend. An Afghani . . . he came to me as an illegal immigrant. So I need to go to him as an illegal immigrant, get it?"

He didn't, but it didn't matter. He was a true salesman and he couldn't let me leave until he sold me something. It was easy enough to nod as if he understood. So Babar nodded and talked at the same time.

"There's this truck! My uncle's truck! You can jump on and leave! Takes apples to Afghanistan. He'll take you too. But it'll cost you! Because this truck, it's like a palace!"

"Deal," I said.

He tried his luck a final time:

"Want a woman?"

Once again, I laughed . . . "From now on, I'm an apple, Babar. What would I do with a woman?"

"Well, there you go! I'll get you a woman so she can bite you!"

"Forget it!" I said. "Wouldn't want to get anyone kicked out of paradise!"

He didn't get this either, but he laughed. This was why I liked salesmen. Life was always a breeze with them and not everything had to mean something. Right then I thought of all the people who cashed in their lives like poker chips for a chance to get into heaven. "Let them all wear down the gates to heaven," I thought. Personally I wouldn't go somewhere I was kicked out of. Ever! I wasn't that audacious. Not that audacious! Not anymore . . .

We'd arrived at the hotel. The hotel, owned by one of Babar's countless fake uncles, was so decrepit it was leaning against the buildings on either side to stay upright. Babar, however, saw something else:

"What d'you think? Like a palace, isn't it?"

It was my turn to pretend I understood. It was the least I could do. Along with Babar, I beheld the palace that wasn't there.

"Yes!" I said. "An absolute palace!"

The place all those people had come from, passing through the reservoir in Kandalı to get to the West, that was where I was now: the East. In the Peshawar region on the Afghanistan border, the Pakistani army clashed with the Taliban, the blood of the casualties spilling into the Bara River. Bara went on to spill into the Kabul, which went on to dry out on its way to other rivers. Then whatever was left of the desert spilled into the Indian Ocean. Considering how many of the world's battlefields were situated next to rivers, the oceans must be filled with fish that fed on human blood. And I sat on the lawn of my hotel and fed on one of them.

The truck Babar arranged for me was due any minute. I was trying to replenish myself before the long journey ahead. Even the migrating birds had changed their route due to the smoke billowing out of Peshawar. So we would pass through the border at a point farther south to head toward Kandahar. There would be no apples in the bed of the truck . . . just me and some artillery . . . according to Babar, several crates of Kalashnikov rifles awaited their owners in Afghanistan. They must be giddy with anticipation. I was sure they were eager as children, waiting for the moment they would get to pick up their Kalashnikovs and fire at everything that moved. After all, a Kalashnikov was never merely a Kalashnikov!

First of all, it was a component of the Mozambique flag since 1983. For a weapon, being featured in a country flag was quite an accomplishment. But then there was also this: so many nations in recent history had been manufactured in labs by the United Kingdom, the USA and at one time the USSR, that I imagined coming up with a unique flag for each one must have posed a problem in itself. In fact, I was also sure that these three nation manufacturers had established *Flag Design Departments for Nations Designed* and filled them with graphic designers. Drawing lines on a map didn't a nation make! You also had to sit around to produce common history and culture as its glue. And design a flag based on it! All that took labor. And when it was Mozambique's turn, due to work overload, the designers had had an eclipse in creativity and drawn out the first flag that came to their minds, ending the matter . . . Yes, there was also this possibility! Could Pakistan's flag have come out of one of those departments as well? After all, I was in a country that hadn't existed until yesterday. A land known as India . . . Really, the situation was quite simple: this was a place people were snatched up and knocked into one another like eggs. This was where *The World Egg Wars* were held. That was the reason for the overpowering stink! For rotten eggs smelled like blood. Or that was just my olfactory hallucination . . .

Half an hour later, a murderer walked onto the hotel's lawn. It was the first time I saw him, of course, but his murders were manifest even in his gait. He looked like Yadigar. Our eyes met.

"Babar?" I said.

"Babar!" he said.

Taking along four bottles of water from the hotel, I followed the murderer. He took me to the truck Babar had referred to as "a palace!" I did lay eyes on one this time. There was a palace among the hundreds of inscriptions and images painted on the vault in oils. The picture of a palace . . .

Despite expecting to go inside the vault, the murderer indicated for me to sit next to him. I'd paid Babar double what he asked. Perhaps that was what earned me the privilege of traveling first class! I opened the door of the truck, which was the same brand as Ahad's but a much older model, and climbed in. As a child I used to open both doors of our truck and stand in front of it to look. It resembled the face of a giant. A face with doors for ears . . . Now I rode the face of another giant, onward.

The roads were so bad that a drive of four hours became eight before we arrived at the city of Multan. The murderer and I didn't speak once the entire way there. We entered the city at nighttime and pulled into a gas station. Actually it was more of a shack than a gas station, ready to scoot off and hunker down elsewhere at any moment. In front was a gas pump. Since we hadn't stopped at any of the more convincing gas stations we'd passed by many times on the way, we must be somewhere with utmost geopolitical significance!

Turning to me, the murderer inclined his head slightly and cupped his cheek with his hand. "We sleep here," he meant to say.

I nodded. But even as I was trying to figure out where we were supposed to sleep, he had the tailgate down, beckoning to me.

So I spent the night sleeping in the bed of a truck, in between crates full of Kalashnikov rifles, with a murderer. At first I didn't think I'd be able to sleep, but then I dwelled on it until I nodded off.

I dreamed that there was an earthquake and a hand roamed over my face. A small hand . . .

That kind of touch would normally make me nauseated, but I felt nothing. No ache bombs went off on various points in my body, nor did my pulse quicken.

"Just a dream, sadly," I said and opened my eyes. I laughed. For the owner of the roaming hand stood right beside me and stared at me with huge eyes. It was a child around five. A boy with a shaved head . . . He had one hand on my brow and the other over my mouth. Right then I also knew the reason for the earthquake in my dream. We were in motion. I'd been sleeping so deeply I hadn't been aware of anything! When in fact people surrounded me and we were already on our way! That makeshift gas station really was a stop after all! A stop for collecting people . . . The women and men sitting on the Kalashnikov crates watched me, the bumpy road making them rattle. Who knows for how long? I sat up quickly. Smiled. Very few of them returned it. So, who were these people? Were we going to Afghanistan together? Seemed like it. My business there was evident but where were these people going? Right then I thought of the seasonal workers in Kandalı. "Maybe they're going to find work," I thought. After all, someone had to work in the opium fields that wielded the harvest anticipated eagerly by the whole world! These people right here must be that someone . . .

Unlike ours, the vault of the truck was open. That is to say, a tarp stretched over iron arches fixed on either side covered the top. I could see the road over the tailgate. The tarp that was supposed to go over that part hadn't been drawn down for the moment. We were apparently legal in the region we were currently in. There was no need to hide.

I noticed that we diverged from the main road. A while later we were making way over a flat plain with just a pair of tire tracks for a road. About a half hour passed before I glimpsed cottages made of stones and dirt. We must have entered a village. Several children that appeared to materialize out of nowhere started to chase us. The truck slowed down, and the fastest of the children grabbed the chain hanging off the tailgate and hoisted himself up. The boy, ten years old at most, found his footing some place on the outside the truck and braced himself by putting his arms over the tailgate. Stuck to the lumbering truck like a barnacle, he grinned at us, displaying the four teeth in his mouth. I might have been the only one who grinned back at him. The others didn't really care. The truck stopped.

I heard the murderer's door open and close. Then he came and shooed away the child that still clung to the tailgate. The boy quickly vanished behind it, grinning even as he ran. The murderer slid open the latches on either side to lower the tailgate and our eyes met. He acknowledged me with a nod, then turned and yelled. From where I was, I couldn't see who he was calling to. A few minutes later, however, I saw and understood all . . .

A woman and man approached the truck. They were both young. Then all of a sudden dozens of people were surging around them. Perhaps the entire village . . . they kissed and hugged everyone. The elderly cried, the children laughed and cavorted. I couldn't make sense of it at first but then it hit me like lightning. They were making farewells in such a way that I knew they would never see one another again. The people around me weren't going to Afghanistan to work but much farther away. I could see now! I was among the *embarkers*, at the point from which they *embarked*. I was at the beginning of the road! I was at the start point of the great journey starting in Pakistan and ending heaven-knows-where in Europe. It was all unfolding right in front of my eyes. I was in the place that the people—who we had picked up from the sixteen-wheeler in Derçisu, held in the reservoir, and handed over to the boats—had left for a better life.

I stood and took the young woman's hand to help her onto the truck bed. Then I took the man's hand and hoisted him up . . . They were both crying. They also knew. They were aware they had no idea what the future held. They were taking the first steps toward darkness on a day like this, when the sun was so bright it practically lit up the insides of our mouths. Then

I looked at their hands. At the small bags they held. I hadn't noticed until then. The others also had small bags next to them, slouching this way and that. One middle-aged, bearded man only had a plastic bag . . . He was embarking on the trip of a lifetime with only a plastic bag . . . a plastic bag would suffice to begin everything over . . . Perhaps it held some food and when that was over, the bag would disappear too. He'd go wherever he was going with nothing. Without a thing to his name. He'd take only himself. And whatever remained on his mind . . . Waving off the young couple, men watched quietly while women sang a keening song in unison. It sounded like keening since both the singers and the audience were weeping. They must all be related. Their faces were nearly identical. Especially the kids. None had more than four teeth in their mouths.

The truck started up like an insult to their moment of farewell. It moved forward slowly. The elderly took a couple of steps and stopped, the middle-aged walked and then ran a bit, and the young trailed us as for as long as they could, waving. Once again the children were last to give up the chase . . . The young couple clung to the tailgate and waved for as long as they could before turning to us and sinking to the ground. They leaned against the tailgate and pulled their knees to their chests. All that remained was the insult of a rumbling engine and the sighs of the young woman and man . . .

Just then I felt a hand on my shoulder. I turned my head and saw the little boy that had woken me up. Picking him up by the underarms so his little feet sailed in the air, I put him in my lap. Or he would have fallen . . . then I said:

"I'm sorry . . ."

Turning my head right and left, I tried to look each of the people in the face. They didn't understand. I tried again.

"Forgive me."

Then again . . .

"Forgive me for the awful things I did!"

And an apple bobbed in my sight. I turned and looked in the direction it came from. At who held it . . . It was plastic bag man. The man who was going to the other side of the world with just a plastic bag . . . he had an apple in his other hand too. He smiled. He must have assumed I was asking for food they could spare. I took the apple and bit. Then I gave it to the boy in my lap. At the same time it dawned on me that there really was a crate of apples among the Kalashnikovs. Not to transport, but to give to the immigrants as provisions . . . like the cheese and tomato sandwiches I had once prepared . . .

The boy and I bit into the apple alternately . . . taking turns. I sat in the center of the vault. I glanced around. Everyone held an apple. They were either biting or chewing. Except for the young couple that had freshly joined us . . . they were trying to get used to forgetting. They grieved for what they'd abandoned . . .

I turned to the man who'd handed me the apple. "Thank you," I said. "Thank you for forgiving me."

Not comprehending, he smiled. I tried again.

"I'm so glad you never knew me!"

Then again . . .

"I'm so glad you never set foot in my reservoir!"

And a smack landed on my cheek! A quick and tiny smack, delivered from a small hand. I'd neglected to hand the apple in my hand to the boy. It was his turn and he couldn't wait! The smack and my consequent widened eyes and raised eyebrows had everyone laughing. At the top of their lungs! I laughed too. Even the young couple sitting across from me cracked a smile . . . Only the boy didn't laugh, because his mouth was filled with apple. He'd delivered my punishment. He'd smacked me in the name of all the people whose lives I'd ruined and that was the end of it. Now the same hand trailed over the bruised veins in my arms. Making it better wherever he touched. I held a child shaman in my lap! From Islamabad to Kabul, spiritual guide to all smugglers! A child who knew and could do anything! I thought of Maxime. The French journalist . . . then I kissed the boy's hand. Just like one ought to do upon meeting a little shaman . . .

We spent the night in a definitive void. In a field surrounded by stars reaching all the way down to the earth to light up the horizon on all four sides . . . It was as straight as if ironed flat by the daytime heat, as silent as if frozen by the nighttime chill.

We tried to sleep. There were some who succeeded. Others blinked in the darkness like flickering flames until daybreak. I was one of them. The little boy was curled up in his mother's lap like a puppy, dreaming of goodness knows what . . .

Toward daybreak, I got off the truck and took a walk. Then I sprawled on the ground to watch the sun appear and the stars vanish. The sun that came up was so enormous it wasn't like any I'd ever seen. Maybe it was a vagabond sun randomly dropping by on its way past the earth. A never before seen sun, a painter . . . It dawned for just us that morning and painted the sky purple first, then red. Once it was clear of the horizon and wholly visible, all that was left was the yellow earth reaching out in every direction and the pale blue of day. I thought of Cuma . . . then of myself . . . then I stood and returned to the truck sitting in the middle of the emptiness.

When I got to the vault, I saw that the sound sleepers and the wide-eyed ones had switched places. It was others' turn to sleep. The remaining looked around with yawning eyelids. Now awake, the little boy chewed on a biscuit he was clutching. I met his mother's eyes. I smiled. Surely she smiled back though I wasn't able to see. Her face was covered with a black veil, leaving only her eyes exposed. The thieves who had said *open sesame!* in their fables said *cover up, woman!* in real life. We were in such a region of the world that each man thought he was *Ali Baba*, believing everyone else to be the *forty thieves*. Being told over and over had made the tale reality.

The murderer, who always looked alert despite the fact that there was no telling if he was able to get some shut-eye, said a few words to those with me and brought the tarp down over the tailgate. This created a curtain between the sun and us. Yet the vagabond sun persisted in leaking through the rips in the rough cloth to blind us.

The truck started up and we moved. Slowly at first . . . then, we picked up speed like a marathon runner coming into his rhythm. It was so jangly that I was sure we were traveling on a nonexistent road. We must be getting close to the border. In a blink I'd enter Cuma's country . . .

"Not much left," I said. "I'm coming!"

Then a gunshot rang out. Then another! And another! The people around me started screaming and the truck accelerated even more. We didn't know who held those guns, but we were clearly in their crosshairs. Finally a bullet ripped through the tarp. By a gigantic stroke of luck, however, it didn't hit anyone and left through another hole it opened in the tarp. Two more beams of light spilled into the vault. I sat up hastily and started shoving everyone I could get my hands on flat on the ground. The others, who'd been frozen in place, thus came to life and started sprawling. I knocked over two women and one man at a loss for what to do other than scream and pray, and no more people remained in the vault that were upright. Then I darted between two crates of weapons and tried to make myself as small as possible. We were now piled on top of one another and rocking as though in a cradle. The gunfire increased. I couldn't figure out where it was coming from. Either the bullets were being unloaded from a high spot overlooking the area or, worse, vehicles whose engines we couldn't hear over the noise were trailing us. I sensed that we were slowing down. Was the murderer shot? But that would've sent the wheel careening and at that speed we would definitely have tipped or turned over! Finally we slowed down and stopped altogether. The gunfire ceased at once. I crawled to the tailgate and cracked the tarp open to peek out. I saw two pickup trucks. With armed men in their beds . . .

I heard the murderer's door open and close hastily. He must've gotten out of the truck. Indeed, he entered my field of vision a few seconds later and faced the men he'd failed to outrun and lose. One of them got off the truck and started talking with the murderer. A few words were exchanged, and the murderer turned and walked toward us. Our eyes met as he unlatched the bolt near me. Hearing the sound of the bolts being opened, the people around me that had fallen silent when the truck stopped started yelling again. They didn't want to confront the armed men. However, it was too late. The tailgate was down and the tarp had been raised. Everyone was in plain sight now. The murderer gestured for us to get out.

I was the first to hop off the bed. Then I helped the others off. The armed men had also gotten off their trucks to line up side by side. There were nine of them. Their faces were covered. We stood still in front of them. The little boy in his mother's arms was crying. He'd been struck dumb with fear through the entire chase and now he couldn't stop even if he wanted to. The man who'd talked to the murderer must've been the leader of the armed men. He was the only one among them whose face was uncovered. He pointed to the hysterical boy and said something. At that, with help from the plastic bag man next to them, the mother and child were put back on the truck. So we were able to meet at a median of compassion after all. The leader of the armed men turned to us and delivered a short speech. As soon as he was finished, the people spun around and started walking back to the truck. Moving faster than everyone else, the plastic bag man got on the truck bed and began dragging the Kalashnikov crates. Two armed men took the crates and loaded them one by one onto the pickup trucks. When the last crate was unloaded, the murderer shouted at the people surrounding the truck. They started climbing in faster. Livid at having been robbed, the murderer kept shouting. Especially at the ones unable to climb in! Right then I said to myself, okay. This is it . . . their beef isn't with us! They're going to leave with the Kalashnikovs . . .

The young couple we'd picked up from the village and I were the only ones that remained. The young man helped his wife onto the truck bed. Just as he was about to follow her, the leader of the armed men spoke. At that the young man turned to gape at him. He started shaking his head. Tears filled his eyes as he did. Whatever it was he'd been told, he didn't want to consent. One of the armed men, however, approached the young Pakistani to grab his arm and start dragging him away. His wife couldn't get off the truck for fear, but begged for them to let her husband go. She screamed and wept. The murderer merely stood by. Apparently this was his agreement with the robbers: to be able to proceed in exchange for the Kalashnikovs and a man . . .

Right then I thought of Rastin and took a step forward, shouting. What I said didn't matter because they wouldn't understand me anyway. But when I shouted and beat my chest with the palm of my hand at the same time, they were able to figure out that I was telling them to take me instead of him. Ignoring me, the leader of the armed men looked at the murderer. As though to say, "All right with you?" I was a foreigner after all. They wouldn't want to be hit by a satellite-operated American missile two days later when all was forgotten. The matter was solved when the murderer nodded his assent. They agreed to take me instead of the young man. The weeping young man was released from their tight grip. At a loss for how to react to the unexpected self-sacrifice, he was unable to react at all. He just lowered his head and passed by me. He couldn't even say thanks. The only thing he could do was to retrieve my bag from the truck bed to hand to me. In turn I took the paper frog out of my pocket where I'd carried it for the past sixteen years and gave it to him. He peered at the frog in his hand, then at me. I pointed to the boy who still shed tears in the depths of the vault. He understood what I meant to say. Cuma's frog was passed hand over hand and given to the little boy. The last glimpse I had of the child was of him sighing at the frog in his hand.

As the murderer lowered the tarp over the tailgate, the leader of the armed men touched my arm. We were leaving . . . I spun around and walked to the pickup trucks. I could feel the stares boring into my back. A truckful of people watched me in spite of the curtain that had come between us . . . None of them would forget me. Nor I them . . .

"Go," I said inwardly. "Go at once . . . go wherever it is you desire to go."

I didn't know what would happen to me or where I would be taken. But I'd done what I ought to. The rest was of no concern to me.

No one spoke to me for the entire ride. We passed through endless plots of land and arrived at a village. A village full of houses
flattened by a road roller of a war . . . Dark heads hung from
doorways without doors and windows without panes. Those
who glimpsed us emerged from these *tomb-houses*, yodeling.
Most of them were women. The ones around me replied to the
yodels with raised Kalashnikovs. The looting was being com-
mended. The trucks stopped and we hopped off the crates. We
began walking.

At the edge of the village where the houses started to thin
out, I saw people at work with shovels. It was clear that as a vol-
untary prisoner, I wouldn't be running. So up till then no one
had hit or mistreated me. In fact, the other armed men had gone
off in various directions in the village, leaving only one person
with me. As we approached the area where shovels were being
lifted and lowered laboriously, I saw that a hole was being dug.
All the workers were old. Looking at their faces, I couldn't tell if
the dampness around their eyes was tears or sweat. They were
as likely to die of fatigue as of old age. For whatever end they

were digging, it didn't seem that they'd be able to see the finished product.

I turned to look at the armed man next to me. He made a fist of his free hand and brought it to his mouth like a glass. That's how I knew they were trying to dig a water hole. They needed workers. Someone had to stay behind in the village to work when they were out looting. But there was no one aside from the old men. Those who could leave had all left. The young, the middle-aged, and anyone else with a modicum of hope for the future . . . We were in a place people deserted the first chance they got, without thinking twice about it.

I was given a shovel and the old people withdrew. I took a deep breath and released it. Then I started to dig. A monster with a thousand mouths, the sun bit my back and neck with all its teeth. Being the perpetually congealing wound I was, however, I worked unremittingly. I was familiar with shoveling after all. What's more, this time I wasn't digging a moat to protect myself from people. Even more importantly, I knew I wouldn't be digging up my mother's body. Death wouldn't come out of the hole I opened. On the contrary, life would: water. I was merely digging for water.

I dug for two months. We only found water when we got to the fourth well. We also had to bring the stones to line the walls of the well from a distance of three kilometers. And we only had one wheelbarrow. The pickup trucks came by the village so rarely that we were forced to carry the stones with the wheelbarrow.

At night I slept under the stars. Or rather, on them . . . In the mornings I rose before the sun and started work. I was given food. Meat now, bread then. But never the two at once . . . They themselves mostly went hungry. They didn't have anything except for a few animals. And they had me. That was it . . .

When we found water in the fourth of the wells dug with the most primitive means possible, all wrinkled faces broke into smiles. At a depth of six meters, it was the feeblest of waterbeds. We waited on it all night long. In the morning, however, we saw that the well had only filled up a meter. But we didn't lament as we now had a well at the bottom of which we could see our reflections.

Since there was no one to keep watch over me, I was often waited on by women or sometimes children. Holding Kalashnikovs . . . however, they left me alone once they saw what a hardworking, docile slave I was. I all but became one of them . . . When he saw the water at the bottom of the well, the leader of the looters even embraced me and tried to explain that I could stay in the village if I wanted to. But there was somewhere I needed to be.

At the end of my two months as a convict,[14] I made my farewells with everyone, got on one of the trucks, and went on my way. The only things I had left from the village were two bottles of water. Two bottles of water from a well . . .

The truck stopped in the entrance of Kandahar. My companions indicated that they could go no farther. They didn't want to go into the city. I could sympathize. Everyone had limits around them within which the stories of their lives unfolded. I got off the truck and walked. Toward my own life story . . .

---

14 Pun on the Turkish word for convict, "shovel prisoner."

I'd been on the road for a week. Either on a bus, in the bed of a truck, or on foot. I walked. I knew, however, that there wasn't much left to my destination. I'd asked everyone I came across, "Bamiyan?" In return they'd pointed to a dot on the horizon. The dot grew larger each time and slowly but surely turned into the threshold of the valley. In a few more steps, I'd be there . . .

I ascended a final incline. I stopped at the end of the path and took a deep breath. But I couldn't release it. Like my breath I wanted to hold this moment when I laid eyes on Bamiyan Valley for the first time. The only thing to do in the face of what I was seeing was to stop. To just stop and look. Because I'd found the place I was seeking. The picture Cuma had drawn stretched ahead in front of me.

There it was . . . a valley with trees rising in the midst, surrounded by high crags. There they were! From where I stood, I could see the empty grooves of the two gigantic Buddha statues. There must be a few hundred meters separating them. The rock walls into which they'd been carved were like rippled curtains drawn across the length of the valley. I was seeing dozens of small cave entrances. Dozens of little cavities were speckled around the two gigantic grooves. They looked like eyes on the jagged rock face. And if the caves were eyes, the people living in them, like Cuma had once, must be their pitch-black pupils . . .

I started running. I was on one of the slopes leading down into the valley. I ran and ran without a care. I weaved between boulders. I weaved between trees. I fell. Rose. And ran faster. With each step, everything I looked at grew even larger. The crags grew higher, and the grooves that once housed the Buddhas loomed even more enormously.

I didn't know which one to head toward. I couldn't guess which one the road would take me to. I just ran. And found myself approaching the larger groove. The distance between us was maybe a kilometer, maybe more. I couldn't take my eyes off it all.

Finally, a few hundred meters short of the gigantic groove above me, I stopped and tried to catch my breath. At last, I said inwardly . . . I've made it at last . . . I closed my eyes for an instant and imagined that the fifty-five-meter-tall Buddha statue was still there. Inside the enormous groove . . . Cuma had grown up with that statue. Always watching it . . . Perhaps he'd even climbed the groove in front of me and looked out at the world from between the Buddha's feet. I could see the statue, too, now . . . and a boy named Cuma as he ran right past me . . .

I opened my eyes and the statue vanished. All that remained was its empty groove. I started walking slowly. Then a woman appeared in front of me. An old woman . . . she must have deduced where I was headed from the direction of my stare. She waved her hands and shook her head. "Stop!" she meant to say. "Don't go!"

I just chuckled and walked on . . . but she wouldn't give up. She shouted something in my wake. I think one of the words was Taliban. I kept on chuckling and walking.

There was no one else in sight. Only the smoke rising from the caves in the distance. Smoke that proved that lives were lived inside the caves . . . I drew even nearer to the gigantic groove. From here on it was only a climb. I'd feel my way up the rocks. My hands and feet knew where to go. It was as if I'd spent my life in the valley with Cuma, climbing up to the groove . . . Maybe I really had, since anything I wished could be real.

With a final step, I was in the groove. I raised my head. Spun around. Looked up at its ceiling looming over me like a dome. It made me dizzy. I stopped. Looked at the horizon. Spread my gaze over the mountains and hills corrugating the horizon and the vast emptiness stretching out toward it. Then I bent my head. I was standing on shattered pieces of rock. Perhaps they were the remnants of the destroyed Buddha . . .

I sank to the ground. Sat. Laughed. Then I heard a sound. A familiar voice . . . a voice I hadn't been able to hear in years . . . a voice I'd come all this way just to hear . . .

**Are you OK?**
Yes.
**Tired?**
A little.
**You've been on the road for years . . .**
Yeah . . .
**Well? Does it look like the drawing?**
It does, Cuma . . . it really does.
**Thank you for bringing me home.**
Thank you, Cuma. For inviting me to your home . . .
**What're you going to do now?**
I don't know . . .
**All right . . . what about later?**
Maybe I'll live here in place of those who left . . .

**Gaza . . . I'm only telling you so you'll be prepared: you might dream of morphine sulfate, for a while, when you sleep. But don't you ever surrender . . . please.**
Don't worry.
**Are you going to tell yourself your past again?**
No, no . . . this is the last time.
**You say that every time . . . are you sure?**
Then let me put it this way: I hope I never have to tell it again!
**You won't! I believe in you . . . Gaza . . . I have to go.**
I know.
**Shall we say good-bye?**
Good-bye, Cuma.
**Good-bye, little boy . . . now go and finish your story . . .**
It's finished.

I delivered Cuma home, whom I'd carried inside me since the day I took his life. I heard his voice years later only to say good-bye. I was in the Bamiyan Valley of the Hazarajat region of Afghanistan. Inside the gigantic groove which once housed the fifty-five-meter-tall statue of a Buddha . . . The statue had stood for 1,500 years at the very spot I was now standing and then gone up in a cloud of dust. I looked down and saw a boy. He was fifteen at most. He stood staring at me from between the nearby trees. He held a Kalashnikov. I smiled. The boy raised the gun and fired. I felt warmth bloom in my left shoulder. I looked at the perfect emptiness stretching out in front of me. I stood up.